# THE HERBALIST

Holly Seddon is the international bestselling author of three novels. Alongside fellow author Gillian McAllister, Holly co-hosts the popular *Honest Authors* podcast. After growing up in the English countryside obsessed with music and books, Holly worked in London as a journalist and editor. She now lives in Amsterdam with her family and writes full time.

You can find Holly on:

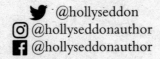

 @hollyseddon
@hollyseddonauthor
@hollyseddonauthor

By the same author:

*Try Not to Breathe*
*Don't Close Your Eyes*
*Love Will Tear Us Apart*

# THE HIT LIST

## Holly Seddon

First published in Great Britain in 2021 by Trapeze
an imprint of The Orion Publishing Group Ltd
Carmelite House, 50 Victoria Embankment
London EC4Y 0DZ

An Hachette UK Company

1 3 5 7 9 10 8 6 4 2

A CIP catalogue record for this book is
available from the British Library.

ISBN (Mass Market Paperback) 978 1 4091 9550 4
ISBN (eBook) 978 1 4091 9551 1

Typeset by Born Group
Printed and bound in Great Britain by Clays Ltd, Elcograf S.p.A.

MIX
Paper from
responsible sources
FSC® C104740
www.fsc.org

www.orionbooks.co.uk

For Gilly, my (book) birth partner
and the keeper of my secrets.

# PART ONE:

## Now

PART ONE

# Marianne

A shadow falls across Marianne's shoulders. Her toes curl on the cool decking and a shiver crawls down her back. Compared to her Hackney flat, Noah's Richmond townhouse is a mansion, but it's this tiny, chilly garden that she loves the most. Walled on all sides and invisible to the neighbours, it's crammed with an ornate cherry blossom tree planted by his late wife that leaves just enough room for a wooden bench.

She tucks into its corner, lighting her cigarette and looking up at the bare branches. When Marianne first sat out here a few months ago, shaking with guilt and exhilaration after their first night together, the tree was alive with pink blossoms. This morning she had to brush the dead flowers away. Subtle waves of old petals, bunched up like little fists.

As she drags the last lungful of smoke, she allows herself the briefest memory of her and Greg's last weekend together. Tea, toast, the *Observer*. No cigarettes, no terrace, nothing new to learn about each other. And no easy chat, no peals of laughter, not like it had been. But under the silence there was still deep affection, a foundation into which they'd both poured years of love and respect.

On the Sunday, they'd eaten a roast dinner, cooked – as always – by Greg.

In their early years he'd cooked so joyfully and she'd eaten so gratefully. But that last time, had she even thanked him?

She can still picture him in their flat, making pastry on Monday evenings. It was a ritual, a leftovers pie made from whatever they hadn't finished of the Sunday roast. Then what was left of the pie, always too big for two, sliced and frozen.

So many Mondays, so many pies that the image is sepia, archetypal rather than specific. But in her most abiding memories of Greg, there he is in their tiny kitchen, flour clinging to his eyebrows and beard, his wedding ring set carefully to the side while he kneads.

She goes inside to find Noah in his kitchen, drinking a protein shake while the coffee pot sits full and steaming for her.

'OK?' he asks over his shoulder, lifting a cup down from the cupboard. She nods, then shakes her head, then pads over to hug him from behind. She feels his muscles contract as he pours her a coffee, precise little movements still new to her.

They stay in silence until Noah swallows to break it. 'It sounds like a cliché,' he says carefully, 'but the first anniversary really is the hardest.' She leans into him more and he carries on softly. 'It's not that it ever gets easy, but it does get better.'

She holds him tighter, grateful for the shorthand of the bereaved, no need to add or explain. Unsure she really could.

According to the kitchen clock, it's just gone eleven thirty. Almost to the minute that a call came through this time last year.

'Marianne Heywood?'

'Yes, who's calling?'

'I'm a sergeant with the Metropolitan Police. Do you have someone with you?'

She thought her heart would collapse in on itself, right there on the floor of the staffroom.

A year ago today, and already her arms have slipped around another man. Last year, she thought she'd never be ready. And yet these last months, the more time she's spent here, the more she's started to picture a whole new life ahead of her. Her things nestling next to Noah's. New routines. A bedrock of in-jokes and references and memories it took years to build with Greg, is now in its glorious infancy with Noah. But today, she can't think about that. Today belongs to Greg.

*

4

Marianne leaves in the late afternoon before Noah's daughter, Daisy, gets home. For all Marianne's growing hopes, it's early days for all of them and she is yet to meet his five-year-old. It's made easier by her maternal grandparents' desperation not to lose their only grandchild as well as their daughter. Daisy stays with them every Friday at least, while Noah and Marianne pretend they're unencumbered lovers, feeling their way in their own time.

'I wasn't ready for anyone new until you,' Noah said, the very first Friday that she stayed over.

'Neither was I,' Marianne replied, choosing an easy lie instead of a complex truth.

Now, in the dimming light, Marianne sees her whisked-up reflection in the black curves of her little car. Her curly brown hair hangs wild and unbrushed. Her blue eyes shine back, new lines feathering their edges. Even her leather jacket is battered and scuffed. She licks her finger and wipes the tide marks from under her eyes, then fumbles for her car key.

The front door re-opens and Noah jogs over on the balls of his socked feet. He has a good foot of height over her; his shoulders are probably a foot wider too. A bear of a man. He hugs her tightly and Marianne feels his heart booming through his thin T-shirt. So very alive. 'I'm here if you need me,' he says, releasing her and heading back inside. 'But I won't pester you.'

The stereo reads 17:37. As she reverses out of Noah's drive, Marianne tries to picture what she would have been doing at this exact time a year ago. The memory is blank, the black box recorder removed for her own good.

A little after seven, Marianne rattles the door key in the sticky lock and shoves her way into her Hackney flat. After an empty night, it smells like the opposite of life. Not quite death, more like the blank space between the two.

They'd bought this place as a first step on the ladder, seven years ago. The best they could get on their salaries. A teacher and a charity worker, their mortgage broker had audibly sighed.

Greg's parents offered to contribute, but Marianne's pride shot that idea straight down.

The building had long been converted from a faded Victorian house into an upstairs flat with a separate greasy spoon underneath. After living here for a month, everything they owned smelt like cooking oil. A few months ago, the café was closed down by health inspectors and Marianne found herself missing the distinctive smell. 'Stockholm Syndrome,' Greg would have joked. Since the closure, the flat has sat above an empty space, a black hole behind a metal shutter.

*A year ago today.*

She pulls open Greg's side of the wardrobe and gingerly takes out his favourite shirt. Sliding it from the hanger, her eyes prickling. She grabs its fabric as though it is flesh and sniffs it deeply, but there is no trace of him now. Just the distant smell of whatever fabric conditioner was on special offer a year ago. It drapes over her as she slips it on, buttoning it carefully. He wasn't tall, but she's shrunk since then.

She can't quite imagine doing this with Noah's clothes. Not yet. He's so much bigger, but it's not that. His world is complete and she is entering it; he is welcoming her in but it is not her world. Marianne and Greg built their world up together; they were a family of two.

She looks in the mirror and wonders what Greg would think if he were standing behind her now. That she's being indulgent? Disrespectful? Her body is still scented from a night with another man. Or maybe, like her, he would remember how they had been for most of their marriage, until it all started to crumble at the very end.

'*I love you*,' she imagines him saying.

'Always,' she replies, into the silence of the flat.

Still wearing the shirt, Marianne struggles to push up the sash kitchen window high enough for her to lean out. The small galley looks out over a jigsaw of other people's yards but she never sees a soul out there. She smokes fast and deep, blowing plumes across the would-be gardens and away into the scrubby trees.

6

They had given up smoking together, after they got married. Planning, as newlyweds always do, for forever. Not wanting cigarettes to plant a cancerous bomb in those dreams. It had been easy for Greg, who was never a heavy smoker, but Marianne had resented how hard she'd found it. A personal affront. Even when she'd officially given up, she cracked frequently, 'borrowing' cigarettes from friends on rare nights out, begging a smoke from colleagues on difficult days and angrily buying a contraband pack of ten from the local shop after rare arguments with Greg. Until the last few months of his life when the arguments stopped being rare and the packs became twenty, barely hidden in the airing cupboard.

And then, a year ago today, she'd arrived at the hospital to be bustled into a small room with a ridiculously floral sofa and no smoking signs everywhere she looked.

'Can I see him?' she asked.

There was a pause, an intake of air. 'I'm very sorry,' the doctor began, holding her own hands together in a practised move.

Marianne sat down hard on that ugly sofa, folded in on herself and barely took in a word. When she finally opened her eyes, all she could think was that she needed a cigarette.

She smoked so much that first week that her fingers turned yellow and well-wishers held their breath when they hugged her. Her mother kept opening the windows, letting September winds blow through the flat so that scraps of paper with Greg's final words fluttered dangerously. Marianne had eventually slammed them shut, screaming god knows what at her mum, pointing to Greg's notepads and doodles, the little notes and receipts that had previously pissed her off as they clogged up the precious surface area of a 'bijou' flat.

Every artefact of life becomes sacrosanct in death.

\*

Forever means less to Marianne now and she has no plan for it. She stubs out the cigarette on the concrete windowsill, a satisfying polka dot to add to the rest. She pushes the butt into the overflowing plant pot she once intended to grow something in and tugs the window back down by its flaky frame.

Marianne opens the bare fridge and then teases open the broken door to the freezer compartment. A small space, she'd never really used it herself. It was only when the cover fell off after a particularly hard slam of the fridge door that she saw inside. One piece of Greg's pie, stuffed there a Monday long ago. Some distant afterthought.

The pie is there still; she takes it out gingerly and holds it like a newborn. A solid piece of proof that he was here, alive once, caring enough to cook for them. Great family meals just for two. Tears fall as she switches the oven on, a musty smell filling the small room. She imagines Greg's voice: '*What are you doing to my kitchen, hen?*'

'Sorry,' Marianne whispers, 'but if I don't eat this soon, I'll have to throw it away.' She defrosts the pie slowly in the microwave – no going back. You don't read about this in those leaflets about grief. When is the right time to take a new lover? And when is it OK to eat the last slice of pie?

She lifts it carefully from the plastic tub, notices with a grimace that it's not just softened and defrosted, the edges have started to bubble. 'I'm sorry,' she whispers again. It had always been a joke between them, how she was all thumbs in the kitchen. 'You could burn a boiled egg,' he used to laugh. 'You're the Rambo of cooking.'

She smiles at the memory as she slides the pie on its baking tray into the oven. She hasn't eaten a proper meal at home in a long time. Still the Rambo of cooking, she tends to buy ready meals, order takeaways or just skip meals rather than bother with proper food. But this is different. She smokes another cigarette while the food cooks and then sets herself a place at the table.

At first, it feels wrong to swallow. As if she's not eating the last remnants of a homemade pie but eating something of

8

Greg himself. It feels cannibalistic. But soon the familiar flavour and the softness of his pastry, missing for the last year, takes over her senses. She weeps as she swallows the final mouthful. The last of him, gone.

'I miss you so much,' she says to the empty plate. 'I just wish you were here every fucking day.'

She looks at the pile of exercise books on the table and her school-issued laptop, but she knows full well that no work will happen tonight. She's too full, too sad.

Instead, she will do what she did on their wedding anniversary and Greg's birthday. What she did on those early widowed nights when the bed seemed so achingly cold and the night so terribly long. And then later when she needed to whip herself with memories, when the bed was still warm from the wrong body.

Tonight she will spend the night drowning herself with everything Greg left behind.

*

For the first few weeks after the funeral, and long before she met Noah, it was just the analogue stuff she sank into. There was plenty of that. The photographs, the little notes from their early days, gifts and clothes. She leafed through Greg's notepads full of indecipherable doodles and lists, even coating herself in a tiny spritz of his cologne here and there.

Eventually she started to crave more and turned to the digital remains. And, god, was there a lot. She'd sat on their bed with her laptop burning her legs, starting with their early email conversations.

Last month, when she'd read everything she could bear to on her own ageing laptop, she opened his.

Tentatively looking through his browser history, wincing at the no-surprises porn, retreating instead to read his emails from their early days, like the announcement to his mum that he'd met a girl. 'She's called Marianne and she's a teacher.

9

I think you'll like her.' Wrong, as it turned out, but Marianne admired his optimism. Greg's mum had always expected him to come home once he'd 'got London out of his system', but Marianne had stuck a spanner in that plan. Never mind that she would have happily considered moving above the border; Greg was always adamant he didn't want to return to Scotland. But it was Marianne who got the blame.

She'd rifled cautiously, more through fear than respect, and when his laptop battery ran out, breaking the spell, she was relieved. But she's here again, as she knew she would be.

Marianne would once have assumed this kind of thing was normal. At the bereavement group that she used to go to, plenty of the 'left behind' had also become archivists, talking about the love letters and mementos that they would grab first in a fire. Some even brought along the last Christmas card or the first Valentine, clutching them nervously as they spoke. But she'd recently asked Noah if he spent time looking through his wife's old emails and files, reading her letters and diaries. They'd been lying on his bed, still clothed and holding hands. How had they even got into the position? She can't remember now but they were basking in each other, sharing secrets and talking urgently.

'Do you look through Louise's things?' she'd asked and he'd propped himself up onto his side.

'What do you mean?' he said. 'I sorted her clothes out and—'

'No,' Marianne pressed. 'I mean, do you look through stuff she didn't show you when she was here? Letters and emails and . . .' Her voice fell away. The look on his face had nearly stopped her heart with shame. She didn't mention it again.

Greg's laptop sits on the table in front of her now. Lumpen. Out of charge. Covered in tides of dust. She uncoils the cable, plugs it in and opens it up. Some of the keys have been rubbed clear of symbols so she feels for the 'on' button as if she's reading braille. A little light blinks and the machine whirrs lazily awake as she opens a bottle of Pinot Noir.

The screen finally comes alive with a freeze frame from last time. And so she pours a glass of wine, taps a Gauloise from the pack and brings the flame close to her face.

\*

They met in July 2013. Greg newly arrived from his native Scotland, where he'd drifted for a few years after finishing his geography degree. Marianne, an émigrée to the East End from South London and from Devon before that. She'd arrived in a hurry. He'd taken his time. They met in the middle on the number forty-eight bus one boozy Friday evening.

That summer in the city. Both mid-twenties. Lives barely begun.

They'd swapped numbers and she'd woken the next morning to three messages. The first, asking if she'd like to see the Tate Modern's exhibition of street art. The second, apologising for being presumptuous. 'I completely understand', he'd written, 'if you woke up and regretted giving your number to some strange man.' And then a third. 'Oh god, I sound like a nutter. I realise this is the third text I've sent. Can I start again? I'd love to meet up some time, at your convenience, but no worries if you're not up for it. Yours, Greg.'

It was the sign-off that did it.

They'd previously met drunk, her recollection of his face blurred at the edges, the details smudged. The man waiting outside the gallery had a sharp nose and high cheekbones. Out of his bus seat, he was around five foot nine, slim but muscular.

He wore a white T-shirt and dark blue jeans. He'd trimmed his beard but still looked like a man who lived in the woods. She wore a blue 1950s rockabilly dress, hair carefully coiled into victory rolls and held in place with pins. Heels to make her feel taller. It was, she realised immediately, too much.

As they left the gallery, Greg let out a long sigh. 'I didn't understand any of that. Do you want to get a beer?'

'I would really love a beer,' she said, unpinning her hair and shaking it out as they walked.

The day turned into evening as they shared a basket of chips and clinked beer bottles. Sitting on the concrete overlooking Bankside Pier and wrapping each other in stories. This is who I am. This is who *I* am. All those words, long lost to the evening sunshine. There were always going to be more words, so she barely bothered to remember.

And then they slid slowly, comfortably, into constant communication. Phone calls at night and emails by day. Hers sent in bursts around lessons; his scattergun and frequent. She pictures him back then, sharing his every thought as he had it. 'You have no inner monologue,' she used to say.

'You should be grateful you get to receive such a waterfall of wisdom,' he'd reply in his soft, staccato Scots. When had the waterfall dried up? Last year. But it had slowed to a trickle before that.

At first, they met on scheduled dates. Cheap dinners with vouchers, too skint to hide it. Films at the Troxy, smuggling in pick 'n' mix from a nearby shop.

Between those moments in the flesh, more words. Strings and strings of emails. Re. Re. Re. Re. Re. Re. Re. Re. Never ending. Until they did.

*

Tonight, of course, there's nothing new in his sent items and that is as painful as ever. She clears the spam, unsubscribes from a few more straggling newsletters. It's like gardening, ripping out the weeds. Widow's work.

Her favourite 'sent item' was the first time Greg told her he loved her. 'By email? How very Noughties,' her colleague Clare had joked. But it wasn't high tech, it was low confidence.

She searches for it now, opening sent items and typing 'love' in the search bar. There are hundreds of results, of course. She takes a swig of wine, switches to sort 'oldest' first, then sits back in surprise. *Jenna.* Of course. His account predates Marianne by several years but it's still a slap in the face to see all these emails.

*Jenna*. The one that got away. She takes a breath and clicks in to the first email containing 'love' that he sent his ex-girlfriend. The 'I love you' is just there amongst general chit-chat. Of course, he opened this email account when they'd been going out for years. He and Jenna had got together during their Highers.

She clicks out and into the next and the next.

The conversations here are briefer than Greg and Marianne's. Jenna the intrepid solicitor, a really modern girl. *Stop it, it doesn't matter now*. She searches for all emails to and from 'Jenna Fairbarn'. Seeing snipey emails from the bitter end would be easier on the heart. Marianne can see already from the subject lines that their relationship had dissolved into accusations and nit-picking. She clicks into one where Jenna is dressing Greg down for forgetting to leave the ten pounds that he owed her. And another where Greg has emailed Jenna to try to explain, clumsily, what he *actually* meant the previous night when she had 'done your legal bit at me instead of letting me talk'. Greg was always more comfortable with emails than text messages, a hangover from the days of 140-character limits. 'I have too much to say,' he'd laugh. There is even the odd email from Greg to Jenna sent after he met Marianne. A vague and half-arsed attempt at staying friends. 'Just checking in!'

The emails had long stopped by the time Marianne and Greg married. All except one. Marianne blinks and takes a thick swig of wine. There is an email to Jenna sent just days before he died but 'archived', so she hadn't seen it before. It was only unearthed through searching. The subject line reads: 'I need you.'

Jenna,

Can we meet? I can come to you? Or we can talk on the phone. I know a lot of time has passed but I'm begging you, please don't turn your back on me.

Greg xxx

13

She can find no reply in his inbox. She checks the archive – nothing. Deleted items then? It's empty. Picked clean before he died. Did he do that to delete Jenna's response?

Outside, the night sky has turned navy, the street below quiet.

'I need you.'

*I needed you, Greg.*

Still she stares, reading it again and again.

Stung, Marianne considers tracking Jenna down. Calling her, screaming at her even. But Jenna hadn't even replied and mustn't she be grieving too? She must have found out about Greg's death – they both came from the same small town. Maybe she'd decided to ignore the email, not feeling the same pull to Greg that he obviously felt to her. And now she has to live with that. Besides, it's too late for that kind of call. It's too dark and she's too frayed with wine.

Three kisses, though, just like in the other 'Jenna' correspondence, instead of the customary two that Marianne and Greg had somehow settled on, wordlessly. Could he have met Jenna and started a very brief affair? Or did he just *want* to cheat on Marianne?

Begging and desperate for the one who got away, years after he'd last seen her? How could he? In those last days of his life, why was he preoccupied with his ex-girlfriend from a million years ago? She would never have expected this from Greg. Principled, relentlessly *good* Greg. But then, he had already started to withdraw at that point, so who knew?

Marianne rubs her hands over her face and clicks through the mess of folders cluttering up his desktop. Looking for what, she's not sure. Photos of Jenna? Plans to divorce? She doesn't know, but in lieu of anything else to do, she picks up pace, feverishly looking under pixelated rocks.

And then she sees it.

Not a photo of Jenna. Not a love letter.

An icon. A name.

*What the fuck?*

She wouldn't even know what it was if she hadn't heard a group of Year 12 pupils talking about it at school. About the depravity. About how everything, *anything*, is available.

Bragging, really. Lying, probably.

It's a browser but not like the one she's been using. A different animal altogether. A wormhole to the dark and dirty place beneath the normal internet. An illegal place, filled with the worst of everything and where anything is available for a price.

Before he died, she realises with a sudden punch to her gut, Greg hadn't just been emailing his ex, he had been accessing the dark web.

# Marianne

It has become dark so quickly that the screen in front of Marianne is lit up like a fire. She leans back in her chair, her shoulders stiff and tight. She blinks, as if a quick slice with her eyelids will wipe away the scene. But of course it doesn't. Marianne is still in the flat, at their table for two. The bottle of red in front of her is empty and her ashtray overflows with little grey caterpillars. And on the screen, an icon for a dark web browser sits where Greg tucked it, hidden away from her eyes.

*What do I do?*

Unable to process the discovery, instead she carries the ashtray into the kitchen and dumps the contents in the bin. A stale cloud rushes up at her.

Clumsily, she rinses a layer of dust from a single heavy glass tumbler that's been unused for a long time. She has to clamber onto the sideboard to grasp the near-empty bottle of Macallan.

'You can take the boy out of Scotland,' he'd say, late at night, then fall asleep after two soft sips while she was still brushing her teeth. The bottle was a gift from her father-in-law to his only son, the Christmas before Greg died. He received one every year and spent the next twelve months slowly finishing it.

Her fingers tremble as she lights another Gauloise and sucks it deeply. Then she takes a sip. She sits back down with a thud, takes another slug of whisky and winces. She stares for a moment as her pale fingers wind around the slim white cigarette as if they belong to someone else.

Somehow, it's nearly eleven at night. Where has the time gone? She should focus on the here and now and close this old laptop down. Maybe even wipe its contents or throw it away.

The thought of destroying everything that's left on here sends her heart racing even harder. But why was he going to that place, and why didn't she know? Could this be connected to Jenna? Some kind of sick obsession that united them?

A creeping fear closes in on her. She'd found porn on his computer last time she went grief-snooping, of course she had. Tell-tale links in his search history, links she didn't need to click on to understand. Nothing weird, though; nothing you'd need to go to the dark web to find.

And, yes, over the years they'd definitely cooled from the feverish, intensely physical early years into something more comfortable, less frequent. They were both so busy and Greg was so stressed. If anything, it was her who was frustrated and occasionally found herself climbing the walls, missing passion and human touch.

What more did he want that Marianne or videos of random glistening bodies weren't able to provide?

She closes her eyes; thoughts of skin and metal, of blood and fear race across her mind. She doesn't even know what she's trying not to imagine.

*Some things are better left unseen.*

But her heart just hammers harder. She opens her eyes and it's still there. This little icon, winking at her like Alice's white rabbit.

Marianne staggers through to the kitchen, pouring the last from the whisky bottle into her glass. She cracks her knuckles, releasing a burst of pressure, and then pulls a fresh carton of cigarettes from the cupboard where food used to be kept.

She lights up and smokes fast, then sits back down, still staring at the screen. The ash spills in knots all over the table as her hands tremble.

*Fuck it.*

Marianne clicks on the icon and holds her breath.

*

It takes far longer than a normal browser to open, so long she thinks it might not work, but then finally it appears. At first it looks familiar. A recognisable browser frame around four tabs open already – presumably from the last time he logged on.

She clicks through them. The first one is an email service she's never heard of. There's no pre-filled information, no way to log in. She tries his usual usernames and passwords, but the site does not yield.

*So he had a secret email address.*

She clicks on, dreading how much worse this could get, the pastry and wine sitting heavily in her stomach. The next tab is filled with chaos. It takes a while to make sense of what she's seeing.

It's not a page of horrific porn at least. Instead, it's rather like an old-fashioned-looking forum divided into sub-forums. She scrolls down carefully. It appears to be some kind of marketplace, with each sub-forum offering a different speciality. Guns, pharmaceuticals, hardcore porn of every flavour, even snuff films. The kind of stuff she'd heard the Year 12s joking about. She'd thought they were exaggerating. It can't be real, surely?

*Why were you here, Greg?*

She stares at the marketplace and tries to make sense of it. Alongside the sale links, it's full of weird lingo, disgusting

17

pictures and gifs. Plus a hodgepodge of inane topics, grim rambling and braggadocio.

And so much of the content shared here seems to be cruel. Greg worked with victims of human trafficking, he helped desperate people access help. He may have been quick to temper in his final months but he was kind and good. He was not the sort of person who would find this entertaining. But then Greg hadn't seemed the type to keep secrets from her, or to know how to use the dark web. He didn't seem the type to contact his ex in a fit of pique, but he did.

*I'm begging you, please don't turn your back on me.*

When Marianne and Greg first met, he worked for an animal charity. He'd turn up on dates with little ribbons of fur on his trousers from the fluffy visitors to the office.

People were who he always wanted to help, though; he'd told her that on their very first date, squinting into the sun overlooking the Thames. People who'd been treated like animals, modern-day slaves.

But when he finally got a role at the small charity Hidden Humans after a few years, he became more serious, more troubled. Every week there were more people he hadn't been able to help as much as he'd wanted, vulnerable people who'd slipped through his fingers and back into the world of cash landlords and paperless jobs – at best. The boomerang back to exploitation was an ever-present risk, even for those who had got out before.

He gave it his all. Turned himself inside out trying to do more and more. Their last holiday, the summer before he died, she'd read thrillers by the pool and knocked back Aperol Spritzes until her head swam. He'd paced around and struggled to relax. He'd been stressed, wondering aloud how long he could keep doing such a thankless, frustrating job. The relentlessness, the sheer numbers in need, had crushed him. He was a rescuer, a doer. In the thick Italian heat, he'd spent his time scooping tiny frogs from the pool and setting them free, while she'd watched from behind her sunglasses. There were more little kickers churned in the filter than he could possibly have saved.

How could *that* Greg have laughed at jokes like the ones she can see right now? How could he have spent time somewhere that offers access to watch live executions?

Then she sees it. Now it starts to make sense. A sub-forum all about buying people. Women, mostly. Available to the highest bidder. No photos, just physical measurements and a 'guarantee' of clean health.

*Oh Greg.* Ever the Good Samaritan, he must have come looking for people who'd slipped away, back to black. She wonders if he ever saved anyone here. Ever disrupted anything. If any of these ads are even real. He never told her anything about this place, never so much as hinted. She often joked that he never stopped talking, always one silly monologue going on. But actually, about the serious stuff, he kept mum.

She clicks away to the next tab, guilty that she'd thought the worst.

It's another chat forum but far more basic, less busy. A meeting point for activists by the looks of it. Others like him, big hearts and wide eyes. Is that fair? For all his naivety, Greg wasn't so blithely trusting. He didn't even talk about this place. *Or maybe he just didn't trust me.*

She thinks again of his email to Jenna, an ache building behind her breast.

Unlike on the other tabs, here she can click back and retrace Greg's steps. She clicks once. The site churns so slowly she imagines hearing cogs turning. Everything is so much slower down here, in this cesspit of a place. Eventually the screen comes alive again.

The subject of the post reads: **ASSASSIN SUPERMARKET HACKED**.

She reads on to the main body of the post, disbelieving and confused:

Usual hoax caveats but apparently someone's hacked the database of the Assassin Supermarket and you can search for anyone with a price on their head.

Worth checking to see if any of the trafficking bosses are on the list, or anyone else that you're looking into.
Unlikely that any of us will have gained that kind of attention but advise you check anyway.

Here's the link.

Her gut reaction is that this is a hoax. It looks like a very strange link, even ignoring the extraordinary claims of what will be found there. It's nothing like normal URLs. An unmemorable spit-up of numbers and letters. She won't click it. Far too cautious, far too wary of technology, and of dangerous secret places that she doesn't understand.

Instead, she clicks into the final tab that Greg left open on this browser. And realises that while she would never click on such a link, a link to a supposed hit-list database, Greg did. Because it's right here in front of her eyes.

*

The site is misleadingly simple for something that deals with death. Roughly chucked together with a search box. It looks like it was created by a child.

'Want to know if you're on a hit list?' It says. 'Search your name here.'

There is no back or forward arrow here so she cannot see who Greg searched for. Presumably the names of traffickers, perhaps other activists. Did he look for himself? *Should* he have looked for himself? Did he make any enemies while he was rummaging around down here, trailing god knows what and god knows who?

For a year, Marianne believed without question that Greg died in an accident. But what if . . .?

She's tapping the keys before she can stop herself. Surely he wasn't killed, surely not. But . . . but. The cursor seems to judder away from her as she types and she wonders if it's the whisky or the website.

*Gregory Darrow.*

*Enter.*

Nothing happens for a moment and then the site wheezes into action and a line of text appears above the search box.

*No results. Try again.*

She tries: *Greg Darrow.*

*Enter.*

*No results. Try again.*

She exhales. Greg was knocked off his bike on a busy London road not far from here, the thirteenth cyclist to die in the city that year. A classic hit-and-run. He was a mild-mannered man who was liked by everyone he met. Yes, he could stretch his remit at work and go above and beyond to help those who needed it. But that meant lending people his own money or going on protest marches; maybe it meant trying to track ex-clients down through this kind of back channel, but not putting himself in the sights of a fucking assassin.

*What is wrong with me?*

Of course his bloody name wasn't on here. He was the victim of a tragic accident and now she's the victim of a stupid hoax.

As if to prove it to herself, she types again.

*Marianne Heywood.*

*Enter.*

Again, nothing happens. She blinks slowly and breathes deeply, deciding in that moment never to come to this terrible place again. Whatever Greg was trying to do down here was his world, not hers. And it was his business, his possibly ham-fisted methods for making the world a better place. And it's the world's loss, and hers, that he's gone. She will file this place away with his grovelling message to Jenna and instead think only of the good times. To mourn the best of him and bury the questions because there's no one here to answer them.

The page changes.

*Search results: Marianne Heywood, Hackney, date of birth: 7 August 1987.*

Next to this sits a tiny greyscale photograph of her face.

A line of text appears above the results with a skull emoji on either side: *Congratulations, someone wants you dead.*

# Sam

I can smell the last dinner that he cooked as I tread carefully through his kitchen in the darkness, twisting this way and that to avoid corners. It smells like a fry-up, a breakfast to prepare him for the upside-down schedule of a night shift.

I cover my nose and breathe silently.

Even if I didn't know for sure, I could tell as soon as I slipped inside that there isn't a living soul in here. The air feels unbroken. No one else's breath, no other body heat but mine. He's deep in the warehouse at a DIY store now – a waste of his talents but the best place for him. Away from the public.

I keep the lights off. No need for a curious neighbour to get involved. I'm through the hallway and up the stairs in seconds. I know my way around from my last visit, and I've spent hours with my eyes closed, walking this route in my head, preparing. There can be no room for error. I'm not getting caught for this one, not for a man like him.

His office door is open, his computer screen now dull and grey. I don't need to see what's on there, I know very well.

I tread lightly into his bedroom. His bed is unmade and it stinks of his body. As before, his prescription sleeping pills are on the side table. I slide out an unused sheet and pop out the twelve pills, cradling them in one gloved palm as I slip the empty foil into my back pocket with the other hand.

I place four pills in the small glass of water next to his bed, swirling the liquid carefully. They'll dissolve by the time he crawls under the covers, hopefully too exhausted to refresh the glass before taking a sip. And one sip should be enough to keep him asleep while the next part of the process kicks in.

Back downstairs, I place another four pills in the open and nearly finished bottle of red wine that sits next to the hob – a back-up. The final four plop noisily into the open pint of milk inside the fridge door. Some people like a milky drink before bed, especially those with sleep issues. The smell of food rushes out at me and I screw back the lid and shut the door quickly, my stomach curdling. Other people's food turns me inside out.

The first part of the job is done now. One way or another, he'll sleep for long enough to ensure the second part will work.

I'm back up the stairs in seconds, silent on soft, clean socks. I don't need to check the floor plan on my phone. I know precisely where to find everything. I've done this part so many times in my mind that I had to remind myself on the drive over that this assignment has not been fulfilled. Wishful thinking, perhaps.

I tease the boiler cover open and unfurl my set of tools.

When the job is done, I take the final photo and upload it. Proof of the penultimate task's completion. I allow myself the slightest smile as I pass the target's office and head back down the stairs.

Then I pull up my mask, lower my hood, slip my boots back on and leave the way I came in.

# Marianne

Marianne sits frozen in her chair, head grinding into the back of it as if she's chained into a wild fairground ride.

Her flat is all shadows, there's just a pale blue light seeping out from the laptop's screen. Outside, someone shrieks. Moments later there is an eruption of laughter.

Heart still thundering, she looks again. It really is her name. And her suburb. Her date of birth. Her face. On a fucking hit list!

Marianne squints at herself, her expression frozen in monochrome. In the pale light, she touches her real flesh, feels the contours of her face as she stares at the tiny facsimile on the screen. When was this photo taken? Her hair is tied back, as it often is for work, and she isn't looking directly at the camera. It could easily be from CCTV, cropped from a group photo on her school's website. Uploaded as one of hundreds on Facebook.

She feels a bead of sweat run down her back, despite the chill.

Who else is on there? She remembers a news story a few years ago about a dating website for married people looking for affairs. It was hacked. The names and email addresses of every member uploaded to a website and searchable – even now – by any concerned spouse. There are apparently thousands of names and email addresses on there, real people's indiscretions preserved forever. A catacomb of shame. But affairs are one thing; being placed on a hit list is quite another.

She clicks the back button, returns to the first page, then back again, but nothing happens. She clicks to the other tab, the one where Greg read about this website and clicks back, back, back but it just ends up at the main chat room for activists; there's no breadcrumb trail that shows what Greg looked at or why.

She's never felt scared at home before, not here in her nest. Even when one of Greg's friends made an ill-advised joke about him haunting the place. Now she's too scared to close her eyes. How is it so dark in here? She rushes from the table and turns on all the lights in the flat, double-locks the door.

If she hadn't drunk so much, she'd run to her car and fly back to Noah's. Taxi? No, he has his daughter home now and falling drunk out of an Uber, ranting about dark webs and assassination attempts is not the introduction she wants to make. For everything happening here tonight, that glimmer of a future is worth protecting. She doesn't want to taint it with this. Whatever *this* is.

A chill creeps up her neck, the hairs standing up as if sensing she's being watched. She spins to look behind her but of course no one is there.

*Did Greg find me on here? Is that what he found a year ago? Why the fuck didn't he warn me? And why the fuck would I have a price on my head?*

But he couldn't warn her, of course he couldn't, because he was knocked off his bike before he had the chance. Maybe he assumed it was a hoax, regretted looking. Maybe he never even searched her name and this is . . . what? A coincidence?

*What the fuck is even real?*

She tries to think strategically. To parent herself into some kind of logical next move. What would Noah do? Laugh it off? But Noah wouldn't look in the first place.

So what should she do? What does one do in a situation like this? Finding yourself listed as a murder target, in a dirty little shithole on the illegal netherworld below the internet?

She clicks back to the initial post about this and reads the replies. Lots of them are disputing the claim of hacking, most of them are calling anyone who searches their real name a grade A moron (in generally more colourful language). But one reply makes her blood freeze.

'Don't do it. Don't look. Seriously. A guy I used to talk to on here, he found his name on another hit list and went to the cops. Fucking idiot. They laughed him out of the station and the next day he was found with his throat cut.'

This sounds like bullshit, but . . . But. Who might watch her if she went to the station? And if she did, what would the police even do? What would they look into, if she made herself known to them? Would they go through her and Greg's computers? Her emails? Would they report their findings to the school? They'd have to, wouldn't they?

And all that for what must be, surely has to be, a hoax.

She shuts everything down. As the light from the screen fades, the room seems to squirm. Her head swims with wine, whisky and what-ifs.

It must be a sick joke. Just a laugh, for someone who finds that kind of thing funny. Not a normal person – one of those trolls who takes pleasure in others' distress. She has a few of those emerging in her older year groups already. Mostly boys, unsure of how to communicate and of who to be – and latching on to the wrong role models. One in particular comes to mind, Robbie. So different to his gentle older brother, Marc. The perennial smirk on Robbie's face telling Marianne that he might know more than he should. About lots of things, including her.

How hard is it to scrape the normal internet for a photo and date of birth? Serve up a result as if someone else has listed her there? It's probably a basic thing to set up if you're into that kind of thing.

*But why my name and not Greg's? Surely any name should bring up a result if it's a prank?*

She rubs a hand over her face, scrabbling for logic and reason. *No, calm down. Maybe it wouldn't find Greg because he's dead.* The finality of that sentiment wakes her with a slap.

This just can't be real. The exhaustion and the whisky have taken her mind. *And you're grieving*, a memory of Greg whispers in her ear.

Yes, grieving. A year ago today, and that's been shoved to one side by the mess of this night. She gets up too fast and the chair tumbles behind her, the noise echoing in the solitude of the flat. She stumbles through to bed, climbing into Greg's side and wrapping his shirt around her, the sleeves long like a straitjacket.

She pictures him again on that last holiday, crouching over the pool, desperately fishing out the frogs. And the mice in their kitchen, oh god, the mice. She'd wanted to put poison down, to get rid of them as soon as she found their shit amongst the ransacked food. He was aghast and bought humane traps.

They hadn't worked. Every time he'd pulled one out to check it was empty. 'Give it time,' he said.

Then they'd multiplied. Great piles of droppings to wipe out every morning, the shrill crescendo of hungry baby vermin seeping through the skirting board and the hole in the back of the food cupboard.

So she'd covered the hole in the cupboard and blocked the gaps in the skirting while he watched, appalled. 'It's poison or starvation,' she said eventually. 'You need to deal with problems head on and not leave them for me to handle.' Did he take her advice too literally?


# Sam


I tease out the little tray and switch the SIM cards in my phone. I can do this in my sleep now, my fingers telling me which SIM is which from the subtle scratches and indentations. Around me, people grind their teeth and stare into smartphones as they queue to collect their takeaway coffees and Sunday-morning muffins. So much caffeine and sugar, it's a wonder the whole coffee shop isn't vibrating.

As the phone whirrs back to life, I close my eyes. I can't remember the last unbroken night's sleep I had, and I can feel exhaustion tugging at my corners.

In my palm, the smooth metal phone vibrates with an encrypted message. The last assignment was a success. Carbon monoxide. A tragic accident. A box ticked. A happy customer.

Now another assignment waits.

I open the file. My face, should anyone look over at my table, is impassive. Bored, even. But the truth has many layers. It's not exhilaration that is creeping up my spine, it's more potent and fragile than that. Hope, perhaps. And a foundation of fear, always at the rock bottom of it all is fear. A pulsing fear that keeps me alert.

A waitress brings my coffee and I smile a thanks but she's already looked away, uninterested. Finally the file opens. I swallow my coffee and scan the details.

Her name is Marianne.

# Marianne

### Sunday, 12 September 2021

Dead sleep swallows Marianne until the early hours of Sunday, when a throbbing head and squirming guts wake her. She's startled by the bright light still on in the bedroom, squinting as she hobbles to turn it off. She downs a pint of water, goes to the bathroom, then weaves her way back to bed, avoiding the entrails from last night. Knots of ash, an overnight bag bursting with unwashed clothes, a chair lying on its side.

In bed, she spends a few more hours thrashing around in the gossamer layer between disturbed sleep and semi-consciousness, groaning with her hangover from under the covers and waking for good while the sky is still an ill-formed sludge.

In the dim distance, the sound of Broadway Market drifts through the curtains. In the park over the road, children play wildly, crackling with life. All Marianne can do is lie as still as a corpse.

*

Yesterday when she woke up, she was in Noah's bed. She'd felt his warmth pressed behind her. His salty smell rising from the duvet that tangled both their legs in the night. They were both half asleep as he pulled her nightdress up. The mid-morning sun drawing a yellow line around the curtains as she pushed against him. Heat, sun, morning salt. She felt something like pleasure. Something like forgetting.

Afterwards, she slid out of bed and his hand caught her wrist, his fingers pushing her skin so hard that white crescents formed. She gasped.

'Oh god, I'm sorry,' Noah said, alert then for the first time. 'I just can't get enough of you.' She looked down and smiled, her hair falling like a stage curtain. As she traced a wrinkle in the sheet, an imperfection they'd just made, he pulled her into him. Thick arms like a cartoon sailor. The kind of man she used to laugh at. *They* used to laugh at. 'Big as a barrel and thick as a brush,' Greg would have said. But Noah isn't thick. And he had kissed her like he could love her. She'd kissed him back in answer, morning breath be damned.

She can see herself loving Noah. And soon. It's early days, but for all the darkness that led to them being available, time together is like a burst of light. She hopes he feels the same.

\*

But now she lies alone, cold and haunted. The whole building is silent but for her. No neighbours on either side; those spaces are weekday offices filled with the crushed dreams of hourly paid temps. Below swells the blackness of a condemned business. The loft above is scattered with spiders and Christmas decorations she'll never use again. She winces at memories of their last Christmas. She was needlessly tetchy, and refused to go to his parents' house. Would they ever forgive her for keeping his last Christmas to herself?

And then in the last December gone, her first Christmas without Greg, she'd flown out to her mother's new house in France. Had spent most of it lying on the spare bed, unable to hold a conversation. She thinks now of Noah. Imagines his thick fingers carefully taping up the presents for Daisy. How will he manage when she's a teenager, angry and unwinding, demanding and needy all at once? Marianne lets herself hope that she could join in with their family Christmas next year. And then in years to come, perhaps she will help Daisy navigate the horrors of adolescence, girl to girl. Not a replacement for her mum but something close. Maybe, if things work out, Daisy could have a little brother or sister.

*If I'm still here.*

*Congratulations, someone wants you dead.*

As a history teacher, death usually arrives in the classroom as a comma, a footnote. Thousands died here, a king died there. It's as disposable as the biros she chews while the class works quietly. Death was not a part of her life for so long, and then it slammed into her at the same time those wheels slammed into Greg. What end could be planned for her? And why? Especially why?

Marianne has spent a year embroidering a new life. New routines, a new boyfriend. A future. And now death is tapping at her window again. *But it can't be true, surely?*

The pulse of her heartbeat drums its way through her brain and her bones. Her stomach growls, only acid and bile left in place of the last piece of sacred pie. Her skin prickles from her scalp to the soles of feet. Every breath is shallow. She didn't charge her phone last night, too drunk and rattled for normal concerns. She finds it tangled in her covers.

She shivers as she reaches over to plug in her phone, seasick from moving. A text from Jane in Dubai, asking if she wants to talk. A missed call from her mum that she must have slept through. A WhatsApp message from Noah. 'Thinking of you x.' It was sent at eleven last night, while she was still crawling down the rabbit hole, yet to reach the end.

On aching legs, Marianne drags herself from the bed and out into the cold morning of the lounge. As she picks up the chair and sits down carefully at the table, her throbbing eyes zone in on Greg's laptop. Not opening it now seems like the easiest thing in the world. So why couldn't she have left it alone last night? Other grieving spouses would have left it alone. Noah would have left it alone.

But for Marianne that great ghoulish box has been opened, its hinges bent and lid torn off. Greg was emailing his ex and going on the dark web, in secret. And now she's been left here by herself to fight whatever is coming, without knowing why it could be coming. Or when. Or if.

And even while she's having these thoughts, trying to tie things together in some kind of logical bow, a tickertape in her mind is running on loop: 'This can't be real, this can't be real, this can't be real.' Because it *can't* be real, surely? Normal people don't end up on hit lists.

*

With the phone still plugged in, she searches for the number of her local police station. Instead, there seems to be a central phone number for non-emergency calls. What's more of an emergency than death? And yet, to call 999 would seem insane.

She taps in 141 on her keypad first – not sure if that even blocks your number anymore – then adds the rest. She's placed in a queue, muzak grinding her hungover head.

A woman eventually answers with a gentle Welsh accent as she reads from her script. Finally: 'And how can we help?'

Marianne swallows. *Where to start?* 'It's about . . .'

'Yes?'

'Well, it's about a threat to my life.'

'If you're in immediate danger, you need to end this call and dial nine—'

'No, I'm not, I mean, I don't know when . . . or if . . .'

'Can I take your name and the address where you're currently situated?'

'No, I'm sorry, you can't. I need to be anonymous.'

'Madam, we can't help you if we don't know who you are and it sounds . . .'

'Are you recording this?' Marianne says suddenly.

31

'Well, yes, calls can be recorded for training purposes, I did say that at the—'

'Can you stop recording it?' *What if someone is tracing this? What if someone can hack into these recordings?*

'I can't control that myself, I'm afraid, but it is only for internal use. Why don't you tell me why you feel your life is in danger?'

'OK. This will sound nuts, but I saw something on the dark web. Something that said an assassin's database had been hacked and you could search it and see if you were on it.'

The woman is silent.

'And I searched my husband's name first, he died last year, but he wasn't on it.'

'Sorry, are you saying your husband was assassinated?' There's a crispness to the voice now.

'No, my husband was killed in a road accident but I searched my name – and my name was on there.'

'Your name was on an assassin's database on the dark web?' The incredulity is barely disguised. The woman's voice has grown louder and Marianne imagines colleagues craning their necks to hear.

'Yes,' Marianne says. 'And I don't know what to do. I'm worried that if I go to the police station, they'll know and it'll make it worse.'

'Who will know?'

'The assassins.'

'The assassins,' the woman repeats.

Marianne ignores her tone. 'But if I go to the police station, what would happen?'

The woman pauses. 'Well, they'd take a statement first. Though you would have to give your name to them. And they would take down the details of why you think you're on an, um, an assassin's database . . .'

'Forget it.'

As Marianne cuts off the call, she hears the tiniest shard of laughter. Because of course this is hilarious. It's downright absurd.

*I must be losing my mind.*

# Sam

There's plenty to work with here. A small flat over a disused café. A second-hand car with a poor safety rating for frontal crashes. A teacher who takes the same journey to and from work every weekday. A widow, sleeping alone at the back of the building. I already know more than enough, but in this bone-tired state I can't get loose or sloppy. I'm too close to the finish line.

Targets are, luckily, just as prone to sloppy moves. Especially the ones who think nothing bad could ever happen to someone like them. Just because it hasn't so far.

They say the turkey always feels safest right before Christmas.

# Marianne

Marianne has hardly lived a controversial life. The standout 'drama' of her youth was her father upping sticks and pissing off. Which is about as bog-standard a trauma as you could find. You could probably have skimmed a stone across the beach of her Devon town and hit someone else in the same situation.

She'd headed for the city as soon as she could, driven away from, rather than to, something. Never really knowing what her 'something' should be. After university she'd drifted into teacher training, finding out she was good at it. To her relief and dismay. She would never set the world alight. Ambitious within her job, sure. But far from ruthless.

Did she piss off the wrong people at university? Not that she could imagine, and not in ways that would come back to haunt her decades later. Maybe a parent at school? It feels like a huge leap.

33

Marianne Heywood is a good teacher, with a comfortable life, a recent tragedy and the optimism of a new relationship. And one secret, sure, but hardly a murderous one. More embarrassing than anything. But still, not something she would want anyone to look into lest they think it suggests worse secrets to be found.

She looks again at Greg's laptop. Greg had no powerful friends. But did he have enemies of some kind? Did he stick his nose into the wrong place? She thinks of the activist message board, of his frustrations with how slowly he could work. Did he cut corners and take risks in his desperation to make things better?

'Greg,' she whispers, looking through to the bedroom, to his empty side of the bed. 'Did you do something really fucking stupid?'

Outside, the grey sky gives way to yellow and a steady rumble of traffic drags night into day. Greg's notepads still litter the dining table, his bag is still propped up against the bed. Traces of him are everywhere. Maybe it's time she looked more closely at them. At him, and her memories of who he was.

Her life could depend on it.

\*

Compared with Noah and his neat angles and designer sofa, Marianne's flat looks like it's been burgled. If things work out between them, she will need to up her tidiness game. Would there be any space in Noah's house for her bric-a-brac? For the detritus of her life?

Greg's notepads sit on the dining table, the 'stuff drawer' in the kitchen bulges more than it ever did and as well as books, the bookcase is filled with newspaper supplements, old diaries, unopened post.

She opens the curtains and the yellowing light picks out every dancing dust particle and misplaced fibre. It feels noisy, a cacophony of things to deal with, and for a brief moment

Marianne imagines herself throwing a match at the lot of it and walking away.

Instead, she makes a coffee and pecks at her first nauseating cigarette. She doesn't hoist up the kitchen window like she normally would and as she paces, she tests again that she locked her front door properly last night. Then Marianne pulls on her softest clothes and pushes Greg's shirt, dank with her night sweat, into the washing machine with the rest of the dirty things.

She looks at the pile of notepads again, imagines for a moment that she can pick out the fingerprints, the dust of her late husband. No, not 'late', no euphemisms – Greg hated euphemisms. Her *dead* husband.

Who will clear away her rubble, when she is dust?

Her best friend from school still lives in Devon, their *Sliding Doors* lives creating a wedge. When did Marianne last go to see Nina? She's met her daughter only a handful of times. And Jane from uni, now living in Dubai and working in an international school. If Marianne called her, as she had after Greg died, Jane would tell her to drop everything and fly out. But she wouldn't mean it. No one really means that.

Abi at work, probably the closest to a friend in the staffroom, is the head of safeguarding. There's no way Marianne can mention anything that involves the dark web. She'd be suspended.

Would it fall to Noah? Not if anything happened now, it's too soon. And god, no one deserves to go through that twice.

With a surge of energised panic, Marianne clears her own mess. Shoving rubbish and bits of paper into a bin bag, while making a pile of everything she finds that belonged to Greg. It fast becomes a chaotic little shrine – receipts and shopping lists, torn out news articles that mean nothing to her. And the notepads, of course.

The first bin bag is already bulging, split down one side by the sharp corner of an ignored envelope. She imagines her own skin splitting, slashed by a knife. Marianne squeezes her eyes shut but the image remains inside her lids, only now a rusty zip in her flesh is being slowly, callously teased down so that the very meat of her is raw and exposed.

She works harder, faster, trying to outrun the images. Outside, clouds tumble and make way for slashes of rain. It turns the pavements dark grey and paints the roads black. Inside, she works with a fever. Stuffing and piling and sorting like a factory robot. Only when everything has been arranged into a teetering tower of Greg's shrapnel and four straining bin bags of her own junk, does she stop. More coffee, more smoke.

Her head bangs a relentless march as Marianne sorts through the scraps of paper and junk on the bookcase where fiction should be. The box file catches her eye on the top shelf. It was bought by her mum, she remembers her sorting paperwork into it. A pretty floral design she would never have chosen. Like the flowers on his coffin that she didn't choose either. Like the flowers she's sure his mum leaves by the grave she tends up in Scotland, where Marianne cannot bring herself to go.

She drops the folder on to the table where it coughs up a cloud of dust.

*

The box file is at odds with the scrappy pile of notepads and paperwork. It had been tucked up there on the shelf all this time like a security camera.

The inquest into Greg's death happened during a school day and despite protests from her mum, she'd gone to work instead of attending. It was too painful, too final. At work, things felt almost normal. She could pretend that at the end of the day he would be there waiting, with a home-cooked meal and years and years of in-jokes and unspoken knowledge. An inquest would have stolen that away.

Greg's father had flown down from Scotland. She could picture him in court, cutting the same shape as his son. Narrow-boned and attentive, with his notepad in hand. Losing himself in the logistics. But Marianne and her mother-in-law stayed away, separately. Every fresh detail was a grain of salt pressed into their raw grief. They knew plenty already, more than they wanted to know. The thick tyres on his narrow chest. The slim bones of his hands, pulled apart. The way his bicycle looked, bent into outsider art by the impact. The lack of CCTV. 'A surveillance black spot', almost unheard of in London.

She catches sight of her pale, haunted reflection in the windowpane and jumps. There is no one else here, no one can get in, but her skin prickles as if she's being watched.

She carefully opens the box file. It's full of papers, some of which Marianne has seen before. Letters from the life insurance company. Copies of police reports and statements. A coroner's report and a death certificate. The end of a whole life summarised in just a few pieces of paper.

Paperwork was never Marianne's forte, she had enough of that at school. Greg took care of everything, jokingly pushing forms in front of her to sign like he was the harried secretary of an important CEO. 'Time is money, Marianne, just sign the thing!'

And then her mother had taken his place in the immediate aftermath. It would fall to her mum, wouldn't it, if something were to happen to Marianne. She casts a guilty eye at the bags of unopened letters. Right now, no one is on top of things.

There's a copy of a claim form that Marianne remembers having to sign sometime after Greg's funeral. Her mum's curly handwriting, spelling out Greg's name, the cause of death, the policy number. Love displayed through diligence, the only method her mother knows. The life insurance policy they were claiming on is here too. Where had her mum found that? The memories from that time are patchy and pockmarked.

Next, there's a letter explaining that the pay-out would be made to the deceased person's estate. It sounds so formal and fancy, so at odds with Greg. His prized possessions were his old vinyls and the wedding ring that she now wears on a necklace. She touches it gingerly. He'd practically vibrated with nerves and excitement when she first pushed it onto his finger, in front of bemused friends and family who didn't understand the choice of music: 'Bonnie and Clyde' performed by Brigitte Bardot and Serge Gainsborough. The breathless French duo singing of the kind of wild love Marianne and Greg had then. A love that would outrun everything.

God, they were young.

Marianne picks up the policy document again. It's a straightforward life cover policy, enough to pay off the mortgage and keep the lights on if one of them should die. No, wait. She looks closer; this isn't a joint policy, this is cover for Greg alone.

She looks again at the date. It was taken out just a few days before Greg died.

# Sam

I clean and polish my tools for what I hope is the last time. Soaking them in vinegar, then applying baking soda, then lemon juice. Drying gently with a brand new cloth, firm and deliberate strokes. The way I was taught long ago.

I take my time over this. Knowing I will dispose of all of these soon means it's even more important to do a perfect job.

Afterwards, I inspect my work, holding each item up to the light with gloved hands. Appraising, as coolly as I can, while trying to find fault. I fix a tiny spot of rust, repeating the vinegar stage. Then I pack them all into their holder, slide it into my pocket and head for the door.

I know everything I need to know about the target in theory. It's time to get practical.

# Marianne

The life insurance policy droops in her shaking hands. Marianne looks again at the date. A dark, urgent vein opens up inside her, poison working its way through to her mind. She tries to ignore it but she can't, it blooms across her skull. *Did Greg know he was going to die?*

'Stop it!' Marianne calls out before she can stop herself. None of this can be true, none of it. It's a hoax. An accident killed Greg and no one will kill her. It was prudent to take out life insurance, and normal. Greg was normal! Even as she tells herself this, an itch creeps up her limbs, deep under the skin where her fingers can't scratch.

Marianne closes her eyes and pictures her thoughts as a nest of ribbons, all knotted together. With her mind's eye she teases one loose, pulls gently at the biggest, rawest one. Greg's death. She keeps her eyes screwed shut, her feelings at arm's length. Greg died and it was an accident. An *official* accident. The police said so, the coroner agreed and the insurance company had no reason to quibble.

She wraps her cardigan tightly around herself but still feels cold, frozen to her core.

*

As she stands up to make another strong coffee, her knees buckle. How different things had been when she woke up at Noah's.

Only yesterday but already another lifetime. *Noah.* She thinks of his breadth, his solidity. His whole life, his whole purpose is to look after his daughter, Daisy, and keep her safe.

*Who will keep me safe?*

Certainly not her dad. Long dead and long useless before that. Greg could never understand her disinterest in his offers of comfort on the anniversary of her dad's death. She tried to explain, 'I don't miss what I never had.' Tried to understand that when Greg pictured dads, he obviously pictured his own. Nevertheless every year, Greg was always ready with cuddles and comfort. Just what she could do with now. And home-cooked food. Nurture and nourishment. The basics, more important than anything.

She hopes that she and Noah could become each other's safety. That out of their cautious beginnings, taken slowly for Daisy's sake and theirs, they might build something new and lasting. Marianne dares not admit it to anyone, but she pictured them as a family one day. Maybe even growing that family. Maybe. *Hopefully*. A second chance she didn't ask for but was holding tentatively nonetheless.

Greg had always been adamant that he didn't want children. The world was too crowded and too cruel, he'd said. She'd agreed in principle, more or less, pushing down the small voice inside her. The one that said maybe she would like to have a child . . . and maybe all the good things that still exist in the world are worth sharing. And then her twenties ticked over to her thirties and she started to press her fingers against his certainty, feeling if there might be any room for compromise. There wasn't, nor was he prepared to even talk about it. It remained an unresolved argument right up until he died.

She orders a takeaway curry through a delivery app. Her hangover and blood sugar crying out for carbs, fat and spice. Technology has enabled her laziness but the tech world is far from a passion. It's more a necessary evil and always, she blanches, more Greg's area than hers. After he died, it took months for her to work out how to use the cable box, realising that she'd deferred to him in so many ways she'd become childlike.

Outside, the wind whips the building. The old window frames rattle like teeth. She's never been scared in Hackney before, not even when someone was mugged just outside. Now every time she catches her reflection in the window she jumps. Today is a house-of-mirrors version of her and Greg's happiest days. Tucked in the flat, no work and nowhere to be, comfy clothes and a takeaway on the way. That feeling of not being needed anywhere else and of having everything you want right here. This cramped, messy flat had once been the place where they could both fully exhale. A fortress for two. She'd have taken that feeling over any level of wealth or status, they both would.

When they'd first moved in together after months of bobbing between their respective flatshares, they'd spent every spare penny setting up home. Catching the train to IKEA, travelling back with bags splitting, flat-pack escapees sliding out from boxes. Everything embossed with newness and hope. 'This is *our* whisk,' Greg had said, holding it aloft like the *Lion King* cub. She smiles at the memory, just for a moment. Then thinks guiltily of that little metal whisk, cold and unused in the drawer. Greg left her everything and nothing.

Greg handled most of the finances and paperwork. But for day-to-day cash, for salary payments, they kept separate accounts. He didn't even get sent paper statements that she could dig out and look through now. What would she even be looking for? A chunk of cash drawn out to pay someone for something? Was he being blackmailed? Did he owe money?

A draught snakes up the stairs from the street and whistles under her front door. She tucks her feet into her lopsided slipper boots and opens Greg's laptop again. Perhaps she could still access his internet banking. She was pretty sure he'd have saved the password to autofill. Convenience over safety.

She opens his normal browser and goes to the bank website. As predicted, his username and password populate the fields but when she tries to log on, she gets a message to say that the account is closed and to contact the branch during opening hours. Someone must have notified them about his death, possibly her mother or Greg's dad. Marianne was probably told, in that netherworld between death and starting to live again. Either way, she doesn't remember.

She sets a reminder on her phone to call Greg's bank in her lunchbreak tomorrow and turns back to his laptop. *Reminders*. It was Greg who convinced her to give up paper organisers after she left her Filofax on the bus and briefly lost control of her life. Greg used his Google account for everything: his email, calendar, contacts, reminders. If he was involved in something dangerous, the details could still be in his calendar.

Her phone buzzes next to her. The delivery app tells her that her food will arrive in just a few minutes.

Marianne reopens Greg's email and clicks the calendar icon on the right. She navigates back to 2020, to 9 September, when he emailed Jenna. There's no mention of his ex but there is an all-day appointment set for 'Bluebell'.

Who is Bluebell? A client, perhaps? Maybe something happened to Bluebell and she needed specialist legal advice, and that's why Greg emailed Jenna that night. *Please let it be that.*

She clicks to the next day:

**Jenna**
**13.33**
**Euston**

The doorbell rings sharply while Marianne stares at the screen; her hollow eyes stare back in the reflection.

# Sam

The delivery guy at Marianne Heywood's door is losing patience. He's rung the bell three times already, shifting from one foot to another and tucking his bike out of the way of irritated passers-by. When the door finally opens, the target is apologetic, gesturing awkwardly and flashing a placatory smile.

She's wearing baggy, old-fashioned pyjamas tucked into woollen boots. No make-up, probably not planning to go out. She matches the photo, there's no doubt it's her. A mane of curly brown hair, dark blue eyes, very pale skin.

She's a slight woman. I know from the dossier that she's five foot two but she looks even smaller than that. Childlike, really. But they are often the ones who will surprise you. The ones with a blind fury in their bones and something dark and rotten crawling just below the surface. I know the power of that latent fury better than anyone.

Marianne takes the plastic bag of food, practically curtsying as the guy leaves. She takes a quick look around the street from side to side, then shuts the door.

She didn't notice me sitting on a bench in the small scrub of lawn across the road, scattering bread for the dirty pigeons.

I noticed everything that I've trained myself to notice. The shuttered-up space beneath her flat. The single lock on her street door. The thin windows at the front, companion pieces to the shaky sash panes at the back, all of their thin strings frayed and creaking.

And I noticed the fragility of her bones. I saw every trickle of red blood and bead of blue that was right there beneath her translucent skin. I sat perfectly still, breathing calmly, blinking slowly, and I watched the very life of her throbbing and bursting to get out.

# Marianne

The food congeals in foil trays, untouched on the table. A cold chill creeps up Marianne's spine; her eyes water with exhaustion. She knows she should eat or she won't be able to function properly, and as she scoops out lukewarm rice, her empty gut swills with acid. The grains have clumped together and insect-like flecks of yellow and pink loosen and tumble down.

They used to get a takeaway every Friday. A shared marital treat, one they limped towards through hard weeks. Now it's just a utilitarian solution for laziness.

Marianne dumps spoonfuls of bright red tikka masala on top until it seeps into the rice, a greasy ribbon of oil catching the light. Stomach churning, she plunges her fork in and stares at the red mess on the steel prongs. Her mouth fills with saliva but she can't bring herself to part her lips.

On the Wednesday before he died, Greg had emailed Jenna out of the blue.

By 8 a.m. on the Thursday, Jenna was on a train, bound for Euston.

Where did the ex-lovers go? Greg didn't have money for secret assignations in hotel rooms, although Jenna did. When Greg came home that night she'd barely noticed. Glared into her marking while he reheated Thursday's lasagne for what would be their last supper.

She almost turned Noah down when he asked her out those few months ago. It was too soon after Greg, it wasn't fair to his memory. And she was already carrying the guilt of one regrettable assignation.

Noah had coloured red as she opened her mouth but said nothing, gaping at him like an idiot. 'I'm sorry,' he said. 'It was inappropriate to ask you, will you just forget I said anything?' He'd turned to go and she'd reached out, brushed the skin on his arm with her fingertips and then snapped her hand away, wondering if he too had felt the electric charge fizz between them.

'Don't say sorry,' she said. 'I'd love to go for a drink with you.'

She felt so conflicted, so guilty, that she nearly denied herself a second chance. And all the while Greg had been meeting up with his ex on the side. But why?

Marianne slides her food away with a long exhalation. The fork drops, flecking an angry line of red across the table. The ribbons are all knotted again.

Jenna could answer at least some of these questions. Greg had reached out to her, while he was pushing Marianne away, keeping her in the dark. Whether it was as simple as missing her, or as complex as needing legal advice, Jenna had clearly been a trusted confidante. Someone he could call on to drop everything.

Marianne searches in Greg's inbox and then writes down Jenna's email address before opening the email app on her own phone. Marianne and Jenna didn't know each other but she could hardly email from Greg's account and haunt the living fuck out of someone who is probably still grieving. The ghosts of first loves tend to linger.

Marianne tries to picture Jenna at Greg's funeral, held up in Scotland because Marianne had no energy to fight about it. Jenna would surely have come to pay her respects – the whole town seemed to turn out, a vague grey mass – but if she did, Marianne was unaware. She'd taken one of her mum's nerve pills and glided through the day half a world away from everyone else.

Dear Jenna,

It's Marianne, Greg Darrow's wife, here.

I'm sorry to email you out of the blue like this and I really hope this doesn't cause you any distress. I was clearing some of Greg's things and I found out that he met with you before he died. I would really like to understand why. I am not judging you in any way for anything, I'd just really appreciate some honesty.

Thank you,

Marianne

45

With a hollow feeling, Marianne replaces 'wife' with 'widow' and then sends it before she can proofread it away to nothing. It's Sunday and Jenna is unlikely to reply, but it feels like *something* at least.

\*

What might Greg have found if it was Marianne who had died and her husband who'd been left to rifle through her digital underwear drawer?

She had secrets of her own. Who didn't? But she'd been careful. She'd created a folder in her email account with a bland and misleading name and tucked everything from her ex-pupil, Marc, in there.

That careful deception, those furtive messages, were a bigger admittance of guilt than anything. And nothing had actually happened, not then.

She'd not always been secretive. The postcards, ironic pictures and pithy little messages she'd received from Marc had been in plain sight.

'Why is *he* sending you postcards?' Greg asked one day in 2019, having never mentioned it before.

'He's just glad I helped him with his A levels,' she said, her cheeks colouring. 'And I think he's finding the transition to university a bit hard.'

Up until that point, she could tell herself whatever story she wished about this thing, this situation. Putting those postcards in a cupboard in the flat, not hiding them. But afterwards, when she switched to email and included the words 'my husband found your postcards and I think email is better', she'd upgraded the unspoken into something more concrete. But still nothing had happened.

There's no one to make excuses to now. But if there were, Marianne would say that Greg was distant where Marc was available. That Greg was brooding, troubled by the world and everyone in it, while Marc was at the sweet stage of barely

46

looking beyond his own adolescent worries. She could say that chatting to Marc, emailing him about thoughts as they drifted to her, sharing jokes that Greg might once have enjoyed were he still paying attention, helped insulate her from what was happening in her marriage. She might even say, troubling a confession though it is, that listening to Marc's worries and encouraging his young mind to stay the course, allowed Marianne to nurture, to mother almost, in a way Greg had curtailed.

And every time she sent and immediately hid an email, nothing had happened. And every time she'd read an email from *him*, in another room to Greg, smiling secretly before she archived it away, still nothing had *actually* happened. She never even saw him again until after Greg had died.

But while he was still alive, Greg barely mentioned it again. Not even as a joke. No references to 'postcards from your fancy piece', no prods in the rib when jokes about toy boys came up. She should have been angry when he first queried those cards, the sides of his mouth twisting down as he held the small stack by their corners as if they were contaminated.

She should have been angry. What he was implying was . . . it was something she should have been angry about. But she couldn't allow herself anger, couldn't allow herself to switch on any feelings because she knew that some of those feelings were simply not OK.

\*

There is so much more to go through. Years and years of calendar appointments and reminders. The hard part is knowing where to start and what to look for. Marianne reopens Greg's calendar and clicks all the way back to 26 July 2014, a date scorched onto her heart.

**THE WEDDING OF THE CENTURY!!!**
**14.00**
**Leyton Great Hall**

Greg had 'invited' her to it so it sat in her Google calendar too, even though she was still living out of a Filofax back then. He'd carefully added the full address of the venue – as if she didn't know.

God, they were young to get married. It hadn't felt like it then, but it certainly feels like it now. London-young anyway; she'd walked down the aisle an old maid by the standards of her native Devon.

Marianne clicks on through his calendar. A zoetrope of memories. Honeymoon flights, mortgage-broker appointments, dinner reservations on anniversaries and birthdays. Milestones embroidered with just a few lines of code.

She slows when she reaches 19 March 2015.

**Interview – Case worker**
**10.00**
**Hidden Humans**
**Lambeth**

That job was everything he wanted. They'd celebrated with sparkling wine and fish and chips when he'd got the call. It was slightly less money than the animal charity paid, but money had never been his driving force. She remembers the acute pride she felt, so sharp it was physical. Her husband, her principled, hard-working, optimistic man. He was the best of them, and she could not have loved him more.

When he got going in the role, he talked optimistically about all the change he hoped would come; the women whose lives had been turned around with support; the solicitors he'd found who would work on cases pro bono; the exploited, homeless runaway who had been rehomed. The change came years later when nothing had improved *despite* him doing that work.

'Every month, there are more people in need and the government don't do anything. In fact, they make it worse. I had three trafficked people last month who were being made to clean schools, never seeing proper wages – that's not just apathy, that's fucking profiting from slavery. If the local government aren't even checking their suppliers, what hope do we have?'

'What do you want me to say, Greg?'

'Which cleaning contractors does *your* school use?'

Marianne had tried not to sigh. 'I don't know. I'll ask.'

She'd forgotten though, hadn't she.

Marianne scrolls on through months and years, watching the number of personal appointments sputter to nothing, crowded out by work. He gave it his all, but it was never enough.

She reaches Friday, 27 September 2019 and sees a whole day for 'Bluebell' again. No other details, but this is the first occurrence. She clicks on, faster and faster, finding more and more Bluebell days as she goes. 'Bluebell' at least once a month right up until the day he contacted Jenna.

*Who the fuck is Bluebell?*

# Sam

I tap my unregistered Oyster card along the same little strip of London that I always travel through. Then I am seen by traffic cameras on the A3 as I drive, a frown scoring my forehead. I buy a modest dinner for later, paying with cash. My undisguised head with its grey temples gives a nod to the security guard manning the door of the miniature supermarket, one of the many I visit that are laced along the A-roads snaking their way out of the city. I am so completely visible that I am almost transparent, tugged along on the tides of middle-class life.

I am seen in all these places, wearing my true face, because I need to be a functioning human. *I need to be normal.* I have routines that make sense because I need alibis. And when I have to switch off my humanity and slip below the line into

49

the deepest darkness, these strings of normality dangling through my days are all I have to pull me back up.

Sometimes, they slip from my grasp altogether.

# Marianne

'Bluebell?'

Marianne says it out loud, hoping to dislodge something, some tiny little petal of a memory but there's nothing there.

'Bluebell.'

It could be a client. Perhaps. Or a nickname for a lover. Or a favourite prostitute. It could be a dog or a fucking boat for all she knows. Bluebell. Every month, for over a year.

This time yesterday she was still mourning him acutely, simply. Now a whole new raft of feelings are flooding in. Fear and confusion at the helm, followed shortly by a nagging sense of stupidity at trusting someone so completely. Even shades of jealousy. Greg, her open book, was anything but. And she has no idea of her place in his story. Or whether she's really going to be the victim of its bad ending. There's nothing else to do but keep looking. No one else will have any answers for her. Marianne thinks again of calling Noah, but what would she say? In the early months a relationship is a fragile thing; one gust of wind could send it scattering. Let alone a great storm of paranoia and fear.

No, there's nothing else for it. She searches in Greg's email for 'Bluebell'. Nothing comes up beyond the appointments she'd already found in his calendar. If he was emailing someone called Bluebell, he was doing it from his work account. *Or that secret dark web email account that I can't get into.*

Above her, she hears a scratching sound. It's very slight at first and she has to strain to hear it. It sounds like the cautious scraping of a knife on wood, growing more frenzied. For one dark second, she imagines it belongs to metal on wood, a hook, Death's sceptre.

*Mice*.

The scratching spreads. It sounds like a fleet of discrete blades working their way down the wall, trying to carve their way into the room. The offices either side of her are empty, but apparently the old crumbling walls and the roof are not. She imagines their fast little bodies, scrambling over each other and slinking around inside the wall.

On her hand, Marianne writes 'poison' in black ink.

She stares at the letters she's just written, so casual in their murderous intent. Is that how easy it is? Is she vermin as far as someone is concerned?

Turning the stereo on to drown out the mice, she searches in Greg's laptop's documents folder. It's a wild mess of work notes, old job applications, out-of-date CVs and wedding speeches. Odds and sods.

Bluebell is not hiding here.

She opens his photos and scrolls through, barely able to look. His beautiful face, guileless and optimistic. The two of them, young and stupid with love. Their wedding day, faces aching from smiles, his hair growing more tousled as the day drew on, her hair unpinned and loose by the end. Make-up slipping from her happy wet eyes. The two of them dancing and laughing to 'Come On Eileen', her wedding dress hitched up around her knees. The way he looks at her. Like she's the only person in the whole world. Like she is his world. *Who took this picture?* Who cares now?

She closes the photos down, raw and shaking. Those people, those moments, they've become something different. Characters rather than memories. A loss so deep she can't look at it.

Instead, Marianne searches the internet. She discovers the Latin name for the common bluebell, a few celebrities whose daughters are called Bluebell and not much else.

'Bluebell Greg Darrow', *search*.

'Bluebell slavery victim', *search*.

'Bluebell charity', *search*.

'Bluebell slang', *search*.

'Bluebell prostitute', *search*.

'Bluebell betting', *search*.

'Bluebell fucking help me here', *search*.

*Nothing. Absolutely nothing. Where else?*

The white rabbit winks at her as Marianne's fingers find their way back. In minutes she's staring at the dark web browser again, snapping back to it despite all her earnest intentions. First she tries the marketplace forum. The screen seems to crawl and metamorphose in front of her, updating, *pulsing* as hundreds of cockroaches around the world ply their hateful wares. She doesn't read any of it. Instead, she clicks into the search box.

*Bluebell. Search.*

The site flexes and blinks while she holds her breath.

*No results found.*

Next, she goes to the activist chat room, searches there too. The wait is painful. But no result there either.

She goes to the email login screen, tries 'Bluebell' as a password, as a username, a frenzy of attempts with desperate combinations. Nothing.

Marianne goes to the final tab, the hacked hit-list database. Despite hoping it will be gone, a figment of her drunken imagination, the website is still there.

She types 'Bluebell' carefully, one finger at a time. *Search.*

She can barely stand to look at this site, its simplicity hiding the viper's nest underneath.

*No results. Try again.*

She types angrily, hopefully, fast. Marianne Heywood. Search. Please, please, please let it be gone. Let me have imagined it. Let it be a hoax. A randomly generated response that won't come up this time. Please. The site seems to freeze, and Marianne holds her breath until her chest hurts.

*Search results: Marianne Heywood, Hackney, date of birth: 7 August 1987.*

*Her face.*

That damn skull emoji again. *Congratulations, someone wants you dead.*

*

Marianne imagines Greg heading out to work on his final day. She'd already gone. She always left before him during term time, throwing a goodbye at him as she pulled the door closed.

When he died, he was wearing an old black hoodie that she'd more or less commandeered over the years, not the reflective jacket she'd bought him. Time was, they would wear each other's clothes interchangeably. His hoodies hanging baggy on her, his joggers swimming on her legs, her old T-shirts tight to his chest, worn with boxers while they curled up to watch TV. *Time was.*

She knows precisely what he was wearing that final morning because she received it back afterwards, ripped and tattered, laced with gravel and blood.

On that last day, Greg must have closed their flat door around half past eight, having dragged his bike down from the stairs where it was awkwardly balanced. He only got three streets away. An accident, by every measure.

Her back runs cold with sweat. Did Greg see her name on the list and try to fool them by wearing a hoodie she'd been recently wearing? Surely he wouldn't do something that stupid, he'd just tell her what he'd found?

Unless he did something to put her on that list and then tried, in a round-about and fucked-up way, to put it right? *Is that why he took out insurance on himself, by way of goddamn apology?* Either way it didn't work.

*My name is still on there, Greg!*

*

Marianne goes to the kitchen to get a blast of fresh air. She slides the window open and an autumn chill puckers her skin. Anyone could be standing in the rat run of alleyways behind

53

her building, she'd never know. The city had always felt so safe to her. Yes, there's an edge to it, but it offered protection in numbers too. Now those numbers are all faceless murderers, able to get right up close to her, crawling around her life like the mice in the roof.

She closes the window tightly again and pulls down the blind. She's out of fags but there's a pack in her car. There's no way she can cope with everything without cigarettes.

Outside, the street is quiet and damp. A bus lurches past, its windows steamed opaque. Silhouettes move lazily inside. A few couples walk arm in arm down the pavement, or stomp in the single file of an imminent break-up. A dog walker briskly marches a Labrador, headed for the grass with a knot of poo bags coiled around his lead. A group of teenagers smoke weed in the scrubby parkland.

Her car is two streets away and she holds her keys in her left hand, spiked through her fingers like Freddy Krueger. Her phone sits heavily in her coat pocket and her pyjamas trail along the stained street. Marianne looks around, trying to be subtle, while her heart crashes around in her chest. She's feeling her way, unused to being in any danger beyond the baseline fear that all women are handed as children.

She turns the corner and sees her little Fiat 500 where she left it. It looks infantile and she feels a pang of protectiveness. Its roof has a scattering of leaves while a flyer flaps lazily from under the windscreen wiper. The same takeaway advert that is fluttering around on all the neighbouring cars. She opens the door, looking furtively around, and snatches the cigarette carton, locks up and rushes back along the streets, slipping inside her front door and locking it. She presses the timer light so it bursts into life, ticking like a heartbeat.

She starts to mount the stairs and catches the black sight of a spider, scuttling into the corner of one of the steps. Fuck. She'll have to go past it but, god, she hates them so much. The way they move, the sheer darkness of them. Jagged scribbles of evil.

The weekend before last, a daddy-long-legs had clattered its haphazard way towards her as she lay under Noah's warm duvet. Before she'd had time to freak out, Noah had leapt naked from the bed, cupped the insect in his big hand, unlocked the window with the other and clapped it outside. 'That was something else,' she'd laughed.

'Here to protect and serve, ma'am,' he'd said, doffing an imaginary cap.

If only he were here now.

She waits for the spider to take the hint, to just disappear without any input from her, but he just sits in her eye line, taunting her.

'OK,' she says, and rushes past him, up the next couple of steps, then slows to regain her composure.

The timer light switches off and plunges her into darkness in the windowless space. Her stomach drops and she crouches in fear. In the darkness, she imagines the spider crawling into her hair. Shadowy hands cling to her and mouths hang open in silent screams. There's no one to help her fight her own imagination, let alone any real danger lurking.

She takes a breath and rushes up the steps, her feet finding the well-worn dips in the carpet and her hand reaching for the light switch on the landing. The hallway grows reassuringly yellow again. She's still alone. Still safe. No hands or mouths or eyes, and she can no longer see the spider. She hurries back into the flat and locks the inner door as well.

# Sam

I take a circuitous route back to Hackney. I'm seen in a base-ball cap driving into the bruised bit of Greater London where Essex and London bleed into each other. The plates on my car are not real.

I am seen in a thin jacket and sunglasses, tapping an unregistered Oyster card at an unmanned station and settling into a train that boils me at my ankles thanks to unnecessary radiators. I dismount and dump my charity-shop jacket in a waste bin.

As I stroll through Hackney Wick, I pull a fresh fold-up anorak from my pocket and over my head.

The weather rolls over me, the air swells with damp and the sky hangs dull and grey. I turn sharply and join the path alongside the Thames, a thin metal fence on my left, the bold graffiti wall of an old warehouse on my right. I whistle a nameless unknowable tune that is probably a distant cousin of an old radio jingle or a song my son once sang. The thought stops me for a moment and I blink out at the brightly coloured houseboats of Fish Island, bobbing on the water like bath toys. The scene blends with the remnants of old summer days spent in a garden I'm not allowed in anymore. There is no one watching as I slap my face, hard, and shake myself sensible again.

I arrive back on Marianne's road just as she slips inside her front door, closing it with a slam. I stroll past the door without changing pace and pass in time to hear her footsteps. All alone.

# Marianne

Marianne makes a cup of herbal tea and some toast. She's brought the gloom back in with her and wraps a knitted blanket around her shoulders as she sits heavily on the sofa. Greg's mum made this for them. A moving-in present, brought down by plane as an extra piece of hand luggage. Marianne had hated it on sight. Too fussy, too old fashioned, not *them* at all.

Greg had guessed as much but she grew to love it in the end. Did she ever tell him that? Did Marianne thank his mum properly or could she tell that her daughter-in-law was unimpressed? Ungrateful too.

She thinks guiltily of his parents up there, in Greg's childhood home. She'd ribbed him about his old bedroom the first time she'd visited. 'This is like a shrine! It's fucking creepy!' She hopes it brings them comfort now. More comfort than her own little museum has brought her.

While picking at the food, Marianne takes in the room as if looking through someone else's eyes. It's a scene of total dysfunction. The dining table still covered in laptops, notepads and scraps of paper. Four large bin bags straining with their contents. A tote bag full of essays to mark, long overdue.

The sofa dips in two spots but she only ever takes the right-hand side, leaving Greg's corner covered in mismatched cushions. Like a teenager sneaking out, leaving a fake pillow-person under the covers. She tucks her knees under her and lets her eyes close for just a moment.

*Congratulations, someone wants you dead.*

Her eyes snap open with the sickly click of a doll's. This isn't the time for rest. Marianne hauls herself from her nest to grab the pile of notepads and paper from the table and takes it back to the sofa, flicking on the light as she goes.

There are so many pieces of him here, so many thoughts scored into these scraps. No beginning or end, just an infinite paper snake eating itself. She thinks of Greg's soft fingers around a pen. Remembers the little crease in his forehead when he was concentrating. It appeared when he was stressed and anxious too. She saw it more and more during his final months, unaware that there was anything going on besides the uphill battle of an impossible job.

She opens the first of Greg's notepads. Always proper hardback notepads, never jotters. She touches the cover just lightly, imagines him picking it from the stationery cupboard at work. *Are you in here, Bluebell?*

It's full of doodles, scraps of names and telephone numbers. All meaningless to her. These are the notepads of a feverish, busy mind, catching every fleeting thought; it's impossible to know what is important. She keeps flipping, sees dates of birth she doesn't recognise, some kind of grading – A, B, D, O. Clients, no doubt. Some kind of shorthand for their status or needs. Almost always undocumented, names and dates of birth are often the only identifying information that people escaping trafficking have got. She remembers that much at least.

There are probably hundreds of names across all of these notepads. Among them are drawings of little mice, minutes from meetings with actions starred with asterisks and calls arranged with related organisations. Hard, tight circles scored in frustration.

Greg has dated some of the pages. The notepad she's looking at right now seems to be from 2014, so she sets it aside and picks up another to flip through. This one is 2013. Fewer scored angry circles the further back she goes; neater writing too. A simmer rather than a boil. The notebook she picks up now is from late 2018 and she flips to the end but it's just more meaningless scrawl, even as the year ticks over into 2020 – the year he didn't see out.

This last notepad she's just picked up carries on where the other left off – summer 2020, a couple of months before he died. Only a third of it is full. The last used page is a series of work actions that Greg never came back to complete. Numbers. People to call, clients to check on, meetings to arrange with related charities that support forced-marriage victims or sex workers. As she flips through, she sees nothing that hints at life and death questions – for her or for Greg. Nothing relating to Bluebell either.

*Breathe, do this properly.*

Marianne leafs slowly through the notepad again, this time taking one page at a time. This is the notepad Greg was using just before he died, it's too important to just thumb through. She even continues looking through the blank pages after the writing stops, just in case.

As Marianne reaches the dead centre, she can see that a page has been ripped out, a little fringe remaining along the inner spine. She holds the pad up to the light. The imprint of whatever was written on the missing page has been pressed into its neighbour.

She runs her fingertips along it. It's no good, it's impossible to decipher. She gropes around the room for a pencil and sits back down with the notepad on her lap, using a feather-light touch to rub the soft pencil stub over the indentations, watching the words come back to life.

# Sam

Through the gap in the curtains, from across the road in the park, I see Marianne Heywood leap up into view like she's been shot.

In her hands, she clutches a small book and struggles to keep hold of it, as if it's grown hot to the touch. Now she holds it out in front of her and stares at it, her mouth hanging open.

A plot twist, perhaps. Maybe a death.

I know a lot about Marianne Heywood already but not the kind of books she reads and I wonder, pointlessly, about her tastes. Is this book in her hands some kind of modern-day bodice ripper? Or perhaps an action thriller, filled with a dizzying body count and a distinct lack of logic?

My mother was a big reader, always thinking and dreaming. My father the opposite, practical, logical and prepared. I am more like my father, through nature and nurture.

I wonder what my parents would think of my life now. They might understand the pragmatism, I think. But this is not the life they would want for me, any more than I would want this for my son.

Marianne has disappeared already. Sinking out of view and back into her story. A little ship, bobbing up and down on a tide, and completely oblivious that she's sailing in a direction from which there is no return.

# Marianne

Pencil dust coats her fingers. She has made a frame of anxious charcoal smudges around the page. There isn't much here. No doodles, dates of birth or angry scored circles. She's stared at it for so long now that when Marianne closes her eyes, she can still see the words imprinted on her eyelids.

Just five names, four of whom are total strangers. One who isn't:

Andrew Mackintosh
Rosie Parsons
David Ross
Pavel Bourean
Marianne Heywood

There's not even a glimmer of familiarity, no matter how hard she stares at the other four names on this list. *Did I know* anything *about my husband?*

She looks at Greg's Facebook profile, but none of those people are listed among his friends. With the exception of Pavel Bourean, they sound too British to be clients, who mostly come from outside the country. Marianne logs into Greg's Gmail, searching for full names then just first names. Greg knew plenty of Andrews, none of them with the surname Mackintosh though. The rest come up totally empty, apart from, of course, Marianne Heywood.

*Why did you put me on this list, Greg? Who did you write it for?*

Back on Facebook, she finds thousands of people called Andrew Mackintosh, Rosie Parsons and David Ross. Too many to contact and none with any connections to her or Greg. She finds no Pavel Bourean at all. Off-grid or made-up, the name is just as useless to her. It's all useless to her.

She tries Google but it's the same story, a whole lot of nothing. And, in Pavel Bourean's case, literally nothing.

The light has faded, everything shrouded in shadow. She stares at the dark corner of the room and knows there is somewhere else to look for these names.

This will be her third visit to the dark web in twenty-four hours, something bordering on a habit. Is this how it starts? *Is this how it ends?*

*

The wait is painful but the now familiar site is hardly a reassurance when it does reappear in front of her. She shivers despite the ambient temperature of the room.

She copies the first name from the list carefully. How many people could be on this database in total, obliviously dancing towards the edge of something?

*Search results: Andrew Mackintosh, Godalming, date of birth: 2 July 1964.*

The black-and-white picture shows a middle-aged man in glasses. Marianne has never seen him before, but Greg had put him and her on a secret list.

She searches the next, exhausted by the knowledge, some dreadful intuition, that she will find the next name too. And she does.

*Search results: Rosie Parsons, Tottenham, date of birth: 23 April 1993.*

A woman's face looks directly at the camera, her blonde hair rendered silver in the monochrome image.

Marianne searches the rest, writing down the dates of birth and locations until she knows the skeletal facts.

Andrew Mackintosh, Godalming,
    date of birth: 2 July 1964.

Rosie Parsons, Tottenham,
    date of birth: 23 April 1993.

David Ross, Reigate,
    date of birth: 18 October 1976.

Pavel Bourean, unknown,
    date of birth: unknown.

The individual details are not so important right now; just one simple fact is clouding out every other thought: *Greg wrote a hit list and put my name on it.*

\*

When Marianne crawls under her covers, she can still think of nothing but this.

The bed is cold and unwelcoming, the sheets creased and gritty. She thinks now of Noah's clean sheets and warm skin. The smell of sandalwood and orange. And his double-glazed windows and Neighbourhood Watch signs. She considers messaging him to ask for help. 'Save me from my dead husband, from whoever he really was.'

Her fingers tap the screen to life and hover over the WhatsApp icon. She imagines him rubbing his eyes and sitting up, his face folding into a frown as he reads her message.

Then she imagines trying to explain what started all this, how she went rooting around on the dark web after finding out Greg had been on there. Noah is brunch and sunshine, optimism and future. He's not darkness and mistrust, he's not the past. And what would he say anyway?

*'Why don't you go to the police? Do you have something to hide?'*

Noah, and hopefully his daughter too, are her prize for getting through this unscathed. She cannot risk dragging them into it.

Marianne puts her phone down hard on top of a pile of books that teeters next to her bed. She wraps her duvet around herself, shuffles into the middle of the bed and listens to the night outside. The babble of nightlife has always calmed her. She and Greg used to make up little stories to accompany the sounds of footsteps, snatches of conversations. 'Do you think they love each other as much as we do?' she'd say, when they heard couples.

'Impossible,' he would reply.

She listens to taxis taking lovers home to bed, distant police cars patrolling. Drunk friends staggering home, their heavy footsteps slapping arrhythmically. People, lots and lots of people, a safety net of ears and eyes.

Only now she imagines that those slow, crunching tyres belong to someone keeping surveillance on her flat. That those hard footsteps belong to a killer, with a flaming bottle ready to throw through her window. The sound of someone in the alley is no longer a drunk pissing in the dark, but a man with a knife clamped between his teeth shinning up the drainpipe. Risk rippling through every tiny sound, terror hiding in every creak of this old building.

She closes her eyes tight, grinds her head back into her pillow and knows that sleep will not come.

# Sam

The grey stones of the alley are slick with drizzle and the high walls of the neighbouring yards rise up to block out the light. There's not a soul around. Everyone tucked up inside on this Sunday night, feet in their warmest socks, pyjamas straining over bellies full of roast dinner. They've bathed the kids, ironed work uniforms and school shirts, made tomorrow's sandwiches. Maybe there's been an argument or two; Sundays are like that for some.

But the heating is back on and thank god for that, they think. At last that strange sticky summer is behind us and we can turn our misty eyes to Bonfire Night or Christmas or New Year. To something nice and good and wholesome twinkling on the horizon.

Tonight, the whole city glows in a picture-perfect scene while I creep quietly in the dark shadows underneath.

Even if they did leave their cosy homes and brave the damp, they would not see me. They don't want to consider that people like me exist, stealing oxygen from the mouths of babes, planning wicked things. And so I walk in plain sight while they look straight through me. A ghost in a house that refuses to be haunted.

I head to the flat by the back way, watching for witnesses while a fat raindrop works its way down my neck. No eyes, no ears. I'm silent as a snake easing my way along the ground, closing the gate in a practised move and avoiding the puddles that dot the small yard.

The key twists in the door's lock and the tiny metallic sound is lost to the wind. Inside is black and I listen for life. There is none. I switch on the kitchen light and my home is filled with amber yellow.

I dump my keys on the table. Then I slide out of my boots, peel off my socks and stretch my toes on the floor. When did I last rest? Truly, properly rest? Not the one-eye-open sleep of the damned. Not waking at dawn to place myself in someone else's world, ready to shred it from inside out. I can't remember the last time I actually slept all night until I woke up naturally. I lust for it. I want to feast on sleep, gorge on unconsciousness. That kind of sleep has been beyond my grasp for years.

I pull off my damp jeans and walk bare-legged into my bedroom, where I change into pyjamas. In the bathroom, I stand over the sink and rub my hands through my hair, shaking out the dust and cobwebs I accumulated in her loft.

My heating has also come on for the first time this year. In the lounge, my nose wrinkles at the tell-tale smell of burning dust and last year's dead insects warming to a crisp. I pour a glass of red into a heavy, ornate wine glass. One of the only relics of my former life. It was a long time before I dared to drink again and it weighs heavy in my hand.

I light a fire and sit in the armchair next to it, sipping my drink and picking up a book I've tried to read for months. Picture-postcard, just like them. But nothing like them at all.

# Marianne

*Monday, 13 September 2021*

Sometime between two and three, Marianne's wild heart slows enough for her to pass out. She wakes to her alarm just four hours later, groaning into the morning air. She smokes a cigarette still lying flat on her bed, staring into the morning, feeling just as bewildered as she did last night.

She pulls herself loose from the covers, downs a coffee and tries to shower herself human. It is a display reminiscent of those early weeks after Greg died. Robotic rituals. Going through the motions. One foot in front of the other. All the other clichés that bubble up around death.

One of the first times she'd really listened to Noah at the bereavement group was when he spoke about this. He talked about the early months after Louise's kidneys finally gave up. How the routines his daughter demanded, just by being a baby, had been his salvation. They kept him going until he wanted to keep himself going. Was that when she'd first noticed his body, as he stood to talk? The muscular thighs, the slabs of chest under muted but expensive T-shirts? Realising in the process that her own blood was still pumping? Oh, for those days of pedestrian grief.

She dries her hair, paints a mask over her ghoulish face and pulls on clothes. Despite waking up on time, the morning has slipped from her grasp and she's already running late. Marianne stuffs everything haphazardly into her bag, including Greg's notepad and her own list of names, and forces herself out of the door.

\*

Twisting the key with trembling fingers, Marianne manages to start the engine of her car. She drives, somehow, on the correct side of the road and in the right direction. The sunshine feels like a joke. She stares at the other drivers aghast. *Ignorant bastards.* They frown, they glare, they beep, they forget to indicate. It's as if *they* have the weight of the world on their shoulders. *So you have some chores to do, a job you don't like, you're late, your kids are annoying, so fucking what,* she thinks. *So fucking what. Someone wants* me *dead!*

She is reminded, quite out of the blue, of her father. How he had called on her mother's landline, just before Marianne took her A levels. 'Who *is* this?' Marianne asked pointedly, although she knew.

'It's Dad,' he said. 'I have some health news.'

Terminal.

She'd not thought of him in a long time. William Heywood, a partial dad and then an unvisited headstone. Marianne was eighteen when he died, and he was never much cop before that. Even when he'd tried to make last-ditch amends – and he really had – she'd refused to accept the sticking plaster. The girl who needed those efforts was no longer around, she'd grown up a little harder for it.

Besides, cancer doesn't override who you are, and he had been a rubbish dad so then he became a rubbish dad with cancer. But that word. *Terminal.* An ending in sight. She'd never thought of how he must have felt to hear that. To

66

receive that knowledge. And when he told her, wheezing down the line, she'd let it pass through her like everything else he'd ever said.

'There's so much I wish I'd done,' he said, his voice pleading. She'd assumed he meant keeping his family.

Now she knows he was referring to much more than that. All those opportunities lost. There's so much she's never done, never dared. Treading water instead of swimming. So now she knows the unique terror her father must have felt. And for her, there is an utterly unique sense of isolation. An end in sight, and no one else can see it. If it's even true. That old caveat, messing with her mind more than ever.

A horn beeps and she slams on her brakes just before the nose of her car is wiped off by a van overshooting some lights. Her body rattles with adrenaline, the class-A surge of a near miss. Is that how it will feel, before she feels nothing?

Do the others on the list share this knowledge? Are they driving around in a daze, wondering how the axe will fall? Or are they oblivious? Still cocooned in the blanket-soft ignorance that she'd existed in, until she went snooping through Greg's things. Until she pulled that damn thread.

*

The secondary school where she's worked for nearly ten years is a big Brutalist building that wasn't fit for purpose even when it was built in the fifties. The large school hall in the centre and the upper classrooms are accessed by seams of staircases that create a kind of Spaghetti Junction experience during the morning rush. Normally Marianne makes sure she's safely ensconced in the staffroom before the kids arrive. Not today. She pushes against a tide of rucksacks and zombie teens.

Abi tries to make conversation over coffee, her eyes kind and concerned. But it's her job to safeguard the kids; if she knew anything Marianne had seen or done . . . and besides, there are other secrets she doesn't want Abi to unearth. If Abi knew about Marc, knew how close to the sun Marianne had flown before, her career could be over anyway.

She ricochets through the morning, late to staff meetings, spilling water down herself and having to rush out to the bathroom mid-lesson. She's ill-prepared and stilted in class and her students eye her suspiciously; is this shambolic act a trick? But her colleagues don't seem to mind. At lunchtime, a biology teacher and prized gossip called Susan Abbot puts her hand over Marianne's in the staffroom and asks how she's doing. *Oh.* They're making allowances because of the anniversary, of course. A memo probably went around the staff. Don't upset the Widow Heywood. 'I'm OK,' Marianne lies, freeing her hand from Susan's and abandoning the ham sandwich she's been nibbling. Marianne's phone buzzes with a reminder. 'Just need to make a call.'

It takes ten minutes but she finally gets through to the right department at Greg's bank. 'We can send those statements out,' the friendly voice says.

'Oh, thank you,' Marianne sighs, unsure if the statements will tell her anything helpful but hoping they will somehow prove her worries wrong.

'All you need to do,' the woman continues, 'is to write in to the head office, listing the precise dates of the statements you'd like.'

'OK . . .'

'And you need to enclose a cheque for ten pounds—'

'A cheque? I don't think I have any cheque books. Who uses cheques anymore?'

A less friendly pause. 'Do you bank with us too?'

'No,' Marianne says. 'Sorry.'

'We can't take a payment any other way then, I'm afraid, but if you go into your bank and ask, I'm sure they can order you a cheque book.'

'OK,' she says, trying to mask her impatience. 'I'll do that then. Thank you.'

'Sorry, madam, there's more I'm afraid. You also need to enclose a death certificate, proof of your own identification,

68

which can be a copy of your passport or driving licence, and proof of address.'

Marianne pauses, deflated. 'Is that it?'

'Yes, madam, that's it.'

'And how long will it take when I've sent in all that?'

'Well, it depends on whether it's straightforward and how far back the statements need to go,' the woman answers brightly. 'But it should be within a month.'

'A month? Oh, Jesus Christ.'

'Can I help you with anything else today, madam?'

Marianne pinches her nose. Since seeing her name on that list, she's not been able to think beyond one day, let alone a month.

'Madam?'

'Sorry, no. But thank you.'

\*

Marianne has a free period after lunch. She's horribly behind on her work in a way that would usually have her working every second, staying late tonight, hobbling home and working on the sofa. Instead, as the staffroom thins out, Marianne pulls the notepad from her bag and looks again at the list of names that she's copied.

Andrew Mackintosh, Godalming,
    date of birth: 2 July 1964.

Rosie Parsons, Tottenham,
    date of birth: 23 April 1993.

David Ross, Reigate,
    date of birth: 18 October 1976.

Pavel Bourean, unknown,
    date of birth: unknown.

She wonders again if they know they are in danger. Their names look so benign, just three average people living in average places. And someone almost unknown who might as well not exist at all. Surely they can't know anything, Marianne reasons. It's only through sick chance that she stumbled upon her own name. Unless, of course, these are people Greg knew from his dark web activities, but from what she could tell, no real names are ever used.

Except, she shivers, in hit lists.

She should find them and warn them, that's the right thing to do. That's what Greg would do – her idea of Greg, anyway. More than that, she wants to find out how they knew her husband, how they were all connected, why someone – maybe even Greg – wanted them dead. Or maybe, just maybe, they can tell her it's all a misunderstanding.

'Are you OK?'

A brilliant supply teacher called Hayley hovers next to her, concerned eyes peering out from under a vibrant red fringe.

'What?' Marianne says, turning to stare at the woman.

'Sorry,' Hayley says, 'but you were, I don't know, hyper-ventilating, I guess.'

'Oh god, was I?'

She nods, eyes searching Marianne's.

'Asthma,' Marianne says, looking away. 'I'm fine.'

# Sam

I sleep until I wake up. No alarms.

I take a shower somewhere near the boiling point and make a strong coffee. In my sleep, I dreamt, as I often do, about the ones that came before. This strange net of connected targets that seems to be tightening around this final woman.

All of these people are knotted together in some way. Caught through their own behaviour in the same sticky spider's web. I shouldn't care, it's not my mystery to solve, but it chews at me just a little.

I had thought them individual stones but now I see them all laid out in my mind like a row of pebbles. The way that a child's fat little fingers might lay them out. *Stop. Don't.*

I've been looking at them too closely to make out the connections but the powers-that-be are always one step ahead. And the customer is always right. I snort at memories of myself, back when I needed to know who, why . . . A motive by proxy.

Now I just turn up, clock in and get the job done.

No feelings. Life is so much easier that way.

# Marianne

The final period is with Year 10. They're knees deep in World War Two, which takes a toll at the best of times. The sheer waste of young life. And it's happening still, of course, *out there,* which makes teaching this group even tougher. Something teachers are expected to teach in retrospect and ignore contemporarily. A discussion she and Greg had often, almost always growing heated. 'I'm doing what I can to make the past relevant to today's crises,' she'd say. 'But these kids need to pass their exams, *that's* my priority.' His dark eyes would blaze but he'd drop it.

As the textbooks open on pictures of bright shiny buttons and new uniforms, she thinks, of course, of Greg. Just thirty-four.

'Miss?'

Like all those wasted soldiers, he was in his prime. He ran, cycled, ate wholesomely, didn't really drink. Even when they'd smoked, he'd smoked far less than her. He was squeaky clean, inside and out. She'd thought so, anyway.

'Miss?'

At least, unlike the war dead, his tip-top organs were salvaged to help other people. She thinks of them sometimes, little parts of him scattered on the breeze, alive in their way. A legacy that's something like children, but not. Not close enough.

'Miss Heywood, are you in there?' The laughter of the class snaps her to attention and Marianne arches an eyebrow.

*'Excuse me?'*

The laughter stops suddenly and the tall teenager in front of Marianne shrinks.

'What can I do for you, Tamsin?'

*

While the pupils work, sniffling and smirking with the excitement of home time looming, Marianne eases her phone out of her bag and holds it cautiously under the desk. Phones are banned, not just for pupils but teachers too. Safeguarding is taken so seriously now that she could be suspended if she was found doing this, but every second Marianne waits feels like the tick of a bomb.

Glancing up every few minutes to check that her charges are still eyes down, Marianne fumbles to unlock her screen and search Facebook for the names and places engraved on her itching brain. Now she has dates of birth and locations, it should be easier to sift the right people from the hundreds of results.

She quickly finds, she's pretty sure, the right Rosie Parsons from Tottenham. She looks similar to the thumbnail at least: pretty, blonde, youngish. In her profile picture she wears a nurse's outfit that Marianne thinks looks genuine rather than fancy dress, but who the hell knows? Maybe she's an actress. Or a stripper. Rosie's account is locked down tight and her friends list is invisible to the public. Marianne's thumb hovers over the 'add friend' button but something stops her. Does she really want to announce her interest in this way?

David Ross appears easily, a more smiley picture than the one on the dark web site. He has his arms around two young boys and all of them wear matching rugby tops. That's as far as she can get; photos, friends, profile are all private. Just like Rosie.

There is no Andrew Mackintosh on Facebook that fits either the age, the thumbnail or the location. And of course, no Pavel Bourean.

*Eyes flick up.*

'OK, settle down,' Marianne murmurs in the direction of whispering mouths at the side of the classroom.

*Eyes down again.*

Marianne taps to wake her phone up in the dark space on her lap. She goes back to Rosie's locked profile and stares at her. She's undeniably pretty. London-based too. Marianne's heart lurches – was Greg sleeping with her? If so, why were the other names on that list? Jesus fucking Christ, was he sleeping with *all* of them? Some kind of group thing? *Shit, should I be tested? Should Noah?* It could have been a list of people who needed to be informed that Greg had caught something? Is that why he needed to see Jenna, did it go back that far?

Marianne shakes her head. He'd hardly write those names down, not in full like that. It would just be first names surely, if this was a list of lovers. And why would that put them on a hit list? It wouldn't.

*Why does it have to be about sex?*

*Eyes flick up.* They're all working. Or at least pretending to.

Marianne turns to Google, searches 'Rosie Parsons London nurse'. Marianne stares out at the class and then looks down, as surreptitiously as she can. She'd searched Google before but not specifically, not with a place and profession. This time, the results are news articles, a lot of news articles.

'Oh god.' It's out before she can stop it and thirty-five heads look up.

'You all right, miss?' a small voice from the front asks.

'I . . .' Marianne swallows, the phone on her lap. 'I, um, I'm fine. Just ripped a nail. Thank you, though, Mia.' She waits for the children to stop staring, every second painful. 'On with your work, you lot.'

A dizzying number of articles, and they all form a three-act tragedy.

**LONDON NURSE STRUCK OFF FOLLOWING PATIENT DEATH**
**FAMILY SUE NEGLIGENT NURSE**
**DISGRACED NURSE FOUND DEAD AFTER SUSPECTED**
**DRUG OVERDOSE**

A bolt slides across Marianne's chest. Her heart bangs angrily against it.

*Rosie Parsons is already dead.*

# Sam

Guilt is a potent weapon and it was stamped through Rosie Parsons like Brighton rock.

*Do no harm.* The very first principle of nursing. And yet she had. So much harm. And however angry the parents of her victim were, they couldn't match the guilt she already felt. She didn't seem surprised to see me again; I wonder how long she'd been expecting me.

Marianne Heywood looks guilty too. I don't know how or why but it's written across her face. The hunted look in her eyes when I walked past her yesterday, creeping along the street in her coat and pyjamas. The way she chews her nails when she's held up at traffic lights. The furtive glances over her shoulder as she walks into school, her hair sticking to the sweat misting on her forehead.

74

What I do know very well is that she is widowed. That she is already sleeping with someone new. And that he has a child. Most important of all, I know that upon her death, she, and I, will be free.

# Marianne

The bell shrieks. Marianne stumbles as she stands, gathers up her things and pushes out of the classroom door. She's absorbed into the crush of young bodies fleeing for home.

*Rosie Parsons is dead.*

As she walks to the staffroom, she wraps herself tighter in her cardigan, closing her eyes and smelling the wool to ground herself. *I'm here, I'm safe, I've done nothing wrong.* She opens her eyes. *That's not strictly true.*

\*

In the corner of the staffroom, she gorges on the news on her laptop, circling the details like a vulture. Rosie Parsons was a paediatric nurse at St Clement's Hospital in Tottenham. She was also a drug addict. Six months ago, a seven-year-old patient died in her care, through her negligence. Rosie was high on stolen prescription drugs at the time.

Those same drugs killed her three weeks ago. 'No suspicious circumstances.' Clearly everyone believed it was an accidental overdose, but was Rosie on the hit list as payback? If she was, that didn't explain Greg's list. He died before the child.

*Greg is dead. A child is dead. Rosie Parsons is dead.*

None of this makes sense, but this latest discovery is far from reassuring. A hit list and one of the five is dead. *Did*

*Rosie inject herself, did she swallow pills? Did someone else hold the needle or press the tablets into her hand?*

And a child, *a child?* Any grief Marianne has felt must be a sideshow compared to that. She thinks guiltily of Greg's parents. When did she last call them? The grief of a parent, as unnatural a pain as it must be possible to feel. Born out of a love she'll never—

Marianne doesn't finish the thought because a vacuum cleaner has started nudging at her feet. She looks up at the face of a young cleaner she's not seen before. He looks exhausted. Wordlessly, Marianne lifts up her feet and keeps staring at the screen as the cleaner works on. By the time she's realised she must have seemed like an arsehole, it's too late to apologise. She leaves instead.

Outside, the sky has settled to a dense grey. Her car sits almost alone, swimming in the scrubby carpark that will one day, allegedly, house a new science block. Although this roofless space is behind an automatic gate, she still crosses carefully, listening out for footsteps.

*Did Rosie hear footsteps?*

Inside the cool of her car, Marianne fumbles with the key and drives to the exit, cursing the gates to open faster. The faded letters on her hand catch the light as she waits: poison.

On the way home, Marianne swings into the empty carpark of a Homebase store, a huge monolithic building for the worship of all things handy and homey. Not her natural habitat and a ridiculous juxtaposition to everything else that's happening.

She catches sight of someone in a store uniform and heads over before she realises her mistake.

'Hi, miss.' Robbie, Marc's younger brother, smiles.

Fuck. Her heart has been permanently racing since she first looked at the dark web, but it climbs even faster now, manic in her chest. *Why him? Why now?*

'Robbie,' she says, holding up her scrawled-on skin. 'I didn't know you worked here.' She smiles in what she hopes is an aloof and casual manner. 'Where would I find mice poison?'

He smiles and she looks down. Ordinarily she'd be pleased to see a pupil holding down a part-time job, greeting people politely and willing to help her. In this case, she'd rather have checked every aisle herself.

He clamps his hand onto her elbow despite her obvious discomfort and steers her through several corners and aisles.

'There.' He points to a collection of bottles with euphemistic silhouettes of cartoon mice. 'Choose your weapon.'

'Thanks, Robbie.'

'Do you need any more help, miss?' he grins, rising up and down on the balls of his feet.

'No. No, thank you.'

He turns away and she stares at the bottles, willing her heart to calm down. There's a smorgasbord of murderous methods for little creatures. Behind her, someone clears their throat. She turns and takes in Robbie's smirking face.

'My brother's home for a few more weeks,' he says, the corners of his mouth twitching. Marianne says nothing. 'He'd love it if you looked him up again, y'know?'

He waits, bouncing even faster up and down, energy crackling through him.

'Right,' she says, looking at the shelves.

'Or should I say he'd love it if you hooked up with him again?' Before she can reply, he jogs off, amused with himself. Fuck, does he know? Surely Marc wouldn't have trusted him with . . . anything.

Robbie cut a familiar shape from behind with broad shoulders and messy hair but he wasn't like his older brother. Marc had been far from a star pupil, but he'd desperately wanted to succeed so he could get to university and away from his family.

'I just feel like a fork in a knife drawer, Miss,' he'd said, his eyes filling but making no move to wipe them. It was an honesty that boys his age would never normally risk and before she could even think about it, she'd decided to help him. Nothing much, a little more attention in class, some gentle nudging, a few extra meetings in lunchtimes to guide him with coursework. It wasn't

77

so much the work, she realised after a while; it was the attention that was helping him. It told him that someone thought he could do it and so Marc started to believe it.

She watches Robbie swagger off around a corner. Gifted with the same handsome face, the same athletic build, but ugly nonetheless. Marc had worked himself exhausted and triumphed in his A levels. Then, when he made it to university, he wrote and told her, he realised the real work was just starting. Not the learning but the relentless work of *still* trying to find his tribe, his drawer of forks.

By the time she saw him again in person, he was twenty-one. A proper man. But an ex-pupil nonetheless. An ex-pupil whose little postcards and missives she'd hidden from Greg. An ex-pupil whose emails she'd deleted guiltily, but not before smiling through her reply. The contact had slowed a little when he'd finally found his flock.

By the time she saw him again in the flesh, Greg had been dead a month. Marc had heard about it from someone, Robbie probably, and had called around to see her. He'd brought flowers and a takeaway. She'd poured them both some of Greg's whisky and let him hug her. It had turned into a kiss. They had spent the night swimming in the grey area between right and wrong.

They both knew it could never be repeated. But it was everything she needed at the time.

Marianne breathes out slowly, then grabs a lethal-looking can.


# Sam


The target should be home soon.

I watch across the rooftops. Through tower blocks surging like spires. Layer upon layer of different houses, flats and offices make up this view, pasted one on top of the other like papier mâché.

The air is an ambient temperature, I barely feel it on my skin. The whole sky is matte grey blending into blue, almost invisible.

I stare and I wait.

# Marianne

Marianne manages to park close to her flat. She finishes the last of her cigarettes while sitting in the car with the evening sun streaming through the windscreen, working up the courage to go inside. Her flat – their flat – had always been a safe haven, now it's poisoned. She looks at the Homebase bag on her passenger seat. *Greg poisoned it*, she thinks, before she can stop herself.

She locks up and walks to her front door, looking around for god knows what. Everything out here is the same as ever. The same noise. The same dirt in the creases of the pavement. The metal shutter on the old café with its colourful splash of graffiti.

She opens the door and stoops for the post. Nothing much, a pizza leaflet with deals she'll never take up, a 'dear resident' letter from the water company about digging up the road months from now and a BT bill still addressed to Greg. As a reflex, she pats her pocket for a cigarette and remembers she finished the pack.

Climbing these stairs used to mean something so different. The last few steps before she and Greg could cocoon them-selves away. Unspoken traditions that she only noticed when they were broken. New traditions not yet carved with Noah.

The first working day that she opened the front door as a newly minted widow, one year ago, everything was exactly the same as the day before. The crappy carpet, the magnolia paint, the smell of grease fat from the café. And when she'd opened up the inner door to the flat, it didn't look like a world that had ended. It looked like a still from a film she was no longer allowed to watch. No smell of cooking, no sound of Greg whistling out of tune and yelping as tiny specks of oil splattered his hairy arms while he sautéed potatoes.

Marianne had closed the door and ran back down the stairs on that first evening last year. She'd climbed back in her car and driven away fast. She didn't plan a destination, just needed endless miles under the tyres, radio up loud. Out into Essex, to Harwich and then up the coast. She'd refilled the tank somewhere in East Anglia, standing on an empty forecourt.

She'd eventually driven home through a blackened sky, eyelids sagging, white knuckles on the wheel.

Today, Marianne opens up and puts her bag on the table. The first thing she notices is the smell, which is absolutely not the same as when she left it yesterday nor when she came back in here a year ago. It's the smell of gas.

*

Marianne hangs back for a moment, checking her senses and taking another cautious sniff. It's definitely gas. When was the last time she used the oven? The last piece of pie on Saturday. *Fuck.* She holds her breath, runs into the kitchen and tries to push up the window. It's stuck fast. She tries again, eyes watering. Eventually it relents and whines its way up.

After a few lungfuls of fresh air, Marianne looks at the hob. It's definitely not on. There's no gas escaping from it as far as she can tell. She doesn't dare touch any of the knobs in case she triggers the spark. She pulls open the oven, then remembers that this part is electric. How Greg would laugh if he were here.

She tries to remember what does run on gas in the flat. Her head has started to thump and she sticks her face out of the window again and breathes deeply.

*The boiler.* She takes a lug of air and goes to the bathroom where the airing cupboard sits. The wooden shelves are over-loaded with the same towels and sheets as always, nothing is disturbed and the smell is no stronger. It's strongest when she goes back to the hallway, just below the loft door.

Back out and down on the street, Marianne calls the emergency gas number. She's told to go back in, turn the gas supply off at the meter, open all the windows and then wait outside.

A serious, uniformed man shows up within half an hour and heads straight up with a gas detector. Marianne paces outside, wanting a cigarette more than ever. After another half an hour, she takes a tentative step on to the bottom of the stairs and waits until the uniformed man appears at the top. 'It's safe to come up now.'

The loft ladder hangs from the ceiling, a petticoat of dust around its legs.

'The flue pipes,' the engineer explains, which means nothing to her. 'They'd been leaking up there in your loft space, prob-ably every time you used the boiler.'

'For how long?' she asks.

'It's hard to say, they were very badly damaged so it could have been gradually getting worse or . . .'

'Could mice have done this?' she asks, glancing at the abandoned bag of mouse poison on the table.

'How big are these mice?' he smiles. Before she can answer, he says, 'I didn't see any droppings up there so I'd be surprised. Anyway, I've fixed it now but you should get someone round to do a gas safety check as soon as possible. Do you rent?'

She shakes her head, thinking of the scurrying feet she thought she'd heard above her. They must have been in the walls instead.

'In that case, you'll need to pay for the gas check yourself but it's not something to scrimp on.' She nods. 'And that boiler is pretty old too,' he adds. 'You should replace it as soon as possible.' Like the stairs carpet, the window frames and the old bathroom suite, it was something they'd planned to change at some point in the future.

'I will,' she promises. He packs up his toolkit carefully. 'This is going to sound weird,' she says, her voice low. 'But is there any way a person could have done this?'

'What, damaged a flue?' He smiles like she's told a joke. She nods and he shrugs, 'I'm not sure why anyone would want to do that.'

'But is it possible?'

'Anything's possible. But if someone wanted you to have a gas leak, there are simpler ways to do it. Like turning on the hob.' Marianne nods, and follows his gaze to the overflowing ashtray.

'And you were lucky not to blow yourself up,' he says, frowning. 'Things go wrong all the time on an older set-up like this, I see it every day. They're accidents waiting to happen.'

Marianne thinks of the fresh pack of fags waiting in the living-room cupboard and how close she came. She vows silently that if she survives the rest of the week, she'll give up for good.

Maybe.

# Sam

I swallow my disappointment. It hits my gut and curdles into anger. The emergency gas engineer has just left, instead of the fire engine and ambulance I'd envisaged when I approached her road.

I can see her right now, moving around her living room, opening and closing the windows like it's some kind of game. She's pacing, faffing, dragging her heels. At one point she closes the living-room window, then stares out over here, pressing her forehead on the glass and closing her eyes. Then she disappears, shaking her ponytail loose so her hair spills everywhere. When she comes back and pushes up the window again, I finally see the flame of her lighter.

An hour too late. This job is already taking longer than agreed, longer than I wanted. I should be free by now. I make a fist as I walk past her door, thumping the graffiti shutters on the café below.

# Marianne

A metallic bang from the street makes Marianne jump as she fills her holdall with clothes. She can't think straight and doesn't want to stay here tonight, not by herself. Accidents happen but how often do genuine accidents happen to people who are also named on an apparent hit list?

If she tried the police again, what would they say? They would ask why she was on the dark web, an illegal activity and probably a sackable offence. They would ask if anyone had cause to wish her harm. Could she honestly answer no, even if she doesn't know why?

And if they were to look at Greg's laptop in ways that she cannot, what might they find? Maybe she had only seen the tip of the iceberg, blundering around on there. But the police have experts, don't they? They could find everything, like that email account she's not been able to get into. What might that contain?

She thinks of the nurse who so recklessly ended a young life. Marianne can barely form this new thought but . . . was Greg someone who hurt children, or wanted to? Was that what led him to the dark web? Was that why he didn't want his own children, was he scared he might . . .? The thought disintegrates, too explosive to hold any longer.

She'd trusted him so completely, she thinks, packing underwear and socks. Even when they fell out, even when he questioned her, she still trusted him.

And he was *normal*. His tastes were so . . . vanilla. Too vanilla sometimes. Giggling a few years in when she suggested ways to spice things up. And the porn she found in his browser history was almost *bland*. But perhaps that was just a cover. And if the police did find something, how could she prove it was him and not her who had looked? It's too risky. Everything is too risky.

'Do you mind if I come to stay at yours tonight?' she asks Noah by WhatsApp, keeping it breezy. She sees him typing, then he stops, then starts again. The flicker of activity like a pulse.

'How come?' he replies eventually. A stinging lack of enthusiasm at odds with his usual generosity and joyfulness.

'I had a gas leak earlier,' she writes, which is true at least. 'The smell is making me feel sick.'

'Oh you poor thing. OK, sure. Come on over. X.'

She grabs her keys and bag and is about to leave but as an afterthought she grabs Greg's laptop and shoves it in the bag with the rest of her stuff.

\*

The traffic grinds slowly from east to west. By the time Marianne reaches Richmond, her shoulders and jaw are locked stiff and the base of her spine feels greasy with sweat. She should have got the tube; she thinks it every time, but can't bear the crush of other people.

Noah's Range Rover is on the drive and she pulls in behind it, her car like a toy compared with his. He works from home but there's no answer when she knocks, so she pulls her phone from her bag. He picks up in two rings, the sound of children in the background.

'Hey, I'm outside,' she says. 'Where are you?'

'Sorry, I had to come and get Daisy from a play date. I'll be back as soon as I can.'

Daisy. The penny drops. That's why he'd sounded reluctant about her unplanned visit.

'Shit, I'm sorry. I didn't realise you had her today.'

'It's fine, it's fine.' He pauses. 'It's about time you met her anyway, right?'

Marianne smiles, despite everything. 'Yes. I'd love to meet her.'

'Well, we won't be long. If you reach over the garden gate and unbolt it, you can get into the garden.'

'I don't want to get picked up by Neighbourhood Watch breaking into your garden,' she says.

'Don't worry, Toots, I'll bust you out of jail.'

She's still sitting on the bench, surrounded by pretty little solar lights, when Marianne sees him through the windows. He mooches up the driveway and peers through his own living room and out through the kitchen. The little girl she only knows from photos looks tiny next to him. Marianne waves with relief. A minute or two later, Daisy has been sent upstairs to get changed and Noah is outside in the garden. He hugs Marianne briefly and the relief makes her head swim. *I'm safe.*

'Now, listen,' he says, with the manner of a department head running a meeting. 'Daisy knows I have a friend called Marianne but that's all. She's not—'

'It's fine,' Marianne says. 'I won't do anything overt, don't worry.'

'I'm happy that you're meeting her, but, if it's OK, I know this is weird but can you put your things in the spare room and, um, sleep in there this time? Just while we . . .'

So she's *his* guilty secret. The future she'd imagined together feels further away than she realised, and she wants it more than ever. She hoists up a smile. 'It's fine, honestly.'

They slide open the patio doors with a strange solemnity and when Marianne tries to make coffee, Noah takes over. 'It'll look odd if you seem to be at home here.'

She scoffs before she can catch herself. 'I'm sure Daisy won't think anything of me making a coffee.'

Noah smiles, but doesn't move away from the machine. 'Please, let me do this at my pace,' he says quietly, reaching for a cup. In the hallway, footsteps thunder down the stairs and Marianne jumps before she can stop herself.

Daisy flies around the corner, a flash of gold hair and purple fabric, springing up at her dad. Noah catches her, swinging her around in a swoop and sitting her up on the kitchen side.

'Wow, you're like a gymnast,' Marianne says and Daisy smiles coyly, swinging her legs a little.

'This is my friend, Marianne,' Noah says, gently.

'Hello,' says Marianne. 'It's very nice to meet you.'

'Hello,' Daisy replies, looking at her knees.

'Let me guess, you must be about eleven? Is that right?'

'I'm five,' Daisy giggles.

'You're not, are you? Five? I thought you were at least eleven. Probably even twelve!'

'My next birthday I'll be six,' Daisy adds.

'And when is your birthday?'

'The sixth of August.'

'No way! My birthday is the seventh of August!' Marianne exclaims.

'Is it really?' Daisy looks to her dad for confirmation and Noah laughs and nods. They'd spent Marianne's birthday in a spa hotel in Sussex. Daisy had been having a second birthday party in Surrey with her grandparents. It had been Noah's idea to go away together and while it wasn't the sort of place she'd usually go, certainly not at those prices, it had been wonderful. Sitting in a hot tub, looking out over the South Downs, with an attractive man pouring champagne, it was a life she was happy to play-act for a night. Just like she's happy to play-act this: a family man, a little girl, suburban safety.

Daisy pulls a picture out of her book bag to show them, her eyebrows knitting together as she awaits feedback. 'Is this a castle?' Marianne asks, taking a punt. Daisy smiles. 'It's very good, Daisy, you're a natural.' Daisy smiles wider still and

Marianne smiles back. Greg had been so adamant he didn't want to have kids that it came up on their very first date. She'd laughingly agreed at the time, raised her beer in a toast to lie-ins and controlling the world population when really she was ambivalent, even then. The needle moving in the direction of 'want' some years later, which Greg considered unthinkable.

'Right,' Noah says decisively. 'It's already past your bedtime, Daisy, so go up and brush your pegs.'

She tries to negotiate some TV time as Noah shakes his head. 'No, it's definitely time for bed, Dais, come on, upstairs.'

'Do you mind if I have a shower while you do that?' Marianne asks him.

He pauses. 'Sure. Daisy, say goodnight to Marianne.'

Suddenly, a little body is leaping up and as Marianne catches her, Daisy leans up and kisses her cheek. 'Goodnight!'

'Goodnight, Daisy, sleep tight.'

*

After her shower, hair still wet and make-up soaped off, Marianne walks into the lounge and flops down on the sofa.

'Oi, you,' Noah says from the kitchen, 'come over here.' The dining table is laid and Noah comes out of the kitchen carrying two plates. 'Poached salmon and vegetables,' he says. 'If you're not feeling too sick from the gas?'

'This looks amazing.' If it was left to her they'd have been gathered around a Pot Noodle. Noah is a caregiver, she realises, whether out of parental habit or just his own nature. She smiles up at him and he mirrors her.

'I like looking after you,' he says, his voice soft.

'I like letting you look after me,' she tells Noah, matching the coyness in his voice. It is still new to them, sharing important words and loaded conversations. A high-wire act of emotions, where either one of them could say too much and scare the other.

Bellies full, they move onto the sofa where they have a corner each, feet up and touching. 'Daisy is brilliant,' Marianne says. 'You must be so proud of her.'

Noah smiles, flicking his eyes just briefly to the framed picture of ashen-faced Louise holding a tiny pink newborn. 'She's everything.'

Marianne thinks back to those early moments at the bereavement group. Noah's emotions so forceful that she assumed he must have been widowed more recently than her. He had sobbed but said nothing for several sessions before speaking.

'My wife died four years ago,' he'd said, finally. 'A few months after our daughter was born.' He swallowed, and she thought that was all he would say but then he'd carried on, so slowly it was as if each word hurt his throat. 'Lou had kidney failure. She shouldn't have gone through with the pregnancy but she was amazed she'd conceived in the first place. She spent the whole pregnancy calling it a miracle baby.' He'd screwed up his eyes and then looked down at the wedding ring still on his finger. 'I thought it was the worst thing that could have happened because it accelerated everything . . . I just wanted more time with her. I'll never stop feeling guilty about that because now my daughter is everything to me, *everything*.'

He talked about his health obsessions, his need to stay fit. Marianne noticed the shape of his chest and his arms; twin flickers of desire and shame turned her head away. It was too soon, she thought. And it wasn't appropriate to ogle bereaved men, no matter how attractive they were.

'I can't let Daisy down and I can't let her lose another parent,' he'd said to the group. 'Not ever.'

*

'Shall we watch something?' he asks now, gesturing to the enormous flat TV screen mounted on the wall.

'Just put on whatever you'd watch if I wasn't here,' she says. 'I don't care what's on the screen.'

He fumbles with the remote and chooses a programme about small businesses. It's definitely not what she'd choose but Noah is a self-proclaimed 'entrepreneur' with 'a finger in lots of pies'.

'I'm not very good at holding down a normal job,' he'd joked on their first date. She's still not entirely sure what he does – investing in failing businesses and turning them around, she thinks. Some business partners in the mix somewhere. Sometimes providing money for start-ups with curious ideas that risk-averse banks won't support, something like that – but too much time has passed to ask again.

She leans back and closes her eyes, happily disinterested. Then her brain starts whirring away again.

'Hey,' she sits up after a few minutes. 'Have you got any booze? I really need to blot things out.' He looks at her for a moment, as if reading her face. Then, without saying anything, he heads to the dining room and rummages in a drinks cabinet she's not noticed before – alcohol is usually a once-a-week 'cheat' for Noah – and then into the kitchen, swinging a couple of bottles. A few minutes later, he presents her with a cut-glass tumbler filled with ice, a slice of orange and dark amber liquid that smells like Christmas.

'An Old Fashioned,' he says, 'but I'm afraid I'm out of cherries.'

'I can't drink this without a cherry,' she says. 'Take it away.'

He smiles as she sips it cautiously. It's incredibly strong and surprisingly delicious. She smiles gratefully as he flops back down into his corner and presses play on the remote. She takes a slug, the booze hitting her fast. 'God, that's good. You're a dark horse.'

He smiles and pulls her foot onto his lap, rubbing her big toe gently. 'I'm no stranger to blotting things out,' he says, eyes on the screen.

# Sam

I'm back in the park opposite her flat when Marianne drives past, chewing her thumbnail and staring at the traffic lights ahead. Like everyone around me, I'm looking down at my phone. Keeping my eyes soft and easy, ready to glance up when the right make and model slides past. I watch her now as she indicates and turns left, her silly little car sliding along the northern edge of the park and then out of view.

This is curious. Perhaps the gas scare has put a kink in the typical routine because she would normally be settled for the evening now. It's a school night and she has no gym memberships, no dinner bookings. Her best friend lives in Dubai, other friends in Devon. Her mother moved to France recently. Apparently she keeps co-workers at arm's length; none of them are even social media connections.

She's likely making an unscheduled trip to her boyfriend in Richmond, but it's too risky to hare off to a different part of London without a plan. I'm bone-tired, sloppy in my movements. I need to go home and take stock, re-read the part of the report that deals with her love life.

I stand up slowly. A little boy smiles at me from the top of the slide and I smile back, then stick out my tongue to make him laugh. His mother looks over with heavy lids and we share tired smiles.

*

I've used a zigzag route, inching back and forth through stop-start traffic for what felt like hours. My temples ache from concentrating, my teeth still grinding as I climb out into the evening air.

Once inside, I take off my boots by the door with an involuntary sigh. My heels are sore, gritty with all the miles I've covered. I spread my toes out on the cheap carpet and stretch my arms over my head. I've worked hard and fast, expecting this assignment to be resolved by now. Hoping, despite my inherent caution, that this last box can be ticked and I can put all of this behind me. We've already agreed that Pavel Bourean is not a possible target, long disappeared. This only leaves Marianne.

This should already be job done, a mess cleared up. Justice, I suppose.

But I'm still on the hook and now this 'final' job is growing more complicated by the day. I rub my forehead and tug my coat off.

According to the report, her boyfriend is a businessman called Noah Simpson. A widower with a little girl. I look again at the shots from Google Streetview. It's a family home. I will need to tread very carefully – there can be no collateral damage.

I study the floor layouts, the entry points and those little shards of gold where all neighbours' views are blocked. I make a plan, then head into my kitchen to scare up something to eat.

As I wait for the microwave to ping, I set an early alarm for the morning.

# Marianne

*Tuesday, 14 September 2021*

Marianne becomes aware of her own skin first. The hairs on her arm standing to attention before she even knows she's awake. *Someone is in here, watching me sleep.*

Their breath skims the surface of Marianne's skin. Her arm is draped over the pillow and she tries to keep it from trembling, keeping her eyes closed and breathing level. Buying time while she works out what the fuck to do.

Behind her, in the warm belly of the bed, she feels Noah stir and roll over to spoon her. A big ship, turning slowly. Still asleep, he wraps his heavy arm around her and pins her where she lays. Whoever is standing there continues to watch.

It's early morning but still dark in here. With her eyes screwed shut, Marianne tries to picture the room, the layout. It's both familiar and not. Cushions another woman chose; an en-suite full of men's products; at the foot of the bed, the blanket box that Noah laid her down on during their first, most adventurous, time.

She pictures the double-glazed windows, locked for security in the way that safe suburban people like to do. Even if she could unpin herself from Noah, as soon as she moved she would surely be grabbed. And what of Noah? And Daisy? *Fuck*. She pleads silently. *Don't hurt them.*

'Daddy?'

They throw themselves apart and open their eyes in unison. Daisy is a blur of legs and a tangled nightie as she runs out of the door. Noah pulls on some pyjama bottoms and rushes out after her, casting a pained look back at Marianne as he leaves. She was supposed to go back to the spare room last night, but four Old Fashioneds and a couple of orgasms had knocked her out. And he'd passed out just as easily, clearly. But that was the one condition for her staying and she'd blown it.

The threat of imagined danger lingers in her racing heart and sweaty palms, but reality is a sad slap in the face. From the other bedroom she can hear Daisy's sobs and Noah's soothing, apologetic tones.

Marianne's phone lies on the side table. The alarm starts up and the screen goes black, the last sputter of energy used up. She plugs it in to a spare charger on Noah's side and drags herself to the shower, keeping her hair out of the water and using a body wash that makes her smell of sandalwood and testosterone. She wraps herself in the same towel she used last night, its edges cold and damp. From the other room, she can hear Daisy and Noah talking quietly over the sound of fresh sheets being billowed and fanned.

She dresses guiltily, silently, wishing for a way to slip out unnoticed and somehow rewind to last night and just get into the spare bed instead. Noah appears, grave faced.

'I'm so sorry,' she starts but he waves it away.

'She wet the bed. It was just bad luck.'

'I figured that's what happened. Is she OK now? Did she ask about us?'

He clicks his jaw. 'She's OK,' he says, pulling gym clothes from his drawers and peeling off his pyjamas. She watches him discreetly. When she's stayed over usually, she's felt proprietorial of his body, grabbing his bum when he walks past or squeezing his arms while he cooks. Now she feels like an interloper. Like the other woman.

'I'm sorry, I know I'm being a bit moody. It's just . . . I didn't want it to happen like this,' he says. 'She's never known me be with anyone and I really wanted to get this right, to give us . . .' – he pauses and looks at her – 'to give us the best chance.'

She smiles, she can't help herself. 'You're such a good man,' she says as he turns to leave.

\*

Marianne goes downstairs, nervous to see how Daisy reacts. But when she gets into the kitchen diner, Daisy is smiling and crunching cereal.

'Coffee?' Noah asks, sunnily.

'Yes, thanks.'

'I get nightmares too,' Daisy says. Marianne frowns, unsure how to reply.

'I explained that you got scared and got in with me,' Noah says.

'I do that sometimes,' chirrups Daisy. 'I didn't know grown-ups did, though.'

Marianne stays for the coffee, despite running low on time, and the three of them compare their days ahead.

'I'm playing with knives and fire in the woods,' Daisy says and Marianne stares at her in shock.

'Forest school,' Noah says, smiling. 'And you're not playing with knives *or* fire, Dais, I read the letter. You get to build a campfire and cut sticks.' He looks at Marianne but addresses Daisy. 'And you'll be supervised the whole time, young lady.'

Daisy shrugs. 'What are you doing today, Marianne?'

'Well, I'm going to be teaching lots of smelly teenagers today,' she says. 'But I don't get to take them into the forest, I'm afraid.'

'Oh,' Daisy says, as if genuinely sad. 'Poor them.'

Noah smiles. 'And does no one care what Daddy's doing?'

*Daddy*. The last 'Daddy' Marianne shared breakfast with was her own, decades ago. Daisy shrugs. 'You already told me and it was boring.' The little girl tries to stifle a smile, enjoying the laughter of adults, and lists Noah's day's tasks on her fingers. 'You're taking me to school, then you have a boring meeting and are going to the gym.'

'Something like that,' Noah says as Marianne notices the time.

'Shit, *sugar*, sorry. I really should go.'

By the time she inches on to the Edgware Road, Marianne should have been taking the register for her tutor group. If there was anywhere to park along this jammed artery, perhaps she could pull over and get on the tube. She brings up her mental map of London. No, it wouldn't work anyway, she'd only get as far as Liverpool Street before having to squeeze onto a bus bulging with irritated commuters. And that would take even longer, all told. Whatever way she looks at it, she's running unforgivably late.

She feels a rising tide of claustrophobia and opens her window, jumping in surprise when a moped whines past and nearly clips her mirror.

Swallowing her fear, Marianne calls the school in a flurry of apologies. 'I think I have food poisoning,' she says. 'I've tried to make it in but I'm going to have to go home.'

Noah isn't working from home today, Daisy said so; he has a meeting then the gym. The idea of all that space, the quiet safety of his house, appeals more than anything. It's yet more imposition after a dicey start, though. *Fuck it.* She calls, chewing her lip while she waits for him to pick up. If it's a no, she'll just go for a drive, clear her head. She's certainly not going to go back to her flat, not yet.

'Hey, you.'

'Have you left for your meeting yet?'

He pauses. 'Not yet, why?'

'I was running so late that I called in sick but I don't fancy going back to the gassy flat just yet. Would you mind if I came to yours?'

'Of course not. I'll try to cancel my meeting, it's just been tricky to get a time in the diary with . . .'

'No, don't change your plans,' she shouts into the hands-free speaker, a little louder than she intended. 'I've got work to do anyway and then I'll clear off before Daisy gets back.'

'Oh. OK, if you're sure?'

'Definitely.'

'There's a key for the cleaners under the middle pot on the deck, you can let yourself in the back.'

*

The house is silent and still as she opens up. The wooden shutters are open horizontally so a delicate, warm light covers the scene. The breakfast things are already cleared and there's not a crumb on the side. *He's such a good adult.* She puts on a coffee and slips off her shoes. Upstairs, the bed is made with hospital corners, cushions piled just so. Driven by an old memory, she pulls one of Noah's gym hoodies from a hanger but hesitates. The intimacy of wearing another person's clothes is acute, and an intrusion if it's unwanted. Are they at this stage yet? Maybe she can help nudge them into the next stage. She tugs it on like a cocoon. The sleeves need three rolls just to reveal her hands.

*No one knows I'm here.* She closes her eyes and basks in the fleeting flicker of relief.

Downstairs, she slides the patio doors open and takes her coffee outside, feeling the dappled sun on her face through the cherry blossom tree. The walls rise up all around, boxing her away from prying eyes, CCTV or however else someone might track her down. This is a place she can be calm in, take stock in and hopefully, *hopefully*, work out what this mess really involves so she can claw her way out of it.

# Sam

Noah Simpson left his house after his girlfriend, a little girl swinging on his arm. As he hoisted her up into his ostentatious car, the pictures from that computer in Surrey flashed up on my closed eyelids like after-images, burnt there by a bright and unwanted light. I wonder how many years, if ever, it will take to wash my brain clean again. Was I ever really clean?

I need to stop ricocheting off down memory lane but something about her boyfriend has set off a sense of *déjà vu*. Something about the shoulders. The way he carries himself. But also just the sheer size and confidence of him. I've seen him before, in some other place, but I can't be sure when. It's there, the memory, just out of my sight. Yes, I've definitely seen him before.

I will need to be careful if he's in her corner. He's taller than me, with muscles on muscles. His brow was furrowed, thinking of the day ahead, thinking of his car, maybe the bills he has to pay. I wonder if he's thinking of Marianne. I wonder how much he will miss her. I wonder what he would do to protect her.

I can't place where I've seen him before and it's unsettling, seeing ghosts and unsure where they've come from. The problem is that I have had so many lives now, so many different personas, they're all starting to blend into each other. I ache for a time I can just be me and lock these ghosts up for good.

I wait ten minutes then circle back. I've just pulled my own change of clothes from the back seat when Marianne Heywood's tiny joke car curls back into the cul-de-sac and shakes to a stop on the drive.

Does her boyfriend know she's here? I watch as she looks around furtively and then reaches over the garden gate to let herself inside.

A man walking his frantic spaniel nods to me as he wrestles his dog past my car. I smile broadly then settle back down to wait. This could be interesting.

# Marianne

Her laptop is dying. Marianne left her charger at school and over an hour of unsuccessful internet searches has burnt through nearly all of her battery.

She'd wondered if Andrew Mackintosh's Scottish name hinted at a university lecturer or family friend of Greg's, but there were no connections. David Ross sounds similarly Scottish but there's still no obvious link either; no alumni from the same years, no colleague with that name, nothing. She stares again at David Ross's Facebook profile picture, clicks on it for the hundredth time but it only tells her the same unhelpful information: it was taken five years ago and the children are his sons. *So what?*

Pavel Bourean remains a mystery. Unlike the David Rosses and Andrew Mackintoshes, of whom there are thousands, there is no one called Pavel Bourean *anywhere*. It's as if he never existed. Or it's a fake name. *God, it's obviously just a fake name.*

She snaps the screen closed to save what little energy is left and then pulls Greg's dusty laptop from the holdall, where she'd packed it in haste last night. It seems shameful, infecting Noah's clean family home with the rotten DNA of Greg's netherworld. She opens the screen up reluctantly. There's even less charge on here and she didn't think to bring his cable. *Fuck*.

She'd rather not rip through all her phone battery too, but perhaps Noah has a lead that fits one of the computers.

Marianne is pretty sure he won't mind her using his things – he's made his house available to her after all – but there's something clandestine about climbing upstairs and into his office. She's only seen this room once before on an awkward tour after her first night here. It was hard to take in anything about his space after seeing the spare room/home gym next door, filled with the carefully archived possessions of his late wife, Louise.

Both rooms are in the converted loft, the office almost empty but for the desk and filing cabinet. It's a far cry from her own loft with its damaged gas flues and piles of junk. There is an iMac on the desk here, which is no help cable-wise. She was sure she'd seen Noah using a laptop downstairs at one point, but it's not here so he must have taken it with him.

The desk has a small leather portfolio on it and she flicks through, trying to care. She's been a bad girlfriend, paying almost no attention to the details of his life outside of their relationship. Lured mostly by the shared shorthand of grief and how attractive he is, and then swept up in the buds of romance and dreams of the future. She should make more of an effort – he deserves it.

She looks through the portfolio again, with more care. It's very Noah, neat and fancy. A proposal for a craft beer shop, some artists' renderings of luxury apartments, plans for a shared workspace in Clapham, some kind of electric-scooter sharing scheme Marianne remembers Noah giving her the spiel for a few months back.

'I have a car, thanks,' she'd laughed.

'Gas-guzzling relics cost a bomb, cost the *Earth*,' he'd said, with the exaggerated demeanour of a lay preacher. 'You should sell that little motor and hop on a Buzz.'

'A Buzz?'

'Good name, eh?'

She'd pointed to the huge chunk of Range Rover out on his drive and raised her eyebrows.

'I can't get Daisy on the back of a scooter now, can I?'

She closes the portfolio and heads back downstairs, resolving to ask more about his work. About the gym, about Daisy. About everything that isn't death.

*

With no other option, she switches to Googling on her phone. With Rosie Parsons, she found out about the nurse's death via news articles. As much as she hopes to find everyone else on the list alive and laughing at what a big joke this all is, she steels her nerve and starts typing.

Marianne searches 'David Ross' and clicks to the news section. Nothing. Then 'David Ross dead'. Nope. *Good.* It's still possible to cling on to coincidence, she thinks, as she types the same search but with Andrew Mackintosh.

The results flood the screen.

*Fuck. Not good. Not good at all.*

She breathes in slowly and looks again.

*Surrey man found dead of CO poisoning.*

There are a slew of stories, all highlighting the risks of carbon monoxide. Like the Andrew Mackintosh on her list, this one also lives in Godalming and is exactly the right age. *This must be him.* According to a local newspaper website, until a few years ago he was an anaesthetist at a children's hospital in London. And judging by some of the comments yet to be scraped off by moderators, he'd been ousted from his job after being caught in a child pornography sting.

A paedophile. A dead paedophile. Her stomach clenches.

So Andrew Mackintosh was a paedophile who worked in a children's hospital and Rosie Parsons was a children's nurse whose patient died. What does that make the others on the list? Surely Greg can't have thought she was somehow connected?

But if Greg stumbled upon a child abuse ring and was trying to unravel it, that could explain his anger in the last few months of his life. Perhaps he wanted Jenna to help him build a case. It could explain what he was doing on the dark web too, maybe tracking images of a trafficked child being exploited. It could explain why someone wanted to shut him up.

*By threatening me?*

The pieces feel like they're coming together, but Marianne doesn't like the picture they make one bit. In fact, she preferred it when it seemed too ludicrous to be anything but a hoax. This latest idea seems almost plausible.

A shadow of a thought passes over her. *Was Bluebell a child?*

She types: *Andrew Mackintosh + Bluebell.*

Nothing comes up.

Could Bluebell have been the child that Rosie Parsons fatally neglected?

*Rosie Parsons + Bluebell.*

Nothing.

*David Ross + Bluebell.*

Several results.

She scrolls, and clicks.

Bluebell is not a child. The Bluebell is a hotel out in the Surrey countryside forty minutes from where Andrew Mackintosh lived. And David Ross is its manager.

# Sam

Andrew Mackintosh had long given up hiding who he was. It was all there on the screen, on printouts under the bed, and spooled around the carefully labelled film stacks archived from the dark ages. It was there in his eyes the first time I saw him, so black I'd had to look away.

With some of my targets – the ones who still care, the ones still under cover – they'll do anything to prevent exposure. Sometimes, you're even giving them something they've longed for and haven't had the courage to enact. Rosie Parsons was one of those. She took those pills without blinking. Took the water I handed her. Swallowed.

Mackintosh wouldn't have done that. He'd already lost face to such a degree that most people would seek an end. But not him, he was content to limp along for years, scratching out a shitty little existence, free to indulge himself unseen.

A man like that would have fought back if I'd taken the same route that I did with the nurse. I could have overpowered him, I'm certain, but that's messy and untidy. It leaves breadcrumbs for police and arouses suspicion. A man like that deserves to die a pathetic, hollow death, barely moving the needle of public interest.

I'm still unsure what part in all this Marianne Heywood has played. The longer it takes to end this, the harder it is to quell those questions. There's something out of alignment, something blurred in the corner of my eye. The questions are getting harder to ignore.

The target bursts out of the house looking ashen and grey, slamming the door behind her. She unlocks her car, throws her big leather bag into the boot and practically falls into the driving seat. No furtive glances around now, certainly no looks my way, she just wants to go. I stay upright in my seat, wait for her car to disappear around the bend and then follow slowly behind.

# Marianne

Richmond sits on the throne between Inner London and Surrey, knitting two expensive enclaves together. A rich vein of rich people. It's not a place Marianne would have chosen to live, preferring the texture of Hackney, but she certainly felt safer hiding in Noah's suburban sanctum than she did at home. She can see herself growing comfortable here, if she comes through all of this intact.

Now she's out in the open, a huge swollen sky over her. She imagines her little car from above with a target painted on its roof, as she flies over the suspended road that surges from the city and out towards the countryside.

The Bluebell's website was very basic. A few 'arty' pictures of four-poster beds and what could well have been stock images of countryside. Some text boasting a 'boutique hotel experience amongst rolling hills far away from the stress of modern life'. There was no way to book online and the phone number for reservations rang out.

In lieu of any other thread to pull on, and too anxious to risk turning to the police, driving out to see the Bluebell seems to make sense. Maybe Greg tried the police route and it got him killed. Maybe it got Marianne in someone's cross hairs. Maybe someone in the police is involved in this ring. *It happens*.

Or maybe she's way off the mark and David Ross can explain. Either way, moving feels better than just sitting and waiting for the axe to fall.

The engine whines as she presses the pedal to the floor. It's been so long since she drove an unfamiliar route that Marianne swerves as she tries to find the sat-nav shoved somewhere in her chaotic glove box. She holds up a hand in apology and glances in her rear-view mirror, the car behind pulling back warily.

As they all slow for traffic lights, she types in the address and jams the sat-nav into its holster, waiting for the route to come to life.

The hotel itself isn't in a town or village, it seems to be burrowed in the middle of green nowhere a few miles from a village called Godstone. Ordinarily, the history teacher inside of her would burst forward, wondering about the significance of the name, wanting to know if it was formed from the old English 'goda', meaning farm, or the word 'god'. Today, all she wants to know is how far it is and why someone there appears on the same deadly list as her.

She taps the accelerator as the lights turn green.

*

The M25 is jammed up so the sat-nav has her peel away at Leatherhead. From there, she worms her way onto increasingly thin A-roads. It's so quiet out here. People putter along in no rush and the fields are dotted with disinterested animals. It reminds her of her country childhood.

She glances at the time, 11.29 a.m. She should be wrapping up her Year 9 class and heading to the coffee pot but instead she's here, driving along a road she's never taken before, miles from home. No one knows she is here. She feels simultaneously in extreme risk and far safer than she was in the city. Greg would make a quip about Schrödinger's cat, were he here. *Fuck, I wish you were here. But what the hell were you involved in?*

She grips the steering wheel more tightly and blinks away a shock of tears.

# Sam

The creep of familiarity rolls up my spine. This is not the kind of route you'd end up taking by accident if you lived and worked in London.

I drop back. I know where she's going and there's no need to be seen.

I should not have let doubt creep in. If she's going where I think she's going, she's one of them. Another link in the chain. They *are* all connected, these people. Clustered together like a nasty bunch of boils I've been tasked with lancing.

I let a Land Rover Defender pull out in front of me, a matted and happy sheepdog hanging its head out of the passenger window. I go slower still.

Let her get ahead. Let her worm her way to the heart of the hotel where she won't hear my tyres on the gravel or my key in the lock. Let her feel safe.

# Marianne

Her 3G cuts out somewhere around Godstone. The village itself is small and pretty. A high street strung with pretty cottages and a cricket green wrapped around a shiny duck pond. The bright grass has been grooved and churned by wholesome fun and welly boots.

She drives out of the village again, continuing out along a road dotted with lonely cottages and farms, until she dutifully follows the sat-nav onto a lane so hidden that she almost drives straight past the turning. Her last bar of phone reception sputters to nothing as Marianne picks her way under a canopy of dark, twisted trees loaded with autumn leaves. The thick hedges on either side grow increasingly untamed, thorns bulging out and scratching at the windscreen as she scrapes around the bends.

The lane thins even more, the next turn so sharp the hedge rears up like a bramble barricade in front of her. *Is this really the best way?* Perhaps this is the shortest route *as the crow flies* but it's certainly not an easy drive. Fucking sat-navs. She imagines a bigger car or delivery truck trying to navigate down here and feels a clench of claustrophobia in her chest. Every hundred metres or so, a pull-in has been scraped out on either side to allow cars to pass each other, but she sees no one. No other guests leaving or arriving to check in.

Marianne licks her lips. They're dry and rough. She's smoked too much, and has been breathing heavily through her mouth in concentration. Hasn't drunk any water in . . . all day. Maybe she can get some lunch and a drink at the hotel, get a feel for the place and decide whether asking to see the manager is such a good idea after all. There's comfort and safety in a public place, though, and all she need do is ask David Ross how he knew Greg. She's mentally prepared a couple of opening gambits.

*'I found your name in my late husband's paperwork . . .'*

*'I think you knew my husband, Greg Darrow?'*

*'My husband had made a list of people he owed money to, and you were on it.'*

None of them feel right under closer examination. Of course, there is a chance that David Ross himself is dangerous, but as he's on a list with a bunch of dead people, it seems unlikely he's the one trying to hurt her. And really, what does she have to lose?

She rattles over a cattle grid and then follows the curve of the road, a sign appearing on the left with gold lettering on a duck-egg blue background.

*The Bluebell Hotel*
*100 metres*
*Restaurant. Spa. Carpark.*

It has been painted over with a rough white cross but is still legible. Local vandals, presumably. A far cry from the jubilant colours of Hackney graffiti.

Marianne rolls her stiff shoulders. At least she's going in the right direction. She taps her phone screen awake but there's still no reception. Fuck the sticks, give her street lights and a reliable data network any day. *And broken gas flues and cycling fatalities.* She focuses on the present. Just a few more metres to go, surely.

She pulls around a hedge and sees it, a solid building peeking out over the fields.

Marianne follows another blue sign to the carpark but there isn't a single car here. Just her tiny black Fiat 500, surrounded by gravel and the sporadic stubble of weeds. Marianne tucks into the furthest corner and switches off the engine. She hears the rumble of a car in the distance but nothing appears. In the silence, if she concentrates, she can hear the distant buzz of the A25, usurped by its brother motorway but still busy enough with local traffic.

There is probably a staff carpark around the back but it's still strange. It's lunchtime now, surely there are restaurant diners and people checking in? She thinks back to her birthday, the froufrou hotel in the Downs where Noah took her. At this time of day, it was bustling with honeyed blondes and salt-and-pepper sugar daddies mooching between the spa and the rooms in dressing gowns.

The hotel looks positively closed.

# Sam

I pull into the same derelict barn I used last time and kill the engine. I pull on wellingtons, tug on a waxed jacket and grab my hiking sticks. They and the boots are spotless and I scuff them a little before I set off, but it won't take long for them to blend in with the dull greens and browns, the thick claggy mud of the area.

I climb over a gate and it rattles in protest. Ahead, poking over the brow of this hilled field, I can see the roof of the hotel. A few more slates missing since last time, the recent storm loosening them like baby teeth.

I check my phone: no reception. Just in case, I try switching the cards. My personal SIM has a tiny bar of reception. I switch off location services, data and Wi-Fi radios, though. I can't be placed here.

I start off, marching alongside the tall hedges, unseen from the road. Just me and her for miles around. As if Marianne Heywood and I have the only hearts beating in the whole world.

# Marianne

The hotel is prettier and bigger than it looked from the road. It's a red-brick Edwardian building in the shape of an old ink pot with ivy laced along its seams. It sits solid and reassuring on the top of a slope, shuttered windows overlooking acres of nothing. There's something familiar about it, but she can't think why.

Marianne stays in the car and watches through the window, waiting for signs of life but there's no one here. Perhaps they're doing renovations. Work vans could be parked around the back. In which case, maybe David Ross is here to oversee the work. Hopefully, or she's wasted a lot of time and petrol.

She checks her phone; still no coverage and not much battery, but Marianne slips it into her bag anyway, then climbs out of the car. Her footsteps on gravel crunch through the silence.

The carpark is at the side of the building, so she turns the corner to find the main entrance. The front of the hotel is rendered and painted the same duck-egg blue as the signs that guided her here.

The air has a chill to it, the breeze rolling up the hill and buffeting the hotel despite the mild day. She's glad of Noah's hoodie but wishes she'd worn a jacket, something smarter just in case she does get to meet with the management.

She climbs the five stone steps to the front door and reaches for the big brass handle. It's freezing cold and jammed solid.

*God fucking dammit.*

She shivers and wraps Noah's hoodie more tightly around her. She probably should have left it at his but it feels like a talisman, a little comfort. She's been smoking in it; she hopes he won't mind. Perhaps when she gets back to his she could do a machine wash, contribute for her lodgings last night. The idea of that seems alien compared to her current situation.

Marianne presses her face to the cold glass set into the thick wooden door. Inside, the hallway is dimly lit from the lacklustre sunshine and she can make out an unmanned reception desk and an ornate coat rack left naked. No staff, no workmen. No David Ross.

*What now?*

Out of habit, she reaches into her bag and checks her useless phone again, no reception. Then she looks across at the fields for answers that don't come. Greg came here every month at least, but even if he could have somehow afforded it, he wasn't staying the night. He'd not stayed away from home in years, and only then when he was visiting family in Scotland and she'd wriggled out of going.

Marianne leans against the door and tries to imagine how Greg could have got here. He didn't drive, he surely couldn't ride his bike all this way and the nearest train station is in Godstone, some miles away. Someone must have picked him up. Perhaps David Ross himself or a hotel car service.

Marianne peers into the darkness again. If Greg was a paying customer of some kind, perhaps there is a record of these visits, a visitors' book maybe. Somewhere inside.

*

Marianne walks the perimeter of the building, peering through the windows. It certainly looks like a once-functioning hotel; huge sofas face a dead fireplace and a stack of local leaflets sit on a bureau. One of the tables in the small dining room is even made up for lunch. Silverware and fanned napkins, the rest of the chairs leaning forward onto tables like they're thinking, head in hands. It's as if the world froze between meals one day.

She reaches the back of the building. No work vans, no staff carpark. Just the stink from the big wheelie bin. A smell so thick it's almost chewy, clogging in her throat and nose. When was this last emptied? Oil tubs and old catering jars are stacked up along the wall like a house of cards, and to the side sits a surprising shock of yellow: a sharps box for needles. The back of the building has none of the frills of the front. A single plain white fire door sits dirty and scuffed in the centre of the wall. Two windows are framed with peeling paint. One has vanity glass and she can just make out the outline of some stacked toilet rolls. The other window is smeared in grease and dull with old smoke. The kitchen. She tries the door but it's locked. Just around the corner of the wall, hidden from the other side of the hotel by a small brick extension and an old oak tree, is a metal staircase. She follows it up with her eyes to another fire door, as white and scruffy as the one by the kitchen.

There are no other entrances or exits. She's as alone as she feels. So Marianne steps up – one, two, three – the noise of the metal sharp in the silence, until she's at the top.

She reaches for the handle. This door opens.

# Sam

I watch the fire door swing closed after her. I didn't check it when I left last time and I should have, but my error is also my gain. I give her a little time to look around. It will have changed since the last time she came, whenever that was. I don't know the schedule these people kept but this wasn't your everyday circle, this was an elite service from what I could tell.

Something to savour. David Ross almost said as much as I put him in position, held him until I could stand it no more. 'It wasn't that often,' he'd pleaded. 'It was a needs-must situation.'

I have a needs-must situation of my own right now.

I make my way around to the front of the hotel and pull out the big metal key.

## Marianne

After the hard metal of the staircase, the thick carpet under her feet feels almost alive. The old floorboards whimper with every step. Now she's in, Marianne can tell from the tides of dust and uncompromising cold that the Bluebell has been closed for some time.

The smell is something like the inside of an old Hoover bag mixed with the contents of one of those wheelie bins. Sour, dusty and contaminated. She steps lightly down the hallway, slowly, guiltily. Is it trespassing if a door is open?

Somewhere in the distance, she can hear something buzzing. A generator perhaps, or an air-conditioning unit. It's not doing great work if so; the air is cold but dank.

Any customer records would likely be in an office, so Marianne intends to make her way downstairs, but it's worth looking around for any other hints. She may not get another chance.

She tries the first bedroom – number 18 – and it opens easily. No electric card entry here; there are solid brass keyholes to match the brass numbers on the doors. The room is decorated tastefully, a big sleigh bed stripped down to its striped mattress, flecked with the stains of other people's romantic breaks. A chest of drawers has a tray on it, offering a mini kettle, a bowl of used tea bags and some torn sugar sachets. Two cups sit stained brown and off their saucers.

Marianne backs out and continues to the next room where the scene is almost identical but for a wrought-iron bed. There's an abandoned Tupperware lunchbox, wet with mould. In the bathroom, the basin is ringed with soap scum. Old urine coats the toilet.

Somewhere between check-out time and lunch, the plug was pulled here. Foreclosure? An evacuation from a small fire? A bomb threat? According to his diary, Greg was here two days before he died – was he caught up in the panic?

The last room in the corridor has no number. She assumes it's a supply cupboard and when she tries to open it up, it's locked. Marianne looks behind her. It feels colder inside the building than out, the air unmoved by anyone but her. She peers around the corner to check the next corridor – it's identical but with a staircase cascading from the middle of it.

She crouches down in front of the locked door, feeling about as vulnerable as she's ever felt, and puts her eye cautiously to the keyhole.

At first, the room looks the same as the others, just with twin beds. Wrought iron, bare mattresses. But on the nearest one she can see the bloom of a red stain amongst the fabric stripes and as she stares harder, some kind of strap on each side of the bedstead. She pulls back in shock. Was someone chained up here?

*

She rushes around the corner to the large wooden staircase. A grand thing, almost grotesque in this small hotel.

Marianne takes each carpeted step carefully, treading quietly. If there are ghosts here, they're not going to be happy ones and she doesn't want to disturb anything. She arrives in the foyer that she'd seen from outside. An office door sits behind the abandoned reception desk and she is about to step into it when she hears a sound outside. Footsteps on gravel.

Marianne's brain hums with panic. She is trespassing, apparently wanted by some unknown killer but still in pursuit of vital answers that may be here. Seconds tick past, filled with feverish internal debate. Should she announce herself or hide? *Fight or flight?*

It could be David Ross; he was the manager here, after all. And he'd have a key to every room. Even the one she just saw. *Especially* the one she just saw. No, good god, of course she won't announce herself. The questions will have to wait.

She rushes further into the belly of the hotel, through to the dining room she spotted from outside. Her spine tingles with an ancient feeling. She feels like prey.

Close up, the dining room is even more eerie. As if a siren rang out and everyone fled. It reminds her of Pompeii, where disaster struck so fast it immortalised the scene in volcanic rock. A snapshot of mass death. Here it's a snapshot of exodus. On one table, a woman's purse sits. It is dusty and cold to the touch, not handled by a human hand in months. It's a small embroidered coin purse, almost childlike. The stitching spells out 'Lina'. Marianne picks it up as she passes, and puts it in her pocket. She doesn't know why – some emblem of another life perhaps. A good-luck charm left by someone who got out of here.

Behind her, she hears the metallic click of a chunky key twisting in a lock. Followed by the whoosh of a heavy door being opened.

Marianne considers hiding under one of the tables, pushing herself up to the legs and hoping the tablecloth covers her. But it's too risky, too obvious. She presses on, heart hammering. The footsteps follow at a calm, steady pace. While Marianne is in the grip of fight or flight, the new arrival is in no rush. They stroll through the foyer, seemingly oblivious. *It must be David Ross. Who else could it be?*

A swing door with a porthole window sits at the end of the dining room and Marianne pushes it as carefully as she can, arriving in the dark kitchen and steadying the door to stop its movements giving her away. It's freezing cold in here, the greasy film on the windows holding back the sun and the dead strip-lights on the ceiling coated in bugs and cobwebs. The idea that food was ever prepared here turns her stomach while she casts around madly for somewhere to hide.

A corkscrew lies on the stainless steel worktop and Marianne picks it up slowly, silently. As defensive weapons go, it must be bottom of the charts, but it's better than nothing.

There is a stack of plates on the side next to a dry, dirty sink filled with bowls. The whole room hums with stink. A vague buzz of electricity rumbles from the power points and cables, while standby lights dot the equipment. An industrial dishwasher sits open, its door like a tongue lolling from a metal mouth. If it weren't for the racks inside, and the noise that removing them would generate, she would hide inside it. A metal tomb.

A noise rings out from the dining room, a jingle of cutlery perhaps, the scrape of a chair. A sudden realisation makes her pant with panic. *Her car!* David Ross, or whoever has let themselves into this hotel in the middle of fucking nowhere, knows very well that someone is here. Another chair leg scrapes on the floor. Marianne swallows. Far from oblivious, it sounds like they're looking for her.

The footsteps grow closer.

In the corner, a huge refrigerator shakes from the power snaking into it. How long could a person hide in there safely? It's more of a cool room, about six foot by six foot, but it won't have a fresh oxygen supply.

Another chair scrape, this one just the other side of the porthole door. Praying, panting, sweating like she's diseased, Marianne teases the fridge door open. It's huge and even without the light on, she can make out some food abandoned inside: a block of catering cheese, soured milk, vacuum-sealed chunks of slimy grey meat. She gags at the smell, pleads with her throat to keep everything in and steps inside. As she pulls the door almost closed, Marianne hopes to hell there isn't an alarm set to go off if the door is left ajar too long. She squats down next to a box of vegetables that have turned to goo and tries to calm her breathing. In the back of the small cold room, something large and bulky is propped against the back corner, wedged in place by the shelves from each side. It's too dark at first to realise what she sees, the size and shape of it. Its clothes. Its shoes. Its face.

The scream is out of her mouth before she even realises it is forming.

The sour smell rushes into her open mouth and she's sick, vomiting through her fingers while she tries to stop it and stem the sound of terror rushing from the pit of her belly.

There is a dead man in here. Preserved by the cold, a gruesome scar on one eye and his face contorted in fear. Her brain flashes with images of gargoyles, of terrified victims preserved at Pompeii. Of Greg, and how she sometimes dreams of him as the unknown vehicle hit him then sped off; nightmare visions of how he might have looked at the life-splitting second. She scrunches her eyes as hard as she can but the vision of this man remains. His features sparkle with ice crystals. It's David Ross, no question. She recognises him from the Facebook photo she found. Older. Colder. Stuck in here all by himself. Another 'accident'?

*So if David Ross is in here with me, who has just walked into the kitchen?*

Marianne's heart beats so loudly she imagines it ringing out across the room. *I'm in here, I'm in here, come and get me.* She tries to control her breathing but it's jagged, coughing in and out of her like she's drowning.

Through the tiny crack in the door, the one she'd hoped would bring her fresh oxygen, Marianne watches as a black shape moves around the kitchen as precisely as a puma.

Behind her, David Ross remains frozen while Marianne can hardly stay still. Shaking violently and fighting the need to collapse. To just give in and let death bite her to pieces.

The black shape moves closer. It seems to slink, a controlled slide across the kitchen floor. No rush. In the grey gloom of the kitchen, through the haze of stench and dust, Marianne grips the corkscrew tightly and tries to piece the image together.

It wears black boots fringed with mud.

It's tall, broad and strong-looking. Black jeans strain around muscular calves.

Its black wax jacket has rough rope spilling from the pockets.

One gloved hand hangs relaxed.

The other holds a small knife.

And above it all, smiling with amusement, under a close-cropped hairstyle, is the face of a middle-aged woman.

# PART TWO:

## Before

# Samantha

I've been ready to run for twenty years but I never thought it would happen like this.

I'm forty-one years old, a besotted mother of one. We live very comfortably, in a detached house in a prim and proper Surrey town. I drive a shiny and safe car, have a collection of beautiful handbags, each sitting in their own protective satin bags. We have a weekly cleaner.

Besides being there for my son, Joe, I spend my days looking nice and volunteering at a local charity. A housewife, I suppose the term is. I put a lot of effort into looking the part. My long hair, once naturally black and now naturally grey, is dyed with slices of auburn and chestnut. My forehead is unnaturally smooth. I am always made-up.

When I was younger, I was mistaken for a model. *Or was I?* No, I was propositioned with *lines* about being a model, but at this distance, it's about the same thing.

It was during those 'model' days that I first met Steve. Both of us desperate in different ways. Despite being the son of meticulous accountants, he had never shown any aptitude at school, could barely scrape through his A levels. When his slightly older brother, Jonathan, had graduated impressively and started to scramble up the corporate ladder, Steve opted to learn butchery. Food was his passion, but he'd nursed it like a guilty secret. And he was right to be wary. Though it was never said – because that was the way with his family – the decision to follow that passion came at the cost of their parents' respect. It's unfair, in so many ways, but not least that it showed just how smart he actually is, how analytical. He spotted a gap in the market that has led to five food stores and London-based chefs giving him more nods in their books and TV shows than any other independent food supplier. Steve calls himself an epicure. Sometimes, when Jonathan is being spiky, he calls his younger brother a grocer.

I still remember the first time Steve cooked for me. Trying to hide his nerves, the tips of his ears growing pink as he waited for my reaction. Steak Diane and potato rösti, which dates us far more than the clothes we might have been wearing.

I wolfed it down, the first proper cooked meal I'd had in weeks. And watching me appreciate it, especially the meat he'd hand-cut, was the greatest gift to him. Anything less than marked appreciation still seems to hurt him. He's far more tender than he looks, especially when it comes to me. I still catch him looking shy in his own home. Still so in need of approval and reassurance. His parents have a lot to answer for. All parents do.

Steve's spoken only occasionally about the moment he realised he was never going to follow his brother into the world of shiny corner offices and computers. That his heart, and his abilities, lay elsewhere. Signing the lease on his first shop is right up there alongside Joe's birth.

I'm lucky. Our son, Joe, is healthy and safe. He's training to be a doctor, he rows for the university team. He has had one or two girlfriends and treated them kindly. He's a homebody who still, secretly, tucks his teddy bear under his arm at night. I love him more than anything in the world and he loves me.

We are every inch the middle-class dream.

And it's all a lie.

*

'Mum, are you OK in there?'

Joe's knock is gentle at first, soft on the wood of the door. I open my mouth to reply but I just cough out dust. *Am I OK?*

'Mum?'

He knocks again, a crisper rap, panic drumming the beat.

'I'm fine,' I manage. 'I'll be down in a minute, darling.'

He says nothing but I can tell he doesn't move away. He's been like this since he was a little boy, always preferring to be near me than not. Clinging to my legs every morning when I dropped him at school, long after the other kids had run in. And at secondary school, he would prefer to be driven and dropped just around the corner, hugging me at every single goodbye when the rest of his friends caught the bus without looking back. He even chose to live at home through university.

Even now, six foot four and twenty years old, the invisible string between us is just as taut. The thought of severing it is more painful than any other grief.

I would die.

I stare down at the phone screen again.

'Uncle Jonathan is here,' Joe adds, his voice quieter now. 'And I think Dad's getting a bit stressed.'

Poor Steve. He's cooking all the food and furnishing everyone with drinks by himself. He's never been good when he's alone. I imagine going down there and trying to tell him about the email I've just received. The look on his face, the food burning as the fear takes hold. No. I can't begin to tell him what I've been sent, especially in front of his brother. Steve's business, his reputation, his family. It would all be torched to the ground if anyone knew. When it comes to my past, he made a conscious decision to lock it away so deeply, it's like it never happened.

'Can you go and help Dad?' I say, trying to keep my voice light. 'I'll just be a sec.'

'OK.'

I hear him leave reluctantly, his solid weight testing each of the steps leading down to our kitchen, the belly of our home.

I take a deep breath, more a gulp than anything. My heart quickens, my temples greasy with sweat. I read the words again, unbelieving, unseeing. I had almost forgotten this feeling. Almost.

'We know who you really are,' the message starts.

I read it again one more time. And then I delete it.

Steve gives me a grateful smile as I join the small party gathering around the big island unit at the centre of the kitchen. Jonathan – never John – has his arm draped around his wife, Paula. I squeeze Steve's arm just briefly and see his shoulders relax.

'Sorry to keep you all waiting,' I say. 'I felt a little queasy.' I'm looking at our guests but I'm saying it to Steve. He's wearing his leather butcher's apron and pouring batter into a Yorkshire-pudding tray so hot it's smoking.

'Just glad you're here now,' Steve says, without looking up again. Jonathan flashes me a smile and Paula catches my eye, gives me a look asking if I'm OK. I smile at her, nod to show I'm fine.

I need to get it together and act normally for the rest of the evening or she'll ask me about this when we next get together by ourselves. We tend to meet for coffee or brunch once a month, a chance to chat away from 'the boys'. We're hardly best friends, we're so different after all, but we get along. And it's not easy being in relationships with men whose lives are so entwined, so it's nice to have an ally.

Paula is several years older than Jonathan. She's a safe port in a storm, a capable 'head girl' type of woman who gets stuff done. If she still worked, I've no doubt she'd be a CEO somewhere by now. But I don't think she's worked since she had her daughter and certainly hasn't worked since she lost her child. A fate I hate hearing her talk about, not that she often does, because it feels too contagious, too terrifying. As a result I hardly talk about Joe to her, lest it feel like insensitive bragging.

What would Paula think about the message I've just received? She, with no reason to fear the machinery of her country and the lens of officialdom, would probably march me briskly to the nearest police station to ask for help.

I shudder, catching Paula's eye and rubbing my arms as if I'm chilly. She tilts her head, asking another question with her frown, but I just smile again. I have no other answer.

And what about Jonathan? They know elements of my past: that I wasn't born here, that I arrived by unconventional means. They may even know that I'm still not supposed to be here, that years later I continue to fly under the radar, terrified of being sent back to the country I was born in. Perhaps this message would cause them to fear me, to see me as an interloper, an anomaly in Steve's life. Perhaps they have always seen me this way, if they're honest, and this would confirm their suspicions.

I just hope Steve kept the worst of it from them; he promised he would, but these brothers are so close.

I see Jonathan gamely refilling everyone else's drinks while Steve chops kale. The bottle hovers over Joe's glass but he slides his hand over and shakes his head at his uncle. 'No thanks, I have training tomorrow.'

Jonathan is far slighter than Joe but he steps closer to him, energy crackling through his wiry frame. 'Come on,' he says, smiling like a wolf. 'Don't be a sissy.'

Steve and I look at each other but say nothing. Jonathan has no kids of his own, he's never known how to talk to younger people. I can hardly be cross about that, not with the struggles they've had.

And besides, Joe has to learn some assertiveness without us fighting his battles, but my heart sinks as he gives in, accepting another slug of wine that he'll no doubt sip cautiously. What would he do without me here? What would he allow to happen to him? Who might come creeping out from their hiding place? The thought is too much to bear.

I turn down wine and sip sparkling water instead. My brain is imprinted with the words I've just read. I can see them, hear them, taste them. Whichever way I try, I can't make sense of it. It's all true, and yet, I don't understand how anyone could know my history. Or who these anonymous people are who have contacted me. Or why they would care about a former life so long ago, so hidden, that it feels like a storybook. A really fucked-up fairy tale.

# Greg

## Thursday, 13 June 2019

Greg can feel his wife's gaze on the back of his neck. He swats at it as if it's a fly. *She can't see the screen, can she? No, of course she can't.* He shifts in his seat a little to be sure. Crowds closer to the laptop to block it.

The screen is sparse. It flickers slowly like a candle. Behind him, Marianne is draped on the sofa in her dressing gown, towel turbaned on her head. The lamp nearby casts an oval glow around her and in the corner of his screen the reflected scene hangs like a painting.

'*Wife Marking*, 2019, oil on canvas.'

He studies her briefly, relieved to see she's not looking at him after all but staring down at the sheaf of papers in her lap. He smiles at her but she doesn't notice, frowning intently over her work. Those kids are lucky to have her. He lowers his screen a little – almost a habitual tic now – and looks at her again. Her dark eyebrows drawing a line across her face as she frowns, her wild hair bundled up and hidden from view. The kids at school will never see her wildness; all they get is buttoned-up and dedicated Ms Heywood. Some things are just for him.

Meeting Marianne on that night bus all those years ago, it was like an old memory came back to him. Just in that moment, a tiny little jigsaw piece – so small he hadn't noticed it was missing – settled back in its place and his heart was whole. He had to see her again. To lose that little piece, to have it gouged back out of his heart so soon, would have killed him even then.

How fast it had happened, from meeting to spending their first night together. But it didn't feel fast, it felt like coming home. And that first night she stayed over, they didn't make love. Barely touched. They listened to music all night, Marianne lying next to Greg in his old Lou Reed T-shirt and her knickers.

If he could have captured them in a Polaroid right then, he would have been happy never to look at any other photo again. It would be the album cover for his whole life.

Throughout that first evening, all those years ago, Greg was simultaneously frozen with fear and buzzing with adrenaline. He had brought people back to his shared house before, a slow dribble of nice enough girls with forgettable faces, but this was something else. Marianne was something else. He wanted to play her every song he'd ever loved. To find that Venn diagram of her favourites and his: *their music*. And he didn't want to put a foot wrong, couldn't bear to play the wrong song and extinguish a flame before it really caught light. Still feels like that sometimes. A look in her eye, like she's appraising him.

Of course they were just babies back then. He pulls at his beard; a dusting of grey has started to bloom out from its centre and gobble up all the dark hairs. And Marianne, that frown line that never fully fades now, and her hips with their solidity, a new heft. They're proper adults now. But back then, they were happy little idiots, full of lust and love.

Greg toggles away from what he had been staring at, rubs his eyes and heads back to the usual place.

A lot of them don't work day jobs like he does. And they're not married. He's always the last to log on after work, first to log off. A beat of guilt pulsing as he shifts in his chair again, re-blocking Marianne's view.

There's just so much. He stares down at its darkness like a Fibonacci spiral, an endless loop. A man could get lost down here.

*

### Friday, 14 June 2019

Slapping himself awake, Greg watches from the bed as Marianne gets ready for work.

'I'll be back late tonight,' she says, without turning around. 'I'm doing a revision club for the Year Elevens.'

'Oh, OK.'

'It's their second exam on Monday, Greg,' she snaps, pushing earrings through each ear like little knives.

'I know,' he says, confused by her tone. 'I just like our Fridays.'

'Sorry, I like our Fridays too. I'd rather be here with you than with them, undoing their bloody YouTuber conspiracy theories about . . .'

He pats the bed next to him to cut off this rant and she sits down. He shuffles over and puts his head in her lap, pretending to purr. 'You're so weird,' she laughs, but she strokes his face, his hair, bends over awkwardly to give him a quick kiss then gestures for him to move.

'I love you,' he says as she stands up with a sigh.

'Always,' she says, the door clicking behind her as she goes.

Greg lies back down. He can see track marks of her mascara on the pillow and thinks about stripping the bed, washing it all. When did they last change it? Neither one of them would win awards for housekeeping but sometimes it borders on the embarrassing. 'Our little secret,' they sometimes joke. 'Your kids would be shocked to see what a slatternly wife you are,' he likes to joke.

'Lucky for me no one under the age of ninety knows what "slatternly" means,' she always replies.

He should get up and at least *make* the bed but he doesn't move, exhausted from another fitful night. 'Maybe don't shine that screen into your eyes right before bed,' Marianne shrugged, half joking when he last complained about insomnia. Then in a softer voice: 'We'll catch up at the weekend.' And they always do, every weekend. Sleeping in until at least eleven on both days. How do people with kids manage if they can't catch up then?

They both work at the weekend too, trying to get ahead of the week. He always watches in awe as she marks and files and clicks and uploads and then forgets all about it for the rest of the day while he paws at his guilt and chases his tail. There's never enough time, always too much to do. There are no doors to shut on his thoughts, they're there every moment of the day and piercing through his sleep.

'You can only do so much,' his boss, Eloise, tells him. A repeated mantra in their one-to-ones or when she catches him in the kitchen pulling at his eyebrow or beard distractedly. 'You have to put on your own oxygen mask first.'

He gets up and leaves the bed unmade, makes a coffee and sits down by his laptop. Just a little bit of time before work. The very opposite of an oxygen mask, more like being strung with a drip of poison.

He opens up his computer and climbs back down the black hole.

# Samantha

*Friday, 14 June 2019*

Steve keeps his apron on while he slices the Chateaubriand. The slim slices of beef quiver as his knife coaxes them away from the tenderloin. The middle is pink, dripping with flavour, and my stomach lurches.

I close my eyes and move a hand towards my belly to quell the nausea. It brushes the phone in my pocket and I feel a mask of sweat prickle over my face.

I'm not technical and I'm not canny. I've never even had my own phone contract and Steve set up my email address for me. I don't know how they could have found it. I don't even know who 'they' are.

I could try to tell myself that it's a hoax but the details are pinpoint accurate. Ordinarily, I would ask Steve to help me but that's out of the question. All of this was supposed to be in the past; that was an absolute condition on which everything has been built.

And Joe, I can't even consider telling Joe. I meet his eye and smile. He's always looking for reassurance, even now. Even mildly nudging his world is out of the question, let alone setting fire to it.

I try to catch Steve's eye next, but he's looking forlornly at my almost full plate. 'The food's great,' I tell him and he smiles gratefully. He's at the head of the table, a whole side to himself, presiding over events. He reminds me of an old oil painting, a medieval king and his banquet. No, that's not true. He reminds me of someone pretending to be at a medieval banquet, dressed up at a corporate event perhaps. Or sticking his head through one of those wooden seaside pictures.

*

Jonathan sucks on his cigarette, then blows the smoke into the Surrey sky. 'I only smoke when I drink,' he tells me apologetically, as if I don't know. The houses in this strip were once egalitarian, filled with postmen and teachers as well as bankers in their bowler hats. That was long before my time. Now it's all marketing directors, city accountants and business owners, drawn by the detached ink-pot homes and direct line into Waterloo.

Every other house is having an extension built or a loft converted, builders' skips bulging out of driveways like the caravans that used to squat there. The glow of London sits just over the shoulders of this suburb, lending us its litter, crime and extended licensing hours.

The overpriced bottles we've bought chime against each other as we walk. We needed more wine and I was glad of the chance for some air, but Jonathan offered to squire me. Ordinarily, I would ask Paula if she'd like to come too, hoping she'd say no but keen to appear above board. *Innocent.* I was too distracted, though, and I wonder now what she and Steve are thinking.

There have been moments like this over the years, stolen time when it's just the two of us. Jonathan and me. Within these snatched pockets, the air changes, but we never address it. I look across at him and he smiles, a nervousness that's usually well hidden. His face is flushed with drink but my tongue is mute with sobriety.

I wish I could think of something to say, some way to tell him what's on my mind, but I can't. Even after all this time, I can't risk it. The only thing that has kept me safe for all this time is being a closed book.

London's lights sparkle on the periphery of the view. No different to the London I first saw, all those years ago.

'What are you thinking?' Jonathan asks gently, crushing his cigarette under his brogue. This is a voice he uses only when we're alone. I wonder if Paula ever hears it and feel a prickle of guilt, even though I've done nothing wrong.

'Thinking about London,' I answer, honestly. Steve and Jonathan grew up not far from our current Surrey home so the city holds no magic for them. But for me, it still feels like another country. Such a seductive city, a magnet. I will never fully trust in its promises.

Jonathan stops and leans against a large skip; planks of wood and old fittings jut out of it like teeth. 'You've not seemed yourself tonight,' he says, reaching for my hand. My gut twists, something shooting down to my groin and then up to my heart. All these years and he's never touched me like this, no matter how much I've wanted him to.

'Don't,' I say, almost silently. I let my hand fall from his but I don't step away.

'Samantha,' he says. I don't reply. I can't do this now. All these years, all these moments. And now, as I stand on the edge of a secret abyss, just one gentle blow could push me in. I mustn't get distracted.

I start to walk away, back to the family home I almost take for granted. I can still feel the impression of his fingers on me. So light, it's excruciating.

I can't remember the last time I was touched by Steve. I know that whenever it was, it didn't feel like that.

Steve has gradually retreated to a respectful distance. Maybe he hoped I would follow and pull him back. It's an odd stalemate cushioned with care for each other.

When we first got together, sex was part of the package. It never crossed my mind to demur, but even Steve, with his challenges, could tell I wasn't exactly excited at the prospect. 'Your eyes go blank, like you're a million miles away,' he said afterwards, a few months into our lives together. All I could do was shrug and try harder.

But I was a different person back then. A corpse that these people, 'they', have somehow dug up and reanimated.

As I reach our driveway, I notice Paula watching from the window. I give a small wave and slow for Jonathan to catch up. The curtain falls back into place and the door opens.

'Thanks for coming with me,' I call cheerfully to Jonathan as I step back inside, squeezing Paula's shoulder as I walk past.


# Greg

*Friday, 14 June 2019*


Eloise has been Greg's manager throughout his time at the Hidden Humans charity. Somehow, despite the merciless onslaught of the work, helping thousands of people who have been trafficked and exploited, she manages to be permanently, almost supernaturally, calm and patient. She absorbs the emotions of the team but never collapses under their weight. Which is more than can be said for Greg. Often when he gets home at night, he limps into the flat as if he's run an ultramarathon rather than cycled back from Lambeth.

The hardest, most frustrating part of the job is when the charity helps someone only for them to slip back under again. And when the worst happens – they wind up seriously assaulted or dead – it's all the more punishing for having known them, having met them, having held their eye or their hand. So when Eloise asks to speak to him with *that* tone, he steels his nerve.

Greg can feel Eloise's hand on his back now, waiting for the news to sink in. The heavy silver ring she twists when she's worried presses into his flesh.

'Marija? Seriously?'

'I'm sorry,' she says, her voice soft. 'I just heard.'

'But we'd got her out, we *had*. She and her sister were *out*.'

'It's the job, love. You know this is always a risk.'

'You don't mean that,' Greg says, shaking her hand away.

Sisters Marija and Ana had come to the UK to be au pairs, a long and optimistic journey from Central Europe. They'd lied about their ages numerous times, claiming to be eighteen and nineteen. 'But she's actually fifteen and I'm seventeen,' Marija had told him in a whisper.

It used to be safer, back when there were visas for au pair work, but now it's unchecked. Now girls arrive ready to look after kids, practise their English and do some sightseeing. Instead they're locked in private houses, sometimes skivvying all hours for families, and sometimes there are no children there at all.

Marija and Ana finally got free from their captors due to the vigilance of a postman, who noticed they were always in the house, always looking ill and haunted. 'He said his own daughter was the same age as me,' Ana added at their first meeting, in perfect English.

They couldn't go home but couldn't stay where they were. Greg followed the procedures and referred them to the mechanism for applying for asylum, arranged for them to stay in a B&B the charity often use – the best of a bad bunch. Not ideal, not with the other people staying there, but those are the compromises.

A month later, they had disappeared.

The older girl, Marija, was found dead two nights ago. She'd been dumped at the side of the canal a few metres from a well-known solicitation site. Ana was still missing but apparently – according to the other women and girls working with Marija – she was making films, along with some others who had been scooped up by a regular visitor to the B&B. The owner pleaded ignorance.

'We need to find Ana,' Greg says, finally. Eloise says nothing but shakes her head, almost imperceptibly.

*

Marianne isn't home when he gets in. He forgets for a moment that she's working late and feels the sting of her absence. More than anything, he just wants to hold her, press his body against her beating heart. Ground himself in the safety of the living. Instead the flat is empty, left to boil all day so the air is thick. Little whirlwinds of dust twirl in the evening sun that streams through the window. Fragments of her skin and his, dancing close.

He won't cook tonight. On Fridays they get a takeaway, creatures of habit. He had been looking forward to this all week. Ready to lose himself in a comedy, to drink wine with his wife and toast another week done. He doesn't feel like laughing now.

*How late did she say she'd be?* Greg makes a mug of tea, dumps three sugars in it and logs on.

He tries not to get sucked into the inflated chat that's clearly been rumbling for hours already. So much of it is hot air. He's in two minds about whether coming here is even worth it. There is true, valuable, *critical* activism happening on the dark web, but finding it and getting useful things done comes at a high cost. The things he has to wade through . . . the people he encounters.

This latest lot he's found are more enthusiastic than effective. And their enthusiasm seems to run chiefly to the theoretical rather than the practical. The last group he was a part of were a good bunch, realistic, experienced, but they disbanded after a group of them were arrested and a leak was suspected.

The latest idea, of the many plans that are floated without becoming concrete, is blackmail.

'We can only do so much in the background like this, why don't we shoot for the stars?' someone has written.

'Everyone has a secret. Let's force politicians to change policies, let's bribe asylum-centre managers for better conditions, let's force police to arrest the gangs. Why the fuck not?'

Greg's guts squirm. This kind of thing is never the answer. As ever, he tries to steer them away.

Far better to make change on the ground. Use dark web back channels to help people get back in touch with family through untraceable email accounts, to track down and break up small-time trafficking gangs and to find girls who are obviously not 'starring' in videos and photos out of choice, girls being 'offered' for pennies. Girls like Ana.

He doesn't bother telling them this again – they don't want to know. Let them tire themselves out while he gets on with his own plan. He looks at a recent thread about identifying girls in illegal porn, but that's not what he needs to do. He needs to reverse engineer a fuck-load of porn just to find a specific girl, Ana.

He posts.

'I need to locate a girl. I know her name, date of birth (real and at least one fake one she used) and last whereabouts. I know she's been exploited in videos and maybe other forms too. She wasn't trafficked for sex originally but you all know the story. So what's the best and quickest way to track her down?'

'That's easy,' someone writes back. 'Hacker Supermarket will have that done in a few hours. They do that shit all the time.'

'They find trafficked girls?' he writes, unable to hide his surprise. Why hasn't this come up before? He'd heard of Hacker Supermarket but as far as he knew they were a kind of odd-job service, stealing credit card numbers, generating fake gift cards, doxxing people and so on. Not doing anything approaching humanitarian work.

'They find anything and anyone you want, so they'll be able to find your girl.'

He sees himself in the reflection of the screen. Tired, angry, his beard ever more grey. He thinks of Ana, whether she even knows what's happened to her sister yet. If he's fatigued, how the hell does she feel?

'Can I get a link?' he types.

*

It's nearly nine and Marianne is still not back, but it can't be long. How late do Year 11s stay at school revising? And on a Friday night? The key could rattle in the lock any minute. *Now or never.*

He's been staring at this site for a good hour, but now Greg springs into action. Types in exactly what he wants, fills in every field and tries to work out a reasonable deadline. As an afterthought, he adds that he works to help trafficked women. Who knows if the people behind this site have a conscience, but if they do, it might help expedite things.

He gives his anonymous email address and submits.

*

The door swings open and Marianne walks in, rubbing her shoulders as she dumps her bag on the table next to his closed laptop.

'Good day?' he asks, standing up and moving away from the table.

'Long day,' she says, but smiles. 'I'm so glad to be home.'

He wraps his arms around her, smells the coconut conditioner in her hair and the tang of traffic fumes she's travelled back through.

'I'm so glad you're back,' he says into the curls that she's just released from her hair band.

'Are you OK?' she asks, pulling back to study his face. 'Did something happen?'

He looks at her frown, sees that little line scored ever deeper. He opens his mouth but where to start? And where to stop?

'I'm starving,' he says eventually, rolling his eyes and kissing her forehead. 'Let's order a curry.'

*

Marianne sleeps on her belly, one arm cast over the side of their bed. Greg inches down his side of the bed and flops onto the carpet carefully, but she doesn't stir. He takes his laptop into the kitchen and closes the door after him.

He's pretty full of wine and curry but he still needs something. He pulls down the bottle of Christmas whisky from his dad and pours a thick measure in a dusty tumbler. Then he opens his computer on the sideboard.

The quote is waiting for him. He throws the liquid down his neck, his eyes and throat burning in unison. There's a link to accept the offer, to get things started. Greg has enough cryptocurrency, 'money' he still doesn't really believe in but has gathered.

He pours another measure, adding a splash of tap water just like his dad. What would his dad think about *this*? He drinks it in one, feeling his head fuzz over almost immediately.

*It's for the greater good.*

*Accept quote.*

# Samantha

*Monday, 17 June 2019*

I get the second email while stirring milk into three mismatched mugs in the office kitchen of the animal charity where I volunteer. I've been expecting one, refreshing my inbox constantly since I received the first on Saturday and barely sleeping for the last two nights. Thank god Steve and I have our own rooms now.

In that very first message, they told me they wouldn't give up.

This email contains a scanned copy of old papers. Mine. Filled with details that no one in my life now would recognise. A different name. A different date of birth. Place. Parents. All of it. I don't delete it this time. They'll only send more if I do – and if they can find this, I dread to think what else they have on me.

After spending most of today putting on a brave face, my eyes sting with exhaustion, my movements are sluggish and I expect I've done a bodge job on everything I've touched. I'm only cushioned from complaints by my voluntary status. And maybe my long service; I've been helping out at the charity a few days a week since Joe started secondary school.

I carry a trembling tray of drinks through to the little office I share. By the time I place a mug down on Alice's desk, a pool of grey coffee surrounds it.

'You OK?' she asks, frowning up at me from under her thick curly fringe. Sensible, solid Alice.

'I'm fine.'

She doesn't believe me, but we're both adults so she lets me lie.

I put my own mug down on my desk and then take the other to the corner seat where Ruth is on the phone, handset clamped between ear and shoulder. She winks her thanks at me.

Back at my desk, I wiggle my mouse and the monitor comes back to life. The Facebook update I've been writing on the charity page is still there. I add a few more photos of small pets for adoption, drop in an extra 'donate' link and post it.

As I sip my lukewarm coffee, counting down the time until I can leave and hide away at home, my 'work' email dings. I toggle to the old version of Microsoft Outlook, an uneasy feeling growing. Could they know I'm here? Of course they could, they seem to know everything.

**What will your son do if you're sent back? Will he come to visit you in jail?**

We will report you to the authorities in 24-hours' time.
Unless you do the one simple task we have assigned you.
Go here now:

E-Z Luggage & Lockers – London Waterloo
Pear Place, SE1
Locker number 49
Key code to open locker: 160399
Further instructions will follow.

And Samantha, if you tell anyone about this, the offer is
rescinded and a file on who you really are will be sent to
everyone you know, as well as the authorities.

\*

The train into Waterloo snakes slowly through South West London. I still feel uneasy on trains, still furtively look around.

When I first arrived in Britain, the trains looked like toys. But I learnt that they were no more benign than back home. Still laced with officials, people checking tickets, people asking where I'd come from. They wore smiles but it was the same deal. There were police hiding in normal clothes. Guards looking closely. Nosy businessmen with bulky mobile phones.

I learnt what to say, coached first by the men who 'looked after me' and then by my friend Cristina. I learnt about hiding in the toilet when I couldn't pay the fare, and how to seem younger to get a child ticket if there was no toilet. How to get the money for the ticket from other passengers, the sob stories that worked. I learnt the tube map, the overland and all the rat runs; it's still there like muscle memory. It was so long ago that none of those people from my early days in London would recognise me, but I still can't settle.

At Wimbledon the train wheezes to a stop and sits, vibrating, for an unnecessary amount of time. If someone is watching me, they're hiding well. I tear both tips of my thumbnails off with my teeth then start to bite away at the flesh around my other nails. The varnish I've just scraped with my teeth is bitter on my tongue.

By the time we arrive at Waterloo, my fingertips are raw and throbbing. I pace in circles by the train door, then jab repeatedly at the button until it finally lights up. The doors creak open. It's nearly five o'clock and I'm thrusting myself into a main London station just as commuters start to pour in for their journeys home. They move in one slow mass like tipped jelly as I elbow through them.

My unregistered Oyster card is barely used these days and it's taken my last credit to get here. I tap out of the barriers, wondering if I should top it up now or after. But after what?

As I look for the right exit, I see other women my age looking around or distractedly staring at phones. I see a man in his fifties close to tears. Are they in the same situation? On the run, living lies? Ripe for manipulation?

E-Z Luggage & Lockers is not in the station itself; it's not even attached to the station. I have to follow a complex pathway of arches and turns, using my phone map to navigate. There is nothing very 'E-Z' about this place and my nerves have frayed to snapping point by the time I see the sign.

It sits under an archway, two stinking wheelie bins on either side of the doorway. At first I think the storefront is made from smoked privacy glass but as I get closer, I realise it's thick with dirt.

Inside, the carpet is balding and the smell of smoke and coffee lingers in lieu of staff behind the counter. Lockers of every size fill the walls but at first I can't find number 49 in the sea of grey metal. Behind me, a lad of around Joe's age strolls out from the back and leans on the counter.

'Number forty-nine?' I ask, trying to sound normal.

He rolls his eyes, points to one of the larger lockers and then disappears back to his cigarettes. He's nothing like Joe.

*

My fingers tap out the key code automatically – Joe's date of birth, a staple part of most of my passwords since he was tiny. A stupid, complacent choice. How did they know? And what else have they gained access to?

The door opens and I'm staring into an empty locker. My heart pounds, is this a prank? Has someone from *back then* tracked me down, determined to pull me back in? Are they coming to take me? Surely I have no value to them now – they were paid off years ago by Steve. And any 'value' we have now is Steve's, not mine. The house, the business, the cars.

I sit down heavily on the ground next to the locker, my knees clicking as I fold in two. Steve is a good man who tried to do the right thing. And now I'm calculating his worth from the point of view of a blackmailer. He doesn't deserve this. Our nuclear family is developing a dangerous half-life.

I'm about to give up, unsure what the hell to do next, when I see it. An unmarked manila envelope at the back. I reach in, open it hurriedly before the boy comes back for another sneer.

Inside is a stack of gift cards for Electronic Superstore. This makes no sense, why would someone blackmail me but then give me something? I turn the envelope up and shake it. There are no instructions inside but a tiny black rectangle slides out. A SIM card.

I stuff everything back inside the envelope and shove it into my handbag. Then I stand up to leave as elegantly as I can manage. As I burst out into the relatively fresh air of Pear Place, I brush my trousers off. Tiny fragments of carpet remain, like DNA.

I bring my phone screen to life to check train times home and see that I have an unread email.

Put the SIM card in your phone, download the Whispa app and use the same key code as before to access. It will only work when the correct SIM is in your device. All communication will take place there from now on. It is encrypted end to end to keep all parties safe – do not contact us any other way.

I lean against the brick archway, traffic rumbling nearby. Despite the muggy weather, it's started to drizzle and my hands are slippery. It takes several attempts with the spike of my earring to open the SIM tray. I put my own SIM card into the zipped pocket of my handbag and then insert the plain black SIM into the tray, closing it furtively. I feel like a sitting duck, waiting to be caught red-handed.

I find and download Whispa from the App Store while I walk back towards Waterloo Station, unsure if I should be getting on a train or whether there will be other lockers, gift cards to collect all around the city. *What the hell am I doing?*

London still belongs to that other girl, the one I was. Wide-eyed and hopeful despite everything and everyone I'd left behind. I was still a teenager when I arrived, believing somehow that this city would offer a new start, a bigger life. So I took a leap of faith back then, knowing I had no other option, and I landed hard. I soon found that young women like me were simply a commodity.

An overwhelming urge to cry wells up and I push it back down. I need to stay sharp, I know that much. I walk into Starbucks and join a queue, buying myself time and a seat as well as a coffee. By the time my latte is ready, the app has downloaded. I enter the key code and open it up.

*One new message.*

# Greg

### Sunday, 16 June 2019

Despite nerves churning in his belly every time he thinks of Ana, Greg and Marianne have had a nice weekend.

Yesterday, they'd gone to Kew Gardens, breathing in nature.

Then they'd bought fat field mushrooms, thick spicy sausages and fresh pasta from a fancy food store. Greg had cooked it all with hot chillies and almost too much garlic, while Marianne sat on the counter nearby, swinging her legs in pyjamas and reading her book.

This morning, they'd slept in and then decamped to Victoria Park to squint at the paper through the sunshine and eat lunch at the Pavilion café. Look at us, he wanted to shout at the young lovers warming themselves in the sun, we're just like you. After all this time, she's still my favourite.

He crawled across the grass to lay his head in her lap, sinking into her flesh like a memory. Something ancient and hard to reach. Childhood and his mother. Or Jenna. School summers, locked away.

This afternoon, they'd had sex on the sofa as if nothing bad had ever happened.

As he cooks dinner now, he looks out at his wife in the lounge, one leg tucked under her in her corner of the sofa, breasts loose under an old T-shirt. A body he knows so well, a brain he can never fully unlock. A lifelong challenge he'd relished on their wedding day. Better that than boring.

*Ouch! Fuck!*

He's stared too long and burnt his fingers on hot oil. He nurses the little red welts, sucking his fingers.

As the sun goes down, she packs her things for school the next day and kisses him goodnight. 'I'll be in soon,' he murmurs, reaching to stroke her hip as she stands over him. 'I love you.'

'Always,' she says, shuffling into the bathroom to brush her teeth.

\*

She'll be asleep now. There's no sound from the bedroom and the door is pulled to, the light off. He is conscious of his fingers on the keyboard, every tap ringing out in the silence. But she rarely stirs when she's asleep. He's both impressed and envious.

As promised, Ana has apparently been traced and her information is waiting for him. Everything he asked for. Plus a video clip. How have they done this? This kind of black magic is beyond the grasp of his understanding.

He writes down all the details in his notepad and then checks the sound is off on his laptop, casts an eye at the bedroom door and clicks play.

\*

It's certainly not Hollywood. Nor is it a scripted, cheesy porno. This is something rougher, uglier. At first Greg can't make sense of what he's seeing. Like watching one half of a Skype conversation, a static image of a face filling the screen. One camera angle only, catching a small mirror over the bed that reflects a flimsy wardrobe in the corner.

Then it comes to life. And it all becomes clear. This is saved footage from a live stream, pay per view perhaps or the shared spoils of a small network. She is alone, at first. Those same sad grey eyes that had looked up at him in their meeting room, now pretending to be lust-filled and wanting. Painful to watch.

A man enters the room, his face blurred. Greg watches until he cannot.

It's her, that's the important thing.

Now he can use the address he's been given to find her, and try to forget what he's just seen.

\*

*Tuesday, 18 June 2019*

'I'm sorry but I can't tell you,' he says. 'I can't reveal my sources.'

Eloise, patient, sane, *grown-up* Eloise, slaps her hand on the desk. 'For fuck's sake, Greg, this isn't how we do things.'

He can feel the gaze of his colleagues and colours red. *Well, what are you lot doing?* he thinks. *At least I'm making a difference, not just treading water.*

'She's out of there, isn't she?' he says, quietly.

Eloise breathes deeply. 'Yes, but at what—'

'And she's not dead like her sister,' he snaps. More angrily than he intended. Twisted images of that wardrobe, that mirror. The place they found her in yesterday. The way she had clung to him, almost animal-like in her fear.

He doesn't care what Eloise says, doesn't care how much it costs him. He plans to use that Hacker Supermarket service again, and again, and again.

In the work loo, he washes his face in the mirror and smiles as the water drips from his nose. Finally he's making headway. To hell with the risks.

# Samantha

*Monday, 17 June 2019*

*Is this for real?* I look around the dark archway, the sounds of trains thundering in and out of Waterloo just behind me. I stare at the dirty bricks and rowdy pigeons as if they might help me decipher this. I'm reminded still of that much younger me, eyes acclimatising to the tight, dirty bricks of London. The knotty little streets and mismatched houses, the bird shit everywhere.

At first my eyes had been wide and full of wonder. And then I met Cristina, my first and only real friend here. Her own eyes had matched mine but were just a slight shade darker, more jaded. She'd arrived earlier, had experienced rougher treatment. She schooled me in the realities of my situation and helped me to stay safe. I wish she was here now.

I look again at the message on this strange app.

I've never used anything like this. Social media is far too much of a risk. I have a closed and careful circle, my family and my fair-weather friends at the charity; being able to call or email is enough. This new world carries a steep learning curve.

There is only one contact in this app, 'A Friend', and just this one message. At the top of it is a shopping list. I count twenty items: various mobile phones and tablets totalling thousands of pounds. I read on, trying to make sense of it.

In your envelope you have twenty gift cards. Each one is worth £1000. Do not buy more than one item from any one store. Destroy all your receipts but retain the gift cards.

You have 48 hours to buy every item on this list, no excuses. Place the items and the gift cards in a locker at another London branch of E-Z Luggage & Lockers. Send the branch address, locker number and key code to us through this app.

If you are late or do not follow these instructions exactly, you know what will happen.

Confirm receipt of this message.

Do not tell anyone about this.

Your 48 hours starts now.

*

My train home is loaded with commuters, drizzle-damp rising from their clothes as they twist and squat, fitting themselves in like Tetris pieces. I feel numb, sitting amongst these real humans like an alien. It's not a new feeling, but it hasn't been so acute in years.

The journey feels sped up, a rollercoaster compared to the one that brought me to the city earlier. I think of that me, the one I was just a few hours ago, scrabbling at the door. Frantic, desperate, my toes poking over the edge of an unknown ravine. I didn't know what awaited me, I didn't know what I would find. And actually, I thought it would be worse.

Now I feel calm.

I've decided that I can do this. I *will* do this. Buying a few things, putting them in a locker. To do something so simple, that will keep me here with Joe? Of course I can do this for Joe. And really, I can do this for myself. Because I cannot be parted from him any more than he can be parted from me. And I sure as hell can't go back.

Outside, the last entrails of London have given way to the first sprigs of Surrey. The people who get off at these stops look like me but they're not me. I'm sure none of them are carrying what must be stolen goods and secret SIM cards.

I reply to the Whispa message with just one word: 'OK.'

I put my own SIM card back in the tray, tuck the new one behind my phone case where it sits throbbing like a black heart.

A text from Paula comes through asking if I'm really OK. 'You didn't seem yourself last night,' she says. I need to work on my mask, I think, as I reply chattily.

\*

I pick at my dinner, while trying to reassure Steve. I can tell his feelings are hurt – he takes so much pride in his cooking – and he pushes his own plate away without saying anything. I mumble apologetically about another headache.

'Are you OK? You're getting a lot of headaches,' Steve says as I leave the kitchen. 'Maybe we should . . .' He stops. Going to the doctor is out of the question, and he knows it.

'I'm fine,' I say, trying to smile reassuringly. 'I think it's this sticky weather. I need to drink more water.'

In bed, I switch SIMs to look at the list again, copying it carefully onto a note on my phone before putting my own SIM back in.

Twenty items in forty-eight hours, buying from a different Electronics Superstore each time. Of course there's not forty-eight hours now; it's more like forty-three hours. And I'll lose more hours overnight. Then I need to get to a different locker place. And how many stores does Electronics Superstore even have? The calm acceptance I felt on the train has given away to something very different. Have I signed up to an impossible task? *What have I done?*

I hear Joe shutting the front door as he comes home. He's so delicate for his size but he can never quite get it to click quietly enough. I still listen out for his click, not fully sleeping until I hear him return. Even after all these years, I'm still on high alert. The same panic that someone else will scoop him up at school home-time, or grab him on an errand to the shop.

'Did I wake you?' I hear him ask his dad on the landing.

'Not at all,' Steve lies and I can't help but smile.

Joe's getting back from rowing practice and normally I'd sit with him and talk it over. A herbal tea for me, an orange juice for him. But I can't bear to see his face. No, that's not true. I just can't bear to show him mine.

There are forty-seven Electronics Superstores across the UK, the twenty nearest ones are still scattered over an area of several hundred miles. My heartbeat cranks up again but I close my eyes and breathe. I can do this.

Organisation has always been my strength, along with staying calm and thinking clearly. I take after my dad like that, and he groomed me to take his place for that reason.

I close my eyes and try to focus.

After a few hours checking opening times, road closures and routes, I have the most efficient itinerary for visiting the stores. Rather than visit the twenty nearest, I will visit ten heading in a north-west then north-east direction – an arc to the left of London. Then I will mirror this route by heading south-east then south-west, tracing my way back to end in East London. I should have all twenty items before closing time and be able to get them into the E-Z Luggage & Lockers near City Airport. I'll be well ahead of schedule and, I hope, free from this. Just do this one thing, that's what they said.

The first store on the list opens at 7 a.m. so I set my alarm for 6 a.m., swallow some melatonin so I know I'll sleep and switch off the light. My lids are heavy but my mind is whirling through a non-stop replay of the last few days.

Just as I finally feel sleepy, my door opens suddenly. Steve is hovering there in his pyjamas.

'Sorry, love, I know you're not feeling well but I need you in the Reigate store tomorrow,' he says. 'They've all gone down with gastric flu.'

# Greg

*Wednesday, 19 June 2019*

In his notepad, Greg has a hastily scrawled list of girls to try to find through the Hacker Supermarket. He doesn't have much money, but maybe he could scratch up some more. All of the names on his list have been sucked back into exploitation, most of it sexual. They need to be found.

Marianne has spread a layer of paper and card over the table, bits spilling over. 'Year Seven,' she says as she sees him looking. 'Posters about the Black Death.'

'Nice,' he says, flipping open his screen as he sits in his corner of the sofa. 'Let me know if you find out how it started.' She smiles.

It takes a while to get on tonight but he's left the Hacker Supermarket open from last time and toggles straight to it. To hell with all those wannabes and their grand plans, this is real activism, making a difference on the ground.

He opens his messages, wonders if he should just email or go through the whole process the same as last time.

*One new message.*

Greg Darrow,

We can help you save many more girls than Ana. All we need is one healthy young woman a month, who fits certain criteria, and in exchange she will receive a life-changing sum of money and you will receive an address filled with more girls ready to be saved. What do you say? It's win–win, right?

He stares at the screen. They want him to provide women in exchange for being able to help more women? What?

He writes back: '*I'm sorry but I don't understand. What do you need one woman a month for? And what criteria are you looking for?*'

'What are we having for tea?' Marianne calls over. 'I'm starving.'

He can't eat. Can't think about food. Can barely see straight. He shakes his head. 'I don't know,' he says. 'I'll see what we've got.'

He takes the laptop with him into the kitchen and shuts the door. Rifling in the fridge and cupboards, he pulls out the stuff to make pesto pasta. He sets a pan of water boiling and checks the inbox.

*One new message.*

He reads it. Then reads it again. Bile rises.

All those young bodies that he comes into contact with. They're always looking for a way out, a way to pay for themselves, to buy their freedom. To disappear. All they have is their bodies. Often undernourished, always tired, but alive, available.

In the loopholes and gaps, they stumble and fall. Plucked by canny observers, slick operators. Pimped out, carved up and spat out. And now these people, this Hacker Supermarket bunch, they want him to do the same.

It's not prostitution this time, it's organ harvesting.

'Thank you for the offer,' he writes back as the pasta pot bubbles. 'But I'm not interested. I'm willing to pay to find more girls, like we did with Ana. But I'm not prepared to do what you ask. I hope you understand.' It's only after he clicks send that Greg realises they used his real name. They know who he is.

*

He gives up at two in the morning and gets back up. Marianne is in her customary sprawl, dead to the world as he tiptoes out of their room and into the lounge. He knows, even before he checks the inbox, that there will be a reply. Do people like this take no for an answer? Well, tough, they have to, he has no reason to comply. Even though, no, he stops himself. One woman in exchange for many others' freedom is still too much. Isn't it?

*One new message.*

This is disappointing. We were under the impression that you wanted to help these women. But perhaps we should not have been surprised. Your intentions are far from honourable, aren't they?

What would your wife, Marianne Heywood, think if we sent her the attached video?

What would your boss, Eloise D'Arby, think? What would the police think?

*How do they know who I am?*

With shaking hands, he plugs his earphones into the laptop. Checking the earphones are in, he clicks play on the attachment.

It looks similar to the room that Ana was in, another grimy bedroom somewhere. A young girl, younger than Ana, sits on the mattress in underwear. Her wide eyes are glassy, deep shadows underneath as she pouts unconvincingly. She looks exhausted.

Greg doesn't understand.

A man enters the shot, just as in the other video. Only this time, the face is not obscured. The girl crawls towards him on the bed, moving slowly through either a drugged stupor or grim resignation. The man walks closer, slaps her legs and flips her onto her back. Then he looks at the camera and smiles.

Greg stares, scrubbing at his eyes with his hands, but no, there's no mistaking it. It's Greg's face. It's Greg violating a young girl right there on the video.

Anyone seeing this would be absolutely convinced. If it wasn't his own face bearing down on that young girl, if it was someone he knew and trusted, he'd be certain it was them. He can't stand it anymore and closes the video. Sits for a moment with his eyes closed, mind spinning like he's just stumbled from a fairground ride.

He wasn't there, he didn't do it, he wouldn't want to, and yet the video has already taken root in his brain, infecting and twisting his own memory. God, these people are slick. And far more dangerous than he realised.

He reads the rest of the message in disbelief.

It will all become clear how you knew where to find Ana, won't it? After all, you were a frequent visitor to those places. We can easily slip some messages onto your phone. Bookings, if you will, hidden where police can easily find them and you cannot.

Or you could just make it easy on yourself. Do as we ask and save your marriage, your job and your freedom. We know you fancy yourself as a hero, and you will be. You'll get to rescue plenty more women. And the women and girls you provide will receive more money than they could ever earn on the streets or in videos like this. They'll be safer too.

Isn't that what you people want?

# Samantha

*Tuesday, 18 June 2019*

All day in the Reigate store I pace, chew my nails and wait for closing time. I figure I'll wrap up at 5.30 p.m., which is only half an hour early. If Steve questions it, I'll blame my headache again.

He deserves more than this. He asks for very little and gives so much. I think he hoped that what started as a lie might grow into something real, but we have been in this holding pattern for years. I love and care for him deeply. We are each other's rescuers and my affection for him is real. As is the protectiveness I feel for his tender heart. But that's not the same as the way he loves me. So he deserves far more than a headache excuse, but I can barely think of anything except the deadline ticking and what will happen if I miss it.

If I can get at least eight of the items from the different Electronics Superstores before they close at 9 p.m., I can get the rest tomorrow and still make the 6 p.m. deadline. Just as I'm about to close, a woman comes up to the counter with a list in her hand. My shoulders fall and I feel sweat pooling between my breasts and in the groove of my lower back, but I plaster on a smile and manage to get her everything she wants.

Last night, before the melatonin dragged me to sleep, I rejigged my itinerary so I would start near this branch of Steve's store and then coil around the nearest stores leading back to my house.

The first stop is in Redhill, just a few miles away, and I'm in such a hurry when I arrive at Electronics Superstore that I don't have time to consider what I'm doing. In and out within ten minutes, a brand new iPhone in my bag. It's only when I sit down in my car – a Volvo bought by Steve and chosen for safety, not speed – that it hits me. If those gift cards are stolen – which surely they are or why get me to use them? – I've just committed a crime. A serious crime. Way worse than driving without updating my old, foreign licence.

And it was so very easy. Like a warm knife through butter.

*

The next five follow the same pattern. I park near the entrance, stroll in and head to the phones and tablets section. I pick up a couple of different models, all of which are connected to a secure base by a thick coiled cord, then I'll catch the eye of an employee and beckon them over.

'I'd like to get a tablet,' I say. Adding that my daughter/niece/step-son told me which one to get. 'Sorry, let me get my notes, I wrote it down.' They smile, rub their hands together and then ring up the sale. I hand over the gift card, smiling adoringly as I tell them it's a gift from said daughter/niece/step-son . . . they don't care. They hand over the bagged gadget and the receipt, which I tear to pieces once I'm outside.

Of course, it was all going too well. I was feeling something close to confidence. But now the penultimate store doesn't have the tablet I ask for. I scan my list for another tablet to buy but when I ask for it, the eager sales assistant tells me that it's very different to the one I first asked for. 'The storage is about a third, barely enough to download the basics. You really should look at the Samsung—'

I shake my head. 'No Samsungs,' I say. There are none on my list and I'm running out of time.

'Not a fan?' he asks, bemused.

'I don't like the Japanese,' I say. It's the first thing I can think of and I recoil when I see his expression understandably change. He barely says another word as he sells me what I asked for, his mouth twisted as if tasting something sour.

Outside, I exhale fully. At least he only thinks I'm a xeno-phobe and not a criminal. But a sick feeling continues to swell. Steve will be home in an hour and I still have one more store to visit if I'm to stay on track. I drive just slightly over the speed limit. My riskiest yet – the Electronics Superstore nearest my house. As I leave the store with my booty, giddy with relief, Steve rings. 'Dinner's nearly ready,' he says. 'Did you lock up properly?'

'I did and I'm nearly home,' I say as I shut the last gadget in the boot. 'Traffic is murder.'

*

### Wednesday, 19 June 2019

At 5 a.m. I wake up with a brain wave: I could check stock at individual stores on the website and plan the rest of the purchases accordingly. By 4.30 p.m., after a day of strategic shopping, I have all twenty items.

A tiny bead of pride wells somewhere in my chest as I pull into the carpark of an East London E-Z Luggage & Lockers an hour ahead of schedule.

I told Alice, truthfully, that Steve needed me in one of his shops yesterday, so I couldn't come in to the charity and I'd see her next week instead. I told Steve that Alice asked if I could make it up the next day. He shook his head sadly. 'I don't want them to take advantage of your situation,' he said, his eyes searching mine. 'They're so lucky to have you,' he adds.

They don't *know* my situation, I wanted to say. But I just kissed him on the cheek. 'Don't worry about me,' I said. 'I can look after myself.' I saw the flex of his throat and the small gap open between his lips as he tried to tell me that he wanted to look after me, tried to say something that would open things up between us, get us back to the early days. But he said nothing so I left.

Right now, no one knows where I am. Even my handlers, whoever they are, those damn puppet masters won't know where I am until I message them. Until I tell them I've done what they ask, and to please, please leave me alone.

This branch of E-Z Luggage & Lockers is cleaner than the last, busier too. Overhead, planes hit the sky in rapid succession from City Airport. Like shelled peas. One, two, three, bam, bam, bam.

These little jets keep taking off like it's no big deal, as if humans were born to fly. But I watch them roaring up into the clouds and marvel that it's even possible. I wonder what it's like to be inside one of those planes, being spirited away and feeling the ground fall away under my feet.

When Joe was little, he used to ask why our holidays were never abroad like his friends' or his uncle and aunt's. 'I'm scared of flying,' I'd say. 'And isn't Cornwall a lovely place to visit anyway?'

He'd think about it, his little forehead creasing into a line. 'Yes,' he'd say eventually, 'I like Cornwall.'

Only once did he ask why we don't just go by ferry, like when his friend Adam went to France. 'I get seasick,' I'd managed to splutter, the blood draining from my face at the memory of my one-way channel trip. He didn't ask again.

I have never had a passport. Not a British one – of course – nor one from my birth country. To apply for one now, from back home, would be to make myself known to the authorities back there. That alone could spell the end of my life here. And how could I ever trust someone in uniform to understand?

I would need to give my real name, my birth name. And that name is not clean. It sits on files now decades old but serious enough to be dusted off. Serious enough to drag me back. And how would I then get permission to stay here, all these years too late?

My only hope is to finish this task, get these people off my back and get back into hiding.

*

Inside the storage place, a young couple are stuffing shopping bags into a large locker, bickering over the job. Behind the counter, a young woman in a bright yellow headscarf watches them with amusement and then smiles over at me. I smile back but she's already looking back at the couple as they struggle with their toppling bags.

I have the boxed products stuffed in a large sports bag that I haven't used in years. I thought this might be less conspicuous than some shiny Electronics Superstore bags. I needn't have worried, no one is remotely interested in me. I look at the counter girl, but she is still stifling her laughter at the scrapping couple. I follow the faded instructions on the inside of the door.

*Credit card swipe.* I cringe, using Steve's second card as I always have.

*PIN.*

*Key code.*

*Repeat key code.*

*Press the padlock icon.*

I leave as the couple slam their door shut and bicker over which of their maxed-out cards to use.

Back in the car, the planes still pitching relentlessly into the sky over me, I switch SIMs and carefully compose a message.

E-Z Luggage & Lockers - City Airport
Locker 62
Key code: 999999

I send it and two ticks pop up immediately, which, I think, means it's been read. No reply comes.

'Please don't contact me again,' I write. 'I've completed the task like you asked.'

Moments later a message arrives.

> You will receive your next assignment soon. And don't even think about telling anyone, or your little crime spree will become public.

# Greg

## *Thursday, 20 June 2019*

He hasn't slept. Marianne had tried to initiate sex last night, a lazy stroke of his back as he lay in bed trying and failing to wash the images from that video away. When he'd not responded to her touch, she'd started to kiss his arm and tug at his T-shirt. He'd frozen until she stopped. Unable to articulate why the thought horrified him.

All day he thinks of it. Ana's name is still written up on a board, still popping up on emails. Every time he sees it, he flinches. Imagines Eloise seeing the video. Straight-as-a-die Eloise, who will always follow the rules to the letter. She would notify the police. And it would hurt her. Her trust in him would be shattered. She would go home to her wife and cry, he knows, and be permanently changed. The charity would suffer. And then Marianne. He can't even allow himself to picture her seeing it.

After Marianne left for work this morning, with only a sombre goodbye, he logged back on. Took a huge lungful of air and pretended to feel confidence while replying that the video is a provable fake, that he'd done nothing wrong.

He finally reads the reply when he gets home, barely able to remember his day, his journey home. It's a miracle he wasn't knocked off his bike.

> Cut the bullshit, you don't want to test us. If we release this video you'll be fired from work and your wife would never believe you. Especially when she finds the stash of images you keep on your computer. We found them in My Documents > Photos > Greg's goodies.

How could they have . . . he's created no such folder but . . . he clicks through his computer.

*No, no, no, no.*

He did not put this folder here, these are not his images. Hideous, violent images, women hurt and bleeding. Young women like Ana, raging bruises and bony bodies. He didn't download them but they're here nonetheless. Oozing their poison.

He deletes the folder, empties his trash and flips back to the messages.

'Who the hell are you?' Greg writes back. 'How did you put those there? And how do you know who I am?'

Marianne is due back soon. How would they send her the video? Could he get to her phone before she sees it? Her email? Would she believe him, if he told her what happened? She's never shown any jealousy, even when he mentions Jenna. Even when an over-attached client turned up on their doorstep, working out his address from his clumsy mention of the café downstairs. *That* story would be seen in a new light.

She'd always trusted him, always supported him too. When he took a pay cut to move from the animal charity to his current job, she never questioned it.

He could show her the emails, he realises. That would prove he was telling the truth. As the reply comes, he decides he will tell his wife everything tonight.

We will be back in touch when everything is in place.
Start testing for suitable candidates now. And remember,
you'll be 'rescuing' far more women this way.

No, I won't, he thinks. But he doesn't reply. Instead, he starts
to clear up. A fresh start. He'll tidy, clean, make a nice supper
and then tell her everything, stop this before it snowballs even
more. He'll sit Marianne down in their clean flat and he'll start
at the beginning. They'll decide what to do together. A team.

*I was trying to do the right thing,* he'll say. *And I cut some corners.*

He picks up some newspaper supplements, tucks pens in
an old pen pot and pulls the overstuffed black sack from the
kitchen bin. It's been a while since either of them tidied, but
he's in the flat more and he generates more mess so he should
make more of an effort. Yes, this is a good plan.

*I know you're going to be angry when I tell you that I went on
the dark web,* he'll say. *But please just let me explain. It's not just
for bad things, it's for whistle-blowers and activists. It's a safe place
if you know how to use it. Well, I thought it was.*

He neatens his notepads and drifts into the bedroom to
pick up their clothes from the floor, tangled like lovers. He
pulls off the duvet cover, unpeels the pillow cases and yanks
at the sheet, dumping it all in the washing basket. He should
put on a wash too.

*One of my teenage clients died,* he'll tell her. *A girl who had
escaped so much already but got chewed up anyway. But her sister
was still out there. And I needed to find her, to tell her about her
sister and to protect her. So I used a service on the dark web and I
tracked her down. We got her out of a really bad situation.*

When the fresh linen is on the bed, he thinks just briefly
of the mattress in the video. Thinks of how Ana smelt when
he found her. Ammonia, the smell of panic and pain. Hacker
Supermarket were able to find her, when no one else could.

*But the people that helped me find her didn't want to help in
that way again. They wanted me to help them instead. And they
wouldn't take no for an answer.*

Back in the living room, he tucks some of his older paperwork in the overloaded cupboards under the bookshelves. But the more he shoves in, the more sheaves of paper come sliding back out. He needs to sort this out too. He starts by piling up old Tesco Clubcard vouchers, long redundant. They're hardly flush now but once upon a time they lived on those at month's end. Value sausages in Value white bread, slathered in Value brown sauce. Sometimes he'd mix his sauce with vinegar, the way the chippy back home did. Marianne would wrinkle her nose. 'You can take the boy out of Scotland,' he'd say and it always got a smile.

*I promise you I was trying to do the right thing. I offered to pay for information about more girls but they didn't want money. And when I said no to their plan, they threatened me. They threatened us. They even made a fake video, making it look like I'd abused a girl. You know I would never do something like that, don't you?*

Old water bills, old magazines. All on the pile to throw out. Marianne's job offer letter from years ago, a brochure for their honeymoon hotel, an old photo of her university friends, piled to keep. A clutch of postcards next, which he doesn't recognise. Probably from her mum.

*You do trust me, don't you?* he will ask. *I know I should have trusted you. I should have told you what happened but I wanted to fix it. I wanted to keep you out of it. I was scared, Marianne. And now I'm in a hell of a mess.*

He flips the first postcard over. The handwriting is messy, he squints to decipher it and still doesn't understand. Then the next. And the next. There's not much on them, just checking in. Thanking Marianne. A kiss after the name. Some of them seem like replies. Why is her ex-pupil sending her little post-cards and why has she kept them amongst other keepsakes?

\*

The flat is spotless when Marianne gets home and she rushes to hug him but he can barely look at her.

'The flat looks beautiful, what's this in aid of?'

'Nothing.' He shakes her away.

The idea of telling her everything, of trusting her and believing they can overcome anything, that idea has gone cold. Instead, Greg deals the postcards on the table like a poker hand while she watches, fidgeting.

'Why is *he* sending you postcards?'

'He's just glad that I helped him,' she says, but her skin flushes pink. 'And I think he's finding the transition a bit hard.'

'Do any of your other pupils send you postcards from university?'

'Not postcards, no, but cards sometimes. I showed you that letter from Afua who got into Manchester; she was—'

'It's not the same.'

She opens her mouth to protest but closes it again.

'Have you been sending postcards back?' he asks, bracing for the reply. She pauses, her cheeks flushing, but shakes her head.

'I've never mistrusted you, Marianne,' he says, his voice breaking. More than ever they need trust, but how can he risk telling her the truth? How can he trust her and ask her to trust him? Everything is fucked right down the middle.

'You have no reason to mistrust me,' she protests, her eyes growing wet as she holds his gaze, unblinking. No yelling, no anger at him for reading them. Instead, she reaches for him but he pulls away and goes into the kitchen.

They eat in silence. As he clears away, she flips open her marking and avoids his eye. He does not try to meet her gaze. The images of 'himself' in that video play frantically in his mind, so vivid he imagines that his wife would see them if she were to look at him.

How could he expect her to believe him over her own eyes? If she were to be shown that video, she would be bags packed and out the door in seconds. These postcards, over the line as they may be, are nothing in comparison.

If he were to show her the emails, show her what he's mixed up in . . . it would make everything worse. After all, the emails never admit to the video being fake.

He's trapped.

*

## Friday, 21 June 2019

'Eighteen of them were in the brothel fire.'

'Eighteen?'

Eloise nods and Greg puts his head in his hands. There's just always more people out there, at risk, in danger.

'Anyone we know among them?'

'We don't know yet.'

The room they're in was painted by volunteers three years ago and the sunshine yellow is chipped. The sofa has holes picked in it by urgent, worried fingers. All around, posters cheerfully remind anyone here that they have rights, that there are safe places. He makes a fist under the table, feels his nailbeds straining, the ragged edges cutting into his skin.

Another poster highlights the numbers. He stares at them, thinking how pointless all of this is. Just window dressing. Anyone sitting in the room knows the reality. Thirteen thousand estimated to be here through trafficking? Whatever the precise figure is, they can strike eighteen off it.

What would those eighteen women, or Ana or Marija or any of the thirteen thousand, say to the proposal? What about the girl in the video, the girl 'he' was supposed to have violated? Would they actually *welcome* the lump sum being offered, regardless of what they'd be giving up in exchange for it? Would they willingly step up so he could get the locations of more people?

'Greg?'

'Sorry, what did you say?'

'Hun,' Eloise says, softly, 'I know. *I do*. I feel it too, so deeply I could scream. But we have to do things right. We have to.'

'I know.'

'So none of this secret stuff, OK? We do things by the book. We *have* to.'

'I know.'

'Promise?' He nods his head and looks away. He already knows what he's going to do. There's no way out for him, but at least he might save some more women along the way.

# Samantha

## Monday, 1 July 2019

I tried to protest. To appeal to some anonymous bully's human nature. But the more I protested, the tighter their chain twisted around my neck. They had an answer for everything, all in the form of questions. All building the picture of me, swinging on their hook.

*Did you use Steven Redfern's card to secure a locker full of stolen goods?*
*Did you drive his car to those superstores?*
*Do you even have a legal driving licence?*
*Did you disguise yourself for the CCTV?*
*Does Joseph know the truth about his mother?*

I'm on my second assignment now.

*

This time, there is no locker. No mad race against the clock. Instead, I received a photograph of a thirty-something woman called Rosie Parsons. I was given her address and basic background information. I was to watch her three days in a row from morning to evening and write down her movements.

Where she went, at what time, where she ate lunch and so on. If she met anyone, I was to take a discreet photograph. I could even choose the days that I 'worked' and opted for

Tuesday, Wednesday and Thursday, using my charity work as cover.

On Monday, I told Alice I wasn't available for the rest of the week, not bothering to elaborate. If years of unpaid work wasn't enough to buy some time off then Steve was right, they were treating me unfairly. As it turned out, Alice was very kind about it and said I deserved a break.

So for the last three days I have driven to London and parked in a different spot each time, within watching distance of the woman's flat.

I've been there to see her leave at 8.23 a.m., 8.22 a.m. and 8.19 a.m. respectively. Each day she shuffles from the communal door wearing a hoodie and jeans and walks ten minutes until she reaches the grounds of a sprawling hospital.

The first day, I assumed she was visiting someone, but when I followed her through reception, into a lift and then onto a ward, she swiped a card and entered an area restricted to staff. I sat on the chairs outside as if waiting for an appointment and ten minutes later caught sight of her through the porthole of a door, wearing a uniform and striding busily towards a group of beds.

For lunch she normally has a sandwich and can of Diet Coke in the canteen, taking less than fifteen minutes each day. By the time she sits down it's halfway through the afternoon and I'm starving as I trail a few places behind her in the line and pay with cash.

Today, though, she leaves her ward early and walks in a different direction and outside into the grounds. She lights a rolled-up cigarette and slips between two buildings. She looks around furtively and I continue past without breaking my pace.

I look back. There is something skittish about her, almost childlike. She reminds me of Cristina.

Cristina and I were roommates, not far from where Rosie Parsons lives now. Rosie has her own studio flat but Cristina and I slept top and tail, the whole house carved up into anchovy tins for tens of other people.

Of course, that was nearly twenty years ago. We didn't choose each other; it was dumb luck that I'd be shoved into that room with her after I first unfurled myself from the agonising trip in the back of a van.

It was yet more luck that Cristina, this tiny girl eyeing me from under her hair, also spoke English. We were from different countries originally, she from Romania, and it was our lingua franca. She talked like a veteran, an old hand who could no longer be shocked or delighted.

She was younger than Joe is now.

I do a loop of the smaller building and when I come back to the alley from the other angle, I notice a man is in there with Rosie Parsons. He sits on the lid of a huge bin, knees tucked up under his chin and elbows at an angle. He looks like a spider carcass, motionless as he blows smoke. She paces, he laughs and when she eventually stops and stands still in front of him, he says, 'Here y'are then.'

I take a photo as he hands her a paper bag. The kind you might get in a pharmacy, bunched at the top by his long fingers. She snatches it, opening it fast and looking inside. I take one more photo over my shoulder as I walk away but she's not looking anyway, her eyes fixed with relief on whatever is in the bag. When I check the photos later, I'm struck that my first thought isn't 'she looks so small and desperate'. No, my first thought is 'this is great evidence, I've done a good job'. I am steeped in shame as I upload my notes and photographs.

As instructed, I stay in the area and wait for a response. It's a beautiful July day, even London smells green and perfumed. I sit in a park near the hospital, rolling up my jeans and tanning my calves in the sun like everybody else. It's past lunchtime and I'm empty and shaky but too riddled with adrenaline and self-disgust to eat.

I sip from my water bottle, draining the last drop, and then check my messages.

*One new message.*

Your report confirmed what we already knew. Rosie
Parsons is addicted to pharmaceutical drugs. If her
employers were to find out, she would lose her job and
risk arrest. You need to explain this to her, show her the
photographs you took and tell her that she's to report for
training at a place and time of our choosing. We will
notify her in due course. And Samantha, make it clear this
is *non-negotiable*.

\*

I wait in the canteen, unable to eat the sandwich I bought.
Rosie arrives at around three and when I ask for a word, she
comes with me to the corner without a fuss. She's wary but
compliant, almost as if she was expecting something like this.

She visibly shudders when I show her the photographs but
doesn't defend herself, just listens with grim acceptance settling
on her face.

'Training for what?' she asks, when I reach that part of the
spiel. But I don't know.

'Who sent you?' Rosie suddenly thinks to ask.

'We'll be in touch,' I say. 'And if you tell *anyone*, your
employers will be sent these photographs and you know as
well as I do that you'd fail a drug test.'

I walk out before my legs give way from under me.

I send a debrief on the way home and am rewarded with
uncharacteristic praise.

*This is very good work.*

'Thank you,' I reply. 'Now surely I have done enough for
you?'

I do not receive another message for hours. I switch between
SIMs every half an hour, until finally giving up and taking a
scalding bath. When I get out, my legs are puce from the heat.
My whole body throbs like a bruise.

I wrap myself in the dressing gown that Joe bought me
last Christmas and switch the SIM cards again. I can do this

165

in my sleep now. Maybe I do, my dreams a continuation of the constant alertness I've had to cultivate. Sometimes waiting weeks for an order but ready to go nonetheless.

There is a message.

E-Z Luggage & Lockers – London Waterloo
Locker number 63
Key code to open locker: 160399
Further instructions will follow.

My heart drops. They're sending me right back to the beginning.

*

Inside the locker is a bag containing car plates for a registration number I've never seen before. I close the locker again and approach the help desk, an idea forming. The man working in this branch looks slightly more switched on than most and he's watching me intently. 'Excuse me,' I say, trying to sound as respectable as possible. 'Did you happen to see who left these items in my locker?'

He frowns. His thick dark hair shifts with his scalp as his brow furrows. He's probably only twenty-five but he looks done in. 'Wasn't it you?' he says. I see him fumbling for something behind the counter. Fuck, is it some kind of panic button?

'No, yes, I mean that . . .' I just want to stop him pressing whatever he's pressing. But before I can carry on, he pulls out a packet of tobacco and starts to roll a cigarette.

'If this isn't your locker,' he says, pausing to lick the paper, his tongue darting out like a lizard, 'then you shouldn't be opening it.'

I laugh in what I hope is a casual fashion and smile. 'No, it's my locker but I wasn't sure if my husband or son had filled it.' I lean on the counter conspiratorially while the man taps his rolled cigarette on the top. 'I asked my son to do it but I think he might have fobbed it off on his dad.'

'I didn't notice, sorry.' The worker shrugs. He just wants me to hurry up so he can go and smoke. I grab the contents and leave, whispering a silent apology to Joe for dragging his name through the mud.

I confirm that I've collected the goods and then I'm given an address and a list of items, many of which mean nothing to me. Most worrisome, I'm to collect them from an actual person rather than a locker.

*

Michael Sutherland lives in Tunbridge Wells in a small terraced house in Axminster Road. I park a few doors up, squeezing my car into a space barely big enough to open the boot. My new registration plates are safely in position.

When he opens the door, I say I am here to collect the items. He holds my gaze for a moment, then looks down and gestures for me to follow him through the hall into a kitchen diner, and then out into a small neat garden. Baby toys dot the lawn and a cat tumbles lazily around in a pool of sunlight.

Michael opens his shed. He's not said a word to me yet.

The shed is stuffed with boxes.

'I have a list,' I say eventually. 'I need to check it.'

'There's no time, my wife is due back any minute.'

'I have to,' I say.

'Please. I'm hardly going to double-cross you, am I? With what you're holding over me.'

I want to say that I'm not holding anything over him, that I'm the one dangling from a hook, but it won't do any good. Michael needs to hand this over, I need to take it. We're swinging from the same hook.

'If there's anything missing . . .' I say.

'There isn't. Just please, hurry up.'

It takes several trips to the car, and soon my boot and back seat are filled. I realise as I start the engine that I don't know

167

where to take it all. I sure as hell can't turn up at home with it. What would I tell Steve?

I drive off, Michael watching nervously from the window, but pull in a few roads away to check my phone. I'm about to message and ask what's next when I see I have already received instructions.

'Take the supplies to the Bluebell Hotel near Godstone. Drive into the carpark and then ask at the reception for the manager, David Ross. He knows what to do.'

*

It takes a long time to find this place, hidden down winding roads that seem better designed to keep people out than invite them in. My car is battered by brambles as I pass a sign for the Bluebell. I hope there's no damage, I'll have a tough time explaining it to Steve.

Creeping along in second gear, I finally see the building emerge over the brow of a hill.

It has that rustic look that costs a bomb. Dressed down with faux informality, offering a make-believe rural life secreted away from normal people. The Hunter boots of hotels.

It's the kind of place Paula loves. She's been trying to get the brothers to agree to a spa trip one weekend soon. Jonathan seems relatively willing but the idea horrifies Steve. 'I don't want to be cooked like a langoustine,' was his first reaction. We'd all laughed.

'There's more to it than a steam room,' Paula had assured him, but he was hurt at being a figure of fun and doubled down, refusing to consider it.

Now I'm glad nothing has been arranged. The more concrete plans I have, the more I risk letting people down as I'm called away for no good reason.

I swing into the carpark carefully. There are a few cars here already: an Audi, a BMW and an old Ford. I can guess which one belongs to a staff member.

I lock the car and check myself in the reflection of the window. I look presentable enough but out of place. A lone woman arriving at a romantic hotel. I reapply my lipstick and stand tall, pulling my hair out of its ponytail and swishing it over my shoulders.

There are no other guests around outside and when I push open the heavy door, I'm greeted by an empty reception. Behind the desk, through a slightly open office door, I hear raised voices and shift uncomfortably from foot to foot. I don't have time for this, but to interrupt seems rude. Besides, I don't know anything about this David Ross. Maybe he's volatile.

'I can't keep doing this, David,' a woman's voice is saying.

'You'll get it at the end of the week, I promise.'

'We've all got bills,' she says, exasperated. Through the crack in the door I can see a sliver of a computer, some kind of card game on the screen. Shadows flicker as whoever is in there moves around, pacing and pleading.

The man starts again. 'We've got a skeleton staff now, and—'

'Everyone else has left! I need my wages.'

I reopen the front door and shut it loudly. The woman comes out of the office with a tired smile. She's elegant, top to toe in black, and tiny. Her hair is whipped up into a chignon, the kind I could never master and have often paid someone else to do.

'Can I help you, madam?'

'I'm here to see David Ross,' I say. At this, a man in his forties bounds out of the office and the woman sits down at the computer and closes the card game.

'David Ross,' he says, thrusting a hand at me. He's good-looking in a dishevelled way but there's something off about him. As I shake his hand, one of his fingers caresses my palm and I pull back in shock. He looks me up and down, smirking. 'You have the delivery?' he asks.

# Greg

## Monday, 22 July 2019

'And lastly,' Greg asks the pale and nervous girl curling in on herself in the chair opposite him, 'do you know your blood type?'

She nods, unquestioning. 'I think it's A negative,' she says, so quiet he can barely catch it. He writes it in his notebook next to her name and date of birth. The form he has filled in, the one all new sign-ups at the charity have to answer, will be filed with the rest. The extra details that he's jotted in his notepad will not.

*

That night, he uploads the details of potential girls that he has collected so far.

*Why are there still so few?*

The quiet of his flat is not helping. The air coming through the window is thick with heat, the sweet, sickly smell of traffic and cigarette smoke, weed and warm beer. Summer in the city. While he tries to think of a new way to reply to this now familiar question, he puts on a record. Leonard Cohen suits his mood.

The Hacker Supermarket people never believe him but the only answer he has is the truth. 'I can only ask the ones that speak English for their blood type, otherwise they'll have an interpreter in the room as well.'

*None of these are B positive. We need B positive for the first scheduled client.*

He closes his eyes and grits his teeth before replying. 'But I can't help that. I'm only telling you what they tell me.'

The street door downstairs slams, rattling the front of the building. By the time Marianne gets inside the flat, Greg is measuring out flour to make pastry. His wedding ring on the windowsill, glinting in the evening sunlight. 'Not long now,' he calls out as she sighs, dumping her heavy bag on the floor. Just a few weeks left of the term, his wife is always bloodied and limping at this point. Teachers live in reverse hibernation: Marianne breaks herself into tiny pieces for the kids all year, then spends summer sleeping and putting herself back together.

She kisses his shoulder and rests her head on his back as he starts to cube butter. 'I love you,' he says, trying to twist his neck to see her, but she's clamped on tightly.

'Always,' she murmurs, into the damp dip between his shoulders. 'But isn't it a bit hot for pie night?'

'It's never too hot for pie night.' He thinks again of the postcards. 'I just really want to do something nice and something . . .' *What? Something that doesn't involve you flirting with teenagers and me . . .* he can't finish that thought. 'Something *normal*,' he says and she murmurs agreement, holding on even tighter.

\*

### Thursday, 29 August 2019

'And lastly, Kenza, do you know your blood type?'

'B positive,' she says. He gets up slowly and walks to the door, closing it quietly. She sits rigid, staring at him.

He swallows, cracks his knuckles, then speaks quietly.

'Kenza, have you ever been offered money in exchange for . . .' He falters. Her eyes watch him, expectantly, but she says nothing. 'For parts of your body?'

She frowns and looks down at her chest and stomach as she sits uneasily in the yellow room. 'For having sex?' she says, finally. A matter-of-fact question spoken with a trembling voice. He shakes his head and she breathes out, relieved.

'No, not that. But, say, parts of your body that you could
. . . that you could donate. Organs, like your kidneys, where
you could live healthily with just one.'

'No one has offered me money for that.' She sits up.

'If they did,' Greg says, so quietly she leans forward to hear,
'would you have been interested?'

'Is this a test?'

He shakes his head.

'Would I be healthy afterwards?'

He nods.

'How much money?'

He writes it down on the pad in front of him. When he looks
up she is watching him expectantly, a light in her eyes that wasn't
there before. 'If that was a real offer,' she says, 'I would take it.'

'You would?'

'Most definitely.'

He swallows again, feels his throat constrict as if trying
to stop the words getting out. Stopping him taking this next
step. But he has to.

'The offer is real, Kenza.'

# Samantha

*Friday, 2 August 2019*

I thought about cancelling my brunch with Paula but the
more out of character I act, the closer people will look at me.

She's already seated when I get to the coffee shop, sitting
straight as true north, blowing on her coffee. I notice that while
her face is as smooth as it ever was, her hands look wrinkled
and claw-like. I sometimes forget our age gap but it's twisting
its fingers in front of me right now.

'Hello, darling,' Paula says quietly as she stands to kiss me hello.

She smells of citrus and peonies and wears a cashmere cardigan even in this heat. Whatever the weather, she is always herself. I'm envious of such self-possession.

I tug up my metaphorical mask and plaster on a smile as we hug and sit.

The coffee shop is filled with women like us. This is our domain, both the place and the time. Late morning on a Friday, when the world works, we sit. We feel our way with small talk about the traffic, building up to proper conversation like fighters, pacing the ring.

The hum of background chat is punctuated by the iron clangs of the coffee machine, the calls of baristas, working like machines for minimum wage. I wonder where they sleep, whether they have proper contracts.

'Flat white!'

'Matcha latte!'

Paula cuts me off as I'm about to gossip pointlessly about the 'orangery' that our neighbours are building.

'Samantha, I have to ask,' Paula says. My stomach drops as she pauses and looks me up and down. 'Are you pregnant?'

I laugh before I can stop myself. Of all the things she could have asked.

'Shall I take that as a no?' Her brown eyes bore into mine. She's not laughing.

'It's a definite no,' I say, smiling, giddy in my relief that she's so far off the mark.

'It's not impossible at your age,' she says, looking chastened.

'Oh no, I'm sorry, I'm not laughing at you for asking. I'm just taken aback.'

'You looked so peaky the other night and with empty nest syndrome on the horizon . . .'

'Joe will be at home for years to come,' I say, a little too quickly. 'Hopefully.'

She looks at me again, head tilting like she's trying to read something just under my skin. 'You never wanted another?'

I shake my head. I always said I didn't want *any* children but I don't tell her that. I tell her another truth instead. 'I just love him so much,' I say. 'I feel really lucky to have him and that's enough for me.'

She nods and takes a sip of her coffee, swallowing hard. For a moment we say nothing and a swell of guilt grows in my gut. My luck is inversely proportional to hers. What I gained, she lost. I'm about to apologise when she starts to speak.

'When I had Heidi, I didn't want any more children because I loved her so much too.' For a moment I think that's it, but she leans forward and settles her cup on the saucer. 'But if I had had more children, they might have been a match for her.' She exhales and dusts invisible crumbs from her lap. 'And while she was being treated, I started to imagine them.' She smiles as I struggle to understand. 'The other children, Samantha. I started to imagine the children I was so stupid, so *wicked*, to disregard. I even suggested to Andy, my first husband – I'm sure you know about him – I suggested that we have another baby. He was . . . well, it made things worse. Heidi was in a desperate state, she couldn't have waited that long anyway.' She sighs and I look away. 'Of course, I wasn't being logical by then.'

'I can't imagine,' I managed to splutter. I *have* imagined, and it turns my heart to ashes.

Paula looks into the distance. Wherever she is, she's not here in the coffee shop with me. Perhaps she's back in the children's ward with Heidi, or arguing with her first husband. Perhaps she's thinking of my Joe, the extra years he has had that Paula's daughter never got to see.

'I never forgot those children, Samantha. I thought of them, I *think* of them, alongside Heidi as if I lost them all. And I miss them too, somehow. I spent so many years trying to will them into existence. Jonathan will tell you, it was all I thought about for a long time.'

I don't know what to say. She's never spoken this openly before and I don't want to frighten her, even though it's almost unbearable to hear.

'I really hoped that Jonathan and I would have a different kind of luck to me and Andy,' she says, so quietly I have to lean towards her. 'But we didn't.'

She smiles, her eyes glassy.

'I know I'm incredibly lucky,' I say. 'And I'm so sorry you didn't get to have any more children.'

I want to say it's never too late but I know it is.

'You really don't think you would have another?' she says softly. I shake my head. I'm too old, too exhausted, too haunted. 'Well, if you ever even think of it, just go for it. That's my advice. You never know when all your chances will suddenly dry up and your luck will run out before you even knew you were lucky.'

She holds my gaze until I look down. 'And I'd love to be an aunty again,' she laughs.

*

## Monday, 2 September 2019

About three weeks ago I arrived at yet another E-Z Luggage & Lockers. A different teenager ignored me as I opened the long, thin locker to retrieve the parcel. It was wrapped tightly with brown paper and tied with string. It was heavier than it looked, tricky to carry, and when I got outside with it, it slipped from my hands. I just about managed to stop it hitting the floor, but the paper had torn and inside I could see that it was a carrying case. I rushed to the toilets tucked near the concourse at Waterloo but a poster ground me to the spot.

**LOOK** below the surface - does he or she want to be here?
**ASK** the right questions - offer opportunities to speak alone
**CALL** if you suspect someone could be a victim of trafficking

I thought, of course, of my old friend Cristina. I didn't know her exact route into the UK, but I know she didn't leave her home out of choice. Unlike me, who ran, she was dragged. She was the only person I ever told about what happened before I left. She knew about my family, about the way my dad had prepared me to defend my mother. She knew what happened when that moment came, how I'd let everyone down. She knew I could never return.

The package in Waterloo grew heavy in my arms but I moved slowly. In the furthest toilet cubicle, I carefully laid the paper on the floor, placed the case on top and opened it.

I should not have opened it.

I doubt it means anything legally but morally, personally, I found it so much easier to square this 'job' when I was bathed in ignorance.

But that day, kneeling on the floor in a Waterloo Ladies cubicle, I was confronted by the reality of what I was doing.

That day, I could not claim any ignorance, as a polished shotgun shone up at me. A sight I hadn't seen since my much younger days, one I hoped to never see again. With slippery hands, I fumbled the case closed and wrapped it carefully again. Then I propped it next to the sink as I washed my hands, over and over again.

The next instructions arrived on my phone as I dried each finger carefully.

Two hours later I had collected a case of bullets from a short, squat locker at King's Cross and delivered everything to a third locker on the fraying fringes of Stansted.

But something had changed. Some tiny little tear, not much more than a paper cut, had divided how I used to be with how I was now. I could no longer choose ignorance and denial, so I chose knowledge and self-protection. With every assignment since then, I have unpeeled each coating, checked every detail, done my own research. When I look back at how I operated just a few months ago I am astonished I'm still here, walking around. To act as if I'm merely a benign courier, when I could have been carrying things that would set off alarms. Or blow me to scraps. Or harm people, *children*, standing nearby.

I check every detail these days and I leave nothing to chance. This isn't a new way to live for me, more a life that was lying dormant. I can't remember how old I was when my dad first sat me down and told me what I might need to do. 'Your mother doesn't have it in her, but you do.' I was maybe eight, maybe ten. He seemed to read the future more acutely, and earlier, than the other fathers. 'They'll come for me first,' he'd said, matter of factly. 'So it will fall to you to protect your mother.' He was right.

*

Steve noticed my agitation the day after that trip to Waterloo, asking over breakfast: 'You seem on high alert all the time, are you OK?'

I smiled as warmly as I could manage and touched his arm when I said, 'I'm fine, don't worry.'

'Is there something I should know?' he asked, moving away just slightly so the contact was broken.

'What do you mean?'

'You know what I mean,' he said, looking down. Emotionally charged conversations are torture for him.

Could he have found out? Could he have read my emails? Could he have seen something in my behaviour and picked at that scab? I stared back while my brain turned cartwheels.

'Have you met someone else, Samantha?'

I laughed with relief. 'Oh my god, no! No, I promise.' He hadn't returned the laughter, looking into my eyes instead and holding my gaze until his own turned watery.

'Please don't hurt us,' he said quietly.

'I never, ever want to hurt you,' I said. My laughter had gone and my throat grew thick as he stood and left the kitchen.

Since Waterloo, there have been no more guns, trips to hotels or shopping lists. Instead, for the last five or so weeks my work has involved collecting stacks of prescriptions in neat unmarked envelopes. Along with each package, I receive a separate envelope furnishing me with a fake ID. This ID is far better than the papers I 'bought' years ago. Papers, long lost, that I was nevertheless still paying for when I met Steve.

These are so convincing, I consider getting them to produce something for me as Samantha Redfern, but the idea of asking them for anything sickens me.

While they provide various fake IDs, the backstories and the itineraries are mine to decide as I navigate non-chain pharmacies to collect sheafs of Xanax pills, oxytocin sprays and tubes of Ritalin. And other drugs I've never heard of before – steroids and immunosuppressants.

My latest identity is Jane Douglas. I'm forty-two and take Ritalin for adult ADD, only diagnosed in my thirties. Or I take oxytocin spray for extreme anxiety brought about by PTSD from my time in the armed forces. Or I take Xanax for chronic insomnia. Or I take immunosuppressants following an organ transplant. I'm lucky to be alive.

I'm no stranger to building a backstory and acting a role, but I've never enjoyed it. When I first arrived in London, I painted a picture that was as far as could be from the truth. But that only made the lie more obvious. The trick, I learnt from Cristina, was to stay as close to the truth as possible. Which was how I came to tell her my whole truth. When I got to the worst of it, she gripped my hand. 'Don't ever tell anyone that last part.'

So when I first met Steve, I told him the broad strokes of where I lived, where I came from and why. It was close to the truth but the lies were buried in the details.

It's Jonathan's birthday today and he's turning fifty-four. The four of us are meeting for dinner tonight as we always do on the brothers' birthdays. Jonathan often mentions golf buddies and friends from 'the club', meaning the tennis club he and Paula are members of, and yet he and Steve still gravitate to each other. In all these years, I've never met any of Jonathan's friends. I wonder if he really has time to see them; he rarely talks of anything except business. He's CEO of a company that does something technical for finance companies but is so boring I've stopped asking.

Steve doesn't have friends, I know that much. Friendships, relationships of all kinds actually, are a labyrinthine challenge for him. From early on he found them punishing and dangerous, so now he controls the maze himself. Letting only a few of us into his heart and guarding us with his life.

As a result of their close quarters, the brothers – 'the boys' as Paula calls them, though she herself is in her late fifties – exist in a frozen state of childhood. Best friends but bitter rivals. Events like birthdays seem to take the rivalry up a notch. Both of them vibrating at a higher frequency. Gifts ever more lavish, dinners finer and finer.

Whatever wine we all decide on, Steve will panic and call the waiter back to ask for a more expensive one instead. He will insist we all have dessert regardless of how full we are, how ready for bed. Desperate for everyone to be happy, he will strong-arm us in lieu of knowing how to make it happen naturally. And he'll realise he's doing it but not be able to stop.

It is as well worn as the ruby red dress I ask Joe to zip me into, as I stand in front of the landing mirror and wince at how spindly I've become.

'Mum,' he says into my ear as he so carefully tugs at the zipper. 'Are you OK?'

'I'm fine,' I say softly, watching us both in the mirror and catching his eye.

'You're looking thin,' he says. His thick knuckles brushing the knobbly vertebrae of my back as he seals me in.

'Thank you,' I say, but it's not a compliment. The dress, which I hadn't been able to get into for years, is ill-fitting and loose.

'Maybe it's "the change" coming early,' I say. But he's a medical student and he can diagnose my bullshit. In place of anything better to say, I hug him tightly. 'Remember,' I tell him, just as I have since he was a tiny boy, skinny in his pyjamas, begging us not to go out, 'I'll always come back.' I touch my forehead to his and try not to cry.

*

We arrive in Chobham late. There are no spaces near the restaurant so we have to park down the little high street, and walk back to the restaurant. I am taller than Steve in these heels, something that is no problem when sitting in a car or restaurant but makes me stand out when clattering up the road. I feel as if everyone is turning to stare. Steve is oblivious to my discomfort, stressing about being late, worrying about the present.

'It's a beautiful gift,' I say gently. 'Wouldn't you love to receive it?'

He stares dead ahead as if reading something, then I see his shoulders loosen and he slows his stride just a little. 'I would, you're right. Thank you.'

Like all long-term relationships, we have gradually learnt each other's language. What we need to hear and when, what we are really asking each other. We may not have the electricity of some marriages, but we have a shared shorthand that is our own armour.

Jonathan and Paula are already seated when we walk in. From the angle of the foyer, they can't see us yet and I watch as she snatches her hand from his, while he rolls his eyes just slightly and picks up his phone. She follows suit.

They rise, all smiles, when we approach and there is the usual flurry of four-way kisses and back slaps. Paula looks drawn, and when we hug our clavicles clang into each other. I suspect her own thin frame is due to spinning classes rather than the morbid fear fired up by going on a one-woman crime spree.

In the bathroom, we refresh our make-up together. She's pink-cheeked from wine whereas I've been sipping water, happy to be a designated driver for Steve. It's funny, he's so cautious, so careful, but he lets me drive him around illegally and uninsured. Wilfully choosing to believe in the story we tell others.

I watch in the mirror as Paula paints her smudged features back in place. She sharpens the line of her lips and straightens her hair. Her actions seem hypnotic, as if she's in a trance.

'You look lovely,' I say.

'Tell that to Jonathan,' she mumbles. I don't know how to respond and I watch in the mirror, drying my hands, as she flicks her eyes to me. 'You're lucky Steve is so devoted to you,' she adds.

'I'm very lucky,' I say. On paper, she is far luckier than me and yet she's one of the saddest people I know.

'I don't know how you've managed it,' she says and I freeze. There's something sharp in her tone, a drunken swing hidden in there, and I don't want to get caught in the crossfire of whatever is actually pissing her off. Jonathan, I'm pretty sure.

'Are you OK, Paula?'

She smiles at me in the mirror. 'Just ignore me,' she says. 'Too much to drink, I think.'

Back at the table, conversations roll around business and Brexit, old jokes that are no longer funny and well-worn gripes about taxes and the government. I notice both Paula and Jonathan are trying a little too hard to seem happy. Both of them surreptitiously slip their phones into their laps a few times, tapping furiously. I suspect whatever argument they were having before we arrived is still rumbling on, relegated to below the table.

I slip away to use the toilet again, glad when Paula doesn't follow me.

I haven't dared look at my phone at the table, so now I check the other SIM while buying myself some peace. I have received a message through Whispa.

*Go back to Michael Sutherland's house to collect another consignment.*

'When?' I write back.

*Now.*

'I can't, I'm out for dinner with family. I can't just leave.'

*Collect it before midnight or your family won't want to have dinner with you ever again.*

I stare at myself in the Ladies' mirror, wipe away the make-up that's slid under my eyes like bruises. I'm sweating all over my face and neck, and no amount of dabbing with paper towels stops it.

*You have no choice,* I tell myself. *So just get on with it.* It's a mantra that has carried me through my whole life but it's getting very old now, and I'm so tired. Nevertheless I sigh, refresh my make-up as best I can and rush from the restrooms and straight into Jonathan. He's leaning on the opposite wall, hidden from our table and smiling. I can tell from his glassy expression that he's had way too much to drink. I worry which one of that couple plans to drive home.

'Birthday kiss?' he says, winking.

I laugh it off and try to move past but he catches my arm. His smile has faded and he's staring at me. 'Please?' he says. 'Just one.'

'Just one,' I say, cringing as I think of what Paula said about devotion. 'If you do something for me.'

'What?' he says, leaning in and brushing my lips with his. I kiss him back, eyes wide open and looking out for our respective partners. I don't know if I feel worse for Paula or Steve. This is a moment I've thought about so often and now my secret feelings have been picked raw and transformed into a utilitarian step in a last-minute plan.

'I'm going home,' I say, as we pull away. 'Please keep Steve occupied until at least midnight.'

'Why?' he frowns, but moves his head to kiss me again.

'Just please,' I say, unable to hide my desperation. He nods, looking worried, so I let him kiss me again.

'Happy birthday,' I say, as I walk back towards the table to make my apologies.

*

'She's out with her NCT group,' Michael Sutherland says quietly as he opens the door. 'It's the only time I could do it.'

I'm still wearing my red dress and it catches on the door frame as I go inside and grab the first boxes, already stacked to go in the living room.

I realise as we load that I've forgotten to switch the registration plates over. Shit. Hopefully no one is keeping track.

'Where did you get this stuff from?' I ask, and he shushes me.

'My daughter's asleep,' he hisses. 'And you know where I got it from.'

'I'm not one of them,' I say, my voice catching in my throat. 'They make me do this too.'

He pauses, pulling the door closed as he steps outside with me, carrying the last of the boxes. 'I work here,' he points to the name on the box: Deaman Biomedical Supplies. 'In fulfilment.' He waits for a reaction. 'The warehouse,' he adds as it clicks into place.

'What do they have over you?'

'What do they have over *you*?' he replies. Neither of us says anything else.

He goes back inside to his sleeping daughter as I start the engine and tap on my phone.

*I have the boxes. I can deliver them tomorrow.*

The reply comes straight away: *Deliver them to the Bluebell tonight.*

It's ten thirty already but I've learnt there's no room for negotiation. I head for the A21 as fast as I dare.

*

David Ross is waiting in the carpark when I arrive. He's more baggy and dishevelled than before. His hair tufts out as if he's been woken in a hurry. Perhaps he was.

'Do you live at the hotel?' I ask.

He pulls a hand through his hair and nods, adding: 'Would you like to see my room?'

'No.'

'I love your dress.'

'I'm in a hurry. The boxes are in my car.'

There's no need to point out which car it is, there're only mine and David's here. Business is clearly still slow.

We walk to the side of the hotel and carry the boxes up a flight of metal stairs and in through a fire door. My heels are rubbing my feet and I take them off, leaving them on the staircase. I follow David barefoot down the hallway and load the boxes into the same room as last time.

It takes twenty minutes to get everything out and when it's done, I take a photograph to upload as proof. I'm about to dash back to my car, grabbing my shoes on the way, when David pushes the door closed with his fingertips.

'Do you need to rush off?' he says, standing between me and the door. Another man standing in my way. How tiresome. All I can focus on is the strip of hairy belly that peeps through his too-short rugby shirt every time he breathes.

'Open the door,' I say. He stands for a moment, studying the situation. I don't have time for this stupid little man and I grab and twist his arm the way I was shown a long time back by my father.

He jerks out of the way, rubbing his arm as I yank the door open.

'Just a misunderstanding!' he shouts as I slam the door and run down the main staircase and out into the night air.

*

On the M25, driving barefoot, I push my car to its limits as the clock ticks down. The tarmac rushes under my car like a great black river, too many miles of it in front of me still. I consider calling Jonathan, asking him to delay Steve even longer, but it's too risky. Steve or Paula could easily see who is calling as Jonathan's phone lights up. And it's not fair to use his affections like this, especially on his birthday. I'm no better than 'them' if I do.

Instead I press the pedal to the floor and don't notice the speed camera until it flashes me.

Shit. Shit. Shit.

I scream into the drive just before midnight. The house looms dark. Joe must be in bed and I hope to god that Steve isn't home yet. I wince my way over the tiny stones and let myself in the back door, clawing at my zip as I creep up the stairs. A crumpled Cinderella.

When I'm on the landing, I hear car tyres on gravel outside and rush into my room, diving under the covers just as the taxi drives away again.

My heart thunders as I lie in the dark, still wearing my dress. Downstairs, Steve slams the front door and thumps up the stairs unsteadily. On the landing, I hear him hover outside my room.

When I first moved in, we shared the same bedroom. I brought my little bag of belongings and asked for a drawer to keep things in. Steve opened up the big wardrobe, one half completely cleared already. I had almost nothing to put in it. We went shopping that day, me marvelling at the ease with which he paid for things. And that night, wearing the nightdress we'd both blushed at buying, we lay down together.

I was younger than him, less experienced, but I was eager to please and desperate to make things work. Gradually it became harder for me to enthuse and harder for Steve to ignore that.

Joe was a tricky sleeper and more often than not it made sense for me to sleep in his room, getting up to comfort him or give him milk, until he was far older than many toddlers to need such care. I miss those moments, him in the crook of my arm finally daring to close his eyes. The way his little lips parted as he eventually nodded off, the sweet smell of a warm and well-loved child under clean and soft covers. I was so proud to give him that.

By the time Joe reached primary school, it was just easier for me and Steve to keep to separate beds. Ostensibly mine is another guest bedroom but all of my stuff is here and I've slept nowhere else for years. I wonder if Steve regrets this drift. If he asked to go back to how it was, I would agree. Of course I would. But he's never broached it and if any visitors were to query it, his snoring and my restless insomnia are perfectly good excuses.

My door creaks open now and I feel Steve step inside the room. Under their lids, my eyes dart around in fear. Is any of my dress showing? Can he tell I've just got back?

The air changes while I try desperately to slow my breathing.

'You awake?' he says eventually, his voice muffled, his tongue thick with drink.

I say nothing. He watches me for a while and then I hear the thud of his belt on the floor, a rustle as the shirt is tugged away from his barrel body.

He climbs onto the bed and lies down next to me, one hand flopping across my chest then slipping off again. Seconds later, he's snoring. I wait to be sure and then slip out from under the covers and pull off my dress, stuffing it on a chair in the corner. I tease my pyjamas out from under the pillow and then climb back in and wonder if he'll wake up full of regret or intent.

While he sleeps, I turn my phone screen away so I don't wake him, then upload the photo from the Bluebell and send a confirmation message. I wonder if I should add an addendum, warn them about how flaky David Ross is. How loose with his intentions. I owe them nothing, but I've been tied into the same net as him and I don't want to be pulled down.

Five minutes pass, ten. In the end I send nothing more. The phone sits in my hand like a held breath, Steve groans and rolls over slowly. I reach across and stroke his shoulder in some kind of secret apology. I kissed his brother tonight, his best friend. I kissed his brother and then I didn't even think about it again, because everything else I was doing was even worse.

# Greg

*Friday, 27 September 2019*

At Waterloo they meet like lovers, under the railway arches. In the time since he first offered her the money, Kenza has been sent to collect a parcel containing a syringe and preloaded credit card from some locker store, been told to draw her own blood and then leave it in another locker, using the credit card to seal it and then throwing it away. It all sounded absurd to him but she'd just got on with it. The tests were fine, apparently. And here she is.

He hoped, somehow, that he would feel like a good guy today. Trying to ignore the vicious way he was forced into this; it *is* better that the girls work with him than some predator. Instead he feels like a monster.

He buys tickets from the machine, avoiding human contact wherever possible. Kenza leans on the machine's steel side, watches people streaming past. She makes eye contact with a man in his twenties with one of those long beards, shaved hair at the sides. He looks away, blushing. Those posters Hidden Humans and related organisations petitioned to get into train station toilets are coming back to haunt him.

**LOOK** below the surface – does he or she want to be here?
**ASK** the right questions – offer opportunities to speak alone
**CALL** if you suspect someone could be a victim of trafficking

No one is looking below the surface. No one is wondering whether Kenza wants to be here or not. And she's not being trafficked, she's not being shipped out to another country or locked up in a brothel. Not anymore. But nor has she arrived happy, excited for her adventure. She seems less sure now than when he first suggested this. He wants to ask her, 'Have

187

you changed your mind?' but if the answer is yes, what will happen to him? He'll lose his marriage and his job. He could go to prison.

\*

The train rattles into Godstone station. It's unmanned and they're the only ones to alight. Kenza trails behind him up the steel staircase, over the tracks and down again. He looks back, fearful of her breaking away, but she's used to this. Greg wonders how many similar journeys she's been on with other men, men different to him in shades too close for comfort.

'You remembered not to eat?' he says to her. She nods. 'Or drink?'

'I didn't drink anything.'

The train is already a memory, the station has been swallowed up in silence again. They wait in the flimsy shelter and watch for a black car.

\*

'I might as well tell you my real name,' David Ross shrugs, after doing just that. 'It's easy enough to look it up.'

'Hi, David,' says Greg, lifting Kenza's small carrier bag of neatly folded clothes and a toothbrush into the boot of the Audi.

Kenza says nothing.

They turn from the quiet village road onto a narrow lane that surges up hills and around brambly bends. Kenza affects a look of passive disinterest but she worries at a loose thread on her cardigan until her fingers pick a hole. The car bumps up over a cattle grid and eventually comes to rest in the nearly empty carpark of the hotel.

'We've only got a skeleton staff working today,' David says as he ushers them out of the car. He lifts Kenza's little bag from the boot and hands it to her. She takes it in silence as he points towards the side of the building, away from the main entrance.

They pass a large Lexus as they round a small extension and start to climb a metal staircase. 'Our grateful customer,' David says, gesturing to the fancy car. It takes Greg until the top of the stairs to realise that David does not mean a customer of the hotel.

'Will I meet him?' Kenza asks, suddenly.

David Ross shakes his head. 'Her. And no. You'll be asleep by then.'

The small party walks briskly down a carpeted hall, bedrooms to the right of them, a view over Surrey countryside to the left. At the far end, David unlocks a door with a big brass key, no keycards here. Part of the charm, Greg supposes.

Inside the room is a set of old-fashioned twin beds. They have been stripped of the fancy bedding Greg would expect, replaced with blue disposable bed sheets. Greg stares in alarm at the straps hanging from the bedposts.

As the door is locked behind them, a man and woman in surgical scrubs stand up to attention. They all smile uneasily, like people waiting to be interviewed for the same job. The man and woman talk to Kenza about what will happen next. She doesn't react to any of it, instead slides her bag onto the vanity table in the corner of the room.

'I'll just check on our guest next door,' David says.

'She's been prepared,' the woman says to him. 'She just needs bringing in when the time is right.'

*

Greg waits on the made-up bed in an unused bedroom down the hall. He doesn't dare turn on the boxy television set or make any other noise that could attract attention from the 'skeleton staff'. Instead, he sits back against a nest of over-stuffed cushions and tries to get his phone connected to 3G. He's done his bit, there should be an address and details waiting for him in his secret account, but he can't get to it until he gets home.

There is no Wi-Fi in the hotel – *temporarily*, David claims – but there's not even a bar of phone signal to make calls. Not that Greg has anyone to call. Marianne will be in class and has to have her phone locked away, and he's using a day of annual leave from work and no one ever calls in on their day off.

He plays an old game he'd forgotten he had downloaded months ago, then gives up as it zaps so much battery. Next time, he will bring a charger. *Next time* – how easily that idea formed.

He moves across to the velvet window seat and watches the sky change colour. In a far-off field, just skimming the horizon, a speck of a tractor zigzags like a bug across the brown soil.

Finally, the doctor knocks on the door. He didn't offer Greg his name, but the nurse referred to him as Henry. Henry is older than Greg, wiry grey hair at his temples, bushy eyebrows that seem to grow in all directions. He has the reassuring baritone of an archetypal surgeon. *Life is safe in my hands.*

'It was a success,' his voice rumbles softly, as if delivering news about a loved one. He waits, for applause or dismissal, Greg doesn't know. The doctor has little beads of blood on his scrubs and when Greg looks closer, his skin is coated with a sheen of sweat.

'Good,' Greg says and the doctor nods, then turns on his heel to leave. His big hand shakes as he grips the door handle.

Greg pats down his pocket for his return ticket to London. He watches a sleeping Kenza from the doorway of her room, where she's being monitored by the nurse – a blonde woman around his age with black rings under her eyes.

'How long will Kenza need to stay?' Greg asks the nurse, even though he's been told before.

'Four days,' the nurse says. 'But she'll need to take pain-killers after that.'

'And if something goes wrong?' Greg asks. The doctor and nurse look at each other but say nothing.

Greg hears footsteps behind him and wheels through possible excuses as he turns, expecting a curious porter or cleaner. It's David Ross. He gives a hollow laugh. 'Don't look so jumpy, mate. The skeleton staff is just me, there's no one else here.'

'How long will the client stay?' Greg asks him.

'She'll be our guest for a week but she'll come back for check-ups.'

'What about food and . . .'

'This is a hotel, young Scottie. It's all part of the service. I trained as a chef back along, I think I can handle a few meals. We've even got the dining room set up for when she's ready.'

'But what if she still needs . . .' Greg starts, wishing he'd not read the NHS webpage about this. Wishing he didn't know all the things that could go wrong.

'Trust me,' David says, pointing to the client. 'The money this one has, she's got her own machine ready and waiting at home. She wanted us to do a home visit,' he laughs, 'but *you know who* said no. Too many variables outside of our control that way.'

'I don't know who.'

'You don't know who is employing you?' David looks amused.

'Employing? Twisting my arm up my back more like.' Greg pauses. 'It's not you, is it? The messages?'

David just shakes his head, chuckling softly. 'I'm not the organ grinder, mate. Just another monkey.'

Greg stares across at the beds. The two women have been covered with fresh bedding, wrapped in paper sheets like gifts. The far bed contains the client, honey blonde hair just visible under the surgical cap, mouth agape as she sleeps. She looks to be in her forties or maybe fifties, it's hard to tell when someone has enough money. Despite the rigours of surgery, her complexion has the solidity of a paid-for tan, her cheeks unnaturally smooth and round.

Kenza has the complexion of the eighteen-year-old that she is, her skin greyer than before but unlined, untampered with. Swathes of her black hair are held back by a matching surgical cap, which bulges with the weight of it. Her eyelids are perfectly still, her mouth clamped shut. Even in sleep she looks cautious.

'Right,' David says, unlocking the door again. 'Rosie, I'm going to drop Scottie back to the station and then I'll come and check on you all. Not that it's my place to say but in the absence of our *all powerful overlord*, I'd suggest you get Lady Muck back into her own room and spend most of your time in there. She's paying, after all.'

'When do I get paid?' Rosie says, sharply.

'Take that up with *you know who*.'

'Who is *you know who*?' Greg asks her, but she just scowls.

*

'How much are you getting for this?' David asks as he steers fast into a bend, glancing at Greg in the mirror.

'Nothing.'

'*Nothing* nothing or just not money?'

'Nothing.' Greg shrugs.

'You weren't joking about someone twisting your arm up your back?'

Greg looks across at him. David is wearing that same shit-munching smile he wore earlier. He knows nothing, Greg realises. Nothing at all.

'Eh?' David needles. 'You being bribed then? Been a naughty boy?'

Greg's too tired for this, too worried about Kenza. Should he really be leaving her? Trusting her care and rehabilitation to this bunch of jokers, stuck out in the middle of nowhere? It's dark outside already. He'll be joining the train back to London at commuter time and the idea of an anonymous crowd appeals. To get lost appeals right now. And to get home to his inner sanctum, to cook for his healthy wife, to sleep in a bed that isn't wrapped in paper.

'You're another one like Rosie, then. Interesting,' David says in a voice loaded with accusation.

'I don't know what that means.'

They near the junction back into Godstone; David Ross slows but doesn't stop, swinging out fast and then stepping on the accelerator as he tops forty then fifty miles an hour through the quiet village. 'Come on, mate, you saw the state of her.'

'Does she need—'

'Drugs, Scottie.' David laughs with surprise and shakes his head. 'Not the street kind either. Full-on pharmaceuticals. The kind that could kill a pony.'

'My name isn't Scottie, it's Greg,' he says finally, as the car squeals to a stop in the station carpark. 'And I'm not doing this for *drugs*.'

\*

In the evening, Marianne falls asleep next to him on the sofa, her feet curled up underneath her. She looks peaceful, doll-like; whatever the daily stresses and strains beneath her eyelids, they are normal and above board. He's jealous of her ability to sleep soundly, but why shouldn't she? She's a good person, with a clear conscience. She'd never get herself into this kind of ridiculous jam, no matter what was offered.

He wants to wake her. Shake her foot, grip her ankle, climb up her leg and grip onto it, pleading with her to take this whole shitting shambles away from him and fix it. *Tell me what to do!* He puts his hand on her foot, strokes the skin of it, pulls at one toe. She fidgets but doesn't wake. How could he even begin, anyway?

He leaves her sleeping and takes his laptop into the kitchen, pours a measure of Christmas whisky and opens up the secret email account.

*One new message.*

The transition was a success. Here is the location of eight women you will be interested in. We expect another suitable candidate soon or you know what the consequences will be.

He looks through the door at Marianne sleeping on the sofa. Minutes ago the truth was right there, wadded up in his mouth like chewing tobacco, ready to be spat out. But now, the thought is insanity itself. The words, the truth – my God, he would sound like a lunatic.

*Hey, Marianne, I delivered a trusting young girl to a backstreet butcher to have her organ sliced out today. Surprise!*

And then it hits him. This, today, is far worse than the fake video he was threatened with. Because this isn't fake. He really did take Kenza to the Bluebell. He really did wait on an unmade hotel bed while an illegal operation took place down the hall.

There's no explaining that.

He imagines Marianne packing a bag, shock and repulsion written across her face. Imagines her voice, the voice he knows better than any other, telling him to stay away from her. Imagines the shape she'd leave if she was hacked out of his life. And now that he's gone through with this, he's on *their* hook even more.

'They' – these shadowy figures that operate above him, above Rosie and David and the other 'monkeys' as David calls them. What *can't* they do? They seem to have access to everything, able to fake videos and take over whole hotels and god knows what else.

They could show Marianne what he did, and he'd lose everything. He'll have to keep coming up with fresh meat or he's finished. Everything is finished. How the hell did he end up here?

He writes down the address and details of the eight women of whom 'they' have sent details. He thinks about asking, 'Who is this? How many of you are there?' but they have no reason to reply and plenty of reasons to turn up the heat under him.

Instead he replies: 'You'll get a candidate soon.'

*

This time, he doesn't turn up himself at the dilapidated old villa in Catford for the 'rescue'. Instead, he watches the house for a couple of days on his way back from work, bike propped behind him on the wall. When he's as sure as he can be, he tells Eloise that someone rang in with a tip-off. It's flagged to the police, along with the names of the pimps that the 'caller' provided.

Eight women are found.

'Well done, Greg,' Eloise says, patting his shoulder when they hear the women are out. 'You did good.'

# Samantha

*Monday, 21 October 2019*

'I can't. I can't do that.'

And I can't. I really cannot. The latest assignment involves extracting a list of items from a private address. Burglary in other words. The private address is in Kensington, in a block of apartments that – as far as I can tell from Google Streetview and luxury property websites – has a concierge and a full suite of security cameras.

There's no way I can get in and out without being seen, without being arrested. And if I'm arrested, and my fingerprints are taken, my ID will be requested and all this will be for nothing. I have told them this. What they hold over me will disintegrate if they make me go through with it.

They don't reply at first. I imagine them finding an alternative use for me, though a tiny shard of optimism I still hold hopes that they realise they've taken me as far as they can. That they release me from this rollercoaster I've been strapped into, let me climb back into my small and comfortable life, and lick my wounds.

Instead, they send a photograph of a woman. She's a bit older than me or perhaps less pampered. The caption says: *Look familiar?*

She does. Something around the eyes, the shape of the forehead maybe. I chew my acrylic nails – a supposed barrier to stop me shredding my own fingers – and wrack my brain. I suspect she is someone from my younger days, someone who lived in the same house as Cristina and me or was some part of the chain that brought me here.

We've all aged so much that she could be anyone.

'No,' I reply. 'And I really cannot help you anymore.'

Then they send another message. A name, home address and place of work. And I feel like my heart might turn black and stop.

The woman is called Emily Redfern. She lives in a small cottage in Norfolk. She works in a bookshop. And she's Joe's biological mother.

*You can do this. It's not impossible. Or this information will be sent to your 'son'.*

I feel faint.

I *can* do this. It's *not* impossible. And now I really do have to.

I knew Emily was out there, of course I did. So did Joe, though we never talk about it and we never knew where she was or if she was well. Whenever I've tried to raise it, he shuts me down. 'You're my mum,' he says, emphatically.

I found out more from Paula than Steve, who finds it almost impossible to talk about what happened.

*

Emily left for the last time when Joe was eighteen months old, but she'd come and gone before that. She was ill, in ways they're better at treating now.

Paula told me that she and Steve had taken Emily to the doctor in a mob-handed effort, strapping her into the car as she stared dead ahead like a statue. Paula stayed in the waiting room and when they reappeared, Steve shook his head in disbelief. The GP said it was the baby blues.

'It was nothing like the baby blues,' Paula whispered when she retold it. 'Some days, she would walk out and leave Joe in the house, hungry and crying, and have no recollection of doing so. Steve would come back from work and find him in his playpen. Or I'd pop in to check on them and find him in his crib.'

My heart broke at the thought.

When Emily was well, she would talk about that other Emily as a monster. But she was never a monster, she just needed help. Repeat visits to the GP led to prescription anti-depressants, which numbed her completely. At one stage, Steve's mother – still alive then – paid for a stay in a private facility. After a week, Emily broke out and walked barefoot to the family home. Joe was terrified when she banged on the window to be let in.

And then, Steve told me, one day she packed her things and told him she was leaving. She didn't want to be their problem anymore. She would go and leave them here where they would be better off without her.

He tried to find her. Even Jonathan was roped in to tracking her down, trying to use what was then fledgling internet technology. But she was a ghost. True to her word, Emily stayed away. And Steve's hopes died, replaced by anger that she could leave, and then fear that she could come back and snatch Joe.

For Steve, she was a warning shot. He had tried and failed at the normal route to having a family and a marriage. And it had become so toxic and frightening that he wouldn't risk it again. Not the usual way.

As soon as I knew about Emily, I was prepared to protect Joe at all costs. Ready to fight for him, to do whatever it took. If Emily had shown up when he was little, with all my instincts still at their peak, I know exactly what I would have done. Over the years such panic seemed unfounded and she faded to a sad shadow in Joe's background.

Now, in this photograph, she is made flesh. And if she's working and has a fixed address, if she's finally stable and well, she could feel ready to come back into his life with just a little prompting. Who could resist?

And if he was sent her details, would he really be able to stifle his curiosity?

More than any of that, the most frightening thing for me is that they are now bringing Joe into this. I can't let this escalate, I cannot have him tainted.

I'll do the assignment.

*

'Are you sure the target isn't home?' I message, tugging at my uniform as I approach the moneyed block.

*He will be out until late evening.*

The flat is on the fourth floor of a mansion block not far from Harrods. Each apartment has its own glass balcony, looking out over the traffic fumes towards Kensington Palace Gardens. This is the London that is bottled and sold to people abroad, a million miles from most people's realities. I wonder what the man who lives here did to jump that queue.

Before I left this afternoon, I filled a rucksack with cleaning equipment from home. It had to look well used so I didn't want to buy it fresh. I have a duster poking out of the top of the bag. On the walk from Kensington Station, I called in at Ann Summers and bought a French Maid's outfit two sizes too big to attempt to negate any raunchiness. I feel ridiculous, the uniform peeking out from under my plainest coat. I probably look ridiculous too, but at least nerves work as part of my disguise.

The concierge is playing a game on his phone when I walk in and he places it screen side down and smiles up at me.

I open my mouth and opt to use an accent I've hidden for over twenty years.

'Is Mr Derbyshire in his apartment?' I ask.

'Dr Derbyshire?' the man says, with a frown.

'Yes,' I nod.

'I'm teasing,' the man smiles. 'I'm sure he gets that all the time. Who shall I say is calling?'

'Danja,' I say. 'From the cleaning company.'

'I'm pretty sure he went out earlier, but let me call up for you.'

If he is home, I will have to run – he'll know full well he's not booked a cleaner today – but thankfully, the phone rings out.

The concierge shakes his head and I start to cry, letting a few fat tears roll down my cheeks.

'Oh dear,' he says.

'I'm sorry,' I say, my accent as thick as it was on my very first day in the city. 'I was supposed to bring the key and I left it at home. It's my first time for Mr, I mean Dr Derbyshire and I'll lose my job. What can I do? I can't go back and get the key or I'll be late starting, then I'll be late for the next one too and lose my job.'

The concierge is up and out of his seat before I've cuffed my nose and wiped my eyes.

'Come with me,' he says, patting his pocket and striding to the lift.

'What are we—'

'I need to be quick, I'm only supposed to leave the desk for toilet trips,' he smiles, punching in the floor number and closing the lift doors after us. As the lift rushes up, he pulls out a master key.

*

The computer is easy, it's lying on the badly made bed in the master bedroom. I slip it into my rucksack behind the cleaning things. The SIM card is proving harder. No desk drawers to look through. For such an expensive apartment, there's not a lot in it. In fact, there are indents on the plush lounge carpet where pieces of furniture used to be, marks on the walls where paintings once hung. He's either in the midst of moving out or selling things off.

I look through the kitchen drawers, through the occasional piles of paperwork and behind the last few paintings left. Finally I go back to the bedroom and start to go through his chest of drawers. Boring clothes, well folded. There is some dust on every surface – clearly Dr Derbyshire could do with a real cleaner.

I'm just opening the wardrobe door as I hear the front door to the apartment open.

I freeze, standing prone in front of the open wardrobe. Is it the concierge? If not, has the concierge told the apartment owner that I'm in here?

I hear a man sigh and dump something down on the floor. A bag or a briefcase, it makes a quick leathery slap on the wood. I stay stock still, not trusting that I can do anything without drawing attention to myself. I hear a gush of water and then what sounds like a coffee machine. Still I stand frozen. Next comes the squawk of a chair being pulled out. It must be Dr Derbyshire, and he doesn't seem to know I'm here.

I step lightly into the wardrobe and close the sliding doors after me, so slowly I can barely stand it. At first it's pitch black, but my eyes adjust. Fumbling in the gloom, I open Whispa on my phone and send an urgent message.

'He's come home!!! I'm trapped in the wardrobe!!!'

*Stay calm. He has a reservation for dinner soon, he will leave again.*

'And what if he doesn't?'

*You know what you need to do. Unless you want to get caught?*

It gets later and later. I don't dare relax, don't scrunch into the corner on top of his pile of shoe boxes or make myself a little nest in his clothes. The blood pools in my feet, I have to wriggle my toes to relieve them but I remain ready to move.

I switch my SIM and see that both Steve and Joe have called and texted me. Steve is wondering where I am, wanting to know if I'll be much later as he's cooking. Joe is asking about the whereabouts of a specific sweater. Then asking if I'm OK, asking when I'll be back, then telling me, 'Dad's worried.'

I reply to Joe, then Steve, telling them I went shopping at Westfield and left my phone in the car. I say that I've just got it now and that I'll get dinner out. It's unlike me, and they know it. But what else can I do?

I switch the SIMs back and wait. I hear the kitchen door close, pray that I'll hear the front door next. That the doctor is no longer in the house. Instead, the bedroom door opens and he comes into the room. I hold my breath. I hear the slow slide of a drawer, followed by the sharp clatter of it closing again. He steps closer, my eyes cloud with panic and then, as he starts to open the wardrobe door, calm floods me. The same active numbness I experienced decades ago when faced with a similar yet wildly different situation.

I am standing to the side of the door and I have two main advantages over him. Advantage one, he's shorter and slighter than me. Advantage two, he doesn't know I'm here so he hasn't had a chance to plan his defence, whereas I have already planned my attack.

I close my eyes and breathe slowly. In, out, in, out. I raise my arms slowly over my head, fists ready to thump down on his skull. He's reaching inside the wardrobe now. When his head follows his hand inside, I'll have to strike.

His manicured fingers grapple to pull a chunky cardigan from a hanger and then, in a split second, it's over. The arm, the head, the man, gone. The wardrobe door slides shut. Then the bedroom door. Then the front door.

I rub my hands over my face and try to forget what I was about to do, closing my eyes and counting slowly until my heart rate slows again. As I start to climb back out, I spot an old-style jewellery box in the corner of the wardrobe. I tease it open. It's the kind of little box mothers leave their children when they die. The kind I didn't get to inherit; the few things my mother possessed were ransacked along with everything else.

This box is almost empty, but propped in one of the slots designed for a ring is an identical SIM card to the one I have. I snatch it up, slide it into the front pocket of my rucksack and walk out quietly, past a different concierge.

*

The adrenaline is still surging when I reach the tube station. It's been a long time since I felt like this, and I find it hard to square how pumped up and alive I feel, with the depths I just sank to. Depths I've not visited in Samantha Redfern's lifetime.

I'm about to rush through the turnstile when I hear my name just over my shoulder.

'Samantha?'

I spin around involuntarily, my coat flapping open and my 'uniform' exposed. Jonathan stares back at me, taking in my outfit, the wild look on my face, and clearly not understanding any of it.

'I . . .' What can I say? I had forgotten his office wasn't far from here. I've never visited it. I have no legitimate reason to be here, and I've told outright lies to my family about where I am. The last time I saw my brother-in-law, I asked him to cover for me. I *kissed* him. Now this. And I'm supposed to be meeting his wife tomorrow.

'What are you doing here?' he says finally, as people elbow past us to barge through the metal gates.

I have no answer. Instead I stare back at him. Jonathan is slim and boyish. You'd guess he was in his early forties rather than fifty-four. There's an energy to him that sucks everything into it, like a black hole. His smile suggests the promise of something you shouldn't want, but ache for nonetheless.

Still saying nothing, I gesture for us to walk back out into the dark street, the cold stealing my breath and turning it into steam. I put my hand on his arm and lead him away, down Derry Street and on towards Kensington Square Gardens. He's stopped asking where we're going. Now he's following in silence as I open the metal gate and tug him inside.

There are no lamps in here, just the glow from the nearby buildings. I walk to a thick tree with a bench running around it in a ring, which I tuck my rucksack under. 'Sit down,' I say. The same calm as before settles in my stomach. I smile at his bemused expression. 'I came to find you,' I say.

Afterwards, we sit wrapped in each other for warmth. Neither of us asks what will happen next, we both know nothing else can happen.

'It's a very long time since I've done that,' I say.

'You and Steve don't . . .?'

It's bad enough to betray our partners but to give up their secrets too is acid on the wound. 'I meant, take a big risk,' I say.

He doesn't reply, but rests his head on mine so I can feel the contours of his skull pressing against me when he speaks.

'Can I ask something I've always wondered?' he says.

'OK.'

He lifts his head from mine and looks at me. 'Where's your accent actually from?'

I climb down from the bench and rearrange my ridiculous clothes. 'What accent?'

'It's so faint but . . .' He smiles awkwardly and stands up, rearranging his belt. 'It's still there. I mean, I know vaguely, but Steve is so tight-lipped. I've always been curious about you. In lots of ways.'

I tell him. A country in the Balkans he will have seen on the news and never visited.

He mistakes my reticence for embarrassment and reassures me: 'You shouldn't hide it, it's really sexy.'

*

My accent was stronger when I first arrived. I'd hoped to refine it by talking to the locals but most of my conversations were with other people with all sorts of different accents, so it wasn't easy. Cristina from Romania, two girls from Russia in the room next to us, the men who controlled the house, the passing 'guests' that stayed a handful of nights. Instead, I tried to soften the edges of my accent by listening to Radio 4 on the sticky little radio someone had left in the house.

And I was put to work cleaning offices at night, speaking to almost no one, no English practice there.

It was back-breaking work, starting at 3 a.m. and going on until 8 a.m. when the first worker bees arrived. I then slept patchily during the day, Cristina and I curled up like a basket of kittens in our shared bed, ready to get up in the afternoon. We'd eat a hasty meal in the communal kitchen, and then I'd be back out to clean schools after the children went home. Cristina was sent out to sleep with men for money. Neither of us was spending time exploring the city and chatting with the locals.

After the border agency raided the cleaning company, we were all redeployed. Some of us joined Cristina, getting into men's cars, but I was lucky. Because my English was good, I was sent out to Steve's Surrey home to work as an au pair, armed with fake papers and written references. One of the men in the knotty little network I'd been 'rescued' into ran an au pair agency.

As with the cleaning job, all the money earned was handed over to cover the rent and food that I was somehow always in debt for, and had been since I arrived.

But soon, I was completely and irreparably in love. With Joe. The light of my life, I looked forward to getting to work, picking him up and squidging him, making sticky potato prints with him, cleaning his little clothes, more than I'd looked forward to anything in my life. 'You're not like other girls,' my father had always told me, proudly. 'You're tough, you're a fighter, you've never wanted to play with dolls.' I'd believed him. He was right but he was absolutely wrong.

I didn't meet Jonathan and Paula until I'd been working for Steve for several months. By then I'd anglicised my name from Samanta to Samantha and worked hard to lose the last traces of an accent that stood out like a splinter in moneyed Surrey. Yet still it was noticed. I wonder what else people saw.

I pull a little tree bark from my hair and reach for Jonathan's hand as we walk towards the station.

*

I shouldn't admit this, I shouldn't feel this, but I'm drunk on adrenaline. The lust and the aggression both lying dormant, now awake.

At High Street Kensington tube, Jonathan and I head to different platforms, agreeing in a flurry of soft kisses that this can never happen again. I struggle to see how I can ever hold his gaze in company, or say his name without flushing. How will I meet Paula for brunch?

I change into my clothes and dump my uniform in the toilets at London Victoria. Then I message 'them' to say that I have everything they wanted. 'But what if he reports the theft?' I ask. 'They have me on CCTV, and a witness who spoke to me.'

*He won't report it.*

'How can you be so sure?'

*How much have you reported?*

Touché.

They send back instructions of where to leave it – yet another luggage storage place somewhere near Gatwick – and I spend the rest of the journey home with my eyes closed, reliving the events of the day in shock. A strange swirl of pride in the mix too, and the standard underpinning of rage at being shoved onto this ridiculous rollercoaster.

Before I set off, I check my normal SIM for messages. Paula has confirmed our date for tomorrow, Le Pain Quotidien at eleven o'clock. Any remaining adrenaline and excitement pools cold and damp in my stomach as she adds, 'I could really do with a friendly face. I think Jonathan is cheating on me.'

'Oh my god, I'm so sorry,' I write back. 'Hopefully there's an innocent explanation! X.'

I can't remember the drive home from the station, my brain running through all the possible scenarios with Paula, not to mention how close I came to getting caught in that flat in Kensington.

It's only as I pull my car onto the drive that I realise I should have shopping bags with me. I don't even have a handbag, instead I have a rucksack full of cleaning stuff plus a stolen laptop and SIM card. I'm about to reverse back out and nip to the high street to try to find something, anything, still open for business when the front door opens.

Steve is silhouetted by the hallway light, his stumpy feet hanging from the step in their slippers, his eyes as sad as I've ever seen them. He's aged in the last few years, as if a thread got snagged when he hit fifty and the rest of him unravelled. I get out and go closer, leaving the bag in the car. Any last trace of adrenaline has turned to water, sloshing in my guts.

In his hands, Steve holds a letter with a Surrey Police logo at the top. He hands it to me silently and turns away. I read it as I follow him inside.

A speeding ticket from my journey on the night of Jonathan's birthday. My car number plate but registered to Steve, the only one of us with a valid UK licence. The offence took place at a time when I claimed to be in bed, ill. When I had lied, so easily, so blatantly, to his face.

'I'm so sorry,' I say, but he's already walked away.

# Greg

*Friday, 25 October 2019*

Greg leans against the flock wallpaper. The door behind him is locked, sealing him into the pseudo operating theatre. 'Where's the other doctor?'

'He quit,' Rosie says without looking up, fussing with stir-
rups and swabs.

*Since when was quitting an option?*

Talia, the girl on the bed, offers her hands and feet with
mute resignation. She'd agreed immediately to Greg's offer,
barely a flicker of willingness or reticence, like it was just
another in a long line of events outside of her control.

'I need to prepare the patient next door,' Rosie says quietly,
as she unlocks the door with the big brass key and hands it
to Greg. To settle the acid in his gut, he tries to imagine
Talia's face when she receives the money, smiling through
the discomfort. He imagines another group of women being
led out into the fresh air, getting checked over by a doctor,
getting help from his charity.

Is this enough? To negate everything wrong that he has
done? Not even close. He can feel sweat seeping through his
T-shirt, his heart thundering under the cotton. He's never
been so aware of it before, but for months he's had constant
butterflies in his gut and flurries of heartbeats. Marianne has
noticed too, asking him if he's OK so many times that last
night he snapped at her to get off his back. She'd slunk away,
hurt. He apologised this morning, cobbled together some excuse
about work. She said it was OK but her eyes were sad and
she left without kissing him.

He locks the door again and tries to think of something
comforting to say to Talia; then he notices the man at the
sink is waiting to talk.

'I'm Pavel.' The very young man dressed in scrubs offers
Greg his hand. 'The surgeon,' he adds crisply, through a strong
accent. He looks about nineteen, thin dark hair hanging pointed
like a beak, pale face pocked with faded acne.

'Hi, I'm Greg.'

'I hope that is not your real name,' Pavel laughs, nervously.
Greg shrugs. He wants to add something. He should ask if
Pavel – or whatever he's really called – has actually completed
his medical degree. Or when he first performed surgery. *If* he's

ever performed surgery. He should ask if he's going to wash his hands again before touching the precious insides of a human being. Where are the gloves? Where is his cap?

*Ask something.*

Greg opens his mouth.

*And what will happen if the answers are wrong?* What will Greg do – stop this? Then what? He looks out across the fields. Thinning clumps of grass dot the bald soil, framed by the heavy curtains.

'Good luck,' Greg says to Talia. She blinks but says nothing back.

*

He waits in the same room as last time, this time with a phone charger, newspaper and packed lunch. He sits on the bed, sinking into the cushions that don't seem to have been moved since he was here last month.

He plays Tetris, tears a recipe from the paper that he'll cook for Marianne some time and starts the crossword, before giving up.

Hours later, while both patients sleep under Pavel's watch, Rosie eats her sandwiches in the spare bedroom with Greg. Like colleagues. Which, in a way, they are. 'He gambles,' she tells him of David. 'Fucked this place up 'cos of it, apparently.'

'How do you know?'

'He told me. And he's got a big mouth, *I now know*.'

'You told him about the drugs yourself?'

'Fuck's sake,' she says. 'That man is a leaky sieve.'

Greg laughs despite himself. Despite the surreal surroundings, the dusty bedspread, the unwashed coffee cups and single-serving sugars lying around.

'So was it closed down, then?' he asks.

She shrugs and yawns. 'Sorry,' she says, putting a hand to her mouth. 'So fucking tired, I'm still on shifts at the hospital around this. Yeah, apparently it was sold on for development a couple of months ago and no one knows we're here.

Though he probably lost the deeds in a card game, let's face it.' She bites the final mouthful of cheese and pickle. 'Best get back to it.'

Talia lives. The client lives. There's nothing more to stick around for and Greg allows David Ross to rally drive him back to the station again. As the car emerges into civilisation, David's phone starts to ring from its cockpit dock. He ignores it.

This time, there's no banter, no blethering on. David works his jaw and clicks his tongue as if thousands of angry words are stuck in his throat.

'See you next time,' Greg says, but David just drives away.

*

On the cycle ride back from the station, he picks up the ingredients for the shakshuka with feta that he saw in the paper; he'll make it for brunch tomorrow. Another feeble apology for his crappy behaviour. Tucks it all in his rucksack and hurries home to Marianne, narrowly avoiding a woman with a buggy who crosses the road in front of him without noticing him.

'Shit!' he cries and swerves around her.

'Wanker!' she shouts. Greg realises he forgot to put his lights on. It's a miracle he wasn't hit by a car.

When he gets in, he finds that two of the eggs have cracked. He cleans out his bag and waits for his wife.

When she comes in, he won't ask her about her day. Not because he doesn't care – although he's not really interested in the machinations of secondary school kids – but because he can't bear the question being returned. To lie by omission is one thing, but to make up a whole workday that never happened is in another league. *Sure, Greg, that's what she'd be upset about if she knew the truth. That you didn't go into the office.*

If he were to answer truthfully, to just bluntly reply, would she even believe him?

*I met a girl at the station and escorted her to a hotel in the Surrey countryside where she was paid cash, put to sleep and had an organ removed. But don't worry, Marianne, it was for a good cause. Someone really rich had bought it off her.* He shakes his head; even with the 'sweetener' of receiving the locations of other trafficked women, this whole thing is totally, undeniably wrong.

'Why are you doing this?' Marianne would ask, if she could move past the idea that it's a sick joke and consider that her husband is telling the truth.

*Because I used some dodgy service on the dark web to trace a missing girl and now the people behind it have blackmailed me into joining this far larger scheme.*

'Who are they?' she would say, if she hadn't already started calling the police or packing her bags. And he would shrug, because he doesn't know. There are people at the hotel who seem to be cogs in the machine, like him. And then there are people above them, people never named, only alluded to. One of them, presumably, is the person messaging Greg and pulling his strings, but there are at least two of them; David has said as much.

And they – the shadowy, all-knowing 'they' – haven't messaged yet tonight. No confirmation of the surgery success and no information. He thinks of Talia, berating himself for not thinking of her sooner. If something goes wrong, what happens to her? And deeply, secretly, what worries him more is, *What happens to me? Do I need to rustle up another match? Will they still give me the information? Will they tell Marianne? Eloise?*

The door to the flat opens up as the message finally arrives.

'Hey!' he calls out, closing the laptop.

'Just getting into my comfies,' Marianne calls back. He inhales, lifts the screen and reads. A successful transaction. Information about a cluster of very young women. He'll check it out tomorrow and then 'phone it in'. He exhales, snaps the laptop closed and stares at himself in the reflection of the kitchen window. He looks wired, he looks *guilty*. Like an actor ready to pace the stage, he breathes in and out, closes his eyes to study his lines and his 'motivation'. *I'm Greg, I went to work as usual today and I need to appear normal tonight.*

'I'll order a takeaway now, m'lady,' he calls out, sounding weird rather than relaxed.

'You're a bloody good man,' Marianne calls back. He watches his face recoil in the window. *No, I'm not.*

# Samantha

*Tuesday, 22 October 2019*

I leave the house before Joe or Steve wake up and walk aimlessly around the town, killing time before I meet Paula. On any other day I would have cancelled but to do so when she's confided her concerns would be cruel. And suspicious.

Steve and I barely spoke last night. He still hasn't asked why I was speeding along the M25 after feigning illness. He hasn't asked what I was really doing when I claimed to be out shopping the other night. He hasn't asked me anything at all.

I get to Le Pain Quotidien early and sit in the furthest booth from the door. There are clusters of mothers with young children, older couples enjoying retirement. I stare at them, amazed that they don't run from me. I imagine my dirt seeping everywhere until we're all filthy.

When Paula arrives, she is all smiles. We hug and kiss, I press my lips to her cheek and am shot through with a guilt so sharp I flinch.

'Forgive me,' she says briskly. 'I don't know what I was thinking sending you that message.'

'There's nothing to forgive you for,' I say. *I need you to forgive me!*

She shakes her head. 'I was being so silly.'

'You don't think that Jonathan . . .' I trail off. Do I really want to pursue this?

She laughs. 'No, I don't think that Jonathan is cheating on me. He was being so secretive and crafty, I thought that, well, you know what I thought. But it was nothing of the sort. He's taking me to New York this weekend!'

'Oh!' I say, trying to hide my relief.

'He'd been arranging it on the sly and he surprised me last night, not long after I messaged you. I'm sorry I didn't follow up, but we got distracted.' She smiles wryly and I feel my cheeks colour. How could he go home and do that after what we did?

'Well,' I say. 'I'm very happy for you.' She smiles so brilliantly that my eyes sting.

'I've always wanted to visit New York,' I add.

*

## Wednesday, 30 October 2019

The deadline to pay the speeding fine is approaching, and if Steve doesn't pay it and accept three points on his licence, or worse – if he appeals it – they will look at the photographs to ascertain who was driving. Me. An unlicensed driver, living here illegally under a false name. The stakes are as high as they've ever been, yet this is just a fraction of what could be laid at my feet.

We move in politely wide circles around each other. Still eating dinner as a family, still passing the salt and saying, 'have a nice day'. But everything has changed.

It took time for Steve to trust me as an au pair. He was paranoid about Emily coming back and snatching Joe, but I think he struggled to fully trust anyone. He would come back unannounced during the day and let himself into the house quietly, watching as I played with Joe in the garden or helped him to write his name with fridge magnets. Sometimes I would look up and see him smiling, more with relief than anything. But to really gain his trust, first I risked losing it completely.

I'd gone home from work, late, expecting to find the bed I shared with Cristina empty. Since I changed to day work at Steve's, we'd been in different time zones. And the train journeys from Surrey to North London dragged long days even further. She was still sleeping by day, me a few hours at night. I missed her warmth but was glad of the room. But that evening, Cristina was still in the bed.

She didn't sit up to greet me, she didn't move at all. Curled in on herself like a newborn. Grey. I don't know who had followed her back to that house. Which other 'tenant' had let them in. Maybe it was Cristina herself, maybe it was someone she trusted. Although she didn't seem to trust anyone except me. And I don't know what happened next, what happened to her body, because after I tucked her in, closed her eyes and kissed her cold forehead, I left that house and got the first train back to Steve's.

Joe was in bed where I'd put him before I left hours earlier. Hair fluffy from the bath. Steve was already in his pyjamas when I got back, tugging a dressing gown over them as he opened the door. 'Did you forget something?'

I broke down. The words tumbling out of me so fast he couldn't decipher them. 'Come in,' he said, helping me as if I were wounded. I curled into the arm of the sofa where just that day I'd been tucked with Joe, reading Thomas the Tank Engine stories.

'My friend Cristina died,' I said.

'I'm so sorry,' Steve said. 'Was she ill?'

I told him how I'd found her. Spilt myself open about the way we lived. As he watched in silence, I told him that I couldn't report Cristina's death because if I did, I would be sent back.

'You shouldn't be living in that house,' he said finally. 'You can't go back there.'

'I have nowhere else to go. I don't have any money . . .'

'The wages I pay you, I know they're not a king's ransom but—'

'I owe them money for the journey over and my rent; they add to the debt every week and I've never got anything left. You don't understand, there's no way out for me.'

That night, I lay in Steve's spare room, unable to sleep. I wore one of Emily's old nighties and even though the bed was a double, I scrunched myself into the corner as if Cristina was tucked there with me. When Joe woke in the night, I leapt up to see him, gladly cooing and patting him back to sleep as Steve watched from the doorway.

The next morning, he offered me a deal. He would pay off the debt and I would move in with them.

'As a live-in au pair?'

He shook his head and avoided my eye. 'I was thinking that we could do something different. Joe needs a mum. A family. I think you need a family too.'

He offered me sanctuary even though, really, he should have turned me over to the authorities, not given me a new life. And in nearly twenty years, he's been nothing but kind and generous.

'I don't want another marriage like the last one,' he'd told me, all those years ago. 'I don't ever want to wonder, *When will she leave?*'

'I won't leave, ever,' I said.

'I know you won't,' he said, casting an eye at his son hugging the side of my body like a koala and then joining in an awkward three-way hug. 'We'll get better at this,' he said, and I smiled. And we did get better at it. We created a family for Joe that has formed the scaffolding of his life. And mine. And now it's being disassembled.

*

Joe has left for an early lecture and Steve is fussing around, looking for his keys, when I just say it. 'I was seeing someone.

214

I was with him the night that I got the ticket and I was with him the other day when I said I was shopping. I'm so sorry. You can't begin to imagine how sorry. But it's over now.'

He stops and looks up at me, his eyes drooping with age and something else. Something new.

'I'm just so sorry, Steve,' I say. 'I was stupid and selfish. I just wanted . . . I don't know. I just wanted someone to want me. As a woman, not as a surrogate. Just for a little bit. But it was much too big a risk and I regret it so very much.'

He doesn't react, doesn't look surprised. Just watches me, waiting for what he must know is coming.

'I know I shouldn't ask you this,' I say, avoiding his eye. 'But if I don't, everything unravels and Joe—'

'I've already paid the fine and sent off my licence,' he says. 'So don't try to guilt me into it.'

He pats his pocket and there's a metal rustle. The missing keys. Once upon a time, not long ago, we would have laughed at this.

'You were never just a surrogate to me,' he says, his back to me.

'It really is over,' I say. 'I promise.'

Then he walks out.

*

### Tuesday, 12 November 2019

Since dropping off Dr Derbyshire's laptop and SIM card in the luggage store near Gatwick, I haven't received another assignment. No messages, nothing. I've settled back into a life that looks very like the one I had before: going to the gym, getting my hair done, volunteering at the charity, caring for Joe. I haven't contacted Jonathan or Paula, but I have thought of them endlessly. And Steve, poor Steve, has said nothing more about my indiscretion but has instead thrown himself into work.

I'm in the office toilet at the charity, checking my other SIM. It's been so many weeks since they've been in touch that I'm jarred to see it.

It's in the same flat tone that delivers all my assignments.

You need to get rid of Michael Sutherland. You can choose the method but it must look like an accident. Attached is his weekly timetable and whereabouts. Keep it simple. Deadline is Friday night.

'What do you mean "get rid of"?' I write back. Praying I have misunderstood, that they mean for me to help him leave the country, go into hiding.

*You know what we mean. He needs to be killed.*

'No!' I write back. 'Absolutely not. I'd rather go to jail for everything else than do that.'

*You don't mean that. Remember, it needs to look like an accident.*

'He has a young child,' I write, my fingers tripping over themselves. 'This is over a line. I can't do it.'

I'm about to reply again, panic rising in my chest like acid. Another message comes through.

*This is what we found on his computer.*

I can't delete the cascade of images fast enough. I fumble for the lid of the toilet and throw up until my eyes ache.

\*

It's nearly eleven and I lie in bed, numb. Cold in parts I didn't even know I could feel. A tickertape parade rushes through my head, all his comings and goings, his where-abouts, the possibilities dancing in my head. How do you plan a murder? How do you plan to make a murder look like an accident?

I try to remember everything I was taught all those years ago. Of course, that wasn't about murder. That was about defence, about vigilance, but it ended the same way.

Now, decades on, surely I can't really do this? Maybe I could move on, take a new name and find a bedsit somewhere near Joe's campus, hope that I can keep the truth from him a while longer. Anything better than taking another life.

I flip SIMs and type fast.

'I'm not doing it. You can't make me do this.'

Minutes pass. I close my eyes but still the images are there. I think of Michael Sutherland's child and decide I will track down his wife, tell her somehow. It doesn't have to take a murder to fix this.

I can see that whoever mans the Whispa app for them is typing. It comes in bursts.

CCTV of me arriving at an Electronics Superstore on that very first assignment. A photograph of me entering an E-Z Luggage & Lockers. So what? I try to tell myself. None of this proves anything.

Then, a CCTV freeze frame of me going into that flat in Kensington, another of me coming out with a backpack full of stolen goods.

Another from the tube station, which must have been just before Jonathan saw me.

'Stop,' I write.

Still the messages come. Scans of prescriptions, more CCTV stills from places I don't even recognise. And then the maximum jail terms for each offence.

*Ten years for prescription fraud.*

*Ten years for gift-card fraud.*

*Seven years for shoplifting.*

'Please stop.'

*Six years for burglary.*

'PLEASE STOP'

*And you'd better hope it's in the UK and you're not extradited.*

'Why are you doing this to me?'

*We don't have time for this nonsense today, Samantha. Just get the job done by Friday.*

*

217

On Friday morning, I drive to Tunbridge Wells. My car is disguised with a different set of fake number plates and my face in shadow from a baseball cap. I have a mask ready. As I drive, I run through the plan. I wonder, for a moment, if I can really trust these notes about the target's schedule. But I can, can't I, because this was no doubt put together by some other worm on a hook. And worms like us can't make mistakes.

On my passenger seat is a large carrier bag containing a tub of grapes, a roll of plastic wrapping, a men's jacket from a charity shop and a roll of wire. I have no idea if this will work but time is running out.

I pull up two streets away. It's almost ten o'clock and he's due back from his run around half past. There is no one around and I slip quietly down the alleyway between his road and the one behind. My new boots pinch my feet and I feel hot in all these layers of other people's clothes.

I dodge the wheelie bins and dog mess and then open the gate to his garden. The shed has no more boxes; the kids' toys are now stacked neatly inside.

It's a dull day, the whipping wind too damp for clothes to be hung out. No one is watching as far as I can tell. I slide up the sash window – people so rarely lock these – and slip inside, leaving my boots below the windowsill.

I check every room in the house, my heart beating itself against my ribs like a warning. In the front room, I pull several sheets of the plastic wrap ready and hold them tight. Inside my gloves, even my fingers are sweating. I don't know if I can trust them.

I wait behind the door, calming my breathing as best I can, listening out for neighbours or delivery people. Or, heaven forbid, Michael's wife returning.

Eventually the key rattles in the lock. He pushes it open and steps inside, panting with exhaustion. The door bounces back off me and slams behind him. Shit. He turns to face me and I have to lunge at him, knocking him to the floor and covering his face with the plastic wrapping while he claws at me.

An ancient memory stirs, rippling through me and propelling me forward.

The mask slips over my eyes and I can't see properly but eventually he stops moving. He's not a big man, around five foot five maybe, whereas I'm nearly six foot. But he was stronger than expected and I worry I've left bruises.

*It must look like an accident.*

As I drag him, unconscious, into the kitchen diner, I tell myself that runners fall over and bruise themselves all the time. I don't know how long Michael will stay unconscious, but I wrestle his dead weight backwards into the large coat so it sits like a straitjacket. Then I heave him up into one of the chairs. The sleeves of the old jacket hang loose over his thin arms and I tug them over his hands and tie them tightly at the ends with the wire, twisted behind the chair. No ligature marks, but no escape.

I'm sweating already, my breath ragged. I'm not as fit as I used to be and it shows.

In front of him, the tub of grapes sits ready. I rinse the grapes under the tap – it feels like something he would do and every detail should be plausible.

I'm sweating under my mask and when I walk back over to the table, Michael stirs awake and lurches in fear.

'Who the fuck are you?' he whispers. 'What are you doing here?'

'Shout or scream and I will send your wife the pictures,' I say, my voice low.

'What pictures, what the fuck are you talking about?'

He's shaking so much I fear the wire will loosen.

'The photos. Those poor . . .' I watch the realisation seep across his face like blood in a syringe. I lower my voice to a whisper. 'We're doing the world a favour.'

'You mean porn? I've never, I'm not . . .' He shakes his head, eyes wild. 'They must have put it on my computer.' He gasps for breath like he's underwater. A thought hits him. 'Who is *we*?' he pants. 'It's you, isn't it, that woman?' I don't reply. Sweat pours down his face, his skin is pale grey.

He looks close to fainting. 'Oh god, is this because I lost my job? I never told my bosses who I stole all that stuff for. I don't even fucking know!'

'Lower your voice,' I say. I'm surprised by the stillness that has settled over me, that same ancient calm that has been flowing to the surface unbidden more and more. This is a matter of logistics now. I open his mouth, push a grape inside. 'Chew it,' I say. He complies. 'And another,' I say, nodding with encouragement as I feed him like a child. Then I push the third one in, pushing it as far down his windpipe as I can manage while his teeth gnash at me.

He starts to choke, his chest shaking as he tries to cough, tries to escape, tries to keep hold of the life that is escaping him second by second. I watch his eyes widen, widen until they nearly pop. And then I watch him go limp.

When I'm satisfied that he has gone, I untie the wire, pull off the coat and check his wrists for bruising.

'I didn't say anything about a computer,' I say, as I upload a photograph of him slumped at his table, pack everything back into my carrier bag and leave through the window.

I slide my feet back into my boots and head for home.

# Greg

*Friday, 22 November 2019*

Greg is biting into his last sandwich quarter and playing a game on his phone when he hears the car pull up outside. He rushes to the window and peers out from behind the curtain as two blocky men in dark coats and jeans emerge from a big black car that looks more like a robotic cockroach than a vehicle.

They move slowly but with purpose. Two great meaty tanks rolling at their own speed.

'Lock the doors,' David Ross yells from somewhere nearby. 'And don't make a fucking sound.'

The men slip under the window, out of view, and Greg hears the front door open with a whoosh. It's a heavy thing, chunks of thick wood loaded up with old glass, brass knockers and hinges. It swings shut with a soft thud.

The abandoned bell on the reception desk rings out through the foyer. Greg rushes to the door of his room and twists the brass key as quietly as he can. The room is uncomfortably warm.

A shrill whistle rings out through the silent hotel. Greg imagines dogs barking at it from miles around.

'David Ross!' a new voice shouts, followed by another whistle.

'Come on, cheapskate,' the second voice calls, an amused lilt to it. 'We know you're here.'

*Can these be the people in charge?*

The men sound distant Scouse with a hint of more recent cockney. Like Greg, London has swallowed their original accents, softened and reshaped them.

'Come on, mate, let's be having you.'

They palm the reception bell again, over and over. *Ding, ding, ding.*

*It doesn't ring true that these men are in charge. They act like they're breaking into the situation, not owning it in the first place. So who are they?*

Their voices are more falsetto than you'd expect from such thick throats and sloping backs. Thick muscle plastered over with middle-aged fat. The kind of men Greg would cross the street to avoid. Not the kind of men he would choose to be locked up with in an abandoned hotel.

*If they were running this show, they'd know they were interrupting a delicate operation. And they wouldn't want to risk 'the merchandise'.*

Greg shudders.

The whole building is hushed and he tries to imagine where David Ross is hiding. He worries what stage the surgery is at, activity that can't be so easily hidden. Over the sound of heavy stomping downstairs, Greg imagines Pavel with a scalpel in the air, holding his breath. He tries not to think of Helen opened like a chicken carcass, her body drying in the centrally heated air. Only eighteen and from Eritrea, her eyes hopeful despite everything. She told him that after the operation, when she was better, she would go on the London Eye so she could see the whole city. Until she escaped, she'd seen only slivers of the road in Wood Green where she was worked to the bone.

*How long can they safely pause surgery?*

'David Ross, we know you're here, you daft bastard!'

'Let's get this over with, mate. Unless you're ready to pay up?'

It sounds like the men have split up, one still shouting from downstairs and one heading up to this floor. Greg resists the urge to check his lock again by rattling the door. Instead he squats down and pushes his eye to the mechanism. A solid chunk of brass rivets door to frame. He's safe. He hopes.

A shadow passes by outside the door but then comes back. Footsteps shuffle in the corridor and a fist bangs on the wood, shaking it in its frame. Greg stands still, not risking any movement. He tries to slow his breathing, quieten his heart, swallow the rising bile.

Eventually, the shadow moves along and Greg rushes to the bathroom to throw up.

Some minutes later, the front door swoops open downstairs. From his vantage point in the bathroom, Greg can see just enough through the gap in the blind to make out David Ross legging it across the gravel towards his car. Out of shape but driven by fear, David manages to yank the door open before one of the men is on him.

For such a big man, the thug moves with finesse. A precise form of savagery, more ballet than boxing. The other man catches up and helps to deliver the message. It's over in moments.

As they drive away in their big black car, David Ross – his own car door still optimistically open – sinks to the ground. Even from here, Greg can see the blood running down his face and staining his rugby shirt.

*

'They took my fucking eye,' David manages to cry before passing out on the gravel. Rosie and Greg carry him inside to the foyer and lay him on a banquette where guests would once have sat while waiting to check in.

'He hasn't lost his eye,' Rosie says, her voice terse but her own eyes wild with fear. 'But he could have.'

Greg sits on the floor, resting against the banquette that David is lying on. Rosie rushes upstairs to get supplies but moments later, he hears shouting and follows her up.

The door is open on Helen's room, the noise and mayhem spilling out into the hall. Pavel and Rosie shout incomprehensibly to each other as they try to stem the blood burbling out of Helen's side. 'What the fuck were you doing?' Pavel is saying, his accented words bleeding into each other.

'What nurses do,' Rosie growls. 'David needed help.'

'If she dies, this is on you!'

Rosie presses another gauze down deep into Helen's flesh, muttering, 'So long as the client doesn't, *they* won't care.' Pavel flicks his eyes at the serene lump in the other bed as he elbows Rosie out of the way, attending to Helen as Greg grips the doorframe.

'Is that all that matters?' Pavel says and she looks away.

*

David howls and sobs in another room, his eye patched up by Rosie, who has agreed to drive Greg to the station in David's car.

'I can walk,' Greg says. 'I'd rather you stay with Helen.'

'She's stable,' Rosie says. 'Pavel knows what he's doing.'

223

'And if the client suddenly needs help too?'

Rosie says nothing. David's keys swing from her finger, clicking into each other and ticking like a metronome.

'I'll walk,' Greg says again. She doesn't argue.

He can see it's dark outside. Greg has only a vague idea of how to get to the station and he's going to be hours late. It's particularly shitty timing, with his parents arriving for the weekend tomorrow. He did a bodge job of tidying the flat this morning and he has no hope of getting home before his wife and no phone reception to warn her.

'Your girl has had surgery before,' Rosie says, as he packs up his things. Greg stops what he's doing. 'Bad surgery. Not in a hospital, I'd say. Not even one like . . .'

He turns to face her as she gestures to the room.

'Oh Jesus! The same surgery? She didn't say anything—'

'No, not the same and we were still able to . . .' She trails off. 'But it was a mess in there. Poor girl had been butchered.'

'Fuck. Will she be OK?'

'She'll live but . . . I don't know. She should live.'

He follows the lane back to the village, using his phone as a torch. Thoughts of poor butchered Helen mingle with hazy memories of being her age. Of camping, roaming with a pack, making dens by torch light. Thoughts of her young body, already half-wrecked, mix with nostalgia for his own youth. Drinking regretful amounts of Buckfast Tonic with his mates, underage. Thoughts of home. The home of his bones, not the home of his flesh.

Eventually, gritty feet rubbing against his trainers, one sleeve torn by eager brambles, he reaches the village. Friday night and a slow snake of traffic chugs along the A-road that runs through here, scoring the top of the cricket pitch. Parents returning home with fish and chips; husbands and wives shutting the door for the night, sealing themselves into each other's safety. All anyone really wants is a home.

He thinks of Marianne and checks his phone. Just one bar of reception and still no 3G.

He thinks of Helen, her dreams to see their cruel city. Her hopes for a good life, despite everything that's already been taken from her. Will she see adulthood proper? *What has he done to her?*

A little bus is at a standstill in the traffic. He runs for it and knocks on the door. The driver opens it with a friendly smile. Everything is different out in the sticks.

'Where are you headed?' Greg asks the driver, a moustachioed man in a rumpled jumper.

'Redhill, son.'

'That's got a mainline station, right?'

'It certainly does,' the driver says in mock Scots, eyes twinkling.

\*

Greg brings home fish and chips. Curry sauce, mushy peas, pickled eggs, all of it. A warm package, carefully wrapped, and carried in a thin plastic bag. It's all he could think of, all he could do. Just for a moment to be like those couples in the village, with their normal lives and fish suppers.

When he opens up, Marianne is working at the table.

'Oh, Greg, I was getting worried,' she says, her eyes crinkling as she stands up to hug him.

'I'm sorry,' he says. 'I don't ever want to worry you. My phone died.'

'Good day at work, though?' she asks.

He shakes his head. 'I'm just glad to be home.'

Later, as she sleeps, belly full of fish and chips, knees tucked up to the side like a baby, he slides back out of the bed and heads to the living room. Every time he closes his eyes, he sees the red flesh of David's eye socket. Imagines the scarred meat of Helen's young torso. Imagines his own eye, Marianne's side.

A message waits.

*This can't happen again. You need to get a full medical history from them going forward.*

'It was a very close shave. Surely we don't need to keep doing this? There must be better ways for you to make money! I'll pay for the information about the women, like I did the first time!'

*This isn't about money. And I decide when this is over. Information on approximately ten women will follow.*

\*

### Saturday, 23 November 2019

Every time he falls asleep, Greg's back in the Bluebell. In these dreams, though, it's him being chased. By those men; by Helen, gushing blood; by David, his eye missing. And then by Marianne, running frantically through the building, trying to make sense of it all as he weeps and runs away from her because he has no answers.

He gives up on sleep before dawn and cleans the flat as quietly as he can, airing out the spare duvet and even polishing the bookshelves with some moist toilet paper they bought on special offer.

His parents' flight is due to land at 9.30 a.m. but they'll have been up since dawn, catching a plane first to Amsterdam and then back over to London City. Tracing an elbow in the sky. It's one of his dad's greatest pleasures, masterminding the perfect flight path for minimum cost. It's not about the money, of which they discreetly have plenty; it's the sport of it, the logistics. 'He'd have me out to Dubai and back if it saved a tenner,' his mum likes to say.

It's still only 7.30 a.m. but Greg's itchy, crackling with energy. Fear, he realises, it's fear. He leaves Marianne sleeping and pulls on his coat and trainers.

Hackney is just waking up. The early sun a lazy eye blinking into the sky, warm yellow at its fringes. By the time Greg has walked through Victoria Park and down into Globe Town, day has finally broken. He heads towards Canary Wharf, with its great silverfish skyscrapers. Hundreds of windows blending into scales through his tired eyes. Behind him Mile End, with its skate park and canal, its big old houses carved into flats. Wherever you are in London, you're always wedged between two worlds.

He wonders how many people from their top-floor offices in Canary Wharf could imagine what is happening to women like Helen or Kenza or Talia, squirrelled away out of view. And what's happening to them is largely down to men like him. However he tries to square it off in his head, he is taking from the girls, using them as a commodity and then never seeing them again. He's tumbled from solution to problem and is sinking further and further away from his original intention. *Is there any way out?* For a moment he imagines himself walking forever, never going back. Maybe it would be better for Marianne and his parents if he just disappeared. Better than them ever knowing the truth.

By the time Greg reaches Canning Town, he's exhausted. He wants to know how Helen is doing, wishing he'd taken Rosie's number or Pavel's. 'Your part's over now,' Pavel told him when he left. 'Put it out of your head.' So much younger than Greg but so sanguine already.

His parents' flight hasn't yet landed when he arrives. He goes to the toilet, sees more signs he was instrumental in getting placed.

**LOOK**
**ASK**
**CALL**

From his pocket he pulls the piece of paper detailing the addresses of more women in need, and goes to the public phone to dial the number from the poster. Hood down over his eyes, face turned from the CCTV camera trained on the handset. The number is staffed by volunteers from a consortium of related charities. The fast turnover ensures he won't have met the woman who picks up. Still he changes his accent, aping Marianne's slight Devon tint as he gives the information he has received. Ten women stuffed in an illegally converted houseboat, a monstrous fire risk and the rest.

He's thanked for his information and hangs up in a hurry. Safer this way, another step removed from him and Hidden Humans. Last time, a colleague remarked on the 'luck' of yet another tip-off.

He throws the piece of paper in the bin, then buys a giant coffee in Costa, eyes trained on the arrivals door. Eventually they bustle through, his dad wheeling a little suitcase – packed with military precision – his mum fussing with her handbag.

'Hello, son,' his dad says, patting his shoulder.

'Her Royal Highness not here?' his mum says, kissing him. *Three days of this*, he thinks.

# Samantha

### *Christmas Day, 2019*

I see Jonathan for the first time since we slept together – a grand description for what was a mad moment in a public park – as he steps carefully over our threshold, carrying presents. Paula follows, holding a tray with tin foil over it. Steve won't be pleased; every year he hosts and every year she brings something to contribute to the meal, knocking his plans out of whack. It's practically a tradition.

I can't meet either of their gazes and push my face to their cheeks one by one, then take the tray from Paula's skinny hands.

'You shouldn't have,' I say, and she squirms. 'But it's so kind of you, thank you.'

'I thought dessert might be better than a starter, as Steve didn't like that last time.' She gives a little laugh that is tinged with embarrassment.

'I want to hear all about New York,' I say, realising we've not had a catch-up since they went. After what happened with Jonathan, I've been happy to avoid her.

'I have photos,' she smiles, tapping her phone screen as she follows me into the kitchen.

I smile apologetically to Steve as I tell him that Paula has kindly brought a dessert. 'Oh, how nice of you,' he says. Behind him, the ceramic bowl sits like a cartoon bomb. A plum pudding made months ago and lovingly fed with booze every week up until today.

'Where shall I put these?' Jonathan asks, his voice muffled by the pile of presents.

A flash of a memory makes me blush. 'I'll show you,' I say.

Steve is tubby with red-tinted skin, Jonathan is lean and pale, but they share the same strawberry blond hair and blue-green eyes. Looking at Jonathan is like seeing a hall-of-mirrors version of the man I've spent my adult life with. A man who, somehow, has chosen to forgive my cheating. I'm certain that wouldn't be the case if he knew the details.

As I lead Jonathan through to the living room, and the tree I dressed carefully, Joe comes barrelling down the stairs in his socks. I'm relieved not to be alone with Jonathan and I'm sore with disappointment all the same. A toxic mixture.

'Happy birthday, mate!' Jonathan says. Joe smiles, unsure if this is a joke.

'And happy Christmas to you too,' Joe says, finally.

'Christmas!' laughs Jonathan. 'That's what I meant.'

'Let's put these birthday presents by the tree,' I say, trying to keep things light and punctuate the strange swollen feeling that has settled in the living room.

'Is Aunty Paula in the kitchen?' Joe asks and we both nod, dumb with relief.

With Joe out of earshot, I fuss about arranging the presents, my nose and mouth filled with the oppressive smell of fir trees. 'You need to hold it together,' I say quietly. 'I feel guilty too but they're going to guess if you keep this up.'

'It's not guilt,' he says, and I feel his knee brush mine as he bends down to help me. 'I can't stop thinking about you. You drive me wild.'

I stand up and survey my work. 'There now,' I say briskly, before walking out and into the kitchen.

*

In the kitchen, Steve is bright red with effort. Shaking golden potatoes in their tray of goose fat, glazing carrots, checking the huge bird is still tucked snug under its foil blanket. I hand out drinks, bucks fizz for everyone else and orange juice for me. I've not drunk any alcohol for months, never knowing when I'll be called out on a job. Not wanting my tongue loosened by booze.

'What's this?' Jonathan asks, a little too loudly as he points to my drink. 'This won't do.' I grimace at Joe as my glass is topped up from the champagne bottle.

By the time we sit down to eat, my face feels warm and fuzzy.

Jonathan and Paula have come to ours every Christmas since I came on to the scene. Steve was adamant that we would host – he wanted to cook – and I was glad to stay home. I didn't want my son's Christmases dictated by someone else's rituals.

For Paula, this time of year is visibly difficult. I know that she lost her daughter, Heidi, just before Christmas all those years ago. She never discusses it on the actual day, I think out of respect for everyone else's mood and to allow us to be jolly.

As a double kicker, after years of trying for a baby with Jonathan, it was Christmastime when Paula told me they were done. I assume she had started the menopause but I didn't press for details. I look at her now. Her face is more gaunt than the last time I saw her, but she is smiling at something Steve is saying. Always putting on a brave face, prioritising other people's feelings. I'm caught in a gust of pity for her.

I slip next to Joe and rest my head on his shoulder. As he always does, he wraps his arm around me. Everything has always been so effortless between us, the love so absolute. I dare not look at Paula.

The conversation has turned to politics and Steve is in full flow. It's a well-worn speech about his degree from the university of life. His hands splayed on the table for emphasis like thick pink tarantulas.

I feel a sudden prod between my legs and jolt upwards.

I shake my head as clearly as I can at Jonathan, who has extended his leg between mine. He makes a mock sad face but moves his foot. We agreed this could never happen again, I want to remind him, but he's not playing fair. I gulp down more wine.

After dinner, we sit in the living room and open presents. I offer to make coffee, 'or something stronger', and find Jonathan trailing out after me. I fill the coffee machine with water, change the filter and pour in the beans. He steps closer, still saying nothing. He's drunk, swaying, the same look in his eye that he had in the park: hunger.

'I know you're a bad girl,' he murmurs into my hair.

'Can you get the cups, please?' I say, but instead I feel a hand on my bottom.

'You should be my bad girl again,' he says and I freeze. I breathe in, closing my eyes, as he pushes his crotch into the back of me. I exhale and feel him growing harder as I close up the coffee machine and switch it on.

'I can't do this to Paula,' I say, closing my eyes and summoning up all my willpower. The machine grinds and shrieks as hot black coffee fills the cups.

'I want to see those pictures of New York!' I call into the other room, pointedly.

*

After a supper of leftovers, pickles and cheese, and yet more wine, we all head to our rooms, swaying a little. I scroll through the news sites to see if they've reported on Michael Sutherland's death. But it's just another unfortunate accident and nothing comes up, even on the local Kent news sites. More habit than expectation on Christmas Day, I also check the app.

*One new message.*

For an idiotic moment, I wonder if it will contain season's greetings. It absolutely does not.

I've been given another name, another address, another challenge. The message was sent hours ago and I'm surprised by the slight smile that twitches on my lips as I open it.

Joe is tucked away in his room, his television babbling. In the next room to me, Steve snores loudly enough to rattle the roof struts.

I hear the floorboard outside my room groan just a little and set my phone in its charger as the door handle turns. Jonathan walks in carrying two glasses of red wine, a little unsteady on his feet. I hold my breath as the blood red liquid threatens to spill.

'What are you doing?' I whisper, shutting the door behind him. We have no locks on our bedrooms, have never had any need for them. 'What about Paula?'

He hands me a glass, which I gulp as he appraises me. I'm wearing the red satin pyjamas that Paula bought me for Christmas. They still have the folds from being packaged and wrapped.

'Paula's knocked herself out for the night,' he says, sitting next to me on the bed in his own new Christmas pyjamas. 'Sleeping tablets' – he shrugs at my confused face – 'what would we do without them?'

Before I have a chance to reply, he's taken the glass gently from my hand and pushed me back onto the bed.

# Greg

*Christmas Day, 2019*

'You could have gone up to Scotland,' Marianne tells him, pushing her thumb into the hollow of a satsuma and slowly peeling back its skin.

'What, leave you alone at Christmas, hen?'

And she would have been alone. No dad, a mum she finds hard work at the best of times. And it's not like friends would invite her; there's no one she's close to since Jane moved away and most of her old school friends have young kids now. And if she was alone, maybe she would start to pull at the threads. She's noticed his moods, his stress; of course she has. He catches her frowning at him sometimes, like he's a crossword she's trying to solve. They're barely having sex, that's new. And it's harder and harder to keep a lid on the anger bubbling in his guts all night and all day. Anger at 'them', those people running him into the ground; and anger at himself, for falling into their web.

'It was your choice, Greg. I'm not taking the blame.'

OK, so he's not the only one bubbling with anger. He stares at her, unsure how to proceed. An argument on Christmas Day; well, that would be high stakes. An elevated risk. She stares back, then does a little laugh that is anything but light-hearted and pops an orange segment into her mouth.

'It's no one's fault,' he says, trying to sound gentle. *Normal.* 'I love you and I always want to be with you. I'm just a bit sad, is all.'

'It is *someone's* fault,' Marianne mutters.

With hundreds of miles and a country border between them, the chilly relationship between wife and mother-in-law can generally be ignored. So when it rises to the fore like this, it trips him up. It was easy with Jenna, his mum knew her mum, they all grew up together and – this was the kicker – Jenna wanted to stay in Scotland.

It wasn't Marianne's fault that Greg didn't want to come 'home' permanently, however much he loved visiting. But it was less painful for his mum to blame Marianne than to accept that her son, the love of her life as she would tell *anyone*, wasn't coming back to her out of choice.

His parents' last visit here had been a wash. His mum niggling his wife about anything and everything, turning up the Scots so Marianne had to ask her to repeat what she was saying. And Marianne was patient too, she always tried her best but it was stilted and awkward nonetheless.

'Little English queen,' his mum called her, not quite under her breath.

'Wee Scottish cunt,' Marianne had texted him while standing in the same room, and he'd laughed despite himself. Even against his lovely mum, he liked it best when he and Marianne were in on the same joke.

They're both in their pyjamas still, presents unwrapped, turkey joint for two waiting to go in the oven. Another Christmas bottle from his dad. Greg's playing his Rat Pack Christmas vinyl on his little record player, something that started as an irony, back when they still celebrated Christmas the weekend before and then went to their respective 'homes' – and which then became a tradition. He thinks she likes it too, but he doesn't dare ask now.

He pictures his parents on their own, his dad loading the fire with logs and his mum awaiting the arrival of her widowed sister, his Aunt Audrey. He bites his croissant but can taste the morning roll 'doubler' that he's missing. 'Tattie scone wi' square sausage and brown sauce,' he can hear his mum explaining to a confused Marianne on their first visit, years ago.

'It's just . . .' He exhales. 'I don't know. It feels a bit sad when it's just the two of us,' he says. Then realises his mistake.

*

As a child, when he'd imagined himself as an adult, he'd imagined himself as a father. Didn't everyone? He and Jenna had even had a scare, the summer before university when they were still kids themselves. And hadn't he felt something drop, a little melancholy clang in his heart when it turned out to be a false alarm? However absurd an idea it would have been.

But the older he got, the more he learnt of the world, the more clear it was to him that having a child was obscenely selfish. There are already too many children suffering, too many families breaking apart. And the world wasn't equipped for this many people eating away at its resources. Just the other day, he was reading about the projected numbers of climate-change refugees on the horizon. And how many of them would fall prey to traffickers? It was all connected and it was all bad. He thought Marianne understood but in recent months she'd started dropping hints. Hints he tried to ignore until she came out and said it. 'I want us to at least talk about whether we could consider starting a family,' she'd said the other night in bed.

'I can't do this now,' he'd said, hiding in the bathroom until he was sure she was asleep.

'You always said you felt the same,' he says now.

'I was barely out of university,' she says, as she always does. 'I didn't know I was condemning myself for life.'

'Condemning?' The word stings him. He knows she wants a conversation about this, but the idea that their life together as a twosome is a prison sentence feels like a cold knife in his back.

'I like it just being us,' he says, trying to keep his voice level. 'Aren't we enough?'

'That's not fair, Greg. Wanting children isn't the same as not wanting you. Other people have both without being made to feel guilty about it.'

'So you're outright saying you want to have children now?' he asks. She's never been this overt before and he wonders if it's just seasonal exaggeration or something deeper.

She says nothing for a moment, picks at a little hole in her pyjamas. He meant to buy her new ones for Christmas. Wanted to do a lot of things. 'I'm saying,' she starts, her eyes filling with tears so he has to repress the urge to reach for her. 'I'm just saying that I'd like to be able to at least talk about it without you shutting me down. That's all.'

'But you told me you didn't want children and I believed you.'

'I wasn't lying,' she cries, exasperated. 'I was just really young!'

'So I can't trust anything you said back then,' he says, knowing he's being an arsehole but bolted onto this track now. 'If you can just throw your hands up and say, "I was younger then so it didn't count."' He's being blunt but this isn't fair of her; if he'd said he wanted kids then refused to have them, she would be devastated. Why is it OK this way round?

She opens her mouth to argue but he presses on, trying to make her see his point of view. 'You were younger when we got married,' he pleads. 'You were younger when we said "forever". Younger when we said "I love you". Younger when you said you'd be faithful to me and *only me*.' He thinks of the postcards and doubles down. 'You can't pick and choose when to tell the truth and when to—'

'Lie?' she shouts. 'You accuse me of lying because I don't want to give up on a chance to have a child with my husband?'

He shakes his head slowly, allowing even more disappointment to leak out.

'It doesn't make me a liar not to realise that *everything I said*, in our earliest *fucking days*, was written in stone and never to be revisited! This isn't fucking fair, Greg! I just want a conversation!'

'Life isn't fair, Marianne. Life isn't fucking fair. What kind of cunt wants to bring a child into this shitty, unfair, fucking world?' He steps towards her and she sags, deflated. 'Not. Fucking. Me. That's who.' He jabs his own chest so it hurts. 'And if you don't like it, go an' ask your wee boyfriend to knock you up.'

'Go fuck yourself,' she spits. 'And merry fucking Christmas.'

She slams the door to their bedroom and he hears her body hit the bed. He pictures the warmth of it. The insides of it. Red blood leaking around a scalpel incision, soaking into their sheets. He thinks of Kenza, Talia, Helen, all the others. He thinks of the clients sleeping peacefully, relief settling on their faces, a stay of execution for Christmas even if their bank balances are drained. He thinks of every pair of eyes that have stared back at him over the chipped meeting table at work. He thinks of Ana. Of Marija. Of the thirteen thousand question marks still out there. He thinks of his wife, smiling coyly at her collection of postcards. Big picture, little picture, it's none of it nice to look at.

He stares at the closed bedroom door as the alarm sounds for him to get the turkey into the oven.

Yes, only a cruel bastard would bring a child into this.

# Samantha

### Friday, 31 January 2020

I woke up late and alone on Boxing Day, a furious hangover ricocheting through me. The feeling of stupidity and reckless-ness followed me for weeks, but I've not seen Jonathan since. I haven't heard from him either. They cancelled dinner plans with us last month and the relief was palpable. Whether through his own shame or something else, he seems to want to leave our indiscretions in the past. Since then, I've been focused on my own body rather than his.

'You're looking really good, Mum,' Joe says as I stroll into the kitchen wearing my gym stuff. I'm heading to an early class this morning.

'Thank you, love,' I say quietly. I don't want Steve to hear and investigate. He hasn't asked me any more about my 'affair', and hasn't mentioned the speeding ticket again, but I don't want to ram it in his face either. If he thinks I'm getting in shape for someone else, he'd clearly rather not know.

I wonder how long he imagines us remaining in this limbo now. How far his patience will stretch. Joe was so tiny when we first adopted these roles that decades were the same as forever, but now our son is nearly an adult.

I've gone to the gym a couple of times a week for years but it's always been half-hearted. I've sat in the sauna more than I've lifted any weights. But now I need my body to be ready for anything. I'm not getting in shape for a man, I'm getting in shape for my own protection.

Joe is excited by my new interest in fitness, asking me about weights and running, about the new gym I've joined and why that one over the old one. Have I tried kettlebells? What about spinning? This is his area – I think he'd much rather be a personal trainer than the doctor he's being groomed to be – and it's lovely to be able to pick his brain and, let's be honest, bask in the praise.

Lifting Michael Sutherland nearly wrenched my back out and I've had to run from situations several times now, barely able to see straight for the exertion. My new intense workouts – replacing the mornings I used to spend at the charity – are another way to build my armour. But as far as Steve knows, I'm still being 'mugged' for my time by the kind and horribly paid staff at the animal charity.

I told Alice before Christmas that I wouldn't be back in the new year. I blamed fatigue, the constant onslaught of sadness bleeding into my life in ways that I was struggling to conquer. It wasn't a lie, it just wasn't the only truth – and either way, it didn't matter. She hugged me and thanked me for the years. I drank in the smell of her fabric conditioner and probably stayed in the hug too long. She wouldn't touch me if she knew the full truth.

It's a convenience that Steve doesn't know where I am each day. More than a convenience, it's something of a thrill.

'I feel stronger than I've ever felt,' I tell Joe, as he pretends to arm wrestle me.

\*

## Monday, 3 February 2020

Today's target, Andrew Mackintosh, is shorter than me. The overalls the DIY store has given him trail like pyjamas, two sizes too big. He's loading planks of wood onto a trolley, slow and methodical. It's unfathomable that he was once a trusted professional. He's not like a man at all, wrinkling his nose and shoving his misshapen wire glasses back up it. More like a mole. Something that chews its way through soil in the dark.

His eyes are shadows. I dare not look at them. As if they have sucked in all the light of everything they shouldn't have seen. I don't want it reflected back at me.

In my trolley, I have a small bathroom mirror, discounted by 35 per cent. I've picked up a few house plants and a limp tomato plant that I intend to nurse back to life. Steve would like that, home-grown tomatoes.

In my pocket, wrapped carefully, I have a burner phone pre-loaded with everything Andrew Mackintosh needs. I am simply a courier today.

'Can you help me, please?'

I tower over him and he looks up, annoyed.

'With what?'

I visibly bristle, as if astonished by his insolence. Me, a customer, being treated like *that*. 'Well,' I say, a little shrill. 'There's no need for that tone. Is your manager here?' I look around, hand on my chest. Distressed.

He sighs. 'What can I do for you, madam?'

I have, of course, already worked out the CCTV black spot. It hangs over a very specific section of the nail and screw pick 'n' mix. Too low value to be worth the effort. 'Nine millimetre slotted screws,' he mumbles after leading me there, then makes to leave the aisle. I catch his wrist with my hand, hard. Snapping onto him like the jaws of life.

'Ow,' he says, but quietly. Funny how guilty people react so differently. 'What do you want?'

I press the phone into the pocket of his overalls and step back fast. He smells of talc, taking me back to Joe's toddler bathtimes in a flash. It sharpens my senses and for a moment, I wish I was here to get rid of this nasty little man rather than recruit him.

'What's this?' he shoves the glasses back up his nose and goes to take the phone out.

'Not here,' I say quietly, fingering a tub of screws idly in case anyone were to look. 'Go to the staff toilets, turn it on and go to the Whispa app. There's a message waiting for you.'

'What the hell is that? Do I need a password? How do I—'

'Have you used a mobile phone before?' I hiss, running out of patience with this idiot.

He shakes his head. 'Never risked it,' he says. I don't need to ask what he means. God, I wish I was here to kill him.

I snatch the phone out of the pocket again, look around to check no one is looking, and then switch it on. I'm wearing slim leather driving gloves and it's a brisk temperature in here but I still feel uneasy, *noticeable*.

'There,' I say, handing it back. 'Go to the toilet and read that. You'll receive the next instructions soon.'

'Instructions?' he says, shoving his glasses again, wrinkling his nose. But I don't reply. When I look back, he is reading the screen intently, his face the colour of alabaster emulsion.

# Greg

*Friday, 27 March 2020*

For the last few times, there has been a new man working at the Bluebell. Rosie is openly repulsed by him and the feeling seems to be mutual. He's an anaesthetist, brought in after the drama with Helen to better prepare the patients and as an extra pair of hands, should something happen. Not that he seems particularly dynamic or helpful.

David Ross has finally taken off his eye-patch. 'So fucking pretentious,' Rosie said when she saw he was still wearing it weeks after the incident. 'He needed it for two or three days, tops. What a wanker.' Greg wishes he'd put it back on, the glossy scar turning his stomach.

Rosie sits on the end of the double bed in Greg's 'waiting room', tipping the last crumbs of crisps into her mouth.

'Really getting in there,' Greg says. 'Look at her feast.'

She smiles. A slash across her grey face, her exhausted, lined eyes coming to life.

'Does your pal not want to join us?' he says, biting his sandwich.

'My pal?' She runs her tongue over her teeth to dislodge the wet crumbs and takes a swig of Diet Coke.

'That anaesthetist guy, Andrew,' Greg prompts.

'He's no pal of mine,' she says.

'So what's the deal?'

'You don't want to know.'

'I—'

'Mate,' she says, her voice brittle, 'you do not want to know.' Greg stares back, takes another bite of his sandwich and another. Holding out on conversation until Rosie tells him all about Andrew anyway. Then he wishes he'd paid heed to her warning.

She didn't work directly with him, they were at different hospitals, with different procedures. But she'd heard of him, even before the inquiry. Other colleagues had worked at the same children's hospital where his reputation preceded him and outlasted him. 'Wasn't he sentenced?'

'What, by the police?' she asks, shaking her head. 'Kangaroo court. Fucking shameful.'

'So he's doing this for money, then?'

'You make it sound like any of this is a choice,' Rosie laughs. 'Whatever he's here for, someone – *the big bad you-know-who* – has made it so this is the best of a bad set of options.'

'Is that what happened to you?'

She stares at him, weighing him up. Finally, she nods.

'Stupid really. The whole fucking thing.' She laughs but there's no warmth to it. He follows her as she walks to the window and opens it. 'Mind if I . . .?' She is already making a thin roll-up with a pinch of tobacco from a pouch of Amber Leaf. He shakes his head, considers asking for one but she's nearly out. They lean outside and she taps the little curls of ash onto the windowsill. She's burnt halfway down the cigarette before she speaks again.

'Knackered,' she sniffs. 'I was always knackered. After a shift I'd try to sleep but I'd just lay there. Hours and hours. The nightshifts were worse, trying to fall asleep in the day while the little kids upstairs shrieked and banged their toys on the floor.' She smiles and shrugs. 'It wasn't their fault.'

He says nothing. David Ross had told him she had a drug problem but somehow he thinks it would be worse for her if he cut to the chase.

'I'm a fucking cliché.' She waves her hand in the air and flecks of ash fall onto the carpet. She crushes them with her trainer. 'I started using something to help me sleep. And then something to help wake me up. And it snowballed as it always does. Started buying it from a lad in the pharmacy, but I couldn't afford too many from him. So I started skimming pills as well, just one at a time. From . . .' She exhales and flicks her butt out of the window, closing it with a slam.

'From patients?'

She nods.

'Fuck knows how they knew any of this. They had photos of me buying. I had this funny feeling someone was following me and I ignored it. Stupidly. Then this woman collared me at work, told me they'd send them to my boss if I didn't turn up for "training".'

'You believed her?'

'I believed that my bosses would have had to take it seriously if they did. And I'd have been fucked with a blood test. Some of the stuff . . . it can only come from a few places. Anyway, I was *summoned* for training. Told I could do this once a month and they'd get me the drugs and keep my secrets. "Win–win," they said.'

'Sounds familiar. So who was the woman? Is she the one in charge of this?' He's embarrassed to admit he assumed it was all men at the top. For all his modern-man attempts, he still sees doctors as men, nurses as women. Dogs are boys and cats are girls. Jesus, he's tired.

'I don't know who she was.' Rosie shrugs. 'She seemed nervous. She was like, cagey, I guess. I don't know. She had me bang to rights, and I was right there in my work canteen, I just had to listen.'

'So who *do* you think is in charge of all this?' Greg asks, keeping his voice low.

'I don't know. There's a bloke that comes sometimes, never gets involved with the operations but checks everything is in order. Tall guy, good-looking but knows it.'

'He's the boss?'

'One of them. He always says "we" so he's not the only one.' She yawns and stretches, rubs her eyes and flashes a big fake smile. 'Anyway, best get back to it! You can tell me your sob story next time.'

Greg gets in after Marianne but she doesn't question why he's late. She's at the table, staring intensely at her laptop, a glass of wine by her side.

'Working hard, hen?' he says, kissing her on the forehead as he dumps down his bag, flicking his eyes to the screen. She angles it to show him that she's looking at flights.

'If we don't book something soon, we won't be able to afford much more than a week in Weymouth.'

'Nothing wrong with the Great British Seaside,' he says. Panic starts to chew at him – what the hell would a scheduling conflict mean for either his marriage or, well, still his marriage, but also his personal safety and freedom and everything he holds dear?

'I grew up by the Great British Seaside, remember, and it's a pile of wank.'

He's always liked her acerbity when it's not pointed at him. 'My prickly little pear,' he says, trying to focus on the present and quell the panic. He runs his hand over her shoulder and down to her T-shirt, softened by years of washing. 'My braless prickly pear,' he says and she laughs, twisting her chest away from him.

'How long did it take for that bad boy to come off?'

'I was literally walking up the stairs,' she says. 'I had my work blouse over my head before I hit the bedroom.'

These moments of shorthand in their scruffy sanctum. Why can't it always be like this? Just the two of them, no operations, no postcards, no baby chat.

'Let's have some dinner and book a holiday, then,' he says, as cheerily as he can muster.

She sighs and closes her eyes. 'Two weeks in the sunshine with my favourite.'

He basks in the warmth of her smile and hopes against hope that he's given himself enough time to pre-warn 'them'.

In the kitchen, getting the dinner stuff ready, it hits him. He stands with the fridge door open, his frozen face illuminated like studio lights. He hadn't thought. Fuck, he just hadn't thought!

Too fixed on the now to consider any thens. But he's been using his annual leave to accompany girls to the Bluebell, so will he have enough left to take the two weeks they've been dreaming about? He doesn't get a lot to begin with, and he's been taking a day off once a month, at least. How the hell can he explain to Marianne where it's gone?

The fridge alarm cuts into his thoughts and he slams it shut, trying to think carefully.

How many have there been? He counts them on his fingers, each one fading from a story and a complexity to just a name and then, ultimately, just a number . . .

So this is how it happens.

# Samantha

*Thursday, 4 June 2020*

The company director I've been investigating works out of a 'shared space' in South West London. The outside of the building still has old signage from when it was a bus garage, the swirling letters and old four-digit phone number faded into the tight red bricks. The inside of the building, from what I have seen, is a riot of primary colours and oversized spongy furniture. Like a children's day-care centre.

There's no security as such, no guards or key entry system but there's a clutch of CCTV cameras all around, shiny little pimples on every building. But it's OK, I don't need to go in.

It's been a while since I've done one of these and I'm more adept at it than when I first studiously followed that nurse, months back. This time, I learn to anticipate the movements so I'm in the juice bar before he is; I'm on the bus that he's waiting to join.

He's not rigid but his movements form the same loose pattern each day. Two cigarette breaks in the morning, pacing under the old-fashioned bus shelter that is now a smokers' huddle. Mid-morning, one of his co-workers will join him in a 'break-out room' off the main workspace. It's on the third floor so they close the door but think nothing of the window.

He uses the on-site gym while his employees work through lunch. A meal is generally brought to him on the back of a Deliveroo bike. Another two cigarette breaks, then home, still clutching his promotional headpiece.

I've also seen his employees file out, staring at their phones and following them zombie-fashion as they make their ways to the allocated scooters they've reserved. Presumably it's a perk of the job, free credit, but you wouldn't get me on one of those, not in London traffic. I see he feels the same.

He lives in a new-build, three-bedroom house in Streatham with his partner and two children. The small cul-de-sac sits on the Wandsworth border, its back turned away from the solid little council houses that pepper the rest of his road. Most days, he would be walking into tea time. But on Thursdays, the older child has gymnastics and the house will be empty for another hour.

Inside, their home is brilliant white. His partner must be in a state of constant anxiety over dirt. I wonder whose choice the colour scheme was but I have an idea.

'Rachel didn't tell you I was coming, did she?' I say, conspiratorially. He smiles then too and shakes his head in a coy and practised way. He's a handsome man and arrogant with it. 'No, sorry. To be honest, I have no idea who you are.'

'It's fine,' I laugh. So handy, the British allergy to rudeness. As soon as he'd opened the door to me and I'd smiled, 'Hi!' and shaken his hand and stepped inside, he was sunk.

'It's no problem, she was wrestling Annie when we spoke and I bet she just forgot to put it in her diary or something. Shall I come back another time?'

He frowns, unsure what to do.

'I know you're having a really hard time with Polly's sleep and I've got quite a lot of people waiting for appointments, but—'

'No, it's fine. Let's do this first meeting together and she'll be here next time. I'll make sure of it.'

'Would it be worth calling her, perhaps? It was Rachel who arranged the sleep training after all.'

He shakes his head. 'They have to put their phones in the locker at gymnastics, I can never get hold of her.'

*I know.*

Rachel told me all about it when I befriended her in the café. She'd looked exhausted, struggling to strap the youngest into a highchair. I bought her a flat white and a slice of cake and that was all it took. She spilt everything in one whoosh, like a split bag of sugar. So desperate for someone to finally listen. He doesn't deserve her. But I'm not in a position to judge.

We walk through the house as he talks through the toddler's bedtime routine. 'It all just clicked into place with Annie but Polly . . .' He throws his hands up in the air.

'They're all so different,' I say. 'And I bet you love how spirited she is.'

He says nothing. Polly is a raging handful, I saw that for myself. Joe was never that way, always compliant. I know from my mother that I was not. There was a reason I was an only child. I was more like Polly, spoiling for a fight. It was my father who channelled that into something useful. Something essential.

'Can I see her bedroom? Do they share or . . .'

'They have their own rooms. She's got the littlest one as she's—'

'The littlest one,' I say, smiling.

We're inside the small room when I pat my pocket and then rifle in my bag as if remembering something. The room is small but tidy, with POLLY stencilled on the wall, and what looks like a home-knitted blanket on the back of a rocking chair. I think of Joe's, knitted by his grandmother just before she died. He sees me admiring and says, 'Cath Kidston, I think.'

I tug out the envelope and hand it over, smiling. He takes it, assuming it's an agreement for services or some more information.

'I . . . I don't understand.' He's holding the contents without properly looking at it. He doesn't need to, he knows what's in the photographs. He was there.

My voice hardens, my scalp prickling under the heavy wig. 'Tomorrow, you're going to receive an offer for your majority share in Buzz.'

'What?'

'It'll be a fair offer, considering.' I wait for the realisation to sweep his face. 'And you'll accept it. Won't you?'

I tease one particularly incriminating photograph from the set that flops in his hand. I study it and shake my head. 'You'd risk all this?' I say, looking around. 'For a fling.'

'You don't understand, it's been – I mean – we've not been getting on. Polly won't ever fucking sleep, Rach is always angry, I'm—'

'I don't need your excuses,' I say, cutting him off. I know how differently Rachel would tell this story. 'You will receive an offer . . .'

'What offer?' he says, incredulous.

'An offer from an agent working on behalf of a private buyer. You will accept. You will be allowed to stay on and run the company, provided you hit certain targets. Understand?'

'Who are you?'

'I said, do you understand?'

He stares, looks at his daughter's cot and the mobile hanging over it – little white rabbits, twirling slightly in the air's movement. Then he nods, just once.

'Because it should be quite clear what will happen if you don't accept.'

*

I get home and kick off my shoes. My hair is mussed from the wig and no amount of brushing will fix it. I need a bath and hair wash. Good for nothing besides that hot flannel on my face, the door locked, my body swallowed by bubbles.

'You look tired,' Steve says as I walk into the kitchen.

'Sorry,' I say.

I hang up my coat and hover in the kitchen doorway as he pours me a gin and tonic. He's not asked if I want one. I roll my shoulders back; tension has clamped them up high. Steve has given me a tall measure. Ice, sprig of rosemary, slice of lemon, not much tonic. The glass is slick with condensation and it slips from my grasp. I catch it just before it falls.

'That was close,' I say, as I follow him into the lounge and sit in the armchair.

'Nervous about something, love?'

'No,' I say. 'No, I'm not.' I haven't been nervous in months. Exhilarated, yes. Propelled with adrenaline, definitely. Disgusted with myself, frequently.

It was always there, the ability to do this work. My father saw it and sharpened it into an arrow. I think he knew long before the others that he and many other men from our region would be taken. That it would fall to the strongest of those left behind to defend the other women and children when the soldiers came.

And he and the other men *were* taken and it *was* left to the rest of us to defend ourselves. And afterwards, after I came here and created this new life out of the dust and dirt of the old one, that invisible arrow was still held in my hand, still razor sharp but with nowhere to shoot it.

I didn't ask for this work. I didn't want this work. But I'm very good at it. So no, I'm not nervous.

'I don't believe you.' He sits down on the sofa opposite me and takes a long sip from his own glass. When he looks up, he has tears in his eyes.

'You're still lying to me, aren't you?'

# Greg

*Wednesday, 3 June 2020*

The mice are back. Greg hears them at night when sleep eludes him, Marianne lying open-mouthed beside him, oblivious. They've fallen out about them already, their fast-breeding innocence allegories for things the husband and wife can't handle. They seem to be falling out more, the usual harmony they've had for the last however many years has become a slippery thing.

He hears the mice now, running under the floorboards and squirming around the walls. There are babies in there, their shrill squeaks helping to block out his other thoughts but not helping him to sleep. He falls back on a shameful method he's adopted recently, counting the number of women who have had new starts financed by the physical sacrifices at the Bluebell, plus the number of people who have been given new starts through rescue, through tip-offs and enquiries that would not have otherwise happened.

He holds that swelling figure in his guts like a growing baby. He nurses it in these early hours of fitful and dismal sleep.

In the morning, pin-eyed and exhausted, he tries to make light of the infestation. Naming the mice, making a joke of it. They're nibbling into the food but there are too many little bodies to consider hurting them. They've done nothing wrong; everybody has to eat.

After work, Marianne and Greg move the food into different cupboards, put flour and sugar into Tupperware, block the gaps in the skirting and check for trails of droppings.

'I'll check the airing cupboard in case they're nesting there,' he says and she shifts uneasily.

'I'll do that . . .' she starts, but it's too late. His hand finds the box of cigarettes before his eyes understand. When he looks back at her, she crosses her arms but looks away.

'We need to get some poison for these mice,' she says, colour creeping up her neck.

The thought of poisoning them destroys him, far more than her lying about smoking. He can't begin to explain why.

*

### Thursday, 4 June 2020

'Can I have a word, Eloise?' He keeps it light but he's worked here too long and his boss knows Greg too well.

She nods towards the sunshine-yellow meeting room and they slip inside. He tugs on his shirt sleeves, trying to find comfort in the familiar fabric. It's his favourite shirt, one bought for him by Marianne a couple of birthdays ago. It's looser than he remembered.

'I need to take a bit of extra annual leave this year,' he says. She doesn't reply at first but sits back and studies him.

'You still have some leave left, I think?'

'I need to use that too.'

She twists her heavy silver ring and waits for an explanation.

'Marianne is a teacher,' he laughs. It sounds fake. 'You know how it is, she wants to do things in her time off and I, you know, I can't keep up.'

Eloise looks unconvinced. She studies his face for a moment, focuses on his chin – his fast-greying beard – the scraggy mess of his hair. Her gaze is almost maternal as she searches his eyes, the new lines that seem to burrow deeper every day. He looks down.

'This is a tough job, Greg,' she says, eventually, but he can't meet her eye anymore. 'You throw yourself at it, I know that, you all do. And we give you all as much holiday entitlement as we can afford as an organisation but—'

'Please,' he says, looking up. 'It can be unpaid, I don't care. I just need to take the time off I've booked and I need to book another two weeks in the summer.' Eloise is wrong-footed by his outburst, embarrassed by his pleading. She flicks a long lock of hair back over her shoulder as if it's a naughty infant.

'Greg,' she says softly. 'I'm worried about you.' He opens his mouth to protest but doesn't trust what will come out. Instead, he coughs and shakes his head. Willing the threat of tears back into his throat. 'You know you can tell me if anything is worrying you? No judgement.'

Oh, it's so tempting. To just open himself up and pour it all out. All the badness, seeping into the bright yellow room. Letting someone else tell him what to do, punish him even, call the police. Just let it be over. But it's not that simple.

'Mate,' she says, 'what's wrong?'

*I've been responsible for trafficked women getting chopped up in a dirty hotel room. I've been responsible for their injuries. Maybe even deaths. I've lied to you, my parents and my wife. I've found out that I'm the very fucking opposite of the man I thought I was. Every single bit of good I've ever done amounts to nothing. I've fucked everything up and I've no way out.*

'I think my marriage might be in trouble, Eloise,' he says finally. 'I really need this.'

Her shoulders drop but she nods. 'It will have to be unpaid – and don't you dare tell the others.'

'Thank you,' he pants, barely able to speak for the relief. Relief about the holiday and relief that he managed not to tell her anything, even as the truth presses up against his tongue. 'Thank you so much.'

At night, he holds Marianne tightly as she sleeps and he nurses the growing number of girls until it's tattooed into his eyes and he dreams of a great pile of dolls, with him tossing yet more plastic bodies on top. He dreams that the dolls come to life, shrieking like mice until Marianne pours poison in their mouths.

He wakes coated in sweat and shivering, with Marianne staring and shaking his arm. 'You were calling out in your sleep,' she says. 'That must have been one hell of a nightmare.'

All he can do is nod dumbly.

# Samantha

*Thursday, 4 June 2020*

I focus on keeping my glass still and my face passive. 'What do you mean, Steve?' I say. A gentle half-frown, as if I've misheard.

I take a sip of my drink. It's so strong it might as well be paint thinner. 'Mmm,' I say. 'Thank you for this.'

A silent metronome ticks over the scene. Any moment, any second.

'You've not been going to that charity in months,' he says.

I say nothing, the wheels in my head spinning unhelpfully. How does he know? What else does he know?

'You said you'd made a mistake, you said you'd stopped seeing "him", whoever he is.'

'I have,' I say, turning to face him. He stares back, innocent and hurt. 'I know you don't believe me,' I say. 'But I wouldn't take that risk again. I need you, I need this.' I gesture around me. 'And Joe is my family, you and Joe are my family. I just wanted to be touched, that's all, just for a while. We don't, I mean, it's not been like that with us for a while.'

He stares back but doesn't say anything.

'I promise I've not done anything else. Not since I told you.'

'So where have you been going every day then?' he asks, his eyes pleading for me to convince him and stitch this all back together.

Joe's key hits the lock and we both paint on smiles and move closer on the sofa, stage-hands sliding the set back into place for the audience.

When we've greeted Joe, I go upstairs to the bathroom and lock the door. My hands shake so much I drop the SIM three times before I can get it in the tray.

'You need to get me an alibi,' I write.

*You're responsible for your own activities.*

'Not a legal alibi,' I write, hot tears falling. 'My husband is questioning where I've been going while he's at work. If you don't help me come up with a good excuse – and proof – this life I'm protecting will be over anyway.'

I wait. Outside I hear Joe asking where I've gone, his voice rising with concern. I start running the taps and peeling my clothes off.

'Mum?' I see his long shadow peek under the door. My boy. My heart. 'Hi, love,' I say. 'Just about to get in the bath.'

'You OK?' he says, lips pressed to the door.

'I'm fine, I just need a soak. Actually Joe, could you do me a favour and get me a green tea?'

'Of course.' He lingers a little longer until I eventually hear his reluctant steps heading for the kitchen. A message arrives.

*Leave it with us.*

'I need it now. I need proof for whatever story I give him – and fast! I'm hiding in my bloody bathroom!'

*Wait 30 minutes, then check your email inbox.*

\*

My hair is scooped up on my head by a towelling turban. I'm wearing my dressing gown at the table like an in-patient. Steve won't meet my eye and I don't seek his. The unresolved questions sit at dinner with us. We wait for Joe to scrape his plate clean and put it in the dishwasher, then I reach into my pocket.

The printouts are warm and soft from my body heat and I slide them across the table. I was still printing them as he called us down to eat.

'What's this?'

I carefully unfold them and leave most of them in front of Steve, holding the first one up for him to take.

'I know it's hard for you to believe me after what happened.'

The email he's frowning at now is dated three months ago. I don't know how they did it, but I don't question it. The printout confirms my acceptance as something called a Local

Angel, part of some scheme I've never heard of. It may be a completely fabricated concept for all I know. Steve wrinkles his nose but says nothing. He places it down carefully, then leafs through the rest, studying them the way he would a wine list. Each email contains 'tasks' sent for elderly folk or people with disabilities, errands to run, all generated by 'Local Angel HQ' and all of them, quite staggeringly, matching up to days I've actually spent running errands of a different kind. For the first time since all this began, I realise just how detailed the records are that my handlers are keeping. That this is, in a warped way, a sophisticated and well administrated organisation. The thought freezes any misguided gratitude I felt at the fast fix.

'You're an odd-job woman, then,' Steve says, finally. 'That's what you're doing with your time.'

'Yes,' I say.

'Paid? Surely you can't risk it?'

I shake my head. I've certainly made no money from this.

'And you didn't tell me because . . . why?' His voice is softer now, almost guilty. *Please don't feel guilty.*

'I didn't think it would interest you, that's all. How did you know, anyway?'

'Oh, I couldn't get you on your mobile the other day so I called the charity and asked for you.' He shrugs, the moment over, and flicks the television on. 'I don't think you'll be able to carry on doing it, though, at least for a bit. Sorry.'

I follow him into the lounge and he starts to watch a food show that he'll soon be arguing with.

'Dean's left the Leatherhead shop with immediate effect,' he says, without taking his eyes off the screen.

'What?'

'Yeah, he'd been in the till again. I suspected it before, but he got sloppy.'

'Oh god.'

'So I need you to take on some shifts while I'm recruiting.'

'Me?'

He mistakes my concern for lack of confidence and smiles. 'You'll be great, don't worry!'

'How many shifts?' I ask, trying to keep my voice light while my stomach swoops and spins.

'That's not how you brown butter!' he scoffs at the screen.

'I'll just need to tell the, er, the Local Angel people, Steve.' He ignores me and shakes his head again.

'How many shifts, Steve? How many days a week?'

'Oh, I don't know exactly, but most days. It won't be for long.' Fuck.

# Greg

*Friday, 31 July 2020*

Marianne's body is warm when he wakes up. It's early, the light outside still a thick orange, Hackney's mouth quiet for once. Greg stands in the silent kitchen watching a teabag stew until the liquid is thick. He's burnt out, sluggish. He knows he needs to stay alert but his eyes hang with sleep.

He hears her calling and snaps to attention, scooping out the teabag and slopping in the milk. It's lukewarm when he sips. Revolted, he chucks the lot in the sink and starts again.

Marianne is propped on her side on their bed. It's sticky at night now and the morning room stinks of their bodies. She wears a vest and shorts, her breasts falling to the side, her hip at an angle. She looks momentarily broken. A Picasso wife.

'I was thinking,' she smiles and he knows that smile. 'Maybe you should take a sickie today and we spend it in bed?'

The desire to climb back under the covers, crawl up to her, into her, be consumed and consume is so strong his fingers twitch with it. But he shakes his head. 'I can't.'

She lies back down and stares at the ceiling. 'OK.'

'I'm so sorry, it's just such a busy day and—'

'It feels like they're all busy days at the moment, Greg.'

'I know, but this . . .'

'Surely one day won't make a difference?'

He crouches next to the bed, rests his head on her chest. Her skin is tacky in this heat. The smell of her is more familiar than his own scent. More than a smell, a feeling, a . . . Fuck, what's the word? A state, a temperament, *a disposition*? Something like that.

'Greg?'

'Sorry?' He looks up at her, lifts his head from her skin and kisses her, losing himself for a moment.

'So you'll stay off?' she mumbles into his mouth. *Oh god, Marianne, I want to more than anything.*

'I'm sorry,' he says, pulling away. 'I'm really sorry.'

\*

Lina is exhausted. She sags in her seat next to him on the train to Godstone and allows the window to rattle against her cheek bones. She flops the other way and for a moment Greg imagines her resting her head on his shoulder. He imagines how it would feel to provide her that small comfort. It would feel paternal. The way he feels for the mice, the way he felt for the idea of Jenna and his theoretical teenage accident. The way Marianne so wants him to feel, a feeling he fights giving into.

To give Lina that comfort would be so much better, sweeter, more human an offer than the one he made. A small pile of cash in exchange for a vital chunk of her body.

He's careful to alternate the trains that he takes the girls on but has learnt fast how few ticket inspectors there are.

This middle-aged woman with a rigid perm and concerned eyes has seen him with other girls several times. The decision not to make this proposition to men was a conscious one, one of risk assessment and cowardice, but he would look less suspicious if he weren't always with young, frightened women.

An unease wells in his chest as she lingers in the aisle, clipping some college student's ticket but looking over at him and Lina. Greg inches away, widens the gap between them as if they're strangers but the carriage is half empty and they have identical tickets to the same tiny station.

The inspector walks down to them, payment machine clipped to her belt like a gun, eyes still concerned.

'Tickets please.'

Greg hands his over and Lina copies robotically. The inspector checks them, clipping each one in turn but not handing them back, not yet.

'Are you OK, love?' she asks Lina.

The young woman looks up from under her amber hair. Her eyes are exhausted, purple black rings underneath. She's sleeping in a box room with three others, no proper bed, and this is still far better than where she was before. And before that.

The train rattles on, Lina flicks her eyes to Greg and he smiles what he hopes is a natural, encouraging smile. As they surge into a tunnel and the carriage goes grey, Lina finds a smile and nods.

The inspector watches for a moment more, swaying with the movement of the train. Then she hands the tickets back. 'I'll be in the front carriage if you need anything,' she says.

Lina smiles. 'Thank you,' she says in accented but flawless English. 'I'm fine, though.'

Greg is still smiling when the inspector walks away, his jawbone tight.

'Well done,' he says. Lina says nothing. She's danced this dance before.

\*

He's asleep on the bed when it happens. He hadn't even intended to lie down. He had propped himself up deliberately and kept his shoes on but it was no good. Exhausted from months of nightmares and adrenaline spikes, lies and fears, he'd passed out.

Someone is shouting, that's what must have woken him up. It's Pavel, he thinks, and Rosie as well. Pavel is telling Andrew to do something, grab something, fix something, *help*. Greg can't make it out. Everything falls silent. He gets off the bed and walks to the door but doesn't dare go out into the hall. His presence can't possibly help anything, he can only get in the way. Besides, he's scared shitless of what he'll see.

Instead, he just opens the door a crack and listens, hand gripping the handle. He hears Rosie again.

'She's bleeding out!'

He hears Pavel.

'Andrew! I need you to check her heart rate.'

Whatever the mumbled response was from Andrew, Rosie and Pavel are unhappy with it and the yelling continues. Until it doesn't.

Even before they tell him, he knows. David is barking at Pavel and Rosie to wrap her, get rid of her. Greg stares at them all as they fuss over the client who sleeps obliviously on the next bed. Then he grabs his bag and runs out of the hotel as fast as he can.

# Samantha

*Friday, 31 July 2020*

Karen watches me as I ring up a customer's sale. I'm an underling but I'm the boss's 'wife'. For Steve's most trusted lieutenant, our situation poses a paradox. I've tested her over the last six weeks, taking ten minutes extra on breaks and waiting to see if Steve raises it back at home. So far he hasn't.

I've asked him about recruitment, about how long I'll need to do this, but he's been so generous for so long that it seems churlish not to play ball. And I suspect he still doesn't trust me, and with good reason.

Karen asked me a while back if I had trouble with my 'water works', so frequent were my toilet trips. 'Hormones,' I told her, with a mixture of conspiratorial sharing and melancholy designed to shut the conversation down. The longer I wait with no tasks, the edgier I feel. As if something is growing, bulging, just out of shot. Swollen and ready to burst.

Sure enough, as I sit on the loo in our small staff toilet and change the SIMs, there it is. After weeks of no contact and only a few scant errands before that, the growth I feared has burst all over me.

They want me to dispose of a body.

*

I flew down the motorway to get here, false plates rattling, engine screaming. When I got to the hotel, the parcel was waiting outside on the ground. Someone had wrapped it in old potato sacks and tarpaulin. I have to trust that they've done a good job – I don't have the time to check.

I'm not welcomed by anyone. A tall muscular man, who I saw when I first pulled up, turned away almost immediately and I watched his back as he strode fast around the corner of the building and disappeared.

I've already wasted forty-five minutes of my allotted hour for lunch. I think I can wring it out to ninety minutes without Karen saying anything. But it'll still be tight.

My rear seats are down and coated with plastic that I luckily had in my boot from previous errands. On top lies the cargo. I try not to think about what's inside and instead focus on getting rid of it. I spotted somewhere ideal on the way here and pick my way back along country lanes and quiet wood tracks, eventually opening the gate and tucking my car inside away from the road. It takes longer than I'd hope to unload and unwrap the outer layers, and by the time I've shoved it as far into the pile of manure as I can get it, I'm coated in shit. My hair, eyelashes and fingernails are thick with it. The acrid taste so strong in my mouth I think I must have swallowed some.

I stand back to check my work and pay my respects, wiping thick black ooze onto my forehead as I move my hair out of the way. This should work, the smell disguised, the rot hastened. I have left two potato sacks in place, one on the top and one on the bottom. I know from the size that this was an adult. I hope it was a bad person. I can't think of the alternatives. I can't let myself think that this was what would have happened to Cristina. That perhaps this is what happened to my mother.

*Stop. Come back to the present.*

It's as good as it can be but time has bled away from me. I've been gone over an hour and I'm covered in literal shit, which only just covers the ammonia sweats from all the adrenaline. I can't go to the store like this.

I drag some of the plastic wrapping onto my seat and then drive around until I get some reception.

Karen answers crisply.

'It's me, Samantha.'

'Hello.' I picture her crossing her arms, probably wondering how Steve puts up with such a flaky woman.

'I'm really sorry,' I say, in a smaller voice. 'But I'm not going to be able to come back to work today.'

'May I ask why not?'

'I want to tell you but,' I pause. 'It's just . . . I don't want Steve to know.'

'Oh?' she sounds intrigued, which is better than angry. 'I mean, you can trust me.'

'You're so nice,' I say, letting my voice waver just a little. Almost imperceptible, a touch that only another woman would notice. 'I went to the doctor a few weeks back,' I say. 'About my bladder trouble.' I take a deep breath, let out a sigh. 'They booked me for further tests. Just a precaution.' I laugh thinly. 'That's what they said.'

'Oh.'

'Well, I just had the appointment on my lunchbreak and . . .' I can picture her straining with expectation. 'Well, they found something. I mean, they think. I've had some other, well, *symptoms* they called them. I thought it was just my age, just women's stuff, you know?'

'I know, I know.'

'I need more tests. Another scan. They're sending me to a different ward. I just came out to call you, but, Karen, I just really don't want to worry Steve. I mean, it might be nothing but the growth looked pretty big on the screen they showed me.'

'I'm sure it'll be OK,' she coos, a softness to her voice that is usually reserved for elderly customers. 'But you take as long as you need. OK?'

*

I gun it back up the lane to the hotel, the brambles clawing at my wing mirrors. There is only one other car here now – an expensive sports car with mud splattered as high as the tinted windows.

I park as tightly as possible to the back entrance. Outside, I hide behind the fire escape stairs to peel most of my clothes off, shoving the filth-encrusted layers into a carrier bag and throwing the lot into the wheelie bin near the kitchen door. I spot my old shoes on the floor, abandoned here on Jonathan's birthday, and I scoop those into the bin as well. A gust of foul rot escapes as I close the lid. I gag.

I slide out of my boots and rinse them under the outside tap sticking out of the wall. I leave them tucked around the corner, ready to slip back on.

It's sticky with heat but I'm shivering, stepping near-naked up the iron steps. I have fresh clothes in another carrier bag, hanging from one finger through fear of contamination. Any shame or embarrassment I might have felt have been consigned to history. Chased away by adrenaline.

262

I prise the door open and pace down the corridor, eventually finding an open bedroom. Inside, there are signs of life: a crisp packet, abandoned sandwich wrappers, dirty cups. The thick brass key juts out of the lock and I twist it quietly and then press my ear to the door. No one comes but a few doors down from my temporary room, I can hear a flutter of activity. Several voices, a couple of men and a woman talk urgently. I think one of them is the nurse I recruited, Rosie Parsons.

I shower using half-finished miniatures, scrubbing my skin and scalp raw. It takes longer than I'd like to scrape all the shit off and I can still taste it in my throat, along with something darker.

Finally clean, I dry off and dress fast, bringing the towels with me just in case they have traces of DNA on them. As I creep back down the hall, I hear a door open behind me. I don't look back. No one can see my face.

My hair dries loose and tangled in the heat of the afternoon as I head back towards home. Along the way, I dump the towels in a rubbish bin on the village green and am about to pull away when the reception sputters back and the missed calls start to vibrate.

Steve. And Karen.

There's a voicemail from Steve, his voice hoarse. 'You need to come home, now.'

A text message comes through from Karen. 'I'm really sorry, Steve was trying to find you and I didn't know what to say. I'm so sorry – I'm sure he'll understand.'

For a moment, I imagine taking off. Just leaving their calls to ring out forever more until my phone dies. Better yet, crushing my phone under my heel and leaving it in the dirt.

But Joe. Always Joe.

I get halfway home and then pull in to a truck stop to change the plates back. I drive the rest of the way under the speed limit, forcing myself to keep going. Steve will have known immediately that I'd fed Karen a lie. I've not been registered at a GP surgery the whole time he's known me.

*

I see Paula's car parked haphazardly on our drive and pull in behind it. Why would she be here without telling me? Surely if Steve called her in a moment of crisis, she would have at least messaged me. But I remember that I never got back to her to rearrange a postponed brunch and maybe she's a little sore about that.

Maybe something has happened to Jonathan. *Or Joe – and Steve can't face telling me?* God no, it can't be.

I run from the car to the house and as I pass the living-room window, I see Steve with his arms around our sister-in-law. In her hand is one of Steve's violent gin drinks. Joe hovers in the background. Oh, thank god. But what could it be? What has Karen said?

As I step into the house, I hear Paula sob.

# Greg

## *Monday, 17 August 2020*

He scoops their fat little bodies from the pool as Marianne watches from behind her sunglasses. It's hard to tell if she's amused or annoyed. Her book has been abandoned, splayed spine-up next to the generous Aperol Spritz she made herself at eleven in the morning.

He works tirelessly, refusing to stop until every frog is out and safe, but they seem to have a death wish and just keep appearing. If he can just keep doing this, maybe he can stop thinking about Lina. Maybe tonight he will sleep without nightmares about her. Dreams of his hand holding a rusty scalpel as she looks up at him.

He imagines the frogs piling up, yet more bodies. The pain in his chest squeezes the breath out of him until he feels he could collapse at any moment.

'You have a hero complex,' Marianne calls over to him as she rolls onto her stomach.

*

They eat chunks of focaccia for a late lunch, torn with their hands. On the small wooden table by the pool, Greg has laid out bowls of sliced tomatoes, jewelled with salt. They split open a great bulb of burrata and the cream runs down their chins as they eat it. 'I could eat just this forever,' Marianne says, smiling with her face upturned to the sun.

He gropes for something to say. *Let's just stay here! Let's hide in Italy, eating burrata and working as waiting staff and frog rescuers! Let's hide in each other's arms and forget everything that's gone so insanely, surreally, dangerously wrong!*

'Me too,' he says finally, spearing a slice of tomato with his fork and sucking it thoughtfully.

'You're so quiet,' she says gently, putting her own fork down. 'Are you OK?'

'I'm just tired,' he says, shrugging. 'We were so ready for a holiday, weren't we?'

She nods. 'More than any other year, I think. Maybe we're getting old.'

He snorts but sees his reflection in her sunglasses. 'Maybe we are,' he says quietly.

*Lina will never grow old.*

Marianne looks away, taking his greying reflection with her, then points to a tiny brown frog drifting towards the pool filter.

*

Most evenings, they've walked into the nearby town for dinner, still in flip-flops and shorts. The incomparable Italian light softening their features. These walks have generally settled into what he hopes is companionable silence. Taking in the views, enjoying the slow pace, holding hands sometimes. He's watched her face grow more golden, her freckles emerging and her curls gaining a sheen of gold. Italy suits her.

Tonight, though, Marianne has dressed up. She spent hours straightening her wild hair and has painted make-up on. The make-up she brought is designed for her usually pale face and it sits like a mask over her tan. The result is eerie, corpse-like. All he can see is Lina.

In the restaurant, she scrolls through her phone while his brain wheels around, trying to find something, anything, to talk about. Besides Lina, besides that whole deadly mess, he's also worrying about money – he's had to take half this holiday unpaid.

'What are you thinking about?' she asks, finally putting her phone face down next to her cutlery.

*Lina. Death. Guilt. Regret. Fear.*

'The frogs,' he says, too quickly. She frowns and makes to pick her phone back up. *Why is she cross?* He realises too late that he's not complimented her and his regret is all bundled with irritation. *It was her choice to get dressed up, why am I under pressure?*

'You look beaut—' he starts as the waiter arrives with their wine.

'Sagrantino,' the waiter announces with a gentle flourish and continues to tell them about the vineyard, the grape – but not the price – as he pours a little for Greg to try. Ordinarily Greg would gesture for Marianne to test it – it's a bugbear of hers, that old sexist assumption – but tonight he just gulps it back. 'It's good, fine, thanks.'

Marianne frowns and looks back at her screen as the waiter fills their glasses and moves on to another table.

'What are *you* thinking about?' he asks, noticing that she's checking her personal email. She puts the phone back down again, screen to tablecloth, and looks up. In the heat, her eye make-up has run down her cheeks. Coupled with the unnaturally pale face, she resembles a sad clown. A Pierrot staring back at him, tight-lipped.

'I'm thinking about wasted opportunities,' she says.

*

'I'm sorry,' he says in bed, after trying until he's sore. 'But I don't think I can . . .'

She says nothing, no sitcom platitudes or patient smiles. Instead, she extricates herself from his legs, his body, and goes to the bathroom to pee.

Afterwards, Marianne sleeps angrily. He's never known a person able to channel rage while unconscious. Her eyebrows are locked heavily over her eyes, her hands balled up like fists and her teeth rattle in her head like shaking sceptres.

He's losing her, he can feel it. Sand tipping into the bottom of an hourglass, granule by granule so he barely noticed it at first. And he's losing himself too. He already lost Lina. And for all he knows, the others died too. Not straight away but after, in the days or months that followed, living hard lives with battered bodies and no one checking up on them. He imagines the clients with their new leases of life; what do they tell themselves? Do they ever think of the incomplete bodies that have plugged holes in their own?

The number of 'saved people' has swollen and become a monster inside of him. His naivety hangs like a chain around his throat. Who knows what's happened to the people released from his tip-offs? Only a few have come through the doors at Hidden Humans and to chase the details from other agencies would arouse suspicion. How many people has he actually helped and how many lives has he helped fuck up, one way or another? He thinks of the frogs, churning up in the filter despite his best efforts.

Marianne shifts away from him in her sleep, hugging the side of the bed like a life raft. An escape vessel.

What does he still have to lose that isn't already weeping like a wound? His marriage is on the skids, his reputation at work is shot. Eloise gave him an official warning for aggression following a tense team meeting just the other week. He knew he should stay quiet but the complacency was killing him, all his colleagues sitting around sipping coffee as if they've done enough. All he could think of was Lina. If people like Lina were *actually* helped, they'd not be such rich pickings for . . . for . . . *for people like me*.

He rolls over, the sheets feeling gritty and rough on his sunburnt skin.

*I was supposed to be one of the good guys.*

A hot tear leaks out and he presses his thumbs hard onto his eyelids. He doesn't deserve to cry, to snivel while lying in bed on holiday when he's the one who could stop all this. *I will stop all this.*

He crawls over to Marianne, pulls her towards him and folds himself around her. In her sleep, her waist yields and his fingers sink into her flesh. If she were awake, she'd suck in her stomach or whimper with embarrassment.

He strokes the softness. His wife. Growing, changing, turning over the years together. How could he risk this?

He kisses her shoulder and makes a thousand silent promises.

'I love you,' he whispers into her hair.

'Always,' she murmurs, still asleep.

# Samantha

### Friday, 31 July 2020

I'm pinned to the spot, staring from the hallway into the living room. Joe stares back at me, takes in my damp hair and pink skin, my wild expression. Steve hugs Paula tight to him as she sobs and I go to comfort her but there's no room for me, Steve is wrapped around her.

'What's happened?' I say, addressing it more to her than him, but she's crying too hard to answer.

As I get closer, I see what is laid out on our coffee table, butting up against the coasters. Photos. Printouts of photos. I gasp.

Jonathan must have taken them at Christmas, while I slept. In some, I can see snatches of my satin pyjamas, a Christmas gift from poor Paula, crumpled under me.

I exhale and let the fear break inside me. Joe is staring at his aunt, aghast, and I try to catch his eye. He looks bewildered, mortified. I thought I'd left shame behind but I was wrong, it's eating me alive.

'Steve,' I splutter. 'Paula.'

'There are so many of them,' she sobs, her face still pressed against the meat of Steve's chest.

'I'm so sorry,' I manage, my voice coming out in a whisper. 'Oh god, I'm just so sorry. I never meant to hurt you. Any of you.'

'Videos too, so many videos on his computer,' Paula wails, not listening to me. The words trailing into one another as I struggle to make them out.

'Videos?' I say, my mind cartwheeling as I try to remember that drunken Christmas night. 'He took videos?'

It's Joe who steps forward then.

'Mum,' he says, tears forming in the corners of his eyes. He shakes them away. I look up at him and he screws up his eyes and turns from me.

'What?' Steve says, and Paula pulls away to watch, forehead creasing with confusion.

'Mum,' Joe says more emphatically, pleading now. 'Are you in these photos?'

I thought they already knew and now I don't have time to deny it. They can all see that I'm guilty. I thought they must have recognised me, that Paula would have recognised the gift she'd given me just hours before I slept with Jonathan at Christmas. But they hadn't worked it out.

When I looked at these pictures, I saw myself straight away. But I see now that I was just one of many bodies. And I probably could have got away with it if I'd kept my cool, but my guilt is plastered all over my face.

They didn't know. And now they do.

Paula slips from Steve's arms and sinks to the floor. 'I'm so sorry,' I say.

'But I trusted you completely,' she cries. 'I confided in you!'

'You were seeing *my brother*?' Steve spits. 'He was the man you needed to *touch you*?' His voice is almost mocking, a caricature of me, but driven through with rage and pain.

'Hang on,' he says. 'There must have been more than one man. You were with someone else on Jonathan's birthday, because I was with him.'

I nod, mute. No good excuse, no comeback. What can I say? Paula stares at me, a new expression on her face. It's on the spectrum of satisfaction – perhaps relief that I didn't just target Jonathan? Or maybe some understanding that I stand to lose everything. I don't blame her, it's what I deserve.

'So it was just indiscriminate?' Steve fumes. 'Taking risks all over the place, no thought of the damage? After everything I did for you!'

His hands swing at his side, forming fists as he walks towards me. I'm rooted to the spot, staring at Joe, begging silently for him to understand, for him to forgive me. Steve is nearly on me and reaches for my wet hair, pulling my head down so my neck clicks and twists. 'I should never have taken you in,' he says, marching me towards the door.

I cry out, and Joe rushes to his father, pushing him off me. Paula stares between us and the photographs, her cries now dulled to rolling tears.

'Thank you,' I say to Joe.

'You should go,' he says. I nod, reach to hug him, to comfort him. He pushes me away, his face a mask of revulsion. 'And don't come back.'

# Greg

*Thursday, 27 August 2020*

'Greg, we've started.'

Eloise has already disappeared back into the meeting room when he looks up from his desk, begrudgingly. He clicks away from his search, closes the document he's been adding to and switches off the computer monitor for good measure.

After the meeting, where he'd managed to stay quiet and jot down a few notes without giving away his impatience, he opens it all back up.

He'd found Andrew's details easily enough. Turns out Rosie was right about the man's past, and the thought of his hands anywhere near the vulnerable young women Greg has been taking to the Bluebell makes him sick.

And Rosie is Rosie Parsons, paediatric nurse. Acerbic, brittle, damaged Rosie. In need of nursing herself, really, but he has enough people to worry about already.

David Ross had already given Greg his full name. He's the manager of the Bluebell, as Greg already knew, although he remembers David saying something about a new owner.

Pavel is a ghost, a mystery. Greg couldn't even place the accent – Eastern European maybe but with other flavours. Pavel told him his surname was something like Boulean or Bourean, it lodged in Greg's memory because it sounded so like the gravy – Bouillon – but he'd also said something about not using real names.

*This is the best I can do.*

\*

## Wednesday, 2 September 2020

The office printer takes an age to spit out the warm forms he's filled in online. Now he just needs to sign and post them. *Just in case.*

Should the worst happen to him after he shuts this thing down, at least she'll be taken care of. He feels detached by the concept. His life reduced to a simple number, a pay-out. It's the only cross in the 'pro' column on the ledger of his recent behaviour.

*

## Monday, 7 September 2020

The flat is chilled, the temperature dropping now the sad summer is out of the way. He pulls on the nearby hoodie; Marianne often borrows it and the cuffs smell distantly of the perfume she sometimes wears, the one he bought her for Christmas in lieu of better ideas.

It was cold yesterday too, but neither of them had thought to put the heating on. Some kind of brinkmanship maybe – he was too distracted to notice. He'd cooked a roast dinner, a ridiculous meal just for two, and they'd eaten in near silence.

She's not due back for an hour or so and the light falls away as he taps on the keyboard and makes his way to the dark web.

There is an email, of course there is. Asking about supplies. It's oddly casual, considering what happened last time. Not to mention Greg's lack of communication and the long gap between operations.

'The supply has been cut off,' Greg writes, deleting the 'sorry' he added out of habit. 'After what happened to Lina, I'm not providing any more girls and this whole operation needs to stop.' *Send.*

Nothing happens. The flat grows colder and darker and no reply comes.

Nearly an hour passes. Marianne is due home any second. He refreshes.

*That's not your decision to make.*

He hears the street door open and slam shut, caught on the wind or the tail end of his wife's bad day, he can't tell. He doesn't reply. Instead he closes down the computer, turns on some lights, takes the hoodie off and tries to look casual as she walks in.

'All right?' she says and goes into the bedroom to change without waiting for an answer.

\*

### Tuesday, 8 September 2020

A follow-up message has been waiting since last night, but he could only look at it once Marianne has left for work. He stands up to read it, his legs shaking as he takes in the words.

*Come to the Bluebell tomorrow at 10 a.m. Don't think about standing us up or we'll come for your wife.*

# Samantha

### Thursday, 27 August 2020

I try to call Joe as soon as I wake up, as I always do. He never answers. I pull myself from the bed, another gritty night spent running through my mistakes.

I make coffee in the small kitchen and look out over the yard. A bumble bee bumps lazily into the window, tumbling back and then trying again. I don't know what he wants, there's nothing sweet in here.

I've been hiding in this small flat in an uninspiring backwater for weeks. I took the first place I could find that didn't ask for ID.

I paid for a year's rent upfront in cash, before Steve wised up and had the spare bank card he'd given me blocked. I don't deserve his money but I couldn't see another way. So now I have a bedroom, bathroom, kitchen and living room. There is a front and back entrance, and no nearby neighbours overlooking. There is a small fireplace in the living room, some mismatched furniture that I suspect has been left by previous tenants rather than proactively procured, and I've scratched up some bedding and clothes from charity shops on the crumbling high street.

I should phone up about the jobs I've circled in the free advertiser, the ones I hope will pay cash without questions. And I should go to the supermarket and buy some milk. Some food. Instead I sip black coffee and watch the little furry body smash itself again and again against the glass.

I have almost nothing from my old life. A small box of mismatched glasses and mugs that I grabbed from the garage, some clothes I shoved in a bag. The car belongs to Steve.

I have no ID, no bank account. I've never paid tax, never drawn benefit. I don't exist. I still have my phone at least. The contract is attached to Steve's account and I hope that in the aftermath he is too consumed with hatred for me and Jonathan to spend time picking over his bank statements and cancelling phones. I have sent apology messages to Steve but they go unread. Joe reads but doesn't reply to any of my messages.

I haven't heard from Jonathan since that day and I don't want to. I only hope Paula has thrown him out but she's not answering my messages so I don't know. I've thought of driving over there, pleading for her forgiveness, but why would she give it? I can hardly tell her the wider context and even if I could, it doesn't take her pain away. And she's already suffered so much. Losing her child and then being so savagely betrayed by her 'second chance'.

All those women in Jonathan's photos . . . How many of us had he seduced? How many of us had he taken photos of while we slept? Was it just sport to him? I remember Paula's fears that he was cheating, but still I never imagined this scale. I thought only of myself and my mistakes.

I don't know how long I'll get away with using this phone before Steve wises up and cuts it off, so I really should make those calls. I flip open the paper and trace the first advert with my finger. A part-time job in a newsagent. I hope and pray they might pay cash-in-hand. And that Karen from the Leatherhead branch might give me a reference. I'm sure Steve hasn't told any of his staff that he was cuckolded. Or the truth. The worst truth, that he was never married in the first place. That his 'wife' was here illegally, that she would be arrested if she was ever sent 'home'.

My fingers hover over the numbers but instead, slowly and firmly, I prise off the back of the case, slide open the SIM tray and push my other SIM inside. With everything else gone, this feels like a homecoming of sorts. The last time I was good at something besides being a mother.

I imagine myself in a newsagent, ringing up magazines and chocolate bars at the till for a pittance, coming back to this dingy flat and going to sleep only to get up and do it all again the next day. I think of my dad, the years spent preparing me for anything life would fire in my direction. I think of my mum, her hope that I would get away, that I would live a bigger life than hers. The promises I made to her. I think of Cristina. All the others carving out a life in the cracks where other people didn't want to look. I want more. I want to settle scores. I want to make decisions. I want challenges that make me feel alive. And I want money.

I open the Whispa app. I don't bother to read the messages. Any threats or tasks they might contain have long expired. They have nothing over me now. Any crimes they might try to shop me for would expose a paper trail that could lead to others, could trip them up. Are they so certain they've left no traces? The worst has happened to me, I've lost my son. Everything else is noise.

I'm trapped only by my longing for Joe, but in all other ways I'm free. And I'm damned if I'm going to let anyone box me or any other vulnerable woman in again.

I breathe deeply, my lungs feeling full for the first time since I left my house. I stand up straight, take a final gulp of coffee and I tap out my message.

*

The reply comes as I'm sitting in an anonymous leather salon chair. The floor is covered in my own hair and a teenage girl is brushing it into a pile. It looks animal.

In the mirror, my strong jaw juts back at me. My grey temples are undisguised at this short length. I look like my father, a face I haven't seen in so long it's like staring at a ghost. My eyes, wrinkled with everything they've seen, almost disappear without make-up. My forehead bears the genuine grooves of worry, without the magic wand of Botox. No, it's not like seeing a ghost. It's like seeing myself for the first time.

'What do you think, Samantha? Is this what you wanted?' The hairdresser looks concerned.

'It's perfect,' I tell her. 'And call me Sam.'

I take a deep breath before I read the message. Then I breathe out.

We accept your proposal. You will be paid on an assignment-by-assignment basis for the next twelve months, starting from the next assignment. It is important to note that we owe you nothing, and will not be available to assist in any way if you become subject to a police enquiry. You are responsible for yourself alone, and will be paid only on completion of each task.

Welcome to the team.

# Greg

If he slept at all, it passed in a blink. His eyes are gritty, his chest full of phlegm and fear. Conversation had been stilted last night. He could barely catch what Marianne was saying, dread about today crowding out everything else. She'd asked if he was OK, he'd said he was tired, worried about work, the usual. She didn't believe him but gave up.

All he could do was stare at her and imagine someone slicing into her abdomen, wrapping and dumping her. His slippery, bloody slope leading these shadowy bastards to the person he loves the most.

*What have I done?*

Marianne makes him a tea and puts it on the bedside table before she leaves for work.

'Thanks, hen. You're brilliant, you know.' She looks at him quizzically, bemused more than moved.

'I love you,' he adds.

'Always,' she says, rushing out to get to school.

Before he takes a sip, he calls Eloise, his voice husky from a night of gasping for air. She doesn't doubt his illness story one bit, he sounds at death's door. He shivers at the expression.

\*

The rough seat rubs at his skin and the sunshine seems to attack his eyes rather than warm him, refracted and wrecked by the toughened glass windows of the train. There is that ever-present train smell: sweat, recycled air and bad coffee. The smell of a headache. God, he needs to sleep.

'Tickets, please!'

The same inspector looks at him for a long time as he hands over his ticket. 'On your own today?' she asks and he nods, his anxious smile twists into a grimace. What does she think he's been doing on these trips out to the country? Who has she told about him? A boss? A helpline? Maybe just her husband, debriefing over a cuppa after another long shift. 'That creepy guy was on the 9.12 again . . .'

Eventually she – Joanne by her name tag – gives his ticket back, but casts an extra glance over her shoulder as she sways on down the aisle.

David is not waiting at the station; instead there is a black Range Rover, its engine panting and bonnet shaking, like a giant puma. The man behind the wheel beckons him over. Greg looks around at the empty platform, at the battered old shelter and the houses in the distance. Could he, *should he*, run?

The man inches his car closer. Is he a hired goon from the same bunch who beat up David Ross? Or is he one of the organ grinders? A wave of weariness nearly buckles his legs. He's not running anywhere today. Greg opens the door and climbs up to the warm leather seat.

The man drives more slowly than David, carefully inching along the lane to avoid scratching the paintwork. It seems as if this route is less familiar to him.

'Who are you?' Greg says eventually, as they take another hairpin bend in first gear. The man looks at him but says nothing. He's tall, much taller and broader than Greg, and heavily built. He looks less thuggish than the others, though, and smells expensive.

He parks in the middle of the carpark. In the far corner sits a glossy BMW. David Ross's Audi is near to the back entrance, a scattering of old leaves on its roof and bonnet as if it's been here a while. Maybe he's living here now. Greg's searches on the work computer had suggested David lived in Reigate, which is quite nearby. The woman tagged in old photos with him on Facebook, Amanda Ross, is now listed as single, though. Maybe the eye injury was the final straw. Or maybe the gambling debts. Or maybe the everything.

Greg thinks of his own marriage. They both used to say that their marriage was the thing of which they were most proud. That everything else be damned, they could weather anything. Could they really survive *this*?

*We'll come for your wife.*

*But who is we?*

Greg looks up at his square-jawed companion as they cross the gravel carpark, dotted with weeds forcing their way up. The man walks with the confidence of someone in charge. *Are you part of 'we'? Or is 'we' waiting inside? Does 'we' own the BMW or . . .*

'Is there a client here today?'

The man nods and walks towards the main entrance. Greg scrambles to catch up.

Inside, the hotel is colder than usual, a layer of dust coating every surface. 'David needs to clean up,' the man says, more to himself than Greg. Then he bounds up the stairs. They pass the usual operation room; its door is open and Rosie, Pavel and Andrew sit waiting on the beds in their scrubs. They look surprised to see Greg and fall silent.

'Why are *they* here?' Greg asks, as the man continues down the corridor. 'I've not brought anyone with me.'

'I can see that,' the man replies, opening up one of the bedrooms Greg hasn't seen before. Inside, two girls sit nervously on the bed. He knows only one of them and she turns away from him as he looks questioningly at her. Her name is Alba and she was operated on in July. She huddles closer to her friend but holds her own side as if still in pain.

For a moment, no one says anything. Greg breaks the stand-off. 'I don't understand.'

The man opens the bedside-table drawer and pulls out two sealed envelopes. He gives one to the girl Greg doesn't know.

'And your finder's fee,' he says as he hands Alba's over. She continues to avoid Greg's gaze but her cheeks flush.

'It's just good business to cut out the middleman,' he says to Greg, as they go back out into the hall and the man locks the bedroom door with the girls inside. 'And we don't have the hassle of hacking into that trafficking tip line either,' he mutters as he starts to walk down the corridor.

'What do you mean?' Greg asks.

The man stops then and looks Greg in the eye for the first time, reading his face like a line of code. He seems bemused with what he sees. Almost sympathetic.

'Did you really think someone from our organisation was taking the time to track down women for you?'

Greg doesn't reply. Tries to make sense of what he's being told. 'But—' he starts.

'Jesus Christ, you really are naive.'

'But I . . . they promised. I called them in and—'

'Someone had already called them in, that's where we got them from after the first few times. Do you really not get it? Why do all the work when someone's done it for you? First rule of business.'

So every time he tipped off the helpline about exploited women, he was just doubling up information they already had? 'You're fucking kidding,' Greg says. His voice a strangled whisper.

'Look,' the man says, unlocking Greg's usual waiting room. 'If it helped *you* feel better, what's the harm?'

'What about Ana? How did you . . .'

'Who?'

Greg's stomach lurches as the man leads him inside and locks the door behind them with the heavy-set key. Any feelings of propriety that Greg had formed over this space have evaporated. Greg is very much in this man's domain, and at his mercy. On the bed, Greg can see photographs and sheets of paper.

'What is . . .' Greg moves closer. His nausea threatens to overspill.

'Look for yourself.'

Marianne smiles back from every photograph he touches. Photos from Italy last month, from their wedding day years ago. Photographs from the school website and blog. Photos that exist only on his laptop – at least he thought so.

'What does your wife know about our work here?' the man asks, his voice calm but insistent.

'Nothing. Nothing!'

The man taps his foot on the floor and then sits down heavily on the bed. The photos slide towards his thick thighs.

'Pretty girl,' the man says, fingering one of the earliest photographs. He moves his big hand across to the sheaf of papers, then hands it over. Greg has to hold it with both hands; it's a thick, floppy pile. As encouraged, Greg leafs through, frowning. Emails. Lots of emails, almost all from Marianne. Some from a former pupil.

'What does your wife know?' the man asks again in a flatter tone.

'Nothing! I've not told anyone, I promise.'

'You must realise how naive you sound, Greg. You can't just surgically remove yourself from our business without any consequences.' His voice is deep and paternal. He almost sounds reasonable.

'But I've not told anyone, I've not said—'

'You can't expect me to believe that you've not told your wife where you go every month and what you do.' The man laughs. 'You're trying to tell me that you don't engage in pillow talk with this pretty girl?' He stares at the picture a beat too long.

Greg sags, leaning on the wall. 'We're not . . . we're not getting on so well at the moment. We're barely speaking. About anything. I promise.'

The man laughs, gesturing to the pile of emails. 'I'm not surprised after reading all that. Go on, have a look.'

'I don't want to.'

'Fucking look,' the man growls. The words swim as Greg tries to take it all in.

'How did you get these? Did you hack my, her, Jesus . . .'
Greg trails off, picks up a recent email. His wife complaining
about his anger, his blank expression, his lack of intimacy. Not
to her friends, no, to her teenage suitor.

So many emails to him over the years. About feelings and
thoughts and dreams. Bile surges up in his throat and Greg
runs into the bathroom to throw up.

'Why are you covering for her?' the man calls after him.
'She's not loyal to you.'

Greg hangs over the toilet, exhausted and empty. Acid
gurgles in his throat. He hears the heavy footsteps behind him
but doesn't move.

'We can't have any leaks, you understand?'

'I understand,' Greg coughs.

'If you've told her, if you've told anyone, we'll kill you
and we'll kill them. It's that simple.'

*

Greg walks back to the station, refusing the lift. He shouldn't
have come here today, but if he hadn't . . . He thinks of the
man's threats. At least now he knows what he's up against. A
fucking rock and a hard place, that's what.

On the train, he runs through his options. There are none.
Anywhere he runs, he takes danger with him. These people
know everything about him, every address he would ever go
to. There's no escape, no way around this. He just has to keep
moving forward, covering all the bases and hoping for the best.

At home, Marianne and Greg eat in silence. She stares at
him, expectantly, but doesn't try to start a conversation. They
eat scalding lasagne that he made on autopilot. The thick red
sauce turns his stomach. She goes to bed first, taking her laptop
with her and mumbling a goodnight.

Will she email her old pupil?

*My husband doesn't understand me, not like you do.* How could
she? He's barely old enough to have his own email address!

282

Some jumped-up little shit who struggled at school. Now *he's* her confidante?! Thank fuck Greg didn't open up about all this, she'd have got them both killed with her big mouth. Her cheating heart.

'We can't have any leaks, you understand?' the man had said.

'I haven't told a soul,' Greg had whispered. 'Surely you can see that from these emails?'

But does that mean he's safe so long as he stays quiet? How easily that man had talked of killing. How easily they'd got rid of Lina. And god knows who else. That first doctor, what was he called?

Henry. Henry something. There's no way to find him now, he doesn't know his full name and can barely picture his face. Did he meet an end when he tried to escape?

Greg waits until he's sure Marianne isn't coming back out. Then he opens his laptop and contacts the one person he knows would never break his confidence. The one person whose job it is to keep secrets, no matter what. Jenna.

# Samantha

*Thursday, 10 September 2020*

This will be the first job for which I'm paid and I'm surprised by how ready for it I am. Hungry, almost. It's been weeks since I used my mind, months of working out at home to stay strong and testing myself with bogus little tasks. Following people to keep my hand in, relearning the tube map, the road network, the overground off by heart. Preparation is everything.

For the next year, I will perform the tasks, earn my money and keep myself hidden. And I will be here, ready, whenever Joe is ready to talk. And at the end of twelve months, if I do things right, I will have the money and means to rebuild my life and hope upon hope that it can include my son.

For now, and for the next twenty-four hours, I'm to follow the target. I'm to note everybody he speaks to – and if I'm able, I need to note what is discussed – and then I need to close the case. It must look like an accident, the details are up to me.

Right now, he's standing on the concourse at Euston station, holding a takeaway coffee that trembles in his hands. He stares at the arrivals board, as if willing it to change.

\*

I follow them through Euston Square Gardens but they don't notice me. Why would they? I smile at a man walking a squat little dachshund, its comical legs at odds with its serious face. When they sit down on a park bench, I keep walking. I catch up to the dachshund and its owner and ask a few questions about the breed, the dog's name, his personality. I continue to smile after him as I walk back to the adjacent bench and take in every word that Gregory Darrow is saying.

On his lap is a notepad and he's urgently scribbling in it, copying down the names of everyone who needs to be warned.

'But what's this about, Greg?' she's saying. 'I came all the way down here and you're not telling me anything.'

'I *can't* tell you. You'll be at risk if I tell you.'

'At risk from who?'

He doesn't answer and she falls into an angry silence, looking away from him as he writes.

'Please,' he says, 'you're the only person I can trust.'

She takes the piece of paper cautiously.

'Names,' he says. 'If anything happens to me, I need you to warn these people that they'll be next. Tell them to go into hiding or run or . . . I don't know, just tell them. Please?'

'I guess, I mean . . .'

'Please, Jenna.' He rubs his eyes, his temples. 'The most important name on there is Marianne.'

'Your wife? Why would your wife—'

'I've put her in danger. I hope to fuck I haven't put you in danger too . . .' He looks around so I turn my face up to the late summer sun and smile a little. He doesn't pay me any attention.

'If the worst happens, I have to protect Marianne. I have to warn the others too, but . . .' It's an awkward pause and I wonder what the history is of these two. 'She's the most important thing,' he says, finally.

# Greg

*Friday, 11 September 2020*

He watches as Marianne applies her make-up, the same sweeps and circles she's long used. Twenties experimentation making way for thirties efficiency.

Next she scoops her hair into a bun, cursing the straggling curls. Those deft hands, whisking through all that hair and taking care of it. She glares into the bathroom mirror, plucking a hair from her temple, frowning. 'Another grey,' she mutters.

'Are you waiting to use the loo?' she asks, looking at Greg in the mirror.

He shakes his head. 'Just watching you,' he says softly and she smiles, then frowns as she finds another grey hair.

He wants to tell her she's the only person he ever wanted to grow old with. He wants to see her with her hair full of grey, to be old bones together. At the same time he wants to shake her until she screams. How could she open herself like that, to a young lad no less? Had they met in person? Kissed? *Touched?*

Perhaps they should sell up and move far away from all this. From her former pupil, now kicking his heels at the university she helped him get into. And away from the Bluebell. The girls. *Lina.*

They really could go to Italy. Why wait until they're old? He'll give his notice in today; Eloise will probably be relieved. She's started to refer to him as a loose cannon, has pulled him in for extra one-to-ones every week, staring at him through red-rimmed eyes as if she's not sure who he is anymore.

And it's true, he's not been himself. At work or at home. No wonder Marianne sought validation elsewhere. This is all on him. And only he can fix it. And if he can't, at least he can trust Jenna to warn the others. But that's just panic talking.

Yes, he'll definitely give in his notice today and tell Marianne tonight. Tell her everything. No. Tell her nothing. She's safer that way.

Marianne leaves before him, calling goodbye as the door snaps shut.

'I love you!' he calls, but he hears the street door slam.

\*

He makes a mug of tea and tidies away last night's dishes – reheated lasagne that stuck in his throat. He's barely slept in so long that every movement is sluggish and painful. He opens his laptop and gets on with it. Deleting his secret email account and every message ever sent about this. The girls have more reason than him to stay quiet – it's not like they'll breeze into a police station and talk. And the clients are just as culpable, knowingly taking black market organs. No, they'll want to keep this part of their lives as wrapped as their scars. Focus on the new life they've been given.

That's what he should do too. The life he should have treasured more all along.

He has a quick look at the usual sites, combing them for what he's not sure. Anything that could link him to the Bluebell. Anything that could pull him back in now he's prepared to do whatever it takes to get out.

A new post catches his eye on that shitty forum that led him into this whole mess.

**ASSASSIN SUPERMARKET HACKED**, it says. He reads on to the main body of the post.

> Usual hoax caveats but apparently someone's hacked the database of the Assassin Supermarket and you can search for anyone with a price on their head.

> Worth checking to see if any of the trafficking bosses are on the list, or anyone else that you're looking into. Unlikely that any of us will have gained that kind of attention but advise you check anyway.

> Here's the link.

He's not heard of the site but it could be an offshoot of the Hacker Supermarket – the same people who are threatening his life. He shudders. It would make sense – assassinations are big business. Greg thinks of how easily, how coolly that big blond man had threatened to kill Greg and anyone he told. No wonder he could make that threat if he had the staff readily available.

Either way, it's too similar to ignore. If they've been hacked too, his original messages, his request to find missing girls would be traceable. *Fuck.*

Greg clicks through but there's no mention of the Hacker stuff. In fact, it's so low rent that it looks like a hoax. Not worth the risk of putting in his name. He wonders how many people have fallen for this and have now handed over their data to these devious hands.

Shit. He's running late. He'll have to finish deleting everything else tonight. He slips on their shared hoodie, one that used to be his but has been wrapped around his wife more often. The inside of it smells distantly of shower gel and her body. Not sweat as such, more . . . her warmth. He smells the traces of her perfume on the cuffs.

He walks down the stairs, grabbing his bike on the way, something like gratitude starting to simmer under the fear. Because if he still has her, Greg has everything he needs. As the door closes on their little flat, a burst of September sun warms his face. He feels, for the first time in months, like a lucky man.

# PART THREE:

## Now

# Marianne

*Tuesday, 14 September 2021*

In the Bluebell's kitchen, the woman stares back at Marianne through the crack in the cold-room door. Her well-lined eyes search Marianne's face and her mouth twitches. Less a smile than a rip in her face.

'Hello, there,' the woman says. She slides the knife into her back pocket, out of harm's way, but she doesn't move away. She's tall, very tall, with broad shoulders. The dim kitchen light behind her blends into her grey silhouette so she fills the space entirely.

*Fight, flight or freeze.* It's a split-second reaction. Not even a decision, it's more lizard-brained than that. Marianne's body has curled into a primitive ball before her brain has had a chance to catch up. The useless corkscrew clatters to the ground and Marianne's heartbeat roars in her ears. A great monstrous sound, swallowing her up from the inside.

So this is how it ends.


# Sam

She's tiny, this cowering woman. Of course she reminds me of Cristina. Every small girl with a tough expression does. It ebbs and flows; sometimes days go by, sometimes weeks. I wonder if I'll ever fully stop thinking of her. Of how she covered her mouth when she smiled, awkward about her overlapping teeth. Of how she always offered me her food, always held my hand when I cried. The two of us, huddled under the covers, trying to decipher the noises coming from the rest of the house.

I've seen Marianne Heywood many times but never this close up. I'm near enough to smell her. She has a musky, almost masculine smell – sandalwood and oranges. But creeping underneath it is the unique salty ammonia I know so well. Something like the sea at night. The smell of fear.

This close up, Marianne Heywood is insect-like in her skinny black trousers and grey V-neck T-shirt. Her navy unzipped hoodie dwarfs her, fanning over her like the shiny blue-black of a beetle's wings.

The sleeves are rolled over several times, more security blanket than garment.

Behind her, David Ross stands to attention. A museum exhibit, a grim waxwork. His expression has fallen since I left him here, or maybe I just imagined him wearing that oafish smirk right to the end. He talked about his kids, his sons, how they needed him. 'When did you last see your children?' I'd asked, cocking my head to the side. His faltering reply told me everything.

I do feel for Marianne; it must have been a shock seeing him like this. This is probably one of the better bodies to find. Preserved in the cold with no decomposing sludge, no sour stink. A mannequin made flesh. But it's still going to take a toll. People have become accustomed to separation from the dead. In their final moments, bodies are cared for by a select few, wrapped and cleaned, then presented, ready for a neat disposal. Flowers. Songs. Embalming. Real death no longer touches us. No wonder people feel immortal. Until they don't.

It wasn't that way for me. I had seen death as a raw, gaping wound, a black hole swallowing everything around it. My mother and then one of the men who killed her. Not long after that, it was Cristina. And that was before I started this work and became its architect.

'Hello, there,' I say, and I open the door a few more inches. She looks up at me and then scrunches her eyes tightly shut, as if I'm a monster. She is surrounded by monstrosity, it's true, but then aren't we all?

I don't like seeing my previous work. My chest aches with something akin to claustrophobia. On the cold floor in front of me, Marianne coils tighter, her body letting out a whimper that she's too slow to catch.

I look at her and then back at David Ross. I wonder if Marianne even had time to notice his eye; how the scar looks so shiny, magnified by the crystals of ice decorating his skin.

Not so long ago, I wouldn't have considered myself capable of staring down a dead man like this. But then I wouldn't have considered myself capable of so many things. A female trait, I almost laugh. But I don't think this is what women's magazines mean when they talk of empowerment and *leaning in*.

'It's OK,' I say to Marianne. Her head is tucked into her knees like a child. From her hands, a corkscrew tumbles to the floor. The noise is deadened by the cold room so it seems as useless as a film prop.

I pull the door open a little wider. There's no risk of her running, I doubt she could even walk on those trembling legs. She just curls up tighter, her spine bending almost to a snap. A desire to comfort her stirs in me and I crush it. I have other business with Marianne.

I feel it before I hear it. A tiny flutter in my pocket. Then that ringtone I know so well, once so familiar: 'The Final Countdown'. It's just a little joke, just for me and Joe. *Joe*. I snatch the phone out of my pocket so fast I nearly drop it. One bar of reception. Over a year of ignoring me. And now he calls.

I have to answer.

# Marianne

Marianne's spine shakes so violently she imagines its individual knots shaking loose and scattering across the floor like marbles. Anything is better than this gaping mouth of anticipation, the fear so choking she can barely breathe through it.

*Just do it.*

*Just kill me.*

*Just put me out of my misery.*

Is this how Greg felt, as he saw those tyres coming towards him? Time has slowed to a deadly crawl . . . was it the same for him? The loneliness of this moment swallows her whole and she cries out before she can stop herself. The fear is so acute that she's ready to die just to escape it. But still she waits, curling, burning with anticipation. And then, just outside of the silence of this cold coffin, Marianne hears a song, a ringtone, tinny and muffled in the woman's pocket.

It's familiar and nostalgic, something they played at their wedding, she's sure, but Marianne is too churned up to name it, much less make sense of it. By the time she dares look up, the woman has gone.

Marianne's lizard brain kicks in again. Now she's up and stumbling. She picks her way out of the cold tomb on Bambi legs, vision blurred with fear and adrenaline.

Marianne can hear the woman in the dining room, her voice conciliatory, almost cooing into her phone. Apologies tumbling, a break in her voice. Marianne stumbles on, heading for the dirty fire door set into the back wall of the kitchen.

She pushes hard on the metal lever and bursts out into the sunlight, gasping for air, and then runs to her car in such a mad scramble it's more like she's falling than running. No thoughts, no feelings, just action and adrenaline.

She tugs the keys from her pocket and fumbles to unlock the car. She looks over her shoulder as she yanks the driver's door open but the woman hasn't come after her.

In the quiet of the car, Marianne twists the key in the ignition even before she's properly sitting down. No seatbelt, no time, just panic.

'The Final Countdown', the Final fucking Countdown, she thinks, as she crunches out of the carpark and back down the lane as fast as she's ever driven in her life.

# Sam

'Thank you, Joe,' I whisper into the phone, after he stops talking. 'Thank you so much for calling.'

Joe doesn't reply but I can hear that he's still there. His breathing and his studious attention are crystal clear even down this scratchy line. My voice echoes around the dusty dining room.

'I love you so much,' I say, choking a little on a sob. The line goes dead.

I head back into the kitchen but even before I reach the cold room, I can hear Marianne's car shrieking away from the hotel. I have no hope of catching her, my car is hidden in a barn some distance away.

I can afford to let her get ahead, I have a very good idea of where she's going and right now, there is something else I need to do. Something I've been building to for the last year, without realising it. I've been so determined to get the work done and save the money that I didn't see the bigger picture.

I make my way to the office behind the reception desk and unlock its heavy door with another of the keys I should have returned already. Everything is here: the computer, the paperwork. This hotel is so far out of the way that it failed to thrive as a business, but it has also prevented theft. No one can be bothered, or maybe they never knew it was here.

Wearing gloves as always, I switch the computer on. It doesn't take long to confirm what I already believed.

For a chaotic gambling addict, David Ross kept surprisingly detailed records. I now know everything about the Bluebell's ownership and some more besides. It appears David wasn't as stupid as he seemed. But I was. Until very recently, I sleepwalked my way into the kind of enterprise that girls like Cristina, girls like my younger self, get chewed up by. I even provided most of the medicines, without realising it. My stints as Jane Douglas *et al.* making more sense now.

In the locked drawer of the desk, I find the ledger I suspected would be here. These people are record keepers. In the early days of blackmailing me, they kept *everything*.

I take a deep breath and flip it open, reading the names and numbers. So many names. I wonder which one of them I disposed of, and a waterfall of tears wells up suddenly. I should not have taken that call from Joe – my emotions are charging in all directions now – but how could I not? Over a year since I last saw him, over a year since he accepted any of my calls. Two weeks ago, I finally messaged him to say I would give up. That I wouldn't contact him again. Thank god it worked. 'No promises,' he said just now. 'But I can't not speak to you ever again.'

*

I leave through the front door of the Bluebell. There's no CCTV here and no one for miles around. I walk back down the lane rather than churn through the field. The ledger is in my right hand.

The trail of Marianne's exhaust is still lingering amongst the blackberry brambles. She and I are the only disturbance this building has had in a while, a far cry from the feverish activity it must have seen when clients and girls were still coming here.

As I walk, I keep checking my phone, but it's pointless, really: Joe won't call back. He's said what he needed to say, agreed to all that he could bear to agree to, and now I must wait until he's ready to meet. But it's a start – *thank you, God I don't believe in* – it's a start.

I wipe another tear that's been loosened by the whipping wind, and then switch the SIM cards back. Still no reception or 3G on this one. I slide it back into my pocket and unlock my car. The barn is dusty, every surface covered in insect corpses that crunch underfoot. Marianne is long gone, but like a cat, she only has a small area of patrol and I know exactly where she's headed.

I'm furious at myself for not joining the dots months or even years ago.

# Marianne

Marianne surges onto the A25 and away from the hotel. She should go to the police and tell them everything she knows. The dead body in the cold room, for starters. No, for starters the dark web browser she found and everything that followed.

As she drives, her nerve wobbles. Did she really just face a killer? Did she really stumble upon a murder victim?

If she didn't have an imagined target on her back, would she still have read that scene in the kitchen the same way?

David Ross *could* have trapped himself in that cold room. The door was closed; it was surely easily done with no one there to hear his cries. And did that woman really want to kill her? What had she said? 'Hello, there.' And then: 'It's OK.' Are those really the words of a killer? And hadn't she put the knife away once she saw Marianne? And wasn't it an understandable reaction of a woman on her own to grab something like that to protect herself – like Marianne had picked up the corkscrew?

Perhaps the woman saw David Ross and is calling the police right now to tell them she's found a body. *What would she tell them about me?*

Marianne stares out at the black tarmac ahead of her and tries to soothe herself with its normality. The wind blows, the sun shines, she's still alive.

She imagines Greg in her ear: *'You're talking yourself out of doing the right thing.'*

Marianne shakes him away, his unbending morality not so certain now. But if nothing else, she should tell the police about David Ross. She's a witness, after all. And if that woman has given them a description of her, better to turn up of her own volition. She lights a cigarette and takes a deep drag but her body rejects it, sweeping nausea up and over her. She pictures a police station, a sea of uniforms. Questions. 'And what were you doing on private property, madam?'

The searches through Greg's computer, and hers. Telling work. Telling her mother.

*I can't do this alone.*

The road is filling up with family cars, children in the back staring dumbly at iPads, looking out the window or picking their noses. It must be school-run time. Not that far from here, Daisy will be on her way from her Richmond school to her grandparents' house – her second home. Noah will be alone. In his safe suburban home where nothing can hurt her. No gas leaks, no surprises. She'll head there now and tell him everything. Then she'll trust *his* morality; maybe not as unbending as Greg's but probably more realistic.

She can't imagine Greg's voice in her ear anymore, can only think of Noah. His solidity. Noah will help her decide what to do, and hold her hand while she does it. And if someone *is* following her, if this woman wasn't a benign trespasser checking out a strange noise, well, Noah will help protect her. That's the kind of man he is.

# Sam

The 3G sputters back on between Redhill and Godstone, announced by the trill of a message coming through the Bluetooth speakers. My phone sits in its holster like a gun, a cable trailing down to what was once a cigarette lighter. This car, the most average spec of an average model that I could buy with my budget, has served me well, but I'm dreaming of the day that I ditch it. I bought it no questions asked, and didn't send off the paperwork to change the ownership. I couldn't, I don't exist. When I sell it, it'll be for scrap. Maybe I'll just drive it out to the middle of nowhere and set it alight. Burn everything else from these last couple of years with it. God, yes, that's what I'll do. The SIM card, the phone, the clothes, the boots. Just watch it turning to black smoke and drifting away.

I'll turn up on foot to see Joe. I'll walk for weeks if I need to.

The sun pastes the windscreen with thick orange light as I drive towards it, squinting to make out the message on my phone. I surge onto the M25 and pick up speed. I tap the accelerator and wait for my modest engine to catch up.

The end is still in sight as I weave carefully through the lanes, checking for Marianne's little bug car as I go. Beating her to Richmond would be smart in some ways, but there are too many variables I can't control that way. So I drop back just a little and settle into the middle lane. Aggressive men overtake me as they swerve without indicating, shouting along to their music, parents with carloads of kids trundling along, distracted. Everyone is so very predictable.

# Marianne

The driveway is empty so Noah must still be out. Marianne tries to remember what his plans were for the day. Meetings and the gym, she knows that much, but hopefully he'll be finished soon.

Marianne looks around; no one is outside in the quiet cul-de-sac but the distant sound of kids playing helps ground her. Nothing bad can happen in a place like this, surely?

Still, she doesn't hang around in the open for too long, letting herself into the garden quickly. She fumbles for the cleaner's key that she'd left under the pot earlier. The metallic weight sits like a comfort in her hand now. Marianne unlocks the patio doors, then puts the key back under the pot. Slipping inside, shaking the dried cherry petals from her shoes and tossing them back outside, she pulls the patio doors closed with a grunt. Just in case, she locks them from the inside.

She drinks water from the tap, letting it gush over her chin and neck. She plans to make a coffee, opening the fridge to get milk. A rush of images fly at her and she slams the door shut again, trying to forget the way David Ross looked, the way his skin glistened. Instead of coffee, she pours a measure of whisky from the drinks cabinet.

Outside, a car door slams and she jumps, ducking down behind the sofa and peeking out. It's not Noah or anyone nefarious, just an elderly neighbour, but she feels like a sitting duck all the same.

Marianne steps upstairs, carrying her drink. She uses the bathroom, realising only when she sits down that she's not peed in hours, not eaten in even longer and is shaking so hard she shreds the toilet paper trying to pull some off the roll.

She won't feel safe until Noah is back.

The bathroom locks but there's no window. Just thinking about hiding in here makes her head hum with claustrophobia. *The office.*

*

It's unlocked when she gets up there, the street clearly visible through the window, so she can watch for Noah *or anyone else.* She locks the door, the mechanism is more robust than the bathroom lock, presumably designed to keep out burglars.

Her phone is close to dying but her phone charger is still in the car. She opens WhatsApp and sends a message to Noah. She'll explain everything in person, can't even begin to now, so she keeps it light. 'Just popped back to yours for a bit, hope that's OK. See you soon?'

She drains her whisky and feels the alcohol numb her. She should have brought the bottle up. Almost out of habit, she checks her email with the last sputter of battery.

Dear Marianne,

I was a colleague of Jenna's and all of her emails are being forwarded to me. I'm very sorry to be the bearer of bad news but I'm afraid that Jenna died recently. If your query relates to a case that Jenna worked on, please let me know how I can assist.

Yours,

Kate Williams

Marianne's stomach churns. She wasn't expecting this. A tearful rebuttal. A snippy cold shoulder. No reply at all. But not this. Not another dead body.

Her phone goes black in her hand.

# Sam

I park in a spot I've used before, but I don't think any of the neighbours will notice. They're not looking out for people like me, or cars like this. And after today, they'll never see me again.

I watch as the Range Rover parks next to the Fiat and Noah Simpson jumps down. He has a surprising lightness for a big man and seems to bounce on his toes a little as he walks past Marianne's little Fiat towards the door. I remember that walk from last time, with his little girl, and the time before that. The first time I saw him. At the Bluebell. It took me a while to make the connection.

Of course, that day he was wearing an expensive shirt and smart jeans, every inch the successful entrepreneur. Today he's dressed in gym gear. Great slabs of trap muscles and chest, bulbous biceps and triceps visible through gaps in his vest and a flapping zip-up hoodie. He's an advert for his own strength. I am going to need to be smart.

# Marianne

*Jenna died recently . . .*

A woman she knows only by association. A woman of whom she was secretly jealous. A woman to whom she silently compared herself. A woman Greg trusted when he trusted no one else. A woman who is dead.

Marianne looks out of the window but no one's there. She needs to know more. Needs to understand what happened in this latest horrible development.

*Surely Noah wouldn't mind if . . .*

Marianne switches on the iMac and waits for it to load up. She opens Safari. Some tabs are already open: property sites, fancy men's clothing site Mr Porter, bodybuilding.com. All very Noah. She leaves them undisturbed and opens a new tab to search news about Jenna Fairbarn, a deep note of melancholy chiming in harmony with her base fear. Jenna wasn't on the list; this must just be a sad coincidence, mustn't it?

\*

Jenna lived near Loch Lomond, not far from the village of Killearn where she and Greg grew up. The cliché of a big fish in a small pond, she'd returned with her city law degree to the place that had given her such a happy upbringing.

According to the news, the A809 is home to a notorious traffic blackspot. But Jenna's accident was still a gut punch to the community she had loved and served.

So she wasn't 'killed'. Marianne tries to feel some relief in this sad story.

And the decision to finally turn off the machines that kept her breathing was a choice her family made after months of deterioration. But the car accident happened just days after Greg's death.

*Was Jenna distracted by grief and lost control of her car?*

And it was just days after she had made a special and secret trip to London the day after receiving his email.

*Or did someone run her off the road?*

Marianne hears the familiar growl of the big engine and looks out to see Noah's Range Rover rolling towards the house. *Thank fuck*. She closes Safari, the neatly arranged desktop taking over the screen, its icons organised as precisely as Noah's cupboards. She shuts it down, an unease coming over her as the screen fades.

*Did she imagine it? The same icon, tucked in the corner? Surely not.*

As the front door opens below, Marianne looks again at the portfolio on Noah's desk. The unease grows; something just out of the corner of her mind's eye is fizzing dangerously.

She flips through the pages of the portfolio, each one elegant and quietly persuasive.

When she'd looked through these leather-bound pages last time, she'd not yet been to the Bluebell. Hadn't yet felt that curious shiver of familiarity.

*But there it is.*

The portfolio is open on the artist's rendering of the luxury converted flats that Noah is having redeveloped, each one overlooking acres of unspoilt Surrey countryside.

Downstairs, she hears Noah call her name, but she just stares, mute.

According to these pages, the architects will make the most of the existing ink-pot building, gussying it up with floor-to-ceiling windows and sleek balconies. An on-site gym, a concierge. But underneath it all, it's the same place. The same building that welcomed paying guests as the Bluebell Hotel.

# Sam

He's already upstairs when I enter the house, taking the time to slide the patio doors silently behind me. I slow my breathing and regroup, listening carefully before stepping further inside. This whole floor is open-plan, with the kitchen to the right of the dining area, which sits behind the lounge area. The calm right angles are slashed only by the designer staircase that runs along the wall.

In the lounge area ahead, the grey corner sofa has just one deep groove. Behind it, on cream-coloured shelves, sit photographs of his wife and child, a few of him and his wife alone and some framed baby artwork, flowers and hearts made from pudgy fingers pushed into paint. There are no pictures of Marianne.

One of my deepest regrets is that I have no photographs of either my parents or Cristina. I have hundreds, probably thousands of Joe on my phone. But I can't bear to look at those.

I listen again, standing in the centre of this cavernous space, my eyes closed. I trace the creaks and sighs of the struts and boards on the floor plan that I've committed to memory.

I'd say he's in the family bathroom that sits between the master bedroom and Daisy's room. I wonder if Marianne will run down to him from the office, cower in his arms and bury her head in his chest. Or perhaps she's calling him quietly, just beyond my earshot.

I hear nothing new so I open my eyes and take the time to assess the room fully. It's impeccable, every surface shining. Even the deepest corners, the grooves around the kitchen tiles are spotless. Just some splashes around the sink, which I hazard was her and not him. It's as if the house is a show house, or someone has done a forensic deep clean. This will make things easier, on balance.

A toilet flushes overhead and then heavy steps spell out the route Noah Simpson is taking along the hall and up the narrow staircase to the top level.

*Step.*

*Step.*

*Step.*

And finally they're both trapped.

## Marianne

Marianne's head whistles and she bites hard on her hand to stop herself screaming.

Throughout everything, Noah was the one person she trusted. Believing herself in danger, she fled here as if it was a sanctuary. But this is not a safe place, it's a trap.

'Marianne?'

She doesn't answer. Counts the footsteps as he comes nearer.

'Are you up here?'

He sounds like her Noah. The same gentle man who wept at those bereavement meetings, who carefully makes his daughter's breakfast, packs her lunchbox. He sounds like the man who wraps his arms around Marianne in bed as if he's stopping her from floating away. A man she was starting to love. A man she trusted. *Another man I stupidly trusted.*

Perhaps if she stays quiet, he will assume that she's already left again. She whispers to herself, *perhaps, perhaps, perhaps.* Tries to believe this is just another of those moments, the ones she's been escaping all week. Just another of her nine lives gone.

She put the key back under the plant pot, that's good. And she locked the door from the inside. Yes, she could conceivably have got bored of waiting for him and left. What did she say in her message? She'd popped back here, that was it. Perhaps she popped back out again. Maybe she can stay quiet and bide her time. Wait for him to leave again or jump in the shower, then she can run. Get to the police and tell them everything, consequences be damned.

'Your car's outside, Marianne. I know you're here.'

*Fuck.*

The handle rattles but the door doesn't yield.

'Hey,' he says, a coolness to his voice. 'What's going on?'

A pause. Then a rushing sound and a huge crack as Noah throws himself at the door. It bangs and bends but stays in place. Marianne covers her mouth with both hands.

'You're scaring me now!' he says, his voice panicked rather than angry.

'Leave me alone,' she calls out. 'Please, just let me go.'

'What do you mean?' He laughs in exasperation. 'You came here! You're in my house!'

'I didn't know who you were when I came here, I shouldn't have come here, I didn't know. I just want to leave but I can't open the door with you out there.' Her voice sounds high and hysterical.

'What are you talking about?' He's still disguising his anger well. If she hadn't found the Bluebell in his portfolio, she'd be opening up to him right now. Clinging to him like a life raft while he holds her head under the water.

'You own the Bluebell Hotel,' she says. It's not a question.

'Um, yeah, me and another person. What's that got to do with anything?'

'I know what you did there, at the Bluebell.'

'What? What did I do there?' That cynical laugh again, a blast of exasperation but something new too. *Fear.* 'It's been closed for a couple of years now,' he adds, sounding flustered, the coolness gone. 'We've been waiting for planning permission and it's finally come through. It's just an empty building, it's nothing for you to worry about.'

'Bullshit. I don't know exactly what you did there but I know it was something bad. And I know Greg was involved and I think . . .' She stops. 'I think he was killed because of it. And maybe Jenna too and—'

'Who the hell is Jenna? What are you talking about?'

She feels him push the door carefully, feeling around its edge, testing its strength.

'Why do you have a lock on the inside of your office door, Noah?'

'To protect my valuables and business interests. Why shouldn't I? And what's that got to do with anything? I don't know anyone called Jenna and I only know about Greg through you. Look, let me in and we can talk it all through, address your concerns.' He's switched to business lingo but his voice is soft, pleading almost, while changing the subject.

'Most people would have a lock on the *outside* of their office, not one to lock them in. What didn't you want Daisy walking in on?' she says, her voice small. He doesn't reply and she hears him sigh. A long, slow sigh.

'Look, Marianne. Grief does funny things to people. I should know.'

She shakes her head. 'No. Don't blame this on grief, don't try that. This isn't about me.'

'And it's only been a year,' he continues, dropping his voice to the pitch she recognises as the one he uses when he wants to get her into bed. 'You're still processing everything. Maybe we rushed into things too soon, gave in to our feelings too early. But if you feel guilty, you're lashing out at the wrong person here.'

She says nothing, instead looks at the window, tries to gauge whether anyone could see her if she waved for help.

'I've not done anything wrong,' he says. 'I don't know why you have a problem with one of my investments, but it's hardly a secret. I've told you all about that development. And other businesses too. I've not got any secrets from you, Marianne.'

*Has he told me about the Bluebell?*

She'd not really been interested in his work, hadn't paid a lot of attention when he had talked about profit and loss or opportunities and risk. Maybe he had told her. Maybe. She closes her eyes and presses her eyelids with her thumbs.

'Just open the door and we can talk it all through,' he says.

She stands up, bones aching with fear and tension. Maybe she could open the door. Maybe she could unburden herself, they could unpick these coincidences together. She could test him, ask him to come to the police with her. But . . . But.

It's not just the Bluebell, is it? There's more.

She turns from the door and switches Noah's computer back on. It whirs loudly enough for him to question the noise. 'What are you doing in there?' The gentle voice is gone and he bangs on the door but she ignores it, staring at the screen, willing it to load.

Yes, there it is.

'Why have you been going on the dark web?' she asks, trying to keep her voice under control.

'What?'

'I can see it now, the browser. I can click on it and see what page opens up, so you might as well be honest.'

A long moment passes. He takes a sharp breath but still says nothing. More silence. For a moment she thinks he has slipped away, socked feet padding down the hall.

'I . . .' he starts, 'I went on there because—' He stops. She can hear him sobbing. Enough of this bullshit. She clicks in and waits for it to load. The page is blank, no historical tabs still open.

'It was for Louise,' he says, finally.

# Noah

It started with a kidney.

No, it started with a positive pregnancy test, grasped in Louise's hand.

'I'm pregnant,' she said, fingers trembling as she offered it for him to see. 'Oh my god, I'm pregnant.' He stared at it. Two thick blue lines in a cheap bit of plastic.

'But how?' he finally managed to say and she started to sob. His heart sank as he realised they were happy tears.

'Lou, we can't,' he said, pleading with the back of her head as she turned away from his expression. 'It could kill you.'

But *this* whole mess, this started with a kidney.

Every month of the pregnancy had seen a deterioration. As the apple pip grew to a tennis ball to a grapefruit to a melon, his beautiful, healthy wife turned ever more grey, withering in front of him until only her stomach showed signs of life.

'I'm so happy,' she said. 'I never thought I would be so lucky.'

He begged the universe, held his hands in prayer, threw fistfuls of pennies into the wishing well in the park. But still the baby held on in there, growing ever stronger while its mother, its host, suffered a steep decline.

They went private but it made no difference. Her kidneys were shot and having nicer flowers in the room at the hospital made no fucking difference. She needed a new kidney, there was no other option.

Everyone they knew was tested but there were no matches. Every time a fatal crash hit the news, he hoped and prayed they would get a call. Trawling for tragedy. His moral compass spinning.

Soon he had a tiny baby and a sick wife to look after, and still no kidney was available. At night, he'd held Daisy to his chest while Louise slept, shushing and patting, apologising and crying while he logged on. The dark web. His last hope.

*

You could buy anything there; that was the rumour. It was even more of a Wild West back then than it is now. He followed rat runs and whispered links, combed dingy places while he covered his daughter's eyes. There were false starts, obvious hoaxes and, eventually, an offer.

He sent money. A lot of it. A Macedonian outfit with organs of all kinds, all blood types. A veritable warehouse of working parts. Except it wasn't. There was never any kidney, there was never any hope. He wasted his precious time with her, he wasted savings he would need to rely on. Louise wasted away.

After his wife died, he was held together by his daughter. His burning, angry love for her. His guilt. He told himself the anger would fade, but with every gummy smile from Daisy, every milestone her mother missed, the anger grew. He nursed thoughts of revenge, dared himself to do something. Anything to puncture the swelling balloon of rage.

A couple of years passed. Still he couldn't let it go. They'd robbed him of his time with Louise but more than that, they'd robbed him of hope.

Daisy was sleeping at her grandparents' when he did it. Taking a slug of cognac for nerves, left over from a happier

Christmas. The Macedonian outfit had disappeared when he visited the forum on which he'd first found their advert.

Another cognac sitting hot in his gut, he'd posted a clarion cry. Was anyone else scammed by them? Was anyone else raging? Did anyone want to join forces to stop this happening again?

No one replied.

After he'd called his in-laws to check Daisy had settled fine, he posted again. This time included his anonymised email address.

Someone got in touch. They said they were the founder of Hacker Supermarket, as if he must have heard of that. He hadn't. When he searched for it on the normal web, nothing came up. But they were sympathetic and angry on his behalf. Even hinted that they'd experienced a loss like his. And they wanted to hit those scammers where it hurt – and didn't he?

Noah replied that, yes, he did. He fucking well did want to hit them where it hurt. And then he poured the last of the cognac into his glass as he waited for a response. Perhaps this 'hacker' could track down the scammers, stop them hurting other people. Could he trust them? Should he get his hopes up? Maybe they'd come back asking for money and, god, well, he'd probably throw the bloody computer out the window if they did, he was so snarled up by then.

But no. They didn't want money. And they didn't offer to hack anything, not at that point anyway. The proposal was something very different. Rather than track each scammer down – an impossible task – they would strangle their business another way: by providing an 'ethical' alternative.

It appealed to the businessman in him. But more than anything it appealed to the grieving husband in him. For the first time since Lou held that damned pregnancy test – the best and worst thing that had happened to him – he felt genuinely hopeful. For all the complexity, the murkiness of what was being planned, of what he had signed on for, he felt something clean and pure. He felt renewed.

First, they needed to build capital. Sure, they cut corners and used unconventional methods to take over businesses, but those people didn't have a gun to their heads. Bribery, technically, but it was always their choice. And in exchange for keeping their secrets, Noah and his partner took over. It was for the greater good. Some of the businesses died, some thrived, and gradually Noah had a portfolio of income streams. He'd always had a natural flair for investment and business, but he was taking things to the next level. He was finally building a future for him and Daisy.

The Bluebell came along at just the right moment.

The owner, David Ross, was up to his neck in gambling debt. He didn't need blackmailing, he was an eager seller. David grabbed the low-ball offer and agreed to stay on after the hotel closed down in exchange for a cash-in-hand stipend.

For Noah, this whole endeavour was a passion project, a new way of life. Helping desperate people to source organs, saving other families from suffering like his had.

And when they finally got it up and running, it worked well. His partner took care of the other sides of the online business, sides he didn't ask too much about. But this part was genuinely life-changing for everyone. Everyone who deserved it, anyway. Happy clients got a second chance at life and so did happy donors – once their scars healed.

Noah couldn't save Louise, but he could help other people. And for a while, he really believed he was doing a good thing.

# Sam

I'm on the middle floor. Upstairs, Noah Simpson has been doing everything wrong to try to get inside the office to Marianne. Banging the door, yelling, patronising her with thin excuses and provable lies. Men like him never learn. I was raised surrounded by men like him. My father was an exception. Not that he was hearts and rainbows, but he trusted me. He didn't patronise me. Quite the opposite. He taught me how to handle myself, how to use anything around me to keep myself and my mother safe. If I had a knife when the moment came, I had the skills to use it. But he also taught me about rope, knots and sticks. How to use my body to make it seem stronger, bigger, than it really was. Other girls were not prepared so well.

I think of the girls whose names are in that ledger. The women who were chopped about like they were cheap meat. I think of Cristina, just another cheap life. I think of the news story I read recently. It barely pricked the public's consciousness and was immediately swallowed up and pushed down by articles on celebrity love rats and MP in-fighting. The body of a young girl found rotted under a pile of manure in a field in Surrey. Believed to be the victim of human trafficking but not matching any reported missing persons. No flesh left to examine but her dental work looked Eastern European.

As I listen to Noah's fairy-tale version of what they'd been up to, the final pieces fall into place. I know who is really behind this.

# Marianne

'But what does Greg have to do with . . .' She sucks in the air as the penny drops. 'The donors,' she says to Noah. 'Were they—'

'Yes, he found people willing to donate their organs.'

'You paid him to *find people*?' Greg who rescued the frogs? Who cried for every person he hadn't helped? Who wouldn't bring children into the world because the world was so fucking cruel? Greg who never had any money.

'I don't believe you.'

'But you do, don't you,' Noah replies. 'And for what it's worth, he didn't take payment. He gave it all to them.'

She won't let this point settle, won't concede it. Even though, in the depths of her heart, she can believe it.

'So are you still doing it?' she cries out. 'Still trading in body parts?'

'No,' he says, sounding almost apologetic. 'It got too risky.'

Marianne says nothing but reaches into her pocket and pulls at the unfamiliar little bulge there. A small purse, handmade and embroidered with the name 'Lina'. Inside, there are a few coins, a five-pound note softened by hundreds of hands, and two frayed photographs. A young girl, no more than a teenager, with her arms around what looks like her family. In the second photo, one of the younger children from the family picture standing in front of a small house. It doesn't look English but Marianne can't guess where it is.

'What happened to Lina?' she says.

'How did you—' he starts. 'What?'

She stares at the photos. 'Where is Lina now?'

'Those girls,' he says, quietly. 'They knew the risks. And they kept coming, even after some hiccups.'

'Hiccups.' She feels sick. 'Did they even know about these hiccups?'

He doesn't answer, starts to rattle the handle again. 'Come on, Marianne, it doesn't have to be like this. We can talk it through, I can show you it's over now.'

'If it was working so well, why is it over? Because Greg died? Because you killed him?'

'I didn't kill your husband! And we had another source of supplies then anyway.'

'Supplies,' she repeats. Her blood feels cold as it rushes to her guts. 'Supplies,' she says again, swallowing back nausea.

'I didn't mean it like that, it's just . . . It was easier to handle if I stayed dispassionate. If I got too involved I could have made mistakes and if I'd got caught, who would Daisy have then? And I wanted to go legit, I wanted to stop everything I was involved in that was in any way dodgy—'

'*More* dodgy than black market organs?' Marianne says.

He pauses and she can hear him shuffling position, moving his trainers around on the hardwood floor.

'It got out of hand,' he says eventually. 'And I've spent a lot of time unpicking it all and straightening it out. I don't want to be that person any more, I'm parting ways with my business partner. I want to live a normal life, with Daisy and with you.'

'You must think I'm insane,' she shouts. 'And there's no way it was a coincidence that you just turned up at the same bereavement group on the other side of London.'

'There was no coincidence to any of this,' he says. 'I had to plug any potential leaks, I had to find out if you knew anything. But you didn't. You told me you'd gone through Greg's things and you clearly hadn't found anything, so I knew you were clean. I told my partner that you were clean, you were safe, you could be left alone. You're someone who I might be able to build a future with. And I still want that future with you! Please, I never meant for anyone to get hurt.'

'You're trying to hurt me now!' She thumps the desk.

'I would never hurt you,' he says. 'I love you, I mean, I'm starting to love you anyway. Even with your . . .' – he takes a deep breath – 'even with your past indiscretions.'

'What indiscretions?'

Marianne is sitting on the floor of the office, as far from the door as possible, but now she crawls over, listens closely through the door. Surely he doesn't know?

'I know about your affair, Marianne, with your *pupil*. And it's hard to look past it but I did. I would never have cheated on Louise, not ever, but perhaps our marriage was just stronger.'

'How the hell do you . . . did Greg tell you? I didn't cheat on him, I didn't. Nothing happened until Greg had died. And that was just once. I've not seen him since and I wish I could take it back. But he wasn't my pupil, I hadn't taught him in years. He was an adult by then.' She sounds frantic and she knows it. 'I don't have to explain any of this to you – *bloody hell*, this is *nothing* compared to what you did!'

'I'm not sure your boss or his parents would feel the same,' Noah says.

'Stop trying to distract me!' she shouts, pulling at her hair and standing up. Pressing her forehead to the door. 'Why was I still on the list then, Noah?' Marianne sobs.

'What list?'

'You know what list. A list of all the other "leaks" you needed to permanently plug in this fucking – this network you ran. This company!'

'I didn't run this, not really. I was like a project manager, I wasn't the senior partner. You have to believe me. I was a victim too, I tried to stop it and they wouldn't let me until they decided to move into a more lucrative business. Something I wanted nothing to do with.'

'The Assassin Supermarket?' she asks.

He doesn't reply, just keeps begging. 'You have to believe me, I was just a cog in the machine. Like Greg.'

'So who was in charge then?'

She hears Noah cry out in frustration.


# Sam


It's a clean job but I don't have long before his blood pools, his body stiffens and a tell-tale sheen emerges on his skin. I bend into a squat and try to warm up my muscles. I close my eyes and lean my head to the left and to the right. I crack my knuckles to release the pressure. OK, time to get to work.

Noah weighs far more than me but I've steadily built up my strength, and everything my dad taught me about weight distribution was not wasted. It's all about leverage and pivot points. Which is why we can push far more weight sitting on the leg press at the gym than doing a front squat with the bar resting near our delicate collar bones. Joe would be proud. Of my powerlifting knowledge if nothing else.

Speaking of powerlifting, this spare room I've just dragged Noah Simpson into is an absolute treasure trove. It was hard to choose which kettlebell to use just now; I'm not accustomed to seeing so many pieces of equipment in someone's home. And he has a beautiful squat rack, matte metal finish on the bar and weights polished to a shine. And a fancy rowing machine filled with water. So much money sloshing around. I would like to have a room like this in my new house. I think Joe would appreciate it.

In the end I went for a 24kg kettlebell as it was the only one placed slightly askew from the rest, and likely the one Noah genuinely would have used. So confident at his abilities that he got sloppy and let it slip from his overhead grasp. Plausible accidents, every time.

I position him in front of the mirror, mentally calculating where the kettlebell would have landed if it had slipped at the apex of a clean and jerk. I drop it there now, allowing it to dent the beautiful floor.

I consider going to get the cleaning things, making a start on that unfortunate trail from office door to spare room, but the risk of Marianne letting herself out is too great. She'd ruin everything if she ran now and raised the alarm. I can tell by the condition of this home that plenty of cleaning materials will be in a cupboard in the kitchen and I must have faith that this man, this conscientious man, will have products that are up to the job.

But for now, Marianne. I take out the little leather pouch filled with my tools. Her time is now.

# Marianne

Noah has stopped answering. Marianne presses her ear to the door but hears nothing apart from a slight shuffling noise, like something being dragged.

A loud bang sounds from somewhere, maybe in the spare room, and she jumps back. What is he doing in there? Christ, what weapons does he have?

Marianne looks around desperately, but this office is bare. A desk, leather chair, computer and filing cabinet. There's not even a phone or letter-opener, nothing she might use to defend herself. *What is he doing?*

Marianne looks out of the window; the light has faded to dull grey and a few cars are making their way down the cul-de-sac and nudging onto their drives. If she tried to raise the alarm, it's unlikely they could see her from this angle. She looks at the latch on the dormer window. *Maybe there is a way out.*

The desk is pushed up to the window and she moves it, inches at a time, until she can slip behind it and reach the catch on the window.

Behind her, Noah is now scratching at the lock. They're deliberate noises, like he knows what he's doing. He's not just jamming something in and trying to jimmy it open. The cool confidence terrifies her. *Who is this man?*

Marianne grabs the handle of the window and twists it, pushing the pane away from her. The window only opens six inches or so. There's no way out. Instead, Marianne has pinned herself in place with the desk. She turns around to face the door as it opens.

It's not Noah.

It's the woman from the Bluebell.

Marianne turns to the window, ready to call out, ready to scream. But before she can find her voice, the woman is reaching over the desk and her gloved hands are on Marianne's shoulders, turning her back to face the room.

'Don't do anything stupid, Marianne,' the woman says. Her voice is surprisingly gentle.

'Where's Noah?' Marianne manages. 'Are you working together?'

The woman ignores the question and instead reaches past Marianne to close the window. Her glove skims the side of Marianne's neck. The woman's expression is calm and professional.

'Sit down,' she says, pointing to the floor. Marianne's legs buckle and she crashes down, resting her spine against the wall. A mad montage of archive footage rushes through her mind: all the executions, all the mass deaths she's learnt about, *taught about*, over the years. Guns and bayonets pointing at pencil-thin necks, skulls with eyes bulging. Marianne closes her eyes and braces for the inevitable.

Nothing happens.

When she opens her eyes again, daring only a crack between her lashes, she sees the woman sitting across from her with her own back against the opposite wall.

Marianne tries to look out into the hall. The woman's socked foot shoots across the floor and nudges the office door closed.

'Don't look out there,' she says. 'That's not your problem.'

## Sam

'You're free to go, but there are some conditions,' I say. It's hard to keep the exhaustion from my voice, drawing ragged breaths as I approach the finish line.

Marianne just stares back at me. For a moment I think she's lost the ability to speak, but she finally opens her mouth.

'You killed everyone on that list, didn't you?' Marianne says. There is a clarity to Marianne's voice that surprises me. I should be irritated that she's looking this reprieve in the mouth but I have a grudging respect for her burst of impudence. If she has a bit of grit it will serve her well for the next part.

'How did you know about the others if you weren't involved?'

Marianne stares back, no colour in her face. 'Your website was hacked, the Assassin Supermarket. Every job on there is searchable.'

I hide my surprise.

'Do you want to discuss websites or do you want to live?' I say.

'I want to live,' Marianne says. 'But—'

'Then listen carefully and do exactly as I say.'

I had thought Marianne was one of these bastards. Just another link in their chain. Until I saw her face in the kitchen. Then I knew. She's as innocent as those other women. As innocent as Cristina. My mother. The many, many others.

'Noah is dead,' I say. 'And if you don't want to be in the frame for it, we'll need to move fast.'

Marianne stares back at me. I watch as she starts to shake, just a tremble at first and then a violent vibration. Her jaw is clamped but tears well and roll down her face, soaking her T-shirt and baggy hoodie with thick black blotches.

'I know he was into shady stuff,' she splutters. 'But he has a little girl—'

'Shady stuff? Look, I heard his version earlier too, but believe me, Marianne, you don't know the half of what this guy was into. Save your tears.'

'And Greg? You killed him too? He really was a good guy!'

# Marianne

'A good guy.' The woman takes in a deep breath and lets it percolate.

'My husband, Steve, was a good guy,' she says. 'Well, he wasn't actually my husband. I guess he was my partner.' She laughs a little but Marianne doesn't understand what the joke is. 'And he wasn't really a good guy, he just thought he was. He offered me a way out, a million years ago.' The smile fades. 'Except it wasn't a way out, it was just a softer trap.'

'What has this got to do with—'

'Let me tell you what I've learnt about good guys over the years, Marianne.'

Marianne stares at her, mute. *What the hell is this?*

'We know about bad guys, don't we? Violent men, thugs. Bogeymen. And we know that there are some real monsters out there, don't we? We've all glimpsed those monsters, right Marianne?'

Marianne looks away, refusing to give up her stories. Not to this woman.

'Thought so. Creepy guys, handsy bosses. We all know them. Don't we?' The woman raises her dark eyebrows and waits for Marianne to nod. 'Of course we do. Because these men wear flashing neon signs that read: *beware.*'

The woman closes her eyes and takes another long breath, letting it seep from flared nostrils. She looks older than she did at the Bluebell. Ageing by the minute, wrinkling like a deflated balloon.

'But haven't you realised by now, Marianne' – she makes fists with her strong hands but lets them fall into her lap – 'haven't you realised the kind of drip-drip damage that breaks our dams again and again is the kind that comes from the *nice* men? The ones that, my God, *somehow* have broken down our defences so completely that we're still making excuses for them, no matter what they do! You're doing it now. "Noah's a dad!" and "Greg just got in too deep. He was a *good guy.*"'

Marianne stares at the woman but then looks at the door. If she could just stand up while this woman's eyes are screwed angrily shut, maybe she could get out and make a run for it. She starts to unfold her body, slowly climbs to her feet. The woman's eyes pop open like those of a ventriloquist's dummy. 'Sit *down.*'

Marianne sits back down.

'These men, *Marianne*, have convinced you that up is down. And they manage to do *just enough* to keep you fooled. But they still benefit just the same as the bad guys, right? And yes, sure, these "good guys" shrug apologetically when we get cat-called or screw their faces up in disgust at the news stories, but don't they like to remind you that it's "not all men"?'

Marianne nods, just slightly, before she can stop herself. 'But what has this got to do with Greg? Or Noah?'

'The men who call themselves allies,' the woman goes on, 'who punch up, not down – in fact, never punch at all, because they're not like that. Except the ones who do. Hiding in mild-mannered beige. The ones the papers describe as loving fathers, who just flip. I've met those. I've got rid of those, Marianne. You're welcome, world.'

The woman runs a hand through her cropped grey hair. 'You see it all so clearly when you stop being a woman they like to look at, you know? When they stop paying any attention to you at all.'

'But—'

'Marianne, *none* of them are good guys. They just sit at different points on a spectrum. For god's sake, it doesn't make them good guys because some men are worse. They're not heroes just because they're not rapists or thugs or' – she gestures to the hall beyond the closed door – 'a deadbeat dad. None of these men in this foul little network were good guys, *Marianne*, no matter what they told themselves,' she spits. 'And the sooner you let go of the very idea of good guys, the better chance you have of surviving.'

'And what about Jenna?' Marianne asks. 'You killed her too, right?'

The woman shakes her head, a look of regret on her face. 'I didn't, no. And if I knew then what I know now, there are a lot of things I'd do differently. She didn't deserve to die. They got someone else to do it, someone local, and they bungled it. But Marianne, you're still focusing on the wrong people. You need to focus on yourself or you'll never survive.'

# Sam

I tried. I really tried. It took me over forty years to find out the hard way, the agonising way, not to put any faith in men. I should have opened my eyes years ago. I thought I was smart, *a fighter*, but then I jumped at Steve's kindness, even though it tied a noose around me. I fell for Jonathan's bullshit when his shadiness was barely hidden.

I will never rely on another man. Even Joe turned his back on me, but there's still time to put that right and, hand on heart, I don't blame him. A daughter would have done the same.

I guess every woman has to find out in her own time that you can only ever really rely on yourself. But if she's not convinced by everything that's happened to her so far, I don't fancy Marianne's chances. She looks back at me with those big wide eyes, looking like a ghost of Cristina and all the girls chopped up at the Bluebell. All of their lives would fail the fucking Bechdel test. Rotating around good guy after bad guy, as if they're the answer to a question no one actually asked.

'All right, fine,' I say. Time is ticking.

'These are the conditions, so listen very carefully. You go now, Marianne. You walk carefully along the edge of the hall and down the stairs. Leave through the front door and wave up at this floor of the house as you get into your car.'

'What?'

'Some neighbour will have seen you come in, I'm sure of it. So people need to see you leave again. And when you talk to the police later—'

'The police?'

'Listen to me and don't get sidetracked. When you talk to the police, whenever it is that they come to speak to you, you tell them that you left while Noah was working out in the spare room. Keep everything else true. If you sent him any messages, don't delete them from your phone but be prepared to explain them. Be honest about what time you arrived here and that you stayed over last night. Tell them nothing about the Bluebell and nothing about me. Got it?'

'Yes. But—'

I stand up and she flinches. I offer my hand and she reluctantly lets me pull her up.

'You need to leave now and you need to tell anyone who asks that Noah was still working out when you left.'

'But—'

'I will stay here and make sure the evidence tells the right story.'

'But the neighbours will have seen you too and . . .'

I smile, I can't help myself. 'I'm not an amateur, Marianne. But you're running out of time. So go now, stick to your story and never talk about any of this. Get home, order a takeaway from a usual place, tip the driver. Be seen. Go on and live your life.'

She stares up at me.

'But Marianne, know this. If you decide to do anything stupid, it's never too late for them to lay this all at your feet. Noah Simpson was not in charge of this, and the person who is, is still very much alive, pulling the strings. I will take care of that, then I'm going to enjoy my retirement. And you, of all people, aren't getting in my way.'

'How do I know I can trust you?'

I look at her with a hard expression but I keep my voice soft so she really hears it. 'You should never trust anyone, Marianne.'

# Marianne

The journey from Richmond to Hackney is a blur. God knows how many speed cameras she surges past, how many red lights she zips through. There's a space just a few doors up from the flat and she reverses into it fast, straightens up so she doesn't lose her wing mirror to a passing bus.

From the boot, she pulls out her holdall, with his and her laptops still inside. She fumbles for her keys, bags dangling on her aching arms, and is about to shove her way inside when a thought strikes her. She reloads the holdall into the boot, jumps back into the driver's seat and heads off again.

Just like after Greg died, she heads out east. Gunning up the A12 and on towards the coast.

It's dark by the time she hits Harwich. Its crumbling seafront is deserted, just a few empty cars under the dim lamplight. With the boot open, Marianne takes off Noah's hoodie, shivering as she opens up the holdall and pulls out Greg's laptop. As a light rain starts to fall, she wraps the laptop in the hoodie and carries her bundle onto the Ha'penny Pier.

The wooden floor is slippery under foot and she walks slowly, precisely. Below the pier, the brown seawater sloshes lazily around the old construction; in the distance abandoned cranes watch like iron giants. But she is alone here as she makes her way to the end of the pier.

The laptop comes free of its fabric wrapping almost as soon as it leaves her hands. For a moment it looks like the computer might float on the surface of the water, bobbing dangerously, ready for someone to scoop up. But within seconds both the hoodie and the laptop have disappeared, gobbled up by an indifferent sea. As if they never existed.

# Sam

It's funny that in all those years, I hardly ever saw the inside of Jonathan and Paula's house. A few dinners, the odd coffee in the conservatory with Paula. But they always gravitated to our house and we preferred it that way.

I'd never even seen this home office until I crept in through a back bedroom and made my way silently through their house. I suspect this was once the room earmarked for a child; it's bigger than a typical home office and painted yellow, a small box of toys tucked in the back of the cupboard, where I now wait.

I've been here, silent, for several hours. My breathing slow and steady, my muscles loose and relaxed. I'm wearing all grey and black, my boots left outside and my feet silent in socks.

Finally the office door opens. I wonder why, with only one of them still living here, they have waited until well after dark. Downstairs, I could hear the sounds of dishes, of cooking and at one point Radio 4. I could have announced myself down there, the radio noises a perfect cover. But I wanted to see them here, where it all happened. I was suspicious before I broke in and the puzzle pieces all pointed this way. Only a handful of people knew my truth, fewer still had motive to exploit it and only one of them was angry enough. Now that I've seen the computer, I'm deadly certain.

# Paula

Everything began and ended with Heidi. With the helmet of fluffy black hair she was born with, despite her fair parents. With the tiny curling fingers, the nostrils so delicate they couldn't possibly be real. A little doll, Paula used to call her, barely trusting that she was really for keeps.

Did Paula hold her breath for the whole three years or did it just feel like it? When she thinks of her daughter now, gone so many more years than she was here, she is unable to fully exhale.

For a year, it was the purest and most fearful joy. A year of a healthy baby, through which – as all parents do – Paula and Andy worried endlessly about the temperature of the room, of the air quality outside their suburban home, the schools in the area and how to baby-proof the house ready for wobbly first steps.

They didn't worry about her little face and feet swelling, as fluid trickled and became trapped in tiny nooks and corners of her body. Nor did they worry about her eyes crunching together in pain when she peed. Until those moments arrived.

Just three years together and the last two dominated by hospital visits, waiting lists, unanswered prayers. She was everything Paula wanted and she barely touched her with her fingertips before the little girl was being tugged away. It wasn't fair. And there was no silver lining.

When Andy left, it barely registered. The worst had already happened.

*

Jonathan wasn't a silver lining but he was a new hope. One that, as new hopes do, helped Paula blinker herself to his rougher edges and wish for the best. Tunnel vision focusing on one point: a new family.

Not a replacement for Heidi, no one could be that, but an addition to the story. And then that hope, that tiny fragile flame barely lit, was snuffed out too – he had made it impossible to have children. And with that, everything good in which Paula had placed hope, had placed *trust*, curdled.

Paula blows on her camomile tea as she opens the office door. She takes a cautious sip as she sits at the desk. The tea is still too hot and she puts it down carefully, the tip of her tongue raw and now missing a tiny layer.

The rest of the office is dark, just how she likes it. It's nearly eleven at night. When Jonathan was still living here she'd be in bed by now, in a chemical coma from sleeping pills while he texted fleshy pictures to other women and did who knows what in this room. But now it's her room, her house, her hours, her computer. Her mission control.

Jonathan has been gone for over a year. Living in his office or a hotel or maybe in some other sap's bed. He could be shacked up with Samantha for all Paula cares, though she knows very well that's not the case. After years of wishing, manoeuvring, *begging* him to respect their marriage, she no longer cares. It's that simple.

And it's intoxicating! The sheer freedom that comes when you stop clinging to the idea of family or matrimony. Of colouring inside the lines. Of Botox and blow jobs. Of keeping house or 'normal' hours.

She catches sight of her face in the reflection of the screen. Her forehead creased and her eyes lined. She wears her years these days. And why not? She has accomplished enough, and suffered enough, to wear her war medals.

She threw everything at her second marriage. Giving up work at Jonathan's prompting to become a full-time wife, ready to be a full-time mother again. Letting her brain decay slowly, almost unnoticeably, like unbrushed teeth.

It's embarrassing how many years of false hope and wilful ignorance passed by before she finally accepted what was plain to see. The marriage was a mirage. And Jonathan was so blatant about it! It was practically trolling.

And when, after years of negative pregnancy tests, years of her bending over backwards to be a 'dutiful wife', he was still unwilling to try fertility treatment, something irreversibly broke. *How dare he string her along like this? As if she was just some docile wife, some decorated idiot, who could be kept sweet with necklaces and handbags instead of the only thing she really wanted?*

It was in this office that Paula made the decision. All the wilful ignorance she'd employed and deaf ears she'd turned were retired. It was time to find out everything.

While Jonathan 'worked late', Paula combed through online message boards for suspicious spouses. Soon she'd learnt to hack into his emails, his photos, his calendar app. Paula, who Jonathan wouldn't trust to restart the broadband router, even had a secret phone that replicated Jonathan's. Once the shock of it wore off, and the rage cooled just a few degrees, she was left marvelling at his audacity.

The sheer volume of women, the indiscriminate chasing, the revolting, badly lit pictures he sent that somehow, with at least a few women, had paid dividends. A whole second life, multiple *lives*, right under her nose. He really didn't give a shit! It took an extraordinary level of self-belief and selfishness to commit to such a level of deceit and for so long.

And all the while, she had to watch Steve's young 'immigration bride' reaping rewards to which she had no claim. The house, the son and the marriage. It wasn't fair. Paula didn't exactly blame Samantha, not personally; not until she noticed the furtive looks between Jonathan and Samantha. Not until she noticed the ease with which Samantha enjoyed the life she really had no right to.

Other women would say Paula should have left Jonathan. She had plenty of evidence and no ties to bind. But where would she go? She'd abandoned her career, put all her eggs figuratively and almost literally in one basket. She had no money of her own. No future. And she would never have the family she wanted. Because of him.

No, Paula didn't want to leave. Instead, she wanted to get under the skin of this man, learn everything he had kept from her, before she took everything from him. She'd learnt about the dark web from her online community and thought, *why not?*

She used one of his old laptops from work, followed the instructions on YouTube and downloaded the special browser. It took some getting used to, the slowness, the inability to search, but – painfully – she had nothing but time.

She hacked his finances first, then his medical records. Investments that Jonathan had never told her about were meaningless in comparison to the vasectomy he had had without telling her. Right back when they started trying. When she still stood a chance. Any sweetness was gone, hollowed out. Now she was driven by spite and sadness.

*

The Hacker Supermarket started as a side project when she'd exhausted everything in Project Jonathan. A way to earn money that he had no chance of finding. A nest egg ready for when she left. She planned to get her revenge on him too, some big gesture, his photos sent to everyone at his company, or, screw it, beamed onto the wall of their house. By the time she got round to revenge, he'd given her the perfect opportunity to hit him in the only place it hurt. Showing Steve those photos, knowing Samantha was among them – that beat any grand gesture.

But back then, at the start of her 'kitchen table venture' on the dark web, she was focused on earning money.

She advertised on a few of the message boards she'd found links to, and charged small amounts at first. The equivalent of a few quid to hack into photos or emails, the same kind of thing she'd done to her own husband. The challenges got harder. Beyond a hobby, it took on a life of its own. She would accept requests from people and give higher and higher quotes for the work. They often accepted.

While Jonathan smarmed around his corporate world, Paula out-earned him from the comfort of their house. Running a network of her own, employing a staff of little grub worms to help, moving the kinds of goods and managing the kinds of projects no one could have imagined. It was terrifying, thrilling and lucrative. While Jonathan had his piddly little investments and bits on the side, she was accumulating thousands.

But none of it filled the hole, *the holes*, that life had punched into her. No amount was enough to make her pull that plug and leave. She was still looking for something, and didn't know what it was until she saw it. The message on one of the communities she advertised on showed that Noah was a kindred spirit. A man broken by loss but motivated by money.

She immediately recognised his grief, his rage. Wouldn't she have done anything to find a donor for Heidi? If the dark web had existed back then, she could have easily fallen prey to the same scam Noah had.

She didn't take a sleeping pill that night. Instead, she lay under their White Company sheets, thinking that maybe there was a different way. Maybe this thing she'd started could be used for good? Like the charity arm of a weapons conglomerate.

She got back out of bed and messaged from the laptop she kept hidden in her side of the wardrobe. She could see it all, even as she typed her idea to Noah. She knew he'd respond, knew he'd go for it, because she understood to her bones the way grief had shaped him.

Samantha was a gift. Paula had known about her past, knew she would do anything to keep it secret. Perhaps Paula might not have used her if Samantha hadn't been so blatant in her attraction to Jonathan. Perhaps.

When Greg got in touch, it was all too perfect to ignore.

She thought she knew the ideal doctor as well. Henry Derbyshire was Jonathan's tennis buddy. Deeply in debt through ridiculously bad investments – the rich man's form of gambling. It was an early mistake. Too close to home.

Henry never worked out who was really behind the project, but she was glad to see the back of him.

The scheme was supposed to work well for the girls too. Fresh starts – like the one Samantha had got. Like the one Samantha didn't deserve.

Paula sent the first message to Samantha just before arriving for dinner at their house. Watched her carefully all night to see if she seemed rattled. Paula thought for a moment that she might have told Jonathan when they went for a walk, but clearly they had other things on their minds. And god, Samantha was good. Even on her earliest, wobbliest test run. Collecting electronics that Paula later threw in the Thames. Too traceable to risk selling. Samantha had asked about this more than once, when she plucked up courage to start answering her 'handler' back. But Paula never explained.

Samantha resisted, of course, trying to wriggle from the hook, but there was such a bounty of easily hackable CCTV from the locker places and electronics stores that the hook just burrowed deeper.

*

At first the project was cathartic. People being helped, lives being saved. But good intentions don't always equal good outcomes, and the whole donor network turned into an unwieldy nightmare. Having to man that phone constantly, sending Samantha and the others all over the place, the girls flaking out and not showing up. Lina. That was a regret, though Paula didn't admit she felt that way to Noah.

Greg trying to break loose became infuriating too. He was a weak and silly man. Some clients had second thoughts and cancelled just as a good donor was lined up. And all the while, Paula was trying to keep the other businesses going on the side, Hacker Supermarket and Assassin Supermarket – although the latter generated very few genuine sales. She even created a 'hack' website so people could search for their names. She thought it would be wonderful advertising, the kind that had once put a famous infidelity site on the map. But in the end, she was her own biggest customer.

It was a relief to shut it all down, really. She'd proven she could do it, helped some people and made an absolute stack of money. That was enough.

Now Noah is dead, their shared investments are hers, hidden under layers and layers of umbrella companies. Jonathan has so far let her keep the house and money is no object. Just one more job for Samantha – the unfortunate Marianne – and then that side of the business will be shut down too. And then what will she do? It should be exciting, a whole world of opportunity, but she just feels numb at the thought.

'Was it always you, sending me those messages?'

The voice is familiar and Paula turns slowly to the dark corner, trying to hide her shock.

# Sam

Paula wears cream silk pyjamas and dressing gown, one leg tucked under her, a Cornishware mug in her hand. I see that it's shaking slightly and she puts it down carefully, avoiding my eye.

'The one I'm most proud of,' my sister-in-law says, 'was my husband's birthday dinner. Do you remember that?'

'Of course I do.'

'I sent messages right there at the table and none of you noticed.'

I step out of the shadows and walk towards her chair, keeping an eye on the hot tea in case she tries anything stupid.

'I'm so sorry,' I say, and she tilts her head and then laughs suddenly. It rings out like an alarm in the still night. I haven't heard her voice in over a year and I'm surprised by the affection it stirs in me, even after everything.

'It must have been awful to be ignored all that time,' I say.

Paula was the closest thing I had to a friend in recent years. Since Cristina. The affection fades. Paula would have had Cristina carved up like all the others.

Paula shakes her head but says nothing.

'Did this help?' I ask. 'Did it fill the hole?'

She holds my gaze. Her fingers start to tremble in her lap. A detail most would miss. Still Paula says nothing. For a moment she looks older than her years. Ghostly, I suppose. She shakes her head. 'Nothing helps,' she says, her voice cracking just slightly. 'I've been empty for years. This was just a temporary distraction.'

'I know you don't believe me and really you don't deserve it, but I'm sorry about what I did, Paula.' She looks up at me, I see her eyes taking me in, my hair, my size. She's not seen me in the flesh since I left Steve's home and she recoils just slightly.

'You know I can't leave you alive, though, don't you?' I say, my voice soft. 'Not after what you did to those girls.' I pause. 'And to me and Joe.'

Paula takes a sip from her mug. I can tell she's trying to hold her nerve but her breathing is fast, her eyes darting around the room.

Then suddenly she smiles, the same rictus grin she wore for all those Christmases. She sits up straighter and puts her mug down with no hint of a tremble now.

'What a shame this is coming to an end,' she says, her voice clear and brisk. The same game Paula who joined me for brunches and made small talk with Steve.

'You're very good at what you do,' she says. 'I really struck it lucky there. What chance!'

I hold her gaze as she adds. 'Of course, I was bloody good at my job too. Remember the alibi I rustled up with almost no notice? The Local Angels stuff?' I nod. She's talking as

334

if we're reminiscing, as if we're back in Le Pain Quotidien splitting a cake we'd both skipped lunch for. 'All those details matching up, I was very proud of that.' She pauses. 'We could have been a great team if we'd joined forces properly.'

'Perhaps you should have asked me, instead of forcing me,' I say.

'Perhaps. But how did you know it was me?' Paula asks, brow furrowing.

'There was no one else it could have been.' I shrug. 'No one else knew everything you knew, except Steve and Jonathan. Steve wouldn't do that to Joe and Jonathan isn't smart enough.'

She smiles at this and takes a sip of her tea. She's even thinner than when I last saw her, her skin a dull grey as if she's not seen sunlight in a while. Her hair, no longer dyed blonde, is luminous silver. Like moonlight. I wonder when she last went outside.

'He didn't deserve you,' I say, and she nods.

'He didn't deserve any of us,' she says. 'But we could still be a team, you know. You've been working for me for a long time now and you've made excellent money. I was winding it all up, but there's still plenty of work for your talents.'

'Paula,' I say, shaking my head.

She looks down at her hands. 'What was I going to do with my time, anyway?' She laughs. It's a fleeting, shallow sound. 'Just, please, make it quick.'

I start to tie her silk dressing-gown cord gently around her neck, squeezing her shoulder with apology, with reassurance, with welling regret. Things could have been so different between us, but they're not. And they never can be after I learnt what they were doing at the Bluebell, what they had dragged me into. It just needs to end.

'This isn't retribution,' I whisper, as I move her hands to the cord and help her pull. 'This is a full stop.'

# Marianne

*Friday, 17 September 2021*

'I don't know what to say.' Jane's face is temporarily frozen on the screen, but her voice is still audible through Skype.

'I know,' Marianne says. 'What are the chances?'

A husband and then a new boyfriend dying almost one year apart. What *are* the chances? Jane has barely said a word since Marianne called, she's just let her friend talk. But both of them were crying all the same.

It had been a long time since they'd actually spoken face to face, but the years have faded and it's as if they're back in their halls of residence, promising to always have each other's back.

'Pack a fucking bag,' Jane says, decisively, wiping her eyes with the back of one hand. 'Book a fucking ticket and get your arse out here.'

It's tempting. Marianne has been signed off work, something she should have done when Greg died but barrelled straight back to work instead. This time it was non-negotiable and she'd put up no fight.

'The flat's on the market,' Marianne says instead. 'And I've handed in my notice.'

'Good,' Jane says. 'You shouldn't be living in a mausoleum.'

Marianne nods.

'So what do you want to do next?'

# Sam

## Sunday, 24 October 2021

I'm in the kitchen when Joe arrives. To say I feel nervous doesn't come close. I look so different to when he last saw me that I've changed clothes maybe ten times today, trying to find some way to resemble the way he expects me to look. I have worn make-up for the first time since I left Steve's house, but my hair is still growing back and is still in a pixie crop. The lion's mane he'd always loved winding his fingers through as a little boy is a distant memory.

I've cooked a roast dinner, not a patch on one of Steve's, my shaking hands slipping as I peeled the potatoes. Thick plasters now coat two fingertips.

I let him in, unsure whether to hug him, holding my arms out but letting them fall.

He kisses my cheeks briefly, like an acquaintance. We stare at each other in silence until I look away.

'Your house is really nice,' he says, as I lead him through to the small but bright kitchen with its table for two.

'It's your house,' I say. 'Well, it's our house.' He looks at me strangely. A look I've not seen before on his face as he stares at me. At my hair, at my kitchen.

'Can I start at beginning?' I ask. 'And I'll get to that.'

*

I wasn't born here. You know that anyway, even though you've never said. I wasn't born somewhere good or bad, but it was unlucky. And my old country is small and beautiful. It has mountains, rivers and canyons that would make you gasp.

I swore to my mother that I would never have children of my own, not after everything that I saw. She died believing

337

me. And she didn't die in peace, Joe. After everything my dad taught me, everything he prepared me for, when the time came I just froze. I was younger than you by some years and I watched what happened to my mother, I watched a group of soldiers hurting her in ways I can't begin to tell you. And only when it was over did I do anything.

Most of them had left. From my hiding place, I watched their backs shaking with laughter and adrenaline as they left. I don't think they knew or cared that they had killed her.

One of them lingered, one of the younger ones who had held her down. He was watching me as I lay myself on my mother's chest and wept my apologies. All that time preparing, all that time my father spent training me so that I could protect others, and I had let everyone down.

I was barely aware of him, his uniform in the corner of my eye. But he was staring at me. He looked at me as if I was one of the carcasses swinging in the back of your dad's butcher's shops. Meat. Nothing more. Something to be taken, consumed, sliced and spat out. Perhaps because I was young, he thought it would be easy.

He must have heard me move as he walked towards me, and only then did I act. I killed him, Joe. Using my bare fists to knock him unconscious. I hit him in the exact spot on his skull that my father taught me, and then wrapped my hands around his throat.

When I was sure he was dead, I ran for my life.

\*

When I ran from my home, I didn't care where I ended up. I was offered a place in a truck returning to the UK and I said yes. It wasn't exactly altruistic of them – when we arrived, seasick, dehydrated and disoriented, the man driving handed us over to a gang almost as bad as the people I'd run from, but I would have said yes to a one-way rocket to the moon.

I didn't have time to grieve for my mother and I still don't know what happened to my father, but survival had to come first. I think I've leaked that grief out every day since, but the one thing that saved me, Joe, was you. My mother died believing I would never have children because I couldn't bear the thought of them being poisoned by the grief and fear that poisoned me. But then I met you. And you have been the sunshine and the hope and everything good in my life ever since.

I'm so sorry that I broke your father's trust and I'm so sorry that I let you down. Your uncle and I were selfish and disgusting, and I have no excuse. People and circumstances have made me do bad things in the course of my life, but this is one mistake I have to own. I'm sorry.

But I want you to know that I have stayed here for you and worked hard for you, and I will be here for as long as you will let me. I have no real home, not legally, but you are my home. And this is your house.

It's all owned in your name, bought and paid for in cash. If you want me to leave, you can kick me out. Or you can stay here, whenever you like and for as long as you like.

I just hope you know that I would do anything for you and, remember, no matter what happens, I'll always come back for you.

\*

Joe doesn't look at me. Not for a long moment. I can smell that the potatoes have started to burn in the oven but I dare not look at them or break this spell. I don't want to frighten him away. He has just found out that I am a killer, after all.

Eventually Joe stands up and clenches his fists, just like he did when he was little and trying to be brave. He steps towards the kitchen door and my heart prepares to shatter. But then he turns, walks towards me and presses his forehead to mine.

'It's OK, Mum.'

# Marianne

*Sunday, 24 October 2021*

Marianne shuts the inner door, double-locking it for the last time. She'll drop the keys through the estate agent's letterbox on the way. She carries the suitcases down, hurrying as the Uber driver beeps. Her little car was sold last week and most of her furniture has already gone, donated or taken to the tip. She left the bed for the couple who have bought this place. It's their sanctuary now.

All she really has left is in these cases. Mostly they're filled with her clothes and toiletries, but she does have a few of Greg's favourite T-shirts and shirts carefully folded, and some mementos of their marriage. Of the happiest moments. That still counts for something.

When she gets out at the airport, she resists the urge to buy cigarettes. Two weeks and counting, maybe she'll make it stick this time.

Inside, the airport is thick with people, commuters heading back to the European offices, ready for the new working week. Boomeranging between the cities, exhausted and modern.

Unlike them, Marianne has a one-way ticket. Jane was a bit disappointed that Marianne chose not to head to Dubai and work in a school out there, to rekindle their friendship under a boiling tax-free sun. But she understood.

\*

'Passengers for British Airways flight to Florence, please go straight to gate nine. Final call for British Airways to Florence.'

She watches them file by, heading out where she and Greg had honeymooned. Where, on that last holiday, she had watched through squinting eyes as he scooped frogs feverishly

340

from the pool. A Sisyphean undertaking that makes more sense, and cuts deeper, in light of everything she knows.

As the last of the passengers rush down the gangway to gate nine, she whispers a silent message for them to carry with them to Tuscany. She considered going to Italy, trying to find a job in an international school, living a half-life of the one they'd dreamt about. But no. That was *their* dream, not hers.

Greg is gone and with him the life she thought she would lead. But unlike him, she has another chance at life. A life threatened and then saved by the same strange woman. Marianne wonders what happened to her; hopes, despite everything, that she is OK. And that she stays the hell away.

But she was right, in her little monologue, which Marianne was too terrified to take in at the time. Marianne has compromised and settled, limped through life as if she had all the time in the world. As if it couldn't be snuffed out in a moment, the wick pinched between unseen fingers.

Tonight, she will fly to Paris, the proceeds of the flat hitting her bank account just in time for breakfast. And then, who knows? Maybe Madrid, maybe Athens. Maybe New York. Or maybe she'll stay in Paris until she is old and crazy, telling stories about assassination attempts and bluebells that no one would believe. But whatever she does, it will be up to Marianne.

This is her life.

# Acknowledgements

I had been trying to find the right book idea for a long time, growing increasingly frustrated and miserable. I knew it was there, just outside my eye line, but the more I tried to see it, the more obscure it grew.

The case of the Ashley Madison infidelity site hack had horrified and fascinated me ever since the story broke. I was mulling that tawdry story over yet again on 28 March 2018, when the idea for *The Hit List* finally came into view.

I sent it first to Gilly (to whom this book is dedicated). Our WhatsApp messages read:

[16:02, 28/03/2018] Holly Seddon: So . . . on the dark web there are 'murder for hire' websites.

[16:03, 28/03/2018] Holly Seddon: What if instead of an infidelity site hack, you found out your name was on that. And no idea who had put it there.

[16:27, 28/03/2018] Gillian McAllister: That's SUCH a good idea!!!

[16:27, 28/03/2018] Gillian McAllister: Holy shit.

Every writer needs a friend who will discuss dark-web hit lists with them endlessly until the plot comes together. Then rally them when it feels too hard to write. And then celebrate with them when it finally works. I'm not sure everyone is that lucky, though. So to Gilly, thank you, thank you, thank you.

And to Tony McAllister, Gilly's dad, who helped me on detail, plot and even naming ideas. Tony, Gilly, Ilana Fox and Hayley Webster were among the first to read the full manuscript. Their encouragement meant the world.

While writing *The Hit List*, I signed with the wonderful Sophie Lambert from C+W. Her patience, precision and professionalism make me so grateful every day that I have her in my corner.

Phoebe Morgan, who bought this book while she was at Trapeze, is another star I am so lucky to have worked with. She instinctively knew how to elevate the story and her vision for the novel blew me away. Sam Eades, who championed the book even while on maternity leave, thank you!

The whole team at Trapeze is mind-bogglingly brilliant, I'm so happy to call Trapeze and Orion my publishing home.

I have used a lot of artistic licence in the writing of this book, especially with the dark web elements. That's not to say it isn't a Wild West, but the specifics and logistics are entirely made up. And not that I think anyone would look . . . but there is definitely no Assassin Supermarket. There is, however, a webcam on Ha'penny Pier (a great spot by my copy-editor) that would have picked up Marianne lobbing a laptop into the water. Forgive me, but I'm going to pretend it doesn't exist. Or perhaps it was on the blink that day.

I have tried to be sensitive in my featuring of the trafficked women, and in particular Samantha, whose background I researched extensively and am very clear about in my own head, but for sensitivity have been vague about in the text. Any mistakes are my own.

Four books. Bloody hell. I still love this job more than any other in the world. It's a privilege to tell stories for a living. But it's not easy, and I'm not easy to live with while I do it. So most of all, and forever, my thanks go to James, Mia, Alfie, Elliot and Finch. For putting up with me, for loving me and for being my reasons for everything. I love you, I love you, I love you.

# Credits

Trapeze would like to thank everyone at Orion who worked on the publication of *The Hit List* in the UK.

**Agent**
Sophie Lambert

Paul Bulos
Jake Alderson

**Editor**
Phoebe Morgan
Sam Eades

**Design**
Debbie Holmes
Joanna Ridley
Nick May

**Copy-editor**
Sue Lascelles

Clare Sivell
Helen Ewing

**Proofreader**
Holly Kyte

**Finance**
Jennifer Muchan
Jasdip Nandra

**Editorial Management**
Rosie Pearce
Charlie Panayiotou
Jane Hughes
Alice Davis
Claire Boyle

Ibukun Ademefun
Rabale Mustafa
Sue Baker
Tom Costello

**Marketing**
Brittany Sankey

**Audio**
Paul Stark
Amber Bates

**Production**
Claire Keep
Fiona McIntosh

**Contracts**
Anne Goddard